Starlaw

Candace Sams

author of *The Peacekeeper's Soul* and *Fusion*

CRIMSON
ROMANCE

F+W Media, Inc.

Published by
Crimson Romance
an imprint of F+W Media, Inc.
10151 Carver Road, Suite 200
Blue Ash, OH 45242. U.S.A.
www.crimsonromance.com

ISBN 10: 1-4405-8188-6
ISBN 13: 978-1-4405-8188-5
eISBN 10: 1-4405-8189-4
eISBN 13: 978-1-4405-8189-2

This is a work of fiction. Names, characters, corporations, institutions, organizations, events, or locales in this novel are either the product of the author's imagination or, if real, used fictitiously. The resemblance of any character to actual persons (living or dead) is entirely coincidental.

Cover art © iStockphoto.com/clearviewstock and 123RF/yeko

For Lee and for anyone who imagines other worlds.

Chapter 1

"Christ … it's frickin' eerie out here," Cory Martinez whispered.

"And colder than it was supposed to be," Laurel Blake added.

Along with what was normally on their belts, such as side arms, flashlights, extra ammo, and handcuffs, they had special radio equipment that only allowed certain shift members—including the dispatch supervisor—to hear what was going on. Besides all that, she and Cory were dressed in navy-blue jumpsuits with matching PD jackets and baseball caps. They'd added black gloves and combat boots to easily move through the park undergrowth. At the moment, their radios were silent, indicating the undercover detective pretending to be asleep in a clearing was all right so far. He was posing as a homeless man in order catch someone who'd been murdering them and literally draining their blood for the past three weeks.

"So where's the bachelorette party?" Cory asked as he nudged her.

"Why the hell are you asking about that? Pay attention, butt-munch!"

Cory grinned and ignored the reprimand. "Come on. Maria won't tell me."

"That's because she doesn't want you to know."

"But you'll tell your partner, right?" Cory prompted as he nudged her several more times.

Laurel pressed her lips together to keep from smiling. "I might be your partner but I'm *her* best friend and the maid of honor. And she asked me to keep my big mouth shut. So chew on that and keep your mind on the job."

"That's not fair. You guys know where I'm having my bachelor party—"

"That's because there's not a single man at the station who could keep his lips zipped. I swear … when it comes to gossip male cops are worse than any woman I've ever known."

"Laurel—"

"No! Shut up and pay attention."

She saw his scowl even in the dim light filtering through the trees.

"She didn't hire those male strippers, did she? You know … the ones who jerk their junk while movin' around in skimpy costumes and letting women stuff twenties down their G-strings?"

She simply smiled back, deciding to let him sweat the answer.

"Oh man … that's not right!" he groused.

"What's not right? The overstuffed G-strings, or a lot of turned-on women having a good time while tossing back enough tequila to go toxic?" she teased.

He moved closer. "Did you say tequila? Maria gets crazy when she drinks tequila. She gets horny as hell and doesn't remember anything—"

"Okay … that's enough information," Laurel advised as she held up one hand to stop him. "You need to talk to her, not me. And we need to keep our mouths shut … *really*," she insisted as she pulled the collar of her jacket higher.

They sat in mutual silence for another fifteen minutes. Cory finally broke it again with more commiserations concerning his upcoming nuptials.

"I hate the invitations. They suck."

"Then why didn't you help her pick 'em out?"

"I did. Her mother overrode my opinion. She wanted red roses all over everything. I can't stand red roses."

Laurel finally turned to look at him. "What in hell did you choose?"

He grinned. "Daisies."

She pressed her lips together. "In all the years we've known each other … I've never thought of you as a daisy kind of guy."

"Everybody does roses. I read in *Weddings Today* magazine that it's the most used flower in the world where weddings are concerned. I wanted something bright. Something uncommon. Something yellow and 'camera friendly in darkened churches,' like the magazine says."

"Which is why your wedding colors are burgundy and black," she responded while shaking her head in mirth.

The idea of Cory perusing a wedding magazine was too much. But he was all about marrying the girl he'd loved since high school. In the end it wouldn't matter *how* he got Maria down the aisle as long as he got her there.

"My future mother-in-law took every opinion I had and tossed it right in the crapper, like my ideas don't matter." He snorted in derision then let out a few curses in Spanish. "She and I are gonna have a long talk after the wedding. There's not gonna be any of that shit where she tells us how to live our lives, what to name our kids, and how to decorate our house."

"Says the man who likes daisies."

"Excuse me … daisies symbolize love, patience, purity, and simplicity. They're perfect for weddings," he insisted.

A scrambled message over their earpieces made them both sit up at the same time.

"Did you make that out?" he asked as he gently tapped his earpiece.

"Say again," Laurel requested as she keyed the microphone hanging from her jacket epaulet.

There was no sound.

Cory made a second attempt. "210 Adam from 115 King … say again … over."

"For the love of God … help."

Laurel and Cory stared at each other when the clear but panic-stricken voice of one of their comrades sounded through their earpieces.

Without waiting one second longer, Laurel relayed their need for backup as she stood and ran to their comrade's aid.

As she bolted forward, she put her hand on her weapon and mentally plotted the shortest distance between their spot and the assigned location of the caller.

Cory pounded through the brush behind her. She knew he had her back as she picked up the pace.

Through her earpiece, she heard orders being issued from the nearest officers including the dispatch supervisor. It didn't matter if the perp heard them coming now. If a cop was in need, scaring away an attacker might save a life.

Tonight's assignment should have been simple.

Moments later they crashed through the undergrowth into a nearby clearing.

Laurel stopped in her tracks as she saw a tall figure straighten. He'd been bending over someone lying on the ground.

The light wasn't that good but she knew damned well the man in the dirt was one of *theirs*. The old, patched clothing was the same as what he'd been wearing when tonight's assignment had been issued.

She pulled her weapon at the same time Cory did. Despite the cold of the night and the breeze blowing through the trees, sweat broke out on her forehead.

"Police! Put your hands on your head. Interlace your fingers and don't move," she loudly ordered as Cory repeated the message in Spanish.

The language repetition was something they did any time there was a chance for misunderstanding. It wasn't required by standard operating procedure, but it'd saved them a lot of trouble on numerous occasions. She simply waited to see if the man in front of them would comply whether he understood in English *or* Spanish. Her concern was less for his safety, more about the downed cop's injuries.

When the stranger slowly did as she ordered while turning toward them, Cory switched on his flashlight. Laurel gasped and felt her pounding heart lurch. Both of them backed away as Cory spit out a low, feral curse.

The illuminated figure before them was the most grotesque thing she'd ever seen. As Cory's flashlight kept their suspect clearly visible, the man gazing at them then presented a fanged grin. Blood dripped from his mouth as if he'd just cannibalized something. His face bore an unholy resemblance to a movie vampire. His body and even his skull seemed emaciated beyond explanation. There was no reason for how anyone could survive and look so horribly gaunt. His angular face personified evil. There was a wickedly hollow gleam spilling from his eyes. But if the man was insane and an escapee from some facility, he was at least cogent enough to know he'd be shot if he moved. He glared back at her and her blood almost ran cold. The savagery in his expression was palpable and the long, leather-looking duster he wore augmented his thin, tall appearance. Her brain reasoned he couldn't possibly look as bad in daylight.

From the full moon now gleaming through the clearing as clouds moved away, as well as the glow from the flashlight Cory held, their suspect's appearance looked damned hideous.

Cory slowly moved forward. "Watch this son-of-a-bitch!" he commanded. "I've gotta check Mac."

Laurel swallowed hard and tried not to gaze right in their suspect's eyes. Her training made her pivot to keep Cory out of her line of fire. That same training kept her rooted to the spot when her gut told her to run away.

"All right … Batman … or whoever the hell you are … if you move, one of us is gonna put a hole in you as big as a fuckin' house!" Cory tersely promised as he carefully moved toward the downed undercover officer.

Laurel noted there was no repetition in any second language this time. As with her, Cory's concern was for the undercover cop on the ground, not on the ghastly suspect and certainly not on using proper language when addressing what might very well be their killer.

She was aware of her partner kneeling but she still kept her attention on the monstrosity in front of her. What he was, why he looked the way he did, or whether this was the same murderer they'd been looking for wasn't as important as Mac's safety.

"Christ! He's *dead*. His throat is torn out!"

Other officers burst into the clearing.

Laurel heard them drawing weapons and letting loose a barrage of questions Cory tried to answer. Still, her attention was fixed on the horrible sight of what had to be a nightmare torn from her brain, a man with blood dripping from his jaws and down his pale neck.

He stared back and she actually started to shake. The voices of those around her dimmed as the suspect grinned sickeningly. She heard the rattle of handcuffs.

She and Cory had only been there a few seconds before help arrived but it seemed like hours. Their suspect's hands were still on his head but she saw his gaze shift. Before she could utter the warning instinct pulled from her gut, the corpse-like entity moved and was suddenly no longer there.

Shouts rang out as others tried to train their lights on the man, relocate and then subdue him. She knew it was too late. Terror filled her and almost cut off her air. She lifted the muzzle of her weapon, unable to fire in the ensuing mêlée. Fear she'd strike a comrade made her freeze.

In a split second that reminded her of an old movie reel, the perpetrator seemed to materialize and run from one side of the clearing to the other. Something shiny came from beneath his flying leather duster. Whatever the object was, it emitted a light beam and a high-pitched, vibrating sound.

The beam shot forward in a straight stream and struck Cory first. She saw his flashlight fly out of his hand and roll away.

More shouts and cries broke what should have been the calm of the midnight air. She finally responded. Nothing she did was fast enough. Nothing anyone did kept the wraith-like being from moving at a speed defying explanation.

Cory's body hit the dirt.

Two detectives tried to jump the suspect but they had no better chance than her partner. They were struck by the suspect's strange beam weapon and both slumped to the ground. Random shots were fired. She knew triggers were being pulled in panic. Logic was lost on the scene as she followed her compatriots' example and shot at the empty space left by the fast-moving suspect. She heard dull thuds as the bullets of other officers hit the man but nothing slowed him down.

Three other detectives fell near Cory. Her distress on their behalf was almost overwhelming. This was what it felt like to face death. She was next.

In the matter of a few seconds—in a scenario playing out in light speed—no one stood but the attacker and her. At least one cop was dead, according to Cory's shouted description.

"Stay back!" she yelled and knew the warning would do her no good, even as she made it. Her brain, body, and emotions were reacting to training. There wasn't anything left from which to draw. Nothing they'd fired slowed the monstrosity down. And when a person could move at some unholy, inhuman pace, and take a shitload of bullets while putting an entire undercover operation on the ground, he didn't have to follow her commands or anyone else's.

It suddenly occurred to her they'd been set up. The thing with her waited until every cop in the vicinity was there.

The dispatch supervisor had to have sent backup but all the yelling and shooting had kept her from hearing what happened through her earpiece. Surely there'd be sirens any moment. But passing seconds seemed like an eternity as their attacker slowly advanced.

"I will feast well tonight," the gruesome entity rasped out in a grinding, hissing voice.

Laurel swallowed hard.

She opened her mouth to warn him again, as her index finger felt the cold metal of her trigger. There was only one way she'd get out of this.

Warnings had done no good. Following the rules hadn't made a difference. She had no idea who on the ground might be unconscious or dead. And she desperately wanted to live.

"Fuck it!" she whispered as she emptied what was left of her ammo into the tall man.

When he kept strolling forward, grinning as her efforts were a game, she knew all her childhood nightmares concerning Halloween-like creatures were real. There really were things in the night that couldn't be stopped by the best weapons available. There really were otherworldly creatures.

He stopped only a few feet away, seemingly savoring his victory. His glowing eyes looked her over, assessing her. The brightness of them was terrible and menacing. This monstrosity had no fear of anything. If she ran, he'd drop her in the next beat of her heart.

She was out of her league, without any options. This thing was a beast of prey. He enjoyed the hunt and had set the entire scene to suit his taste. A thousand things went through her mind. Chief among these was the thought of her best friend lying a few feet on the ground, and her sorrow for his parents, who'd never really know the truth of what'd happened to their son.

"Very nice … pretty, pretty," he slowly whispered in broken English. Then he licked his lips and made a loud sucking sound as he did so. "I learn your human words so you will understand … because you are a woman and the flesh of such is always sweeter, I will take you slowly. I will slake my lust on your body as I eat. And it will be *good*, little enforcer. There may even be enough life left to feel me inside you. Perhaps I'll hear you scream in fear as you lie beneath me." He nodded. "That would be most pleasurable. Most pleasurable indeed!"

Under the bright light of a full moon, his raised weapon looked like something out of a science fiction movie. Laurel knew she had only seconds left to breathe. But there were ways to go that were preferable than letting this beast take her as he wanted.

She gathered her strength and prepared to lunge. She'd either knock him to the ground or take a chest shot from his space-age looking weapon and end it.

His long, bony finger curled around what looked like a trigger. It seemed like the darkness hid nothing now though she mentally begged for total blackness.

A low whining sound came from the brush. He jerked his head to the left, as if shocked by the sound. Then her would-be killer cried out loud and long; the sound of his feral scream echoed everywhere.

A burst of light sliced through the night. It was similar to the illumination created by the monster's weapon except it seemed far more powerful. Sudden glow lit everything around them almost as bright as noontime.

The horrible entity before her lurched sideways. Long, flowing hair she hadn't noticed before flew around his features as he fell forward yelling in fury.

The muzzle of his weapon was still aimed in her direction. As he dropped toward the dirt, silvery light shot from it and right at her. Sudden, white-hot pain made her cry out in agony. She heard her own voice mingle with that of her attacker's. The sound of her cry seemed strange, as if the outrage it represented belonged elsewhere.

Intense pain flooded every cell of her body.

In weird slow motion that punctuated the agonizing moment, her body flew backward and onto the ground.

Stars shimmered overhead. Except for the breeze coming off the nearby ocean, the night grew silent again. She took one shuddering gasp and pain destroyed her instincts to stay awake. Darkness closed in.

• • •

Darius Starlaw ran forward with his ground crew. Among them were his second-in-command, Barst K'rad, and his medical technician, Gemma Tocurus. All who'd landed on this small rock of a world were chosen because of their previous experience and the knowledge that they'd lay down their lives for one another. In this instance, the danger was most extreme; he'd take no chances.

His weapon was still aimed at his quarry; he didn't dare lower it. Because the criminal he'd just leveled was only stunned, the butcher might still be a threat.

"Hurry," he commanded. "Their technology is primitive but they'll still locate Goll's vessel soon. Barst, we know the general coordinates … find it and take it out. Sear everything indicating a craft was ever present. There's no time to waste."

As Barst hurried to do his bidding, Darius looked at the carnage around him. There was nothing to be done. It took none of Gemma's skill to deem everyone around them was dead. Blood and gore littered the area.

Gemma picked up a metal tube still rolling on the ground. Light came from one end. There were several such devices lying scattered across the dirt. Apparently, these objects were what provided the primitives light in darkness.

Another crewman knelt beside Goll. "He's unconscious, sir. The threat has been mitigated."

"Get that bastard aboard our light shuttle and back to the *Titan*," Darius commanded. "Make sure the decontamination units are on before you enter. Just as we didn't bring any microbes to this backward world, we can't bring as much as a speck of dirt back. Is that clear?"

"Yes, sir."

While the first crewman picked Goll up, threw him over his shoulder, and trudged to his ground transport with another officer assisting, Darius considered the damage. Barst arrived back in record time and made his report.

"Goll's small ship is history. Not so much as a bulkhead bolt is left. No one on this world will know it existed."

Darius nodded. "Good. Before we return, let's get a clear image of what happened here. It can all be used against the prisoner and I want it all to count."

Barst gazed around the clearing even as Darius knelt to get a closer look at the carnage.

"They never had a chance, did they, sir?"

"No … they didn't," Darius muttered. "At least Goll will do no more killing *this* night."

"These victims are physically like you, sir."

Darius's brow rose. What his crewman said was true enough. None of the dead had blue skin or shocking white hair like Gemma. None bore the round-headed and brown, furry countenance displayed by Barst. "Looks are deceiving. On my world they haven't the strength even a child could summon. At least that's what I've been told." He sighed heavily and shook his head in sadness. "Why, by Cronos's balls, would they attack an entity so obviously superior? Surely they must have seen he wasn't like them! Why didn't they back off?"

"Why are some of the victims in similar clothing?" Gemma asked.

Darius sadly shook his head. "I hate to say it, Gemma, but I think they're some kind of enforcers."

"What a terrible end to our quest," Barst offered sadly.

"Barst … follow the others back to the ship. Take personal responsibility for putting Goll in enviro-stasis. I want no mistakes," Darius ordered as he re-holstered his weapon.

Gemma still moved among the victims, making one last check for life signs. Assuming she might find a survivor, Darius knew they wouldn't last long. Earth's technology wasn't advanced enough to undo the damage Goll wrought. He silently cursed himself for not getting to Earth sooner.

"Two still live," Gemma announced. "But one is more seriously injured. If my communo-chip is translating properly, this tag on his clothing says … Martinez. The second one is a woman. Goll's weapon may have been drained by the time he shot her. She's not so badly burned as the others."

Darius moved and knelt beside the surviving male that Gemma identified as *Martinez*. The stricken enforcer opened his eyes and stared straight up at him. Moonlight in the small clearing was quite bright now. It was as if the darkness fled, coinciding with cessation of hostility and the capture of the one responsible for the slaughter.

The Martinez man grabbed the front of his uniform tunic and pulled him closer. Darius didn't fight what was likely to be a whispered last request. He simply gazed back into the dying man's eyes. Life was quickly leaving this injured fighter.

Darius let the man whisper into his ear. The croaked appeal was the same he'd have made to anyone if the situation had been reversed. He only understood the message because his communication chip was attuned to their current surroundings—Earth English, a place called Balboa Park.

Sadly, he couldn't say anything in comfort. The dying human had no such communication device embedded in his body. But he *could* hold the man's shoulders and upper body in such a way as to convey friendship. He wasn't even sure the tubular lighting devices lying on the ground or the moon overhead allowed the victim a good look at *his* face, but body language and gentle physical contact might offer some comfort.

Darius listened intently as a seemingly last request was made. After it was done, the man referred to as Martinez closed his eyes and went limp. He breathed his last.

Gemma tried to revive him, but she soon stared into the darkness, whispering her version of a prayer.

As commander of this sad scene, there was nothing Darius could say or do. He swallowed down a sudden knot that lodged in his throat, and gently lowered the dead man back to the ground. Gemma was the first to speak.

"Commander … what did he say?"

Darius sighed heavily, ran one weary hand across his face and the back of his neck. "He wanted me to 'look after my partner … the woman who was with me.' Those were his exact words."

"Assuming there are no other victims in these woods and that this is the female he spoke of … her life signs are barely stronger than his were," Gemma told him. "I don't know how much longer she can survive. I can barely read in the light from these primitive tube-illuminators, and we can't turn on our own ready beams without summoning every constabulary in the area, but I think the tag on her uniform says … *Blake*. Is that a name or some kind of unit designation?"

"I don't know. I think it's probably her name. Just like Martinez," he surmised.

Gemma glanced at her portable wrist bio scanner then moved closer to the one survivor. "The blast entered this woman's left shoulder and went all the way through. Her breathing has been compromised. She won't survive the night if the primitive physicians here cannot treat this kind of laser injury, and I find it inconceivable that they could."

Piercing alarms tore through the stillness.

"I think those are warnings coming from conveyances. If memory serves, they're called sirens," Darius said. "We're out of time. I don't want to encounter innocents not knowing if even stunners will do permanent damage." He looked down at the unconscious woman. "We need to go now, Gemma."

"Sir, we can't leave her. She'll die if we do," the medical technician insisted.

He slowly shook his head. "You know our orders. We've interfered all we dare. "

"Sir ... *please*. We can't leave her. You said she's probably an enforcer ... like us."

Darius touched the unconscious human woman's face. She was shivering, indicating shock was taking hold.

"Sir? Let me try to help her," Gemma pled.

"Orion's blood!" He gazed down at the still figure before them and made a decision for which his entire crew might suffer.

A dying man had begged for this woman's life. If someone he cared for were lying there, what would he do to give them one more chance?

An old wound opened and he knew the answer to the question. His crew would understand. The punishment, if there was to be any, would be much less harsh for saving a life than if he'd taken Goll's. If he had his way, that penalty was to be his and his alone.

"Get moving. I'll take her aboard but I have one last duty to perform."

"Thank you, Commander!"

He watched as Gemma made her way out of the clearing.

Alone with naught but the dead and one injured human, he stood. Then he set his sidearm to maximum.

"I grieve with those who will never know what happened to you. But know your deaths were not in vain. Justice will be served … you will rest in peace," he murmured just before he fired and incinerated the bodies of the dead around him as well as all their weapons.

There could be no evidence as to the existence of an advanced race. Leaving dead behind—dead whose wounds were produced by highly unconventional weaponry—was in violation of supreme code. Let the local constabularies ponder the burned clearing and conclude what they might. There'd be any number of reasons for such a thing, but none rationally involving advanced races from other worlds.

Like the men he'd just incinerated, no one would ever know what happened to the girl. But if he took her aboard the *Titan* and she *did* live, she could never know this world again. Rules prohibited returning her.

He easily scooped up the injured girl's body then followed Gemma out of the clearing.

"Enough damage has been done this night," he called ahead toward Gemma's quickly retreating form. "We need to be aboard our shuttle, back on the *Titan*, and out of their atmosphere before we're detected."

"Understood. I'll relay the need for alacrity," Gemma said as she picked up her pace. "And I'll have a surgical team standing by for the Earther."

Only a few moments later, but what seemed like a lifetime after the evening's events, Darius entered their rescue shuttle craft with Gemma.

Barst looked up from the flight controls. "By your command, sir … Goll is in enviro-stasis. I saw to that parasite's incarceration myself and will make sure he's secured aboard the *Titan*. He won't be giving us any problems."

Darius saw his crewman's large head tilt in shock. Apparently Barst didn't believe his eyes. The man was staring down at the body in Darius's arms.

"In the name of the Creator of all things … who have you brought aboard?"

"She's an injured Earther," Gemma explained. "If you'll take her to the med lab, once we're aboard, Commander, I'll ready an incu-unit for her and inject a communo-chip."

Darius nodded while firing off another order for Barst. "Lift off as soon as possible or Earthers will be crawling all over us. I don't want any incidents."

"Yes, sir," Barst responded.

In moments, their rescue shuttle landed aboard their command craft—the *Titan*.

As landing bay crews scurried about to make sure the hull of the shuttle was decontaminated, Darius carried the unconscious woman to the med lab. Gemma rushed ahead to get her equipment ready.

By the time he entered the state-of-the art medical facility his technicians were so proud of, an almost imperceptible movement of the ship confirmed Barst had put the *Titan* into quasar drive.

He breathed a sigh of relief. Now they could head home. Their assignment was complete.

"Put her there, Commander." Gemma motioned to the incu-unit closest to her instrument cart.

He lowered the girl into the unit then straightened. His intent was to leave and head to the communication center. Someone needed to speak to the officers there, make sure they monitored Earth transmissions concerning unidentified flying objects. If they were lucky, they'd gotten away with nothing more than a few citizens transmitting news of some small, strange craft in the night sky. It was for that very reason the much smaller crew shuttle had been used as a landing unit.

Just as he was about to turn, something made him glance down. He hesitated then froze in place. Air actually left his lungs when he got his first good look at the woman whose life they'd saved.

There hadn't been enough time, nor enough distance from nearby homes and businesses to properly illuminate the clearing and get a closer look at a planet considered off limits. Nor had there been time for close scrutiny of anything other than who might or might not be breathing. Now, with pressure off, he took stock of the situation.

If anyone on the bridge needed him, they'd call. That part of him that *wasn't* on duty—the part below his waist—stirred at the sight of sudden, breathtaking loveliness. That first good look of the rescued victim was the very thing that froze him to the deck.

If a fusion bomb went off next to the ship, he'd have a hard time distinguishing between his response to that, or to this creature lying so still and pale in the incu-unit.

"She's exquisite," he murmured as Gemma and several of her assistants bustled and moved equipment.

Their injured Earthling had blood spattered over her clothing, neck, and face. Parts of her uniform were in shreds. All that notwithstanding, her skin was perfect, like the lovely smooth and white lunar stones of his home world. Her pinned-up hair was a soft brown color; golden lights shimmered within the strands. Her features were evenly aligned and delicate. Soft brows gently arched over each eye. Her very slightly upturned nose and high cheeks bore a small spattering of freckles. He noted she was more finely bred than half the debutantes his world presented for his perusal. Her body looked lean and toned. She'd probably be tall and athletic if she were standing. And *unlike* many spoiled and selfish beauties his family shoved at him ad nauseum, this woman had dared face a creature many times more powerful, one who'd killed on numerous worlds and who'd been chased to this end of the galaxy before finally being incarcerated.

Sadly, she hadn't been privy to that information but she'd bravely faced Goll down even as her comrades fell.

He leaned closer; curiosity over the color of her eyes gripped him.

"Shame," he softly murmured.

"Commander?" Gemma prompted as she readied her equipment.

"I ... I was just thinking that it's a shame such a beautiful creature might die."

Gemma looked up from her work then briefly studied her patient. "My ... she *is* attractive, isn't she? Even all that blood doesn't hide her attributes. For such a small waist and hips, her breasts appear generously ample. Wouldn't you say so?" she teased.

He straightened and cleared his throat. Now wasn't the time to indulge in flights of sensual fancy. Certainly not over an injured Earther.

"What news of her condition?" he gruffly asked.

"According to the data being correlated by the incu-unit, she has a good chance to recover. I'll need to close her off now so the zerion mist can do its job."

He backed slightly away and watched as Gemma flipped switches that automatically closed the lid to the box-like, silver unit. He stood in silence as the magnetic field modulators were affixed and attuned.

Gemma knew her job. There was no good reason for him to stand there gawking. For the life of him, he simply couldn't make his booted feet turn and leave the medical facility. But when the staff stared at him, as if his presence was no longer necessary, he knew he'd overstepped a few invisible boundaries. His need was showing.

"Uh … I'd … I'd better get back to the bridge," he loudly affirmed.

"I'll relay any changes in her condition," Gemma said as she grinned up at him. "If she looks so good lying there with a big laser hole in 'er, I'm sure she'll clean up *quite* prettily."

He squared his shoulders and glared down at the med-tech.

Good-natured snickers at his discomfort made their way around the space.

"That's of little to no consequence to me!" he declared, a little too forcibly. "Just … just do what you can to help her. I'll speak with you about your lack of decorum later!"

He quickly turned and strode away.

•••

Hours later, Darius ran one hand across the back of his neck and rolled his shoulders in weariness. Since the bridge crew had no immediate need of him or his second-in-command, he and Barst walked to the detainment section. When they got there, they mutually considered their prisoner. Goll was quite thoroughly contained in the stasis cell before them.

"You need to rest," Barst recommended. "It's been many hours since we left Earth and you haven't taken a break."

Darius stared through the icy-looking clear pane of the unit. Through it Goll appeared even more gruesome than when he'd been awake. Hatred for his captive rose within him like morbid pestilence.

Goll couldn't see, hear, or move. He wouldn't need to be fed or removed from the cell for any reason, not until they landed back on Luster. That was the advantage of the stasis technology. A prisoner could be kept there for up to one year, without sustaining permanent injury. Yet, Darius wanted to turn the cell's controls off, jerk the malignant creature from his cryo-slumbering state, and beat him to death with his own two hands. Nothing would have given him greater pleasure than to tear the filthy murderer apart, bone by nasty bone. Something of his thoughts must have become obvious to Barst. His second-in-command kept trying to get him away from the cell before he acted on impulse.

"Commander, everyone in the Constellation League knows of your loss at the hands of Goll's sire, but we're enforcers. We must abide by the law or we become just like those we hunt." Barst paused and waited for a response. When none came, he tried again. "We've been together a long time. I'd hate to see you lose your freedom and your career over *this* bottom-feeding scum. And I'd hate to have to break in another commanding officer. It's hell on my nerves."

"I'll let him live, old friend. Only long enough to see him executed on Luster," Darius muttered.

"There's no doubt that will happen. He killed an ambassador, and we witnessed him destroying Earthers. The penalty for just contacting an isolation-class world is life in prison, never mind the murders."

"I want to be there when he dies," Darius blurted. "Forgive my callousness but I pray it's slower than usual."

"Darius, you need to rest," Barst reiterated as he dropped his superior's title. Perhaps you could stop by the med lab and have Gemma concoct some medication or other to help you sleep. Please, old friend … take my advice?" Barst placed his hand on the larger man's shoulder.

"All right. I'll do as you recommend." Darius turned with a sigh. "I want to see how our passenger is doing anyway. Creator only knows what I'm going to do with that one. I'll stand before High Council for taking her."

"Gemma will vouch for your reasoning. The woman's injury was caused by our prisoner. What can the admiral say? Were we supposed to let her lie there, suffering from a horrible wound before she eventually died? We certainly couldn't kill her, and she had a class one laser wound that could have never been explained to her contemporaries. Worse, she might have been accused of something when she couldn't rationally explain what happened."

"True enough," Darius agreed with a slow nod.

"Besides," Barst continued, "I popped in and took a look at her, just as Gemma was adjusting a communo-chip. Once the admiral sees that beauty he'll probably want her aboard *his* ship."

For some reason, that comment didn't settle Darius's nerves. The admiral's taste concerning young women was notorious. The man wouldn't give a flaming nova whether the girl in question was sexually compatible. A be-feathered, avian denizen from the outer rings of Moriar, Admiral Tel'duc't was nothing if not a hedonist. He liked designing new and exotic ways to pleasure himself, and with females from every conceivable species. Sadly, the bastard openly bragged about it. And though the ladies in his company were always quite willing to serve as arm candy for someone as powerful as a League admiral, those same females weren't well thought of after Tel'duc't was done with them. Darius slowly frowned, then turned away. His destination was the med lab.

Every muscle in his body yearned for rest. He'd been awake for three straight shifts. Thoughts of getting his hands around Goll's emaciated little neck kept him from sleep. Now, thanks to Barst's council, he was seeing things more clearly.

A short time later the med lab hatches opened automatically as he entered the white and silver pristine space. Gemma stood there with her back to him. She was studying a computer screen.

"How's the patient?" Darius asked as he glanced at incubation unit.

Gemma turned to chastise her superior. "When are you going to get some rest?"

He rolled his eyes and shot her a slanted grin. "I must look worse than I actually feel as everyone is so concerned about my sleeping habits! As soon as you brew some of that relaxation potion you have hidden away, I'll head to my quarters. Unfortunately … I've been awake so long I'm not sure I *can* sleep."

"That *potion* is called Turesian tea. It has to be steeped the old-fashioned way for its benefits to be of value." Gemma grinned and got up to heat some water.

He took the opportunity to move closer to the only occupied incubation unit in the lab. According to controls on the outside, the Earther's vital signs were not only stabilized, but they appeared to have dramatically improved from those previously listed on the unit's database. "You were right. She's recovering."

As he spoke, he gazed through the top view port and noted how the woman's color seemed healthier. At least it was better-looking by Lusterian standards. There was no other comparison to be made but to what he knew of other races within League jurisdiction.

The woman's clothing had been removed, as every patient's was when placed inside such units. Without it, the injured rested more comfortably. In its place, a ubiquitous blanket covered her slender form. The top of it rested just over her breasts.

He saw her wound closing. Thanks to the electro-magnetically zerion-altered field within the unit, the flesh was suturing before his eyes. Even the scar would disappear as healing progressed. As he stared, other thoughts took the place of curatives.

He took a small step back when mental meanderings caused his gaze to linger on her perfect, creamy flesh. Her fingers were long and slender. The tips had been meticulously manicured. Her body was athletically lean without being unappealingly thin. Muscle in her upper arms was evident. Her hair shimmered in the light from within the unit. There were streaks of red in it that he hadn't noticed earlier.

How would it feel to run his hands through the long tendrils and curl them around his wrists? What would her voice sound like when she eventually spoke? Again, he wondered about the color of her eyes.

Blue.

He decided they must be a deep, sparkling gem hue, the color of Lusterian midnight stones that were rare and prized.

How soft she looked. How very holdable.

It'd been a long time since he'd viewed a female with such striking, perfect features. Her flesh almost begged to be stroked. A man who could win this courageous creature's affections would live in a universe of passionate yearning. Whispered secrets would be shared in the night. She'd likely have any lover on his knees, begging to take her.

The sound of Gemma's activities brought him out of the delicious reverie.

He blinked quickly, lifted his chin, and tried to regain his composure.

What in the galaxy was wrong with him? The last thing a professional Constellation League supervisor should be doing was ogling some nude victim of a laser attack, even if she was so heartbreakingly lovely, and even if he had been without female companionship for such a long time. In all respects, from the top of her head to the tips of her toes, she appeared just as any woman of his own Lusterian race would. There were only two arms, two legs, two eyes, and two very finely shaped breasts.

"Here, Commander, this should help you get some rest. It's all herbal, nothing harmful."

Darius took the mug Gemma offered and moved away from the unit. He settled onto a nearby lab chair and watched as Gemma worked with the controls on it.

"You know, she'll regain consciousness soon. She's moving her fingertips," Gemma informed him as she carefully lifted the lid.

Darius placed his mug on a table and came to stand by their patient again. He wanted to see if his impression of her eye color was true. Gemma would never know about his interest in that regard, only surmising he was acting with concern.

• • •

Laurel fought her way out of the hazy darkness. Even through closed lids it was clear soft light surrounded her. She felt warm but lethargic, as if she'd been asleep too long. There was a minor twinge in her left temple, as though someone was gently pressing against it. After taking a deep breath and slowly letting it out, she opened her eyes and waited for them to focus. Throbbing in her left shoulder reminded her of the last thing she remembered. She and Cory were in Balboa Park. There was a stakeout and it'd gone bad.

She looked up and shook her head slightly to clear it.

The face of a pretty woman hovered above her own. This person might have been her own age, but who'd really know since the hoverer was a wonderful shade of *aqua-blue*.

Laurel assumed her caretaker *might* be a doctor, but lovely and exotically tilted dark eyes—coupled with pointed ears peeking through a mass of long, snow white hair—made her think twice. What she was seeing, blue skin inclusive, had less to do with any modern medical facility and more to do with Halloween or a little girl's fairy party. Someone was obviously playing a very weird practical joke. Or there was a better explanation.

I'm on some pretty damned good meds.

"Can you hear me?" the blue woman asked.

Laurel tried to speak but only managed a low moan.

"Here … give her some of this," a man's voice offered as the woman took a mug from him. "Are you sure her communo-chip is adjusted properly? One has never been placed in an Earthling as far as I'm aware. Maybe it's not working or something's wrong."

Laurel was helped into a semi-seated position. She tried to sip whatever was being offered. Blue skin girl seemed kind enough. The drink was warm. It was soothing on her throat and tasted like mint.

"Try to speak again," the woman encouraged as she set the mug aside then lowered her patient into a prone position again.

"My partner ... Cory ... is he all right?" Laurel whispered.

"The chip works," the woman said. "I'm happy to turn things over to you, Commander. I just save lives. Explanations are *your* job."

Someone else moved into Laurel's field of vision. Whoever blue girl spoke to was about to address her. She remained absolutely still and tried not to lose it. Something told her she wasn't in Kansas anymore, and that she wasn't going to like the answer to her question.

"Enforcer ... I assume that's your formal occupation ... can you remember anything that happened?"

Laurel stared at the new face hovering over hers. She registered his question, posed in a very deep baritone. Her vision was clearing by the moment but she wasn't prepared to believe anything she was seeing was real. The meds were still onboard. Perception of their presence made her hallucinatory state at least a bit more acceptable.

The man who'd just spoken was much taller than blue girl. He had long, dark hair that was pulled back at the nape of his neck. Strands of it were falling over one shoulder. He sported some kind of uniform. Epaulets on the shoulders of his dark tunic made him look as though he might be a member of some elite police group she'd never heard of. But the gentle kindness in the blue girl's tone wasn't in his. The clench of his tan square jaw, the dark green riveting eyes staring down at her, and the serious set of his handsome, godlike features were off-putting.

"I remember someone attacking us. What about Cory?" Laurel asked again as her voice cleared.

She waited as the two characters consulted. All she wanted was one simple answer. Why weren't they giving it?

"Here, Commander, I found this in her clothing. It appears to be identification of some sort."

That was the second time blue girl referred to tan guy as *commander*. What was that all about?

"This is your identification, isn't it? You *are* an enforcer, aren't you?" he asked.

She gazed at the black badge wallet tan guy had in his right hand. He'd opened it and her ID number and photograph were clearly visible. She was about to ask what idiot on the planet wouldn't recognize a police ID, but tact made her reel in the comment. She licked suddenly dry lips and tried a different angle. Tan guy quickly offered her more tea. She eagerly sipped it if only to gain more time to compose an answer.

For the first time, she noticed the very large, coffin-like box around her. The interior was lined with lights and soft, white padding.

She tamped down panic, swallowed more tea, and amped up her courage. Now wasn't the time to lose composure. Not if she wanted out of this damned container and back into reality. If she screamed or did anything that made them believe she was out of control, they'd likely load her with more drugs. What she had in her was too much as it was.

"I'm with San Diego PD. Please ... tell me where my partner is. His name is Cory Martinez. We were ambushed on a stakeout. What happened to the men with me? Are they all right?"

Something was very wrong, aside from their not answering questions concerning Cory. A supervisor should be present. She saw no one remotely resembling another SDPD cop. Because of their absence, she wondered if anyone had contacted her parents.

Dad was ensconced somewhere in the northern part of the state with a wife two years younger than she was, expecting a baby anytime. Mom was at a law convention in New York with her live-in, architect lover.

As dysfunctional families went, they weren't strongly attached. Still, someone should have contacted them. They might not show up for any mundane reason but surely they'd come if their daughter had almost been killed.

How long had she been lying in the coffin-like box? How bad off was she that such a contrivance was necessary?

She barely turned her head, afraid to see what devices might have been attached to her body. There wasn't enough nerve in her entire arsenal of mettle to ask what hospital this was, and why she'd been placed in the big container. Someone would tell her soon. But she just couldn't ask about the medical side. Not yet.

With every passing moment fear crept into the smallest part of her soul; she was sure it invaded even the smallest cells. Dread made her lie absolutely still.

She clearly saw the faces of her attendants. Garish as blue girl was, big as tan guy seemed from her prone position, their expressions were pretty raw. Neither wanted to speak first. Theirs was the expression cops wore when they knew they had to deliver bad news.

She began to shake.

Stay strong. Don't break. It'll be all right.

• • •

The poignancy of the moment and the look on her face would forever linger in Darius's memory. He knew he'd never rid himself of the haunted gaze so fixed on him. Her eyes *were* a luxurious, gemlike blue that should have been shimmering with laughter. He got the impression she was much more acquainted with happiness than he. She had cared for her friends, they'd likely cared for her. Being as close to her comrades as the concern exhibited, how could she be anything other than contented? At least as long as they were present. But they weren't alive any longer and he needed to say so.

The man who'd died in his arms had asked for this woman's care. He recalled that last wish, even as that brave soul's life force sped into the universe and conjoined with others of equal valor. He owed that man's friend the truth.

He took a deep breath and exhaled before speaking. There was no easy way to tell her, but the responsibility for announcing deaths at the hands of criminals always fell to the most senior officer.

He uttered what was necessary, to dispatch news quickly and as painlessly as possible. "I'm sorry. Your friends didn't make it."

In her gaze he immediately recognized the signs of disbelief. She looked back at him. Then her eyes shifted to Gemma. He could almost hear her thoughts.

Suspicion surely prompted her to question what he'd just said. It was a normal process of denial he was well aware of, having delivered such messages far too many lifetimes in his thirty-three years. But sooner or later, like it or not, the woman lying there would have to come to terms with the truth. It'd been spoken. It was up to time and circumstance now to drive that harsh reality home.

"I *am* sorry," he softly repeated. "But there's no other way to say it. You're an enforcer. You know what can happen when you accept responsibility for defending others."

Laurel shook her head. "You've probably misunderstood. We shot at a man … me and some other officers had to have brought him down. That's who you're talking about. Our suspect is the one who's dead. Not Cory!"

Darius considered her response. Experience in these matters came to his rescue. Because of his communo-chip, he was able to read the primitive writing next to her picture ID. Gemma had already mentioned this woman's name when they'd found her lying on the ground. But he still needed to hear her say it. She needed to maintain a level of consciousness his explanations required. Answering mundane questions compulsory of any enforcer might buy her the time she needed to emotionally acclimate.

"What's your name?"

"Laurel Blake. What's this thing I'm in?" she asked as she glanced at rows of blinking lights inside her container.

"This is an incubation unit or simply an *incu-unit* as we refer to it. It generates energy fields that react with the body's cellular processes. It significantly shortens and augments healing." Then he got back to the meat of the discussion. He moved closer and simultaneously gestured for Gemma to drop the walls of the incubation unit away. Once that was done, he softly repeated the facts she needed to understand.

"The only two people left alive were you and the man who attacked you. I'm sorry."

She searched his face, looking for any break in his gaze. Even now, her instincts kicked in. She was processing as someone with experience in such matters.

He simply waited. There were no tears, no cries of protestation. Just silence.

She eventually turned away. Before she did, he caught the telltale look of even firmer denial. A bit of coldness entered her blue eyes. She wouldn't be convinced easily. But neither was she a collapsing heap of emotion. Primitive as he'd been led to believe her culture was, that was to her credit. He gently squeezed her hand then moved away.

Gemma followed him a short distance before adding an opinion.

"Her vital signs dropped when you told her, Commander."

"Watch her. Make sure she isn't left alone," he ordered.

"Yes, sir."

Darius walked out of the med bay and slowly headed toward his quarters. He unfastened his left shoulder epaulet and let the front of his tunic fall open. As he approached his quarters, the hatch separated to allow him access. He moved into his personal space and quickly pulled the fastener from his hair.

Stripping his clothing off without caring where the garments landed, he numbly stepped into the shower compartment and let the hot water wash away what was left of his emotions. He could only speculate as to what would happen to the woman.

There was one other truth yet to be told.

She could never go back to her world. He and his crew had been given special dispensation to chase Goll "wherever he ran." But Earth—as a world too technologically backward to know about other life forms—was a planet listed as unapproachable for any other reason. Life in prison or even the death penalty might be applied in any case where a violation existed; special permission to go back wasn't obtainable.

Gemma, Barst, and the rest of his crew knew about the *no association* edict. What *he* knew was that it couldn't be augmented for the purposes of returning Laurel. Gemma believed that once the woman's wound was healed, and no evidence extant concerning the existence of otherworldly life forms, her patient could be returned with no harm done.

He hadn't thought the consequences through while he carried the Earther back to the ship. Saving her life came first. That imperative outweighed all others.

Perhaps she'd rather be dead with her friends than on an alien vessel headed to worlds as yet unknown by her kind. Still, he could not have left her there dying. He couldn't have shot her to put her out of her misery. So Gemma's suggestion, as ship's med-tech, had seemed congruent with humanitarian aid. Especially when considering Goll's inhuman attack and her occupation as a fellow enforcer.

In effect, he'd already involved himself and his crew too much. But that was the situation and he was responsible as ship's commander.

He hung his head in weariness. Too tired to consider any thoughts of the future, he moved to his bed and sank onto it. Sleep came quickly.

•••

"Commander, we have a problem in the med bay."

"On my way," Darius responded after Gemma's voice, via the intercom, jerked him from deep sleep. He quickly pulled on a robe and tied it closed as he raced through the passageways.

Once he was in the med bay, he saw Gemma holding down the struggling Earth woman. Barst and several medical staffers ran into the space a split second later.

"What's happened?" Darius asked, maneuvering himself to help contain the struggling Earther.

"She isn't breathing right. A bio-scan shows there's a problem with something in our environment but I can't detect what."

"She was decontaminated when we brought her aboard. All of us were," Darius quickly asserted. "Wouldn't that equipment have indicated a problem?"

Gemma shook her head as she gathered medical equipment on a crash cart. "You need to keep her calm. My job at the moment is to keep her breathing. She went unconscious then awoke again gasping. She's fighting to keep from suffocating. That's all I know for sure."

"I'll hold her," Darius ordered.

As Gemma moved away, Laurel tried to fight her way out of the incu-unit. He held her down though he could see the effects of horrible pain on her face. She acted as though there wasn't any air at all in her lungs or she was being crushed under incredible pressure.

As the others gathered equipment at Gemma's command, he held the patient down with one hand then used his other one to punch buttons that lowered the sides of the incu-unit. Several more moments of fighting took place.

In all his life he'd never seen a gasping person so determined to fight for every bit of air they could get. Clearly, she wasn't ready to give up.

"Almost ready," Gemma called out.

He turned his head to ascertain the staff's whereabouts. When he looked back at the woman he was pinning down, she looked straight at him. Without enough oxygen in her lungs, she couldn't speak. But there was fervent appeal in her pure blue gaze as she stared up at him.

As before, the communication chip embedded in her left temporal lobe made it possible for her to understand his words. He spoke softly, lifted her into his embrace, and cradled her in his arms as he uttered assurances.

"Quiet … we won't let you die. You're safe. You're among friends and you'll be all right. I promise. I promise," he repeated over and over.

Among the bravest of all acts was her brief nod. With that slight movement of her head, she'd given her trust and was trying to calm down even as the last vestiges of air vacated her body.

In moments she'd be unconscious again. If the reason for her medical problem wasn't found quickly his promise of safety couldn't be kept.

"Hurry, Gemma! Hurry," he quietly ordered.

"Keep talking to her," Gemma replied. "I just need a little more time."

He glared at the med-tech, trying to convey urgency without actually saying anything else. A "little more time" might be all she had. He did his best to keep the fear off his face and out of his voice. "Hang on. Gemma is the best medic in six quadrants. That's why she's part of my crew. Just keep looking at me." The woman responded to his command, though she was beginning to turn blue. He held her closer as Gemma approached with a hypo-injection. What seemed like many minutes since he'd entered the med bay were probably only a few seconds. He was holding onto, and responsible for, a dying woman who'd trusted him to keep her safe.

"Why is all this paraphernalia going on your emergency tray?" Barst asked as he quickly decontaminated his hands with bio-spray and pulled on gloves.

"I'm going to sedate her so I can split open her chest," Gemma explained as she repeated Barst's actions.

"*What?*" Both men shouted in unison.

"Readings indicate the decontamination unit we brought her through might have wrongly interpreted something she needs to live as dangerous to us. I don't know what the element was and I don't have time to figure it out among the millions of permutations that might have taken place. Right now I have to deal with the results. She's not breathing so I'm gonna fix it!"

"How could such a thing happen?" Darius asked as he held their patient closer.

"By all my readings her physiology is almost exactly the same as *yours*, Commander. Like I already said … there was something in her the decontamination unit didn't like."

Darius quickly lowered the Earth woman to the incu-unit platform again.

Gemma grabbed her tray, pushed Darius aside, and put an injection gun next to the Earther's neck, just below her left ear. When the med-tech pulled the trigger, the Earther's eyes closed.

Selfishly, he was grateful she'd gone unconscious. He sent a silent prayer to the heavens that all would be well. Everyone around him shared the sentiment evidenced in the urgency being displayed.

"Everyone get out of my way and hand me what I need when I say so. If you haven't scrubbed up, do it now or get out!" Gemma shouted.

"Have you ever done anything like this?" Barst asked.

"I've studied old holo files of such techniques," Gemma responded as she worked. "Usually, this kind of invasive stuff is left to specially designed computer equipment in major trauma facilities. But she's out of time and I'm all she's got."

"The incu-unit can't do what you require?" Barst asked again as he stepped backward.

Gemma didn't respond.

Darius gazed at Barst. The other man displayed a look of pure horror. He wasn't sure his countenance didn't bear the same expression.

He quickly turned to scrub up as the rest of the med bay staff did. It occurred to him that Gemma was risking her career and imprisonment for doing something so dangerous. Only the best surgeons were ever called upon to open a body. Technology was such that invasive surgery wasn't the norm. But Gemma had already pulled down the Earther's blankets, put a laser scalpel to the woman's chest, and was splitting it even as he stood there putting on a pair of sterile gloves and an emergency mask like everyone else in the space. As she cut, one of the other med staff officers slid a mask on Gemma's face, from beneath her chin. It was then affixed behind her head. A sterile gown was tied to her chest and around the back of her neck. Everyone in the med bay who had a reason to help was acting precisely as they should. He'd never been prouder of his crew.

But he still felt impotent. All he could do was watch as blood poured from the new incision in the Earther's open chest. Techs grabbed replacement units of all-blood from Gemma's tray, and began infusing them into Laurel via tubes attached to arm veins.

What if the all-blood didn't match an Earther's needs? Was there enough research to support the use of technologically advanced artificial blood replacement when speaking of a lower species such as an Earther? What if the gaping wound and open, beating heart—a heart that pulsed far too slowly now—was contaminated by atmospheric particulate in the med bay? What if Gemma slipped? What if … what if … what if …

"I can't believe I just closed one hole in her chest only to open 'er up again," Gemma angrily muttered as she worked. "That injection I gave her will keep her out as well as stave off pain and infection."

"But her oxygen intake—"

"Was also temporarily compensated for with the injection, Commander."

Gemma quickly called out for one piece of surgical equipment after another. Staff around the table acted with time-saving efficiency. He heard the frustration in their voices as they communicated with one another. Each of them was frightened they'd lose their patient. Caring wasn't limited to whether an injured person's race was less evolved.

Again, his chest swelled with pride. He turned to his second-in-command knowing he couldn't leave the Earther alone. Her safety was as much his responsibility as Gemma's.

"Barst … man the bridge," he ordered. "We're moving into uncharted space, someone needs to keep an eye on our scanners. I need to stay here."

"Yes, sir. I'll report on any unusual activity," Barst said, then hesitated before leaving the med bay. "I hope she'll be all right. Goll has done enough damage. She'd make an excellent witness at his trial. Diplomats would be hard pressed to ignore her account and use their oily machinations to get Gorm's son free."

"Indeed!" Darius nodded in agreement then put his attention back on the surgical procedure and the bloody, open mess that was now Laurel's chest. He sighed in relief noting how her chest rose and fell more evenly now. Clearly, she was getting oxygen though he wasn't sure what Gemma was doing with her lungs and heart to increase circulation. Such goings on weren't his strong suit. In the med bay, Gemma had total control. It was the only place on the ship where everyone, including him, yielded to her.

"Though I hit her with some heavy meds, she may still be able to hear what's going on so be careful what you say. Audible awareness isn't unheard of in these situations," Gemma softly advised as she kept cutting, snipping, and rearranging organs. "Commander … talk to her while I continue."

Darius's brows rose. He'd just been contemplating a question concerning exactly what Gemma was doing. Instead, he heeded her timely warning and moved closer to the injured woman.

The gore associated with opening Laurel's chest wasn't new to him. The site of it wasn't particularly shocking. He'd seen many casualties while enforcing laws in his assigned quadrant. But something about watching this backward little Earther lying there in the middle of her own blood and incised body tissue was so pathetic. He tried to come up with commentary that sounded intelligent. Something she'd grab onto assuming she *could* hear what was being said. He put one gloved hand on top of her head, noting the thick mass of hair as he conjured words of comfort.

"Don't be afraid. Gemma will have you right in no time," he whispered as he lowered his head to repeat the words through the barrier of the mask he now wore.

As the operation proceeded he actually saw the Earther's entire body tense. Later, she might not be able to remember what he'd said but right now, he was certain she really did hear every syllable spoken, just as Gemma had warned. He got the distinct impression she'd have reached for a hand to hold had she been able to move.

"Just a few more moments," Gemma relayed as she glanced between her surgical handiwork and holographic status updates generated by the incu-unit. "Okay. That's got it. I'll laser-suture the incision. The unit should remove even the smallest trace of the scar."

He recognized the sparkle in his med-tech's bright gaze, and heard the exaltation in her voice. Apparently, she was satisfied with her skills in saving her patient's life.

"She should start breathing deeper soon, sir. Her heart rate is already going back to its original speed. Of course, I don't know what normal is for her. I'm not that up on Earther vital signs but since her biology is almost identical to Lusterian specs, I think it's safe to say she'll be just fine." Gemma pulled off her mask as the incu-unit walls rose around her patient.

Other staff in the med bay sighed with relief and congratulated their head surgeon on a wonderful job. Darius simply stood there trying to hide such utter relief as to be nonsensical given his short acquaintance with the injured Earth woman. She'd fought so hard to live. As on the planet's surface, she'd displayed one more instance of utter courage.

He glanced at the patient and considered the creamy skin of her full breasts and perfect proportions of her body, as it'd been fully exposed when Gemma pulled the blankets back to make her initial incisions.

When one of his other crewmen caught him essentially gawking, he cleared his throat and turned guiltily away. That medical assistant snorted in amusement while pulling clean, thicker coverings over the injured woman's body.

"I ... I was just thinking her physiology and mine might be similar for a reason," he defended. "Lusterian researchers speak of ancestors visiting many worlds in ancient times, before a ban was ever initiated regarding planets that were too backward to be exposed to higher technology. Earth might have been one of those planets. It seems logical to assume some of my home world's travelers might have intermingled with various populations, thereby producing entities whose physiology is similar. Even compatible."

"That's quite true," Gemma maintained as she took off her gloves and bloody surgical apron before handing them to a nearby attendant for sterilization. "Unfortunately ... our decontamination unit didn't see the similarities, only the differences, Commander. The decon-unit actually damaged alveoli in her lungs. That's what I was repairing."

Gemma moved away from the incubation unit, and the presence of staff still cleaning and caring for Laurel. She crooked one finger and Darius bent to hear what she'd say.

"Sir ... I had to add a third lobe to her left lung, move some veins and arteries around and reconstruct them. Primarily, I moved her heart to the back and center of her chest to accommodate the larger lung system." She briefly glanced back and moved further away from Laurel's resting space while lowering her voice. "The thing is ... I can't undo what I've done. Not without killing her. To put her back the way she was would cause her to strangle in our atmosphere, just like you saw. She couldn't diffuse our air for more than a short time ... a couple of hours at most." Gemma shrugged and shook her head in confusion. "I can run a thousand tests and never know exactly what the decontamination unit did. I really don't understand it since our atmosphere is so very close to Earth's. That being said ... she'd be a medical miracle back on her home world. She could survive *there* with what I've done. In fact, her breathing there would be vastly improved. But once her chest was examined she'd never be left alone. I don't have to tell you that her current physical state would in no way resemble her former one. Any youngster with a basic knowledge of anatomy would know there was something very wrong with the placement of her chest organs!"

"But … you said she can survive this way … right?"

"Oh, yes, sir! She'll be fine. The prognosis is great. In fact, no one from an advanced civilization would question the procedure. But, like I've said, an *Earth* physician—"

He raised one hand to stop her. "This shouldn't have happened, Gemma! That decon-unit is supposed to protect us, not destroy the body tissue of other races!"

Gemma shrugged and shook her head. "Maybe someone higher up knows this is exactly why we shouldn't be engaging Earth citizens. But I stand by my decision to bring her aboard."

"That'll be my problem—"

"You won't have to answer for it alone, sir. Whatever's said or done in regards to her presence, I'll be with you. It was as much my call as yours."

He ran one hand through his hair. "I'm sorry to say her return to her home was always a moot point, despite this sudden turn of events."

"Sir?"

"I had orders to categorically stay away from Earth once Goll was caught and restrained. I can't countermand them for any reason, not without risking serious consequences for the entire crew. The law in this regard is standard League code."

Gemma snorted and sadly nodded. "I never really believed the admiral or any other official would give us permission to take her back, including the unusual circumstances. I just *hoped* I might make a case on her behalf." She shrugged. "Not to dwell on the obvious but … she's not going to like it. I wouldn't."

"I wonder if all Earthers would have been as damaged by our decontamination unit," Darius mused.

"I don't know, Commander. We may never know. We're on our way home and that's the way things are."

Gemma put one hand to the back of her neck and tilted her head left then right.

"You'd better get some rest. I'll stay with the woman," Darius offered as he walked to the incu-unit and stood to one side.

"You've barely had enough sleep yourself, Commander."

"Yes, but I've had *some*. When your patient comes out of this unit I fear you and your staff may need all the energy at your disposal. There'll be many questions to answer."

"Aye, sir. The instruments on the unit should alert you to any problems. Call if you need me."

"Good evening," Darius uttered as he watched Gemma walk out of the med bay. He took one last look at the patient then settled back in a nearby examining chair to get some rest. Thoughts of home filled his mind. But then his contemplation turned to Goll.

Unspeakable loathing filled him. He tried to tamp down feelings of vengeance but it was no use. But for their prisoner's sire, life would have been vastly different.

There was a point when harboring such vengeance would have been unthinkable. Something told him that once Goll was dispatched, the emptiness wouldn't heal.

For the minutes the execution lasted he'd have some satisfaction. After that, he wasn't sure of anything.

"I'll watch you die like the blood-sucking, soulless bastard you are!" he whispered. "Any race that would take a child's life deserves the worst punishment."

Bitterness filled him to the brim. It threatened to spill over and drive him to the prisoner section of the ship to do the deed now. It took everything he had to make himself stay right where he was. He mentally repeated his oath to watch the Earther.

No matter how he tried, sleep escaped. It'd been replaced by thoughts of the past, a past he couldn't undo.

His hands gripped the arms of his chair until his knuckles went white. For some reason, all his attention went back to the unit and the woman therein. At least one other on this ship would feel as he did. At least one more soul would have a reason to see Goll dead.

But to keep from making a victim of himself, destroying his family's historic reputation and all it stood for, he'd do his duty.

He dragged air into his lungs and reclined in the chair, trying to think about anything but the hole in his heart.

Chapter 2

"Good morning, Commander. How was your rest?"

Darius blinked, shook his head, and sat up in the examining chair. "If your patient is recovering as expected, I'll welcome my own bed."

Gemma stood by the incu-unit for a moment, examining its readings. "According to what I'm seeing she's progressing remarkably well. Much faster than I would have attributed to an Earther. But then, except for that damned chip I introduced and her injuries from the attack, I perceive she was in fine condition to begin with."

Darius stood and stretched then he shook his hair back. I need a shower. Then I'll relieve Barst on the bridge. Call if you need me." He strode from the space, leaving Gemma to do her job.

• • •

Laurel slowly opened her eyes. There was stiffness in her shoulder and a slight burning sensation in her left temple. She carefully sat up then blinked several times.

She was in some kind of hospital, but it wasn't like any trauma center she'd ever seen.

"Feeling a little better?"

She turned to see the *blue* woman at her side, bearing a mug of something whose steam indicated a hot beverage.

"Who and what the hell're you?" she rudely blurted, shaking her head slightly as if doing so would rid her mind of the Halloween entity in her company.

"I'm Gemma. And you're on board … I'd better let you come to your senses a little more before I unload *that* bomb."

"Look, I know you're trying to help but something isn't right."

"Oh?" Gemma said, looking her patient over in concern. "Any pain should diminish quickly. If you're experiencing discomfort in your temple that will shrink in a—"

"No," Laurel interrupted, "that's not what I'm talking about. It's my eyes!"

"I don't understand. My equipment doesn't indicate anything is wrong with them." Gemma glanced at her readings and shook her head in confusion.

"Well, something is *definitely* wrong. You're blue! And your eyes and ears are pointed. Now, tell me again there isn't something wrong."

"Ohhhh, *that*." Gemma smiled. "No, there's nothing wrong with your eyesight. My eyes and ears are pointed. As to being blue, I actually like to think of myself as a very attractive shade of teal."

Laurel decided she was hallucinating. Or maybe she'd finally gone off the deep end. Police work did that to some people. "Look … let's start over." She took a deep breath and tried to speak rationally. "My name is Laurel Blake. Everything's a little foggy right now, but I do know that I'm an officer with the San Diego PD. Other officers and I were trying to catch a murder suspect when we were attacked. I need to know what happened and where I am. Does my supervisor know what's happened? And where is my partner, Cory?"

"You don't remember what the commander told you?" Gemma slowly asked.

"Who is *the commander*?"

When the woman calling herself Gemma turned her head toward the door Laurel took a good long look at the creature that'd just entered. She automatically grabbed the sheets covering her body, jumped from her bed, and backed to the far wall. Her mouth went completely dry. Joining her and blue girl was a man with features and a build similar to that of a huge brown bear.

Long brown hair fell straight back from his forehead. Larger and more muscular than any man she had ever seen, he looked as if he could cause some serious damage. Crazier still, bear man was wearing a black uniform and high, shiny riding boots. A weapon was strapped to his right side. If she'd seen this on television, she'd have laughed. But nothing about this situation was amusing.

"All right … I've had enough," Laurel muttered. "I don't know who you people are, where I am, or what you think you're doing. I want some answers and I want 'em *now*!"

"Laurel, maybe you'd better sit down and I'll try to tell you whatever you want to know," Gemma gently told her.

"Maybe I'd better come back another time," bear man suggested, as he looked apologetically at Gemma.

"No, Barst. Laurel wants answers. She should have them." Gemma put her attention back on her patient. "Laurel, you were hurt and we had to bring you here. You would have died if we hadn't."

Blue girl walked to a large monitor and pushed a switch mounted on a keypad. A white barrier the size of the entire side of the wall lifted, and the black vastness of open space appeared.

Laurel gasped and felt her heart almost stop. Through the large window she saw stars, enhanced visions of planets and galaxies in the distance—just like those the telescope scenes always displayed on the internet. It felt as though she'd just walked onto the set of one of those science fiction TV shows where the wall wasn't a wall but an open view port, through the bulkhead of a spaceship.

"Okay … okay … this is some kind of joke, right? Somebody put you up to this, didn't they?" Laurel whispered as she dragged her gaze from the scenes of deep space and glanced from one creature to the other. Sadly, blue girl and bear man weren't smiling.

"I can assure you, it's no joke," bear man solemnly told her.

"Laurel, sit down. Let us explain." Gemma held out her hand in a gesture of comfort.

Laurel shook her head in denial. "People are looking for me. The PD will have officers crawling all over the city when I don't show up. Whatever you're doing, you'd *better* let me go. Holding a cop hostage can send you to the big house for the rest of your lives," she warned in her most aggressive tone. "Depending on where you've taken me, you might even face the death penalty if you do anything to me. Is it worth all that?"

Bear man shook his head and looked at blue girl. "Big … house? Gemma, why isn't my communo-chip interpreting that colloquialism—"

"Prison!" Laurel shouted. "You can go to prison for abducting me."

Bear man simply shook his head and left the space.

Gemma sat down in a chair and sighed loudly. "Primitives are always so difficult when they're confronted with something they don't understand. Let me try again."

• • •

"Commander?"

From his seated position in the officer's bridge chair, Darius swiveled around to face Barst. "What is it? You should be getting some rest."

"Commander, our … passenger … is awake and asking a lot of questions."

Darius's brows rose. He shrugged and responded in an absent fashion. "I can imagine. But I wouldn't expect her to comprehend too much. From what our scientists have said, Earthers are quite backward. The best of them are only thought to use about ten percent of their brains. I'm sure Gemma will have her hands full, but she'll cope. I have every faith in her." His gaze went back to the forward view port.

"I don't envy Gemma."

"I'll stop by at the end of my shift," Darius offered. "By then I might have a better idea of what to do with the woman."

"What to do with her, sir?"

"Well … it's obvious we must take her back to Luster. We can't put her on some alien world after only just learning her people aren't the center of the universe. From what I hear, that's what they believe." He paused for a moment before continuing. "It's just that … I'll have to find something for her to do. She can't make the whole trip wandering around aimlessly, can she? Seems prudent to keep her busy. Keep her mind off things … assuming that's remotely possible."

Barst snorted then glanced at a nearby bulkhead monitor. "Sir, someone seems to have changed our heading home. We're still headed for Luster, but not by the course I laid in."

Darius explained his actions so his second-in-command and best friend would understand. "If someone wants to free Goll, they won't expect us to navigate this new course."

"You expect trouble?"

"There's no sense taking chances. I want him back on Luster to face charges and I'll do whatever it takes to see the job done."

"And our new passenger? What will we say concerning her?" Barst asked.

"Given what Goll did to her and her fellow enforcers, I don't foresee a problem with her presence. I've come to the conclusion my superiors will understand. She's just one of the butcher's victims." He waved a hand in a nonchalant gesture. "Besides … as I've already stated, the woman's practically primal. She's incapable of causing much trouble. I'm sure Luster officials will see the situation in the same light."

• • •

"Laurel, stop it! I know you thought it was all a nightmare, but it wasn't. We've been through this dozens of times. Since you awoke and were removed from the incu-unit, I've tried explaining what happened on Earth. I've outlined every detail I can recall, from the time we found you right up to this point. I've told you about the creature that attacked you, but now your anger isn't helping. Besides, if the commander hears about your behavior, he'll place you in confinement." Gemma ducked as Laurel threw another of many medical containers at her.

"Put down that revolver looking thing in your hand and I'll consider it!"

"It's nothing more than a tranquilizer injector. The medication will help you rest."

"Try using that on me and I'll paint the walls with you ... I swear to God!" Laurel angrily threatened.

"Laurel ... please ... I mean you no harm. I know you don't understand, but I can't explain any better. Especially not when you're behaving so irrationally."

"Irrational? I'll give you irrational!" Laurel yelled as she lunged at Gemma.

Unfortunately, blue girl moved too quickly to be caught. She'd put some kind of operating table between them and meant to stay behind it.

Not to be outmaneuvered, Laurel continued to stalk her, intent on getting answers for this farcical situation. "I'm what you called a ... what was the word again? Oh yeah ... a *primitive*. How else would I behave, except irrationally?"

"Laurel, *please* ... " Gemma began, only to find Laurel advancing on her again.

"What did you people ... if you can be *called* people ... plan to do with me? Experiment? Take your probes and dig through my ovaries for a little genetic material to play with? Or does the shit get weirder?" Laurel growled.

"Of course not! We don't experiment on other beings."

"Well, there are a lot of folks on my planet who tell a different story," Laurel objected, then continued her tirade. "I used to think all those UFO types were batshit crazy, but not anymore." She made her repeated demand that had heretofore been ignored. "Now … you take me back to where I came from or I swear I'll make you wish you'd never heard of Earth!"

At that moment the hatch to the med bay opened and bear man walked in. He was accompanied by the big tan guy she remembered from her time in the coffin-looking device.

"Thank the Creator," Gemma gasped. "I didn't know how much longer I could hold her off. She's got the worst temper I've ever seen in one creature."

"*Human!* I am *not* a creature!" Laurel exploded. "I'm human."

Bear man began to chuckle.

"You find something amusing?" Laurel angrily asked. "Because things don't look so funny from where I'm standing."

"Forgive me," bear man calmly told her, "it's just that … for a woman who sustained a very serious injury you seem to be doing remarkably well."

Laurel grabbed at the blanket which currently served as her only clothing. She kept it wrapped around her body with one hand while wielding what looked like a glass specimen jar in the other. Her hair had come loose from the uniform code bun she'd worn the last time she was on duty. It currently lay around her shoulders, causing her to shake it back as it got in her face.

• • •

Darius took a long look at the med bay. He'd never seen it so horribly awry. It looked as though the entire space had been hit by a truncheon blast. Glass was shattered everywhere. Bedding from normal, pristine examining platforms was stripped. That bedding was strewn from every conceivable hanging point. Equipment that should have been contained within sterile shelving units lay on the floor like so many scattered bits of metallic refuse. Carts were overturned; medication containers lay in colorful abandon across countertops. A keypad used to open the main viewer in the port bulkhead had actually been pulled from its containment unit. It lay smoking and flashing on the med bay deck.

"What in the name of … Gemma, what happened?"

Gemma swallowed hard. "We … we had a little difference of opinion. Laurel is under the impression that we mean to harm her. I've tried to tell her otherwise, but she's a bit confused. When I attempted to sedate her she became … upset."

"*Upset?*" Darius growled as he pulled his shoulders back and imperiously clasped his hands together at the base of his spine. "The med bay looks like a Lamarian she-cat barreled through here! Did *she* do this?" He motioned toward Laurel with nothing more than a jerk of his head.

"She's a bit confused," Gemma repeated.

Laurel squared her shoulders and planted her feet apart. "Yeah … I did it!" she admitted, as she lifted her chin in defiance. "Who's askin'?"

Darius looked at the Earther and narrowed his eyes in anger. The woman's posture indicated she was daring him to do something about her behavior. As commander of this ship, he was about to take up that challenge.

"Barst, Gemma … *out!*"

"Commander," Gemma began, "you have to understand. Laurel has been through a great deal. We have to be patient and—"

"Barst, take Gemma to the bridge," Darius ordered as his gaze lingered on Laurel.

"Come on, Gem," Barst said as he used the shortened version of her name. "This isn't going to be pretty."

Barst took the med-tech from the space as Gemma protested in Laurel's defense.

Darius saw their patient looking him over, the way a predator sized up its prey. He almost felt sorry for her. To her, his height must appear massive. She was head and shoulders beneath him, even though she stood quite tall.

She'd obviously seen men and women in uniform. But the black League tunic, pants, and boots he always donned were more officious than the clothing he'd seen on the dead enforcers. And as he recalled, their hair had been shorn quite close to their heads. None sported a long black pelt tied back as was the custom of his world. No, he was sure she'd never seen any other enforcer quite like him.

He took a moment to gaze into her eyes, attempting to judge her reaction. For a split second he thought he saw real fear in her blue, enraged stare. But as he acknowledged that fright with the slightest nod, she rallied and lifted her chin higher. He got the impression she didn't like being studied and presumed weak.

She gripped the glass jar in her left hand with firm resolve. Whatever momentary lapse in courage she'd had, she quickly willed it away and faced him like some demon goddess about to strike.

Anger over her ungracious and childish behavior warred with something in his gut, some instinct to protect. That last emotion was outrageously absurd, especially given her apparent willingness to cause trouble. But it was there all the same.

•••

Laurel forced herself to quit shaking. He sensed it. And when someone knew you were scared they used it. But how could one man possibly be so big? How could a man look so much like the mythical Ares, god of war? Why did she fear someone who looked human enough when bear man and blue girl hadn't frightened her at all?

Towering at least seven feet, the man staring her down had shoulders as broad as the front end of a small sports car and a chest about as thick as most walls. At least that was the way he looked from her current, unclothed position with nothing but a jar to wield in defense.

Though his black tunic, tall black boots, and tight pants were uniform perfect, the darkness of it appeared to match his mood. Hair about pectoral length, currently tied back and left to flow over one shoulder, was in absolute contrast to any uniform code she'd ever heard of.

Like everything else over the past few hours, reality was proving worse than any nightmare. Tan guy was glaring at her with all the love a big panther showed a small rabbit. At almost five feet, nine inches, with all kinds of martial arts titles and trophies, and seven years of police experience, she'd thought herself fully capable of fighting pretty much anything when it came to hand-to-hand battles. Big, tall, and square-jawed, handsome god man stood in front of her reminding her to check that conceit. Dark green eyes drilled holes into and through her. If she'd been anywhere else in the known universe, it wouldn't be far enough away.

She mustered what courage she had left. No one was going to find her wanting in the nerve department. That much she could do for all the other Earthlings who'd been abducted, probed, and disbelieved over the past decades. Poor, poor souls. If the rest of Earth knew what she did, those people wouldn't be made fun of any longer.

Laurel took a deep breath and spoke her piece.

"I'm guessing *you're* the infamous commander I've been hearing so much about? Or did I just dream they'd called you that when I was lying in that coffin?"

Laurel forced herself to glare at him when every instinct told her to run. Once again, she was startled that this mountainous being *looked* human but he could easily be some kind of head-popping insect for all she knew. Maybe these creatures could shapeshift and this one was just holding back until such time as he figured out what to do with her or how to serve her for dinner.

As she'd spoken, his hands came from behind his back and now opened and closed menacingly. As another show of strength, he placed them on hips that appeared to be forged from iron. Like bear man, this human-looking entity wore a weapon that hung from his right side in a low-slung leather-like holster. The angle of it reminded her of old Saturday morning westerns she'd watched on TV as a child. Fortunately, the thing was still holstered. He hadn't aimed it. *Yet.*

She moved away from the wall, hoping he would follow. If she could lure him away from the hatch, there might still be a way to get out of this space. Sad for her, that meant getting around his gravity-defying ass.

Some part of her brain didn't want to believe where she was or what happened. The illusion they were in deep space might just be that.

"So, the little Earther has claws and the inability to thank the people who saved her life." Darius spoke quietly, though ominously.

"*Saved* me? You've *kidnapped* me and I've been told the others who were with me are dead. You want me to thank you for that?"

"We weren't responsible for anyone's death. The man who killed your comrades has been placed in custody. He'll stand trial for what he's done."

As she sidestepped closer and closer to the hatch, hoping he'd think she was just moving out of nervous anxiety, she saw his eyes narrow. He moved to block her. His body was so large there was no way she'd get by him, even if she did drop the only blanket covering her body and ran like hell.

"Let me go," she demanded. "I don't belong here."

"You're right ... you don't. But we'll all have to make concessions. The man we tracked to Earth ... the same man responsible for killing your friends ... has a date to be tried on a planet some distance from our present location. I'm under orders to see this done, and Earth is in the opposite direction. I will ask about returning you to your world when my current assignment is over."

"Yeah? And how do I know you're not lying? Who are *you* that you can make any promises? I want to speak to the highest authority!" She swung her head again to move her hair back over her shoulders.

"I am the highest authority on this ship!" he said as he pointed toward the deck.

• • •

He tried to ignore the soft waves of shimmering brown hair that she'd just tossed back. The thick, soft, and luxuriant textures of those tresses made him want to reach out and stroke them. He shook his head to put his mind on matters at hand and off how tempting her slender body was, all wrapped in that blanket with bare, creamy shoulders exposed and fire flashing from her blue eyes. He'd been in space too long.

Taking time so her anger might abate, he slowly explained who he was. "My name is Darius Starlaw. My surname is in deference to what I do; it's a moniker adopted by one of my ancestors when my family accepted law enforcement as their profession. You'll probably discover from my crew that my real surname is Regalis. This name isn't used outside a few circles on my home world."

He continued speaking slowly and on matters of little consequence to help her calm down. Still, his opinion concerning her behavior must be known. In space, there was no room for tantrum-throwing harridans. If she was an enforcer, she should be used to following orders. Now, whether she liked it or not, she'd follow his. She had no choice.

"I'm the captain of this vessel and by protocol and desire, I require the title of *commander* be employed. As for your not knowing whether I'm lying or not, you don't. You simply have no other choice but to trust us."

Darius paused and looked around the space. It was difficult to control his temper but he did the best he could.

"While I can understand your distress, I must make my feelings concerning your behavior quite clear," he stoically informed her. "If there are any more outbursts like this, I'll confine you to a compartment no larger than the incubation unit by the wall. It's that same *coffin*-like, healing device you referred to previously. If you cannot control yourself, I'll reconsider my promise to ask for your return home. Do I make myself perfectly clear?"

"Yeah ... I understand," she bitterly responded. "And is there any reason why your medical person says she put something in my brain? Something I never permitted?"

Darius sighed loudly, passed a weary hand over his face, and answered quickly. "That was done so you could understand and converse with numerous sentient beings. The chemicals induced in your brain ... by way of the communo-chip's neural stimulation ... will allow you to hear your language being spoken as other tongues are automatically translated. The processes induced by the chip also affect your eyesight in this respect. The most common colloquialisms will be transmitted in a way that will be perfectly clear. In short, you'll hear and see languages spoken in your native, Earth tongue. You'll be able to read many other languages as well. This should make life easier." He lifted his chin in a superior fashion and looked down at her. "This is the advanced technology from which you now benefit, and which could save you a great deal of trouble. Conversely, we all see and hear you speaking in *our* various languages."

"I guess that accounts for how I'm hearing perfect English," she grudgingly acknowledged, "but I've got a few choice phrases for your internal memory banks!"

He looked her over in what he hoped was a deprecating fashion. Then he glanced at the nearly destroyed med bay once more. "Thus far, you've made your feelings abundantly clear, madam. I reiterate that what my medical technician did was standard procedure. The communo-chip must remain in place … unless you *don't* want to communicate for the duration of this trip. This, of course, is up to you. But I wouldn't recommend its removal." He straightened and pulled his shoulders back. "Now … I'd like to consider your infantile behavior a thing of the past. Is it resolved or must I have you incarcerated?"

She opened her mouth to speak but he walked toward the hatch and pushed several buttons on a bulkhead console. "Gemma … return to the med bay, please. Our guest is over her tantrum, and she's agreed to help you put the space back in order." He smiled when he saw the Earth woman's murderous glare.

"Yes, Commander," Gemma responded.

Darius stepped away from the communication console and walked slowly toward the Earther. She refused to back up and stared straight into his eyes as he approached. The creature was trying, with all her might, to show no fear. There was no hint of sniveling. That was a mark in her favor as he disliked those of the fairer sex who succumbed to tearful pleading in order to get their way. His once beloved mate had yielded to that habit and had gotten *her* way. An innocent child paid the price for it.

His trust for the fairer sex wasn't easily given nowadays, but it was easier when the woman in question looked him straight in the eyes. Just as this Earther did.

"One more thing. You'll need to stay in the med bay until I give you permission to leave. There are crew members and equipment aboard that you don't need to see. You wouldn't understand the technology at any rate. But there's simply no need for you to go gallivanting in an area where you might be hurt."

Laurel put the jar she held down, grabbed her blanket closer, and shook her hair back once more. "How long will it be before I'm returned to Earth?" she asked in a furious, low tone.

"I'll ask about your return as soon as we get to our final destination, as promised," he explained. "It could take up to a year for me to convince—"

"*What*! You're going to keep me a prisoner for an entire year?"

"You're not technically a prisoner. At least, we don't consider you such unless your behavior indicates we must keep you locked away." Darius softened his voice slightly. "You'll only be kept in the med bay until such time as I can secure other areas of the ship. As I've said, there're places aboard … and beings among us … that you don't need to see."

"Why? What're you hiding?"

"As I'm sure your Earth law enforcement facilities have places where they wouldn't want civilians wandering, and operatives whose identities should remain secret, it's the same way aboard this vessel. That's standard operating procedure. You don't have a need to know certain things."

"But why will it take so long to get me back home?"

Sadness in her brilliant blue eyes touched Darius and made him feel longings he hadn't experienced for a very long time. He understood the yearning for home, even if hers was a primitive little rock that wasn't worth mentioning. The promise to ask for her return was genuine though he knew what the response would be. For now, all she needed to know was that he would *ask*.

"It isn't the distance from Earth that takes so long to travel, especially not since we have access to wormhole technology. It's the process of trying the man we were sent to capture. Trials can proceed slowly on Luster … that's our destination."

She lifted one hand and tucked a stray strand of hair behind her ear. For a second, she looked like a little girl trying to decide what to do. Pity wasn't something he was used to feeling. Not any longer. The sudden presence of it in his arsenal of stoic control weighed heavily.

"I must warn you, enforcer, it's entirely possible that you'll be called upon to stand as a witness against the man who attacked you and your friends."

She turned her head away. In that instant he knew she wouldn't talk about what had happened back on Earth. At least not yet.

"Y-You talk like you're some kind of cop."

"We're referred to as enforcers, just as I've referenced you. Obviously, we saw your uniform and your identification, hence the mention. As for the word cop, my communo-chip equated words similarly. The difference is that I enforce laws binding a group of planets together. These planets comprise an organization called the Constellation League. The man we chased to your planet was an escaped prisoner from our justice system. He murdered one of our officials."

"He killed a lot of *my* people," she angrily muttered, finally touching on the subject. "What kind of ... *thing* ... attacks the way he did?"

Darius further softened his tone and his demeanor. Now, she was acting more rationally and they could converse, assuming one could speak intelligently with someone of such a mentally inferior race. "The man with whom you came into contact is called Goll. If Gemma hasn't already told you, he's called a *vamphiere*. Though they can exist well enough on other food, they prefer to feed off the flesh and blood of newly killed humanoids. Whenever we come across his race, we keep a very close watch on them. Citizens of most planets report their whereabouts to us whenever they're spotted. There aren't many of them left, but they can be quite dangerous as you've discovered."

"And that's what killed Cory?" she whispered as she stared out the view port.

Again, he felt something akin to pity. He saw a brief glimmer of tears in her eyes before she closed them. Oddly, the presence of them now didn't rile him as it once might have. Her response was entirely warranted as she'd just lost someone who was apparently close to her.

Once again, he grudgingly gave her credit when the woman looked back at him and seemed in control of her emotions. In this particular, rare instance, he was actually sorry she masked her feelings. There would come a time when that control slipped and she'd need help. He knew. He'd been where she was now and understood what she was shoving down and why. The difference was she'd eventually have the opportunity to seek solace in her own way. He hadn't the luxury of accommodating old wounds.

"What will happen to this person? This ... Goll?" Laurel questioned.

"It's my sincerest hope that he dies slowly," Darius answered honestly.

Laurel nodded.

"Commander, I'm outside the bay hatch. May I enter?" Gemma requested via the outer, passageway intercom.

"Yes, Gem. Everything is under control," Darius responded as he uncharacteristically shortened his med-tech's name.

The hatch opened and Gemma stepped into the space.

Laurel turned to the medical technologist spoke quietly. "I'm ... sorry ... about the way I behaved. Thank you for helping me." She paused and searched for the right words. "Many of my kind don't really believe in people from other planets. Can you understand why I acted the way I did even if you can't excuse it?"

Gemma smiled. "Of *course* I can. You've been put in a terrible position because one of our prisoners escaped. The fault isn't yours."

Laurel returned the ready smile Gemma offered and nodded. Then, without acknowledging Darius's presence further, she began to straighten the space and pick up objects that had been strewn about.

Darius spoke quietly so that Laurel wouldn't hear. "Gemma, can I speak to you?" he asked while nodding toward the outer passageway.

Gemma nodded and followed him out of the med bay.

Once they were in the space outside the hatch, Darius leaned against one bulkhead and gave his new orders. "Until I can make arrangements to shield some of our more secure areas, I've restricted her to the med bay. The less she sees the better. She understands that I'll ask for her return to Earth as soon as Goll is taken to Luster and stands trial. What I haven't told her is that such a request will most certainly be denied."

"Sir … she should know—"

"Not yet. Now isn't the time. I don't want to have to lock her up, but I will if she thinks she's out of options. She'll fight and I can't have that kind of behavior aboard this vessel. Besides … it's my hope that once she knows us better, she'll accept the news with greater understanding."

"Ohhhh … I don't think so, sir."

"Be that as it may, this is my decision. I have a ship to run and I can't have this distraction. Understood?"

"Sir … she's not someone to be—"

"The discussion ends now," he commanded.

"Aye, sir."

He sighed when Gemma dropped her head in apparent disapproval. "I promised I'd ask on her behalf, as stated. This I *will* do and I'll put it in the strongest terms to the powers-that-be. There might be a small chance if I can word my request tactfully. So … let's just leave it at that."

"Sir, there's another problem."

"What *else*?"

"When we get to Luster, our own scientists may want to examine her."

"And why is that an issue?" Darius pushed his huge frame away from the bulkhead in concern.

Gemma lifted one shoulder and let it fall. "I'm not about to suggest they'll do anything to her that would be harmful. But they've never come into physical contact with any Earthers that I'm aware of. They'll want to give her an exam outside of any decontamination controls we've already taken. They'll want to make sure I haven't missed something potentially harmful."

"She should expect as much. One of us would most certainly be examined if we'd fallen into Earthers' hands."

"Sir, please try to understand how she must feel," Gemma pled.

"Your heart, as always, is in the right place. But Gemma ... and I cannot stress this enough ... I have a ship to run and we have a trip home that could be dangerous in certain sectors. We can ill afford time spent on infantile dramatics. The woman will have to understand, and I'll tell her what she needs to know when and as I think it's appropriate. She's already proven she can't handle stressful situations. I'm amazed she was ever made an enforcer to begin with, but then Earth *is* as backward as planets come. Even our own scientists and humanists corroborate that sentiment. Now ... this is the last I'll speak of it. You may speak more about how her friends died if she asks; she obviously knows about that part of her sad story. But you and none of the crew are to say anything else. Not one word. I'll make sure this general command is known throughout the ship."

He stalked away, squashing any feelings of remorse, empathy, or even the much-vaunted superior intellect he credited to his Lusterian heritage.

Chapter 3

"I don't understand," Gemma said as she watched Laurel straighten the mess she'd made of the med bay. "What did the commander say to change your demeanor?"

Now sporting a blue robe made of some thick, warm fabric, Laurel stopped picking up surgical tools and stood to speak to the other woman. She sighed heavily and shrugged. "It's simple. I want to get home but I'm out numbered and out-gunned. I realized that even if I were to fight my way out of this place, where would I go? Out there?" She waved a hand toward the vastness of space just outside the view port. "At first, I convinced myself this was all some kind of crazy setup—something to get even with a cop. But no one would go to these lengths over me. I'm just a street pounder. I wouldn't be worth it."

"I know that seeing people from other planets must have been quite a shock. I've done it all my life so it's nothing to me."

"You don't know the half of it," Laurel replied heartily.

"You must be a very good enforcer on Earth. Despite your fears, you've managed to gather yourself quite well."

"What choice do I have?" Laurel responded as she bent to retrieve more equipment.

"Look, after we get this place picked up, maybe you'd like to see where you are and some of the ship's functions," Gemma offered.

"As advanced as you people seem to be, don't you have robots or androids to clean up messes?"

"Not aboard a standard enforcement vessel of this type, no. Our space is limited and everyone is expected to take care of the ship and personally inspect their work stations. We have to report in regularly on any problems. Helps keep us all safe if we don't depend on technology in that respect."

"Sorry … I was being sarcastic," Laurel said. "As to leaving this space, I don't think the commander would approve."

Gemma pursed her lips. "Well, there are things you're going to have to know. How to get food when you're hungry and how to get clothing to wear. These are essential. Your uniform was ruined when you were attacked."

"If I ask a few questions will that get me into trouble?" Laurel tentatively asked.

"Not with me." Gemma smiled. "I have orders concerning certain … issues … but other than those ask away."

"Okay. The first thing I noticed was that you and I are fairly the same as far as body structure. Oh, I'll grant that there are few changes, but not as many as I'd expect."

"Are you asking if there are others who vary greatly from your own form?"

"Yeah. I guess that's what I'm asking," Laurel said with a shrug.

"The answer is yes. There are those aboard who're quite a great deal less humanoid-looking than you, me, and the commander. Barst, the second-in-command you've already seen, is one of those beings. But despite his gruff appearance he's really a sweetheart when you get to know him." Gemma bowed her head coyly.

Laurel registered there might be some romantic connection between the med-tech and the bear man she referred to as Barst. But she kept the obvious questions concerning how-do-you-do-*it* to herself. Besides it being none of her business, she wasn't altogether sure she wanted to know. There were other things she needed to wheedle out of Gemma. These had to do with her immediate safety.

Gemma continued her instruction. "Our teachings tell us that, thousands of years ago, the Creator of all things sent out explorers to inhabit different parts of the known universe. Earth was one of those planets. We're all supposed to have descended from those same explorers though we've evolved, technologically speaking, faster on some worlds than others." Gemma kept speaking when Laurel didn't acknowledge that Earth might be one of those "other" worlds. "Many races have kept their original appearance. Many more have altered theirs as a direct result of breeding with other entities⊠"

"God. I believe in God," Laurel murmured.

"That's one name the Creator has been called. There are others. And I'm glad that you *do* believe. He'll help you on this journey, Laurel. With him, you'll never be alone."

"Yeah, I'm gonna need the company. But, if your teachings are correct, why didn't we advance at the same rate? I mean … if all of us came from a few seed individuals, shouldn't they have all had the same technology to begin with?"

"That's one of the mysteries for the priests to explain. Maybe it has something to do with the Creator's will that we make our own choices." Gemma shrugged. "It's a choice to build a weapon to fight your neighbors. Another to put all your energy into a source of fuel to light cities, then to move into the stars. Perhaps that was where technology began to separate one civilization from another."

"Well, there's one thing your commander is right about. *None* of the technology I've seen should be on Earth yet. We have too many ways to kill each other as it is!"

"I was told, before we were sent on this mission, that Earthers can be excessively violent," Gemma said as she nodded in agreement. "Our scientists have monitored transmissions from your world and they've reported on this tendency. Your statement proves their summation is true. How difficult it must be for you to enforce your laws under such conditions."

"Only sometimes. It's worse when innocent people have to die." Laurel heard the bitterness in her voice but couldn't have curbed it. "I understand the man who killed my partner is in custody on this ship."

"Yes, he is. Goll … the vamphiere who killed your friends … is in a cell, within stasis mist. He's sort of frozen in time. We don't have to worry about any escape attempts or his threatening any of the crew. His species is very volatile."

An idea suddenly popped into Laurel's head.

What if she could find a way to get to Goll and make sure some so-called advanced race *didn't* set him free? The very thought went against everything she believed in as a cop, but something told her she may never see home again. More to the point, she knew Cory would try the same thing she was thinking.

Despite the commander's statement over wishing the vampire-like thing dead, who knew what an advanced culture might do? That he'd murdered primitives—like Earthlings—on a far off planet might not even be a pertinent factor in his sentencing. If she understood the situation correctly, space cops were probably as ineffective when it came to penalizing requests as they were on Earth. Hadn't the commander only *wished* Goll dead? That openly uttered sentiment meant the man in charge of this space ship didn't have a lot of pull in getting his quarry sentenced.

"Uh, Gemma, maybe you could show me how to use the computers now? I'm kind of hungry," Laurel lied.

Gemma smiled brightly and briefly clapped her hands in a show of joyful expectation. "That's a sign your health is improving. Come on. I'll show you how to order food, though the capacity to obtain more than the basics is limited from the med bay."

Laurel hated using blue girl, but what did she really know about her? And what difference did her personal feelings make when one was trying to survive? She had to use her wits. Empathizing might not be the best thing to do.

With that in mind she watched every move Gemma made and made a mental note of each button the woman pushed. To further glean information she might need, she began a casual series of questions.

"Um … I may speak and read a lot of other languages now, but that won't account for customs. I don't want to push anyone the wrong way. I've already had a bad start with your commander. Will you help me learn how to stay out of trouble, Gemma?"

"Of course! That's a very prudent idea," Gemma said as she nodded. "The commander is a fair man, but he does have a temper. He's a little short on compassion these days."

Laurel had no trouble believing that. To get around the commander and commit to her plan, she concentrated on every word Gemma said. If big, tan, muscle-building guy lost his temper over her having trashed one space aboard his precious ship, he was gonna shit a real fury turd before she was done. But there was one thing about cops she guessed might be universal. They didn't do what they did expecting to be popular. With that thought in mind, his good opinion was the last thing she worried about.

• • •

"Commander, we're approaching Chamron," Barst advised, as Darius stepped onto the bridge and took his seat.

"Have we received permission to dock?" Darius asked as he checked the computer readings on the console in front of him.

"Yes, sir. Everything is in order, including our refueling request."

"Good. The sooner we get off this planet, the better. Some of the locals aren't enamored with enforcers. Besides, it's been fifteen days since we left Earth but it feels like a year. I want us home."

Several of the crew heartily murmured in agreement.

The hatch to the bridge opened and Gemma took a position to the left of Darius. "Sir, as soon as we've docked, may I speak with you?"

"Go ahead, speak your mind. Barst can handle things from here on."

"Well … it has to do with Laurel." Gemma hesitated in saying more.

"What's she done *now*?" Darius frowned as he took note of Gemma's concerned expression. The last thing he wanted was trouble while in *this* particular port. Inhabitants of Chamron were known to start fights at the first inclination. He'd have to watch every step they made while dealing with locals. He couldn't spare the time for the Earther's fits of childish temper.

"No, sir, she hasn't done anything. It's just that … given the fact she's got to be assimilated sooner or later, I thought …" Her voice trailed away.

"You're not remotely serious!" he blurted.

"Why not?" Gemma pressed. "She's been cooped up in med bay doing nothing but research on the computer. The isolation and whatever she's looking at in the general library records isn't helping her attitude. She's let it slip on more than one occasion that she's not sure she's really on a ship at all. What better way to make her face reality than to put her in a position she can't deny?" She sighed heavily. "Sir, I think it'd do her mental status some good. As med-tech, it's my professional opinion she'd be better off and so would we all, once she understands there are no schemes, no deceits. She has to recognize the truth about what's happened to her."

From his console, Barst chimed in. "She's *still* confined?"

"She *is*," Darius confirmed. Then he thought for a long moment and actually considered the request and its implications. He stroked his chin and stared out the main view port. "However crazy it sounds and however reluctant I might be to encourage some incident … Gemma may have a point."

"She does?" Barst asked in shock.

"Of course I do!" Gemma defended as she glared at Barst.

Barst shook his head in wonder. "I don't get it."

Darius did his best to explain in light of Gemma's professional counsel. "Our … guest … can't go back to Earth. To contain further displays of irrational rage, she hasn't been told. I reiterate the general order that only I am to discuss certain matters with the woman."

Barst and Gemma nodded in unison as did any bridge crew standing near enough to hear.

Darius tapped the arm of his command chair as he thought on the matter. "I suppose … if she's to be living among cultures that will seem very strange … she must be introduced to them sooner or later. And while Chamron isn't the best place for such an experiment, it's a damn lot better than letting her walk down the gangway on Luster and watch reality hit her *there*. Creator only knows how she'll respond.

"Exactly my thoughts," Gemma said as she eagerly stepped closer to her superior.

"Can you certify this request *is* in her best mental and physical interests?" Darius asked as he stared at Gemma.

"It is, sir. As I've said … I'm not entirely convinced she believes all this has happened to her."

He lifted one shoulder and let it fall. "Gemma's professional opinion is valid."

"Assuming she's properly escorted, and Gemma and I volunteer for that duty, perhaps it could do some good?" Barst relented. "With us right beside her the whole time, what could go wrong? We'll stay away from known trouble spots. The refueling won't take that long."

"She's not a prisoner," Gemma pressed.

"Not *yet*," Darius quickly countered with one brow raised. "I suppose I'd better go too. Not that I don't trust the two of you," he amended, "but the woman is crafty. I can almost see the gears in her brain turning."

"I reiterated that she might be a little more compliant if she's given some freedom, sir. Getting off the ship may reinforce the need to stay close to us, depend on us. It shows a small amount of trust."

"Why does the word *compliant* not even register when I think of that woman?" Darius sarcastically uttered.

Barst snorted.

Gemma glared at the second-in-command.

Darius sighed heavily. "All right. I'll let her out of the med bay; she can leave the ship. But she's to be constantly escorted. Is that clear?"

"Thank you, sir." Gemma smirked as she quickly exited the bridge.

For the briefest moment, Darius felt manipulated but he quickly cast off the idea as impossible. Gemma hadn't a scheming bone in her body. He put his attention back on the approach to Chamron.

"Well … this should prove interesting." Barst grinned broadly. "It'll at least be a break in the monotony of deep space."

"Maybe Gemma's right. Maybe using reverse psychology is the solution."

"Sir?"

"Barst … if she sees what kind of trouble she could really get into, maybe the Earther won't pull any more theatrics and we can have a smooth voyage home."

"You know … she *has* a name," Barst reminded him.

"And we both have business to tend." Darius cleared his throat and adjusted the controls in front of him.

• • •

"I don't understand. I thought he was dead set against me even leaving the med bay much less the ship," Laurel said as she gazed at Gemma suspiciously.

"I just asked nicely and he changed his mind. The commander isn't made of stone, Laurel. He just needed some persuading. Besides … we've got a long journey ahead of us. He really never intended for you to stay locked away for the entire trip, I'm sure of it."

"I still don't get it," Laurel said, remaining steadfastly unconvinced.

"Just accept it as the offering it was meant to be. Now … let's get ready. We'll find something for you to wear. Think of this as a great exploration."

Questions raced through Laurel's mind. She was scared of everything that was happening and couldn't show it. No one was asking about who might be worried about her back home. And now she was about to disembark some sort of alien spacecraft and venture abroad on some world no one from Earth had probably ever heard of. If her gut wasn't hurting so bad, the situation would be comical. No old TV flick could have been plotted any worse. As alone as she'd sometimes felt back home, she truly knew the meaning of the word now and everyone around her was acting as if she should just accept, deal, and get on with what was left of her life. To them, she wasn't a person with feelings. Even Gemma's gaiety was wearing thin. Surely, if blue girl really cared, she'd be asking about things that'd been left behind.

An old training officer had once told her that as long as you're alive, there's a chance to change any bad situation. One just had to look for it.

With every bit of internal strength she possessed, Laurel stuffed down outer signs of fear and turned her mind toward getting home. Something she might see, get her hands on, or hear about might move her closer to that goal. She was sure, beyond any doubt, the big tanned alien running the show had no intention of ever taking her back to Earth. Those around him didn't want to talk about it. That's why Gemma acted so excited about something that, for her, should have been a tedious chore. Refueling a space ship couldn't be that exhilarating for anyone who did it on a regular basis. It'd be like gassing up the family SUV. Blue girl's merry response was forced. Gemma was trying too hard to take her mind off reality.

Laurel took refuge in sarcasm. It'd always saved her composure in the past. Other cops around her had always resorted to it. When life wasn't what you might wish, you had to bide your time until you could turn things around. And existence was as bizarre and serious as she'd ever known it. She now understood that trainer's point. She had herself. No one else. Even as Gemma chattered merrily on, *she* made plans of her own and those had to do with seeking revenge against the Goll creature. Either she'd die carrying them out or these aliens would finally understand the depth of her determination.

"I suppose Major Ass Hard will be coming along?" she asked, affecting a nonchalant air.

"Laurel! If the commander ever heard you call him that, he'd go nova." Gemma laughed, picked up her uniform jacket and changed subjects. "I can't wait to show you some of the shops and there's this tavern I've heard of ... "

Laurel forced herself to listen to Gemma's prattle. How nonsensical was it to stand there talking about such trivialities when someone should have been explaining exactly what had happened to Cory and the rest of her shift. How could something like this have to happen to her?

Utter lack of control almost overcame her. As Gemma kept speaking, she forced herself to breathe deeply and hang on, to act is if she could handle the situation. If there was any time in her life she needed to keep it together, that time was now.

The thing that scared her most—it kept entering her brain over and over again—was the thought that these beings thought her inferior. Even Gemma's attempts to help were colored with the assumption of total ignorance. What if her actions, as the first Earthling among these creatures, were judged and found so inferior as to generate harsh action against her world?

In a strange way, perhaps her plans might change such a judgment, even if they got her killed. If she were able to engage a plot against Goll and accomplish it, despite these creatures' obvious belief in their superiority, maybe they'd have to reconsider their underestimation of Earthlings.

No matter what happened from this moment on, Laurel intended to infuse every word, every gesture, and every action with an air of confidence, competence, and even blasé acceptance. If they thought it strange, let them guess as to her motives.

Strength. She had to be tough. She didn't want to go down in history as the person who caused Earth to be invaded.

Despite her resolve to stand with pride, she tried not to visibly shake when she walked down the ship's gangway an hour later. Gemma had found her a black tunic and leggings to wear, complete with high boots. Her blue companion said it was the best she could do. Unlike Gemma's uniform, there were no insignias on her outfit. As far as she knew, that put her on the bottom of the ship's hierarchy. But then she wasn't relying on any rank to pull her out of trouble. She'd have to do that by wits alone.

"Sure you don't mind my presence?" Barst asked as he approached them from behind.

"Of course we don't." Gemma smiled up at him with affection. "The more there are the more fun we'll have. Right, Laurel?"

Laurel swallowed hard, pasted on her prettiest smile, and held out her hand to the man with features resembling a bear. *Somewhere,* somebody was going to owe her an acting award. It was difficult looking into Barst's face and considering him sentient. This was a flaw she had to get over. Her ability to fool these beings depended on her ability to adapt.

"Sorry for the way I behaved in the med bay," Laurel said to Barst. "I just didn't understand the situation." That was a lame excuse for her behavior but it would have to do. *Show no fear; not ever. The less said the better. Don't let it get back to that commander how afraid you really are, of him and this entire situation.*

"No apology is necessary, Laurel. If I had been you, I would have done much worse than throw a few things around. My species doesn't like captivity. And it wasn't as if you asked to be here." Barst smiled and shook her hand in what was apparently a universally accepted greeting.

Laurel detected sincerity and warmth. But could she ever really trust anyone in this crazy reality?

Take no chances. Show strength.

Gemma grinned as she maneuvered her body between Laurel and Barst and looped her arms through theirs. "Come on, you two. Let's show this place some class."

As they exited the ship, Laurel was stunned by what she saw and almost forgot her self-admonishment to show no fear, have no reaction whatsoever, and give nothing away that could be cause for judgment.

The sky above them was Halloween orange and several planets hovered over purple mountains in the distance. She was unable to tell whether it was day or night on this world Gemma referred to as Chamron. She could see everything around her but that ability didn't imply the real sense of sunlight.

Sentient creatures of every imaginable size, shape, and color milled about what seemed to be an open-air bazaar. It reminded Laurel of a flea market she often went to in San Diego. Objects of all kinds were being offered for trade or sale. And like the people on Earth, everyone seemed to be looking for a bargain. The plant life she viewed was just as strange. There were large pink flowers growing on blue stalks; these were planted in hollowed-out rocky containers. There were other plants of various shapes and sizes, but none of them remotely looked like anything on Earth. Some of them even moved and seemed to follow her progress as she walked.

It occurred to her that some might be sentient and even be carnivorous. For that reason, she kept her hands to herself and didn't dare stop to smell anything.

As Barst and Gemma led her from one stall to the next, explaining what was being sold, she tried to steer away from anyone or any*thing* that looked like it might have a chip on its shoulder. And that was when she was able to discern *if* the creature in question had shoulders.

"Ohhhh, this is gorgeous. It would exactly match your eyes, Laurel." Gemma held up a length of sapphire blue fabric with golden fibers that sparkled in the light of nearby bonfires. These had been lit, as she'd been told, to celebrate the rising of the planet's moons.

In an attempt to feign interest and not appear as mentally unhinged as she felt, Laurel fingered the cloth. Its texture was like silk and cool to the touch. "It's lovely," she complimented.

In truth, she'd never seen anything so perfectly beautiful in her life. The fabric looked as if it'd been spun on the looms of gods. If she recalled history lessons correctly, many on Earth thought much the same thing when silk had first been presented. Still, even when referencing something as innocuous as a bolt of cloth, every word was guarded. Even sarcasm was stowed for the moment. As she'd recalled being told, her communo-chip made her language perfectly understandable. She mustn't do or say anything to give her fear away. It was so very hard when her insides felt like melted butter.

"Where is this from?" Gemma asked the merchant selling the fabric.

"This was spun by spiders in the Corius sector," the vendor explained. "It is the finest quality I have ever sold."

Laurel covertly looked over the gray merchant with four horns on its head. She had to act like she saw this kind of thing all the time.

Before this was over, she'd surely go insane. All she really wanted to do was run to tan man, grab him by the front of his immaculate black tunic, and make him take her back to Earth. Even if she had to hold a knife to his throat to do it. But where on his ship did one go to find a sharp knife?

"We'll take it," Gemma said, handing him coins from a small pouch at her side. "Could you wrap it and have it sent to our ship?"

"Of course, mistress. I know where it is docked. It is the only League ship here," the merchant said as he nodded and turned to wrap the cloth.

"Laurel, that cloth will make the most exquisite gown for you!"

"Gemma, you didn't buy that for *me*, did you? I-I'm very thankful, but I can't take it with me when I get back to Earth. How would I explain it?"

"Don't worry about that. Everything will work out, you'll see."

When Gemma averted her gaze and pointedly looked for Barst who was several stalls away, Laurel knew she was being lied to. And whatever kindness blue girl had shown seemed hypocritical. It was at once saddening and corroborative.

"Look at him, will you?" Gemma asked as she nodded toward Barst. "Here we are, among all these wonderful goods, and all he can think about are those wicked displays of knives and swords! Honestly, men are such single-minded asses."

"It seems there are some things that are universal," Laurel sadly remarked though she hid her despondency with a fake smile.

"I'm telling you, girl, if there were fewer of them and more of us, there'd be far less trouble in the universe." Gemma snickered. "But then, maybe there'd be far less entertainment, too." She grabbed Laurel's hand. "Come on. Let's go get him before he decides to take up residence with that weapons dealer."

Before blue girl could turn and walk away, Laurel placed her hand on Gemma's shoulder. "Thank you for the cloth, Gemma. I don't know if I'll ever have a chance to wear it, but it is beautiful. Maybe we could have it made into something you could wear, too," she absently offered.

"No. I couldn't get away with it. It would clash with my skin," Gemma joked as she presented a broad smile. "Look … I want us to be friends, Laurel. I truly do."

Angered that Gemma might be picking up on her angst, Laurel affected a laugh. "Of course. A person can never have too many friends. That's what I always say."

Gemma turned to catch up with Barst; Laurel followed quickly. She wished these people were genuine, but her cop's instincts warned about their motives. *Stay strong. Show no weakness. Now's not the time to go all soft because somebody gave you a gift.*

Later, hunger forced the three of them to find a tavern Gemma had heard about. They entered the dimly lit, square metal structure and found a quiet spot in a corner. As taverns went, this one reminded her of all those old science fiction movies where alien creatures meandered and partied next to each other. Loud laughter and eerie, wire-sounding music broke out. At least everything looked clean. All the furnishings were made of some bright steel-looking substance, the floor was gray stone. Lighting consisted of some kind of whitish orbs floating above the tables.

Like most cops, Laurel guessed her companions were trying not to expose their backs to an open doorway. Gemma found them a spot near a wall, where they could see everyone or every*thing* that walked or ambled in.

Purple creatures that looked like oversized house cats ordered drinks. Green women who would have otherwise looked like Earthlings served orders. The barkeep was a huge, gray worm-thing with a broad smile pasted on his face. He seemed jovial enough but she had a hard time keeping her eyes off the menagerie, acting like she belonged.

Her companions stared at her then glanced at each other. They knew she wasn't mentally with them. To cast aside doubts concerning her nervousness, anger, and secret desire to get back to Earth, she threw out what she hoped was a benign, conversational question.

"So … your commander didn't feel like a shopping expedition?"

"Normally, he lets the crew have shore leaves alone. It's his way of giving us time to vent without his being present. *This* time, he actually said he'd join us." Gemma shrugged. "I think he may have been held up by the refueling crew."

Barst leaned forward to be heard over the rising din of nearby revelers. "Refueling wasn't the issue. On landing, our consoles showed a glitch in the ship's port security monitors. I would have taken care of it myself, but he insisted on handling it. I'm sure he'll be here soon."

More songs broke out and Laurel glanced at the singers. "What's with all the partying?"

"Aside from this being one of a very few bars on this world, the nearby market is a sales venue for three sectors of space," Barst told her. "Friends are always meeting up in such places, reliving old memories, talking over old times."

Gemma leaned toward him and shot him an impish grin. "And what would you like to talk about, Barst? Something exciting like tactical star navigation, or Simbrium as a new fuel source?"

"Why not?" He laughed heartily. "I'm sorry if I don't find delicate shades of fabric and new makeup techniques of riveting value."

Gemma playfully swatted his arm before turning to Laurel. "Honestly! Here the man is, alone in a bar with two scintillating women and all he wants to talk about is enforcer crap!"

"Don't get saucy, wench," Barst joked. "Maybe I'll have you clapped in irons for insubordination when we get back."

"We haven't had those things aboard for years, unless you've managed to hide a pair for … *special* … occasions," Gemma fired back.

"Could be." Barst leaned toward her as he gazed deeply into her eyes.

Laurel cleared her throat and the two crew members resumed positions less close to one another. "Look, if I could borrow whatever passes for money I could order something for us to eat," Laurel suggested, wanting to get out of their way for a few moments and have a little time to think on her own.

"That's all right. I'll take care of it," Barst said, winking at Gemma.

Gemma snorted. "Don't listen to Mr. Chivalry, Laurel. We don't pay for our meals. The Constellation League gives us food cards. We show those to the proprietor and he gives us anything we want. The League reimburses the tavern owner," Gemma explained. "Here, take my card and get something that looks edible. Don't feel like you can't ask what the food is. When we're on a mission, I do it all the time. There are too many dishes in the universe for anyone to know them all."

Laurel let out a long breath and shrugged. "Okay … we'll all take our chances then." She took the silver-colored, metallic card Gemma offered and walked the short distance to the bar. Luckily, worm guy was as affable as he looked and even helped her place her order.

She had to try harder. Gemma and Barst would go to *Commander Ramjet* and complain about her attitude if she couldn't act normally. It angered her that she was expected to after all that'd happened.

Ordering the food quickly, she waited until it was ready and acted as though she knew exactly what to do when it was finally served on a large round, silver hovering cart. Luckily, one of the cat creatures at the end of the bar had just made a similar meal purchase and she was able to watch what he did with the tray. At least, the creature looked like a he.

God! Why is this happening to me? What the hell did I do to deserve this?

Instant remorse washed through her like a cold wind. What right did she have feeling so sorry for herself when Cory and the rest of her friends were dead?

Then a huge assumption almost brought her to her knees.

What if they weren't dead? What if she'd just been told they were? She shook her head in confusion. Why would the commander and Gemma say her comrades had been killed by something whose name sounded like the mythic vampires of old Earth legend? Why did the alien word *vamphiere* sound like a European pronunciation of the English word *vampire*? Why did that savage who'd attacked them in the park actually look like some movie version of Nosferatu?

These things were points to ponder. The longer she was among these strange beings, the more she was determined to find a way home.

Following the purple cat creature's example, she took her hover tray by one hand and gently guided it toward the table where blue girl and bear guy were happily conversing as if nothing in the universe was wrong.

Resentment almost made her tell them just where to go, using some seriously nasty descriptors in the process. But she reeled in her temper, remembering the commander's threat of what would happen if she didn't.

One minute at a time. Just breathe and hang in there. I might wake up from this nightmare any time now, and Cory and I will have a good laugh over it.

Chapter 4

"That was wonderful," Gemma complemented in reference to Laurel's choice of cuisine.

"I agree. I couldn't have chosen better myself," Barst added.

"Thanks," Laurel said. "I tried to pick something I knew wouldn't hurt us. The menu was a bit broad. There were some things on it I don't even want to talk about."

In truth, she couldn't have cared less what they ate, but sticking to things that looked like vegetation made sense. There'd only been colored protein cubes on the ship. These were pretty damn tasteless, but they'd never made her ill. In this new environment, anything looking like meat was totally off her menu when she didn't know if she'd be eating something bovine-like or some critter that, to her, would constitute a cute house pet.

The round, silver fruit Gemma referred to as marquoi was tasty, reminding Laurel of a margarita. She'd also opted for bread that looked, amazingly enough, like a big artisan wheat loaf. Then, there was cheese the barkeep said had been rendered from ruminants on Arteia—wherever that was. Still, the cheese tasted and looked like cheese. Then, there was the flat and elongated, bright blue romada. This six-inch delicacy, that looked like some fruit roll, was actually a vegetable. Or so she was told. She'd tasted a bit and was surprised at the lentil flavor. All-in-all the food wasn't that bad. She wasn't throwing up or gasping for air. There were no signs of poisoning. That was a *good thing*—as a favorite homemaking guru always said back on Earth. They finished it all off with a bright green beverage Barst referred to as Andurian fizz. It wasn't alcoholic but did taste like sangria.

Barst wiped his mouth with his napkin. "It's probably time we headed back to the ship, he said. "If the commander hasn't shown up by now, he won't. The rest of the crew should be back on board."

Laurel rose when Barst and Gemma did, only to find they were surrounded by angry-looking denizens. Their scowls telegraphed trouble. The one closest to them was a large, philodendron-like leafy man. To her, he smelled like moss. Only two yellow eyes distinguished his face from the fauna all around his shoulders.

"Where go you, enforcer?" plant man demanded from somewhere beneath his greenery.

"We're leaving and don't want any trouble," Barst informed him assertively.

"You leave. Pretties stay," plant man insisted.

Barst glanced at the two women in his company. "What do you say? Do you two want to go back to the ship, or stay here with *him*?"

"I think we'll pass," Gemma wryly insisted.

Laurel simply nodded in agreement. Barst's query was a sarcastic response to their plant nemesis's obvious desire for women. He hadn't intended it to be serious. In asking, he'd made it clear no one wanted to trot off with a piece of musky-smelling shrubbery.

"You heard the women," Barst said with one raised brown hand. "They can't stand being away from duty too long."

"You *sell*," the plant insisted.

Gemma snickered.

Barst smirked and shook his head until his brown mane fluttered around his shoulders. "As tempting as that may be, we don't sell our crew." He then motioned for the women to head for the door.

"No leave." The green figure waived one of its appendages and several of his friends surrounded the women. "Need women for mate on Oboreal. These very pretty," he proclaimed.

Barst let out a sigh of frustration before cracking the knuckles of both his fists. "Look, I'm going to say this one more time. Stand back and let us pass or there's going to be trouble."

One of the plant-like creatures grabbed Gemma and another reached for Laurel.

As a foliage-like paw closed around her wrist, Laurel saw the look on her companions' faces and knew they were a heartbeat away from a fight. Nothing was going to stop it. She planted her feet squarely and prayed she could find something in all the greenery to strike and make count. Before she threw the first punch, however, she waited for a signal telling her when to do her part. It came quickly and painfully.

Without any warning at all and despite his massive size, Barst moved like a wraith. Bear man turned and planted a big fist right in the middle of the plant leader's body.

Gemma followed Barst's lead and did the same thing to her tormentor. Laurel automatically raised one knee into what she hoped was the groin of her own attacker.

When their combined efforts worked and all three of the leafy beings were on the floor, she took a deep breath and winced. The fight was far from over.

Other strange beings approached. Some were shouting commands to leave the enforcers alone, intending to stop the fight before it went further. But some were growling their intent to pummel an enforcer; any of the three of them would do. Laurel was apparently mistaken for some part of a peacekeeping force aligned with Barst and Gemma.

Despite the differences in species and the threat in fighting so many in such a closed space, Laurel actually felt her spirits rise. This was something she knew how to do. And though a fight never ended well for those involved, the three of them clearly had no interest in starting a damn thing. She wasn't about to back off for fear of what sentient critter might barrel toward them. This was her chance to vent. It was also a way to display what an Earthling could do and she really felt like punching something as hard as possible. Now was her chance.

Several more creatures approached and the fight was in full swing.

"Behind you!" Laurel yelled as a large mushroom-looking body approached Barst from behind.

Barst swung and knocked the grayish mass to the floor.

To her left, Gemma fought a huge woman with bovine features.

Laurel turned just in time to see a very tall, half-moon shaped yellow thing—with two neon blue, stalked eyes—coming for her. There was a determined snarl on his thick-skinned face. The being reminded her of a banana with hormone issues.

Great! Gemma and Barst get to fight salad. I get to wrangle dessert!

Using martial arts skills she'd employed on the streets of San Diego, Laurel battered down banana guy with several neat, left roundhouse kicks to the midsection. To her satisfaction, his peel split right where she kicked him, and he went flying some yards backward.

The crowd circled and the action ceased for the moment.

"Anybody *else*?" Laurel invited in a mocking fashion.

She'd been taught to handle herself in a fight. Thankfully, no one had pulled any weapons or the outcome could have been disastrous.

It'd felt good to do something physical, even though the episode should never have happened. According to their inclusive comments, her comrades felt the same.

"Here, bitch! Eat *this*!" Gemma cried as she swung at a spotted woman who carelessly ventured too close. As with all the other foes, this new female attacker hit the floor hard.

Laurel knew they'd only won because a few of the idiots were really drunk. Things seemed to be winding down. But even as she and her two compatriots backed closer together for protection,

Barst took the opportunity to smack one more leaf creature in the face, just for show.

Without affectation, she actually grinned for the first time since being inflicted with this entire fiasco. She noted how Barst and Gemma were smiling too, indicating maybe they'd all been cooped up too long with Commander Butthead.

Sirens blew and anyone else that might have been interested in taking them out quickly backed away. Apparently, someone had called the local authorities when the hostilities began; doors from the far end of the tavern whisked open and humanoid men with heads a few sizes too large rushed in. These newly arrived individuals were all wearing helmets and brown uniforms. Even *she* couldn't have mistaken them for anything other than local cops.

She took a deep breath and let it out. The battle was well and truly done. Unfortunately, what she assumed was the local officers' supervisor strolled from behind the cadre of enforcers. Gold embroidery on this man's gray tunic sleeves indicated someone of higher rank. Her gut started hurting when *another*, very tall, black uniformed presence strode in right behind the supervisor. This latest edition to the crowd was all too familiar; he stood head-and-shoulders above almost everyone else in the room. Darius Starlaw wore an angry scowl so deep that Laurel was sure his face would never recover its once arrogant, superior expression.

"We're gonna catch it now!" Gemma muttered.

"Yeah, but we made a damned good showing for ourselves," Barst softly added. "That makes the punishment worth it."

Bear man suddenly reminded Laurel of Cory. She stuffed down an impulse to cry, then squared her shoulders and prepared to face the intimidating, seven-foot presence of the commanding officer. She'd maintain they hadn't started this fight, but they had damned sure ended it! If big, tanned, and god-like commander didn't like it, he could shove it up his underwear model, perfectly shaped ass.

The three of them stood, shoulder-to-shoulder, glancing at the unconscious beings strewn about the room. No one appeared to be seriously injured. The fight had, indeed, been many to three. The seriousness of the situation was only setting in.

The Chamron enforcer superior stood beside Darius and whined loudly. "Commander Starlaw, you simply *must* control your crew. We can't have this kind of disturbance in our public ale houses." He finished by sticking out his pompous chest, puffing his presence next to the much larger and more muscular commander by his side.

"Perhaps we should find out what happened before placing blame, Council Officer T'mon," Darius suggested.

"It's obvious," T'mon insisted as he looked over the three crewmen from Darius's vessel. "These space-confined socialists of yours entered a peaceful establishment to cause trouble." He planted his hands on his hips and postured though he had to gaze a very long way up to look the *Titan*'s commander in the face.

"Barst ... report," Darius ordered as he turned to his face his crew.

"No excuse, sir," Barst loudly proclaimed.

"Gemma?" Darius asked as he raised one brow and slowly walked to stand before the med-tech.

Laurel noted the unrepentant grin on Gemma's face and struggled to keep one off her own countenance.

"No excuse, sir," Gemma repeated.

Darius took several slow steps toward the third party in the group, then squared his shoulders and gazed down at Laurel.

Laurel wasn't surprised by Gemma's and Barst's responses. They didn't want to show weakness in front of these locals. Making excuses, no matter how righteous, was unacceptable. They'd take what was coming even if they were blameless. And where she'd thought to defend them, they'd really look like complainers if she did so.

"And *you*?" he somberly asked as he gazed down at her.

"No excuse," Laurel firmly responded while lifting her chin and staring back. She'd be damned if she'd throw in the *sir*. His deep green gaze narrowed, somewhat dangerously, and he stepped to within a breath's distance. The invasion of personal space was so blatant, she almost stepped back to keep her breasts from being right up against his midsection.

Gemma gently elbowed Laurel in the ribs.

"*Sir*," Laurel grudgingly added in deference to Gemma's physical prompt.

For a moment—it was only the briefest second in time—she thought he suppressed a smile. But she must have imagined it since he was all business as he turned to T'mon again.

"I'm sorry about the disturbance, Council Officer. I can assure you it won't happen again and my crew will be suitably punished," Darius informed the fuming man.

"Well, that's … that's *acceptable*, Commander. I'll leave you to deal with your people then." T'mon turned away and Darius motioned for Barst, Gemma, and Laurel to follow him.

The four of them strolled silently toward the ship. No one spoke until they were safely aboard and the gangway was closed behind them.

"I was on my way to find you when the local alarm went off. What happened?" Darius asked.

A moment of silence followed.

"Someone had better speak … now!"

"A few Oboreans were looking for women to buy," Barst succinctly explained.

Darius nodded toward Gemma and Laurel. "I take it these two were considered for sale?"

"Yes, sir."

Darius clasped his hands behind his back and shook his head. "You'd think they'd realize they're the only race still using women as a marketable commodity." He gazed into the distance for a moment before putting his gaze back on Barst. "Just for my own edification … what did they offer?"

"Sir?"

"How much would they have paid?" Darius said, enunciating each word carefully.

"We … never got that far, sir. I-I just swung," Barst told him in a confused tone.

Darius lifted one hand and stroked his chin thoughtfully. "Gemma might have brought sixteen-hundred credits. Especially with her knowledge of medicine. But *you* … " he said as he looked Laurel up and down. "The Oboreans would have been asking for a refund when they learned about your temper."

Laurel gasped and glared up at him.

"He's joking," Gemma said in a placating fashion as she put one arm around Laurel's shoulders.

Gemma and Barst began to chuckle.

"I'm glad everyone thinks this is so fucking funny!" Laurel blurted. "Somebody might have gotten killed."

Darius opened his mouth but Laurel cut him off. Her inner regulator was gone; she wasn't reeling things in any longer. Not when *Commander Son-of-a-bitch* had control over everything she did and where she went. Even the food she ate was at his or his organization's discretion. She'd been in space for about fifteen days, by her reckoning. It hadn't taken much to push her buttons after being confined and forgotten in the sick bay by all but Gemma. As far as she was concerned, Darius Starlaw was no better than the greenery that'd just tried to buy her. She was little more than a slave, to live or move by his will.

"This is how it is … *spaceman* … I'll say thank you to Gemma for saving my life. After I woke up in that coffin, she reminded me that you'd locked up that thing that shot me, so I'll thank you as well. But that's the extent of what I owe."

Gemma leaned close to Laurel but Darius raised one hand to stop the med-tech's whispered advice. His eyes narrowed again. "Don't, Gem … let the little nova speak," he angrily ordered.

Laurel took a deep breath and glanced at the two subordinates in the group. Their looks of mutual shock didn't deter. She was sick and damned tired of what she'd endured and the possible, likely probable, death of her friends. And without so much as a clear picture of exactly what'd happened.

"What you think of as amusing in that bar doesn't remotely make me smile, mister. I'm not anyone's joke! And as far as what my history is with you, I've got one version of the story but I don't *really* know what happened to my friends or my partner. I have only your account to go by. And even assuming Gemma and Barst wanted to tell me the truth, it's clear they do or say exactly what you allow them to. If you say jump … they ask how high."

She moved even closer, stood on her toes, and thrust her face very, very close to his. From her current position, she could feel his breath and see the fierce anger in his deep green eyes.

"I suppose you think you're God's gift to interstellar law enforcement, but I've got a P.S. for you. You and no one from your world had any right landing on my planet and interfering with what my friends and I were ordered to do. You might have saved my life, but it occurs to me that if you really do have a lot more technology on this ship, you could have caught up with your man outside our planet's atmosphere, where nobody on the surface could've been hurt, and *before* the fucker even landed! So it's all on you, home boy. If my friends really are dead and their families are grieving, it's because you weren't as good as you damn well think you are!"

Darius's jaw clenched.

"And don't lie to me one more time and tell me you're gonna get me home. Because I know that's not happening!" she added as a final shot.

"*Laurel!*" Gemma whispered again as mortified shock colored her voice.

Barst also murmured her name and put one hand on Laurel's shoulder to gently pull her away from his commanding officer. Even though she stepped back when the prompt was given, she never broke the enraged gaze she bestowed on the man responsible for the worst mess of her life and the horrific events leading up to now.

Darius slowly nodded and spoke in a very soft, infuriated tone that made even his crewmen back away. "Your friends *are* dead. Their families are grieving and that's regrettable. And you're right, Earther. I agreed to *ask* to bring you back to your world but it won't happen. It was my hope that you might acclimate but I can see that's not possible. You haven't the ability to grasp who and what we are and what we do. Lastly … as to catching Goll before he landed, I wish that would have been possible but it wasn't. He was already on your world when we tracked his vessel there. We destroyed it so he couldn't get away. And that was meant to trap him exactly where he was and to keep your authorities from discovering his ship and the technology therein."

"So … you didn't really give a damn about the consequences of an Earth confrontation," she accused.

"I'd have tracked Goll anywhere in the universe no matter where he went. I'd have sold my soul to get my hands on that butchering savage, and collateral damage be damned!"

The growling vehemence in his voice was so palpable that even the air grew hot with raw energy. For a few moments, no one said anything. No one moved.

It was Laurel's turn to slowly shake her head in utter disbelief. "You're no peacekeeper. You're no better than Goll." The fury in his gaze almost made her back up. Instead, she swallowed hard, lifted her chin higher and nodded in understanding. "If this is the future … Earth's a better place without it."

He took one step toward her but Barst held out a hand to separate him from Laurel. "Sir," Barst softly advised, "perhaps we should reconsider saying anything else for the time being, and go our separate ways. Gemma and I will escort Laurel back to the med bay."

Darius turned quickly and strode away, the sound of his boot steps marking his enraged departure.

•••

Darius stood in his quarters looking out the massive view port. It was situated on one entire side of the bulkhead in his quarters. Enhanced visions of stars, nebulae, and planets lent an ethereal air to the space as it was meant to. As with all command-rank quarters, his were more spacious and much more luxuriously appointed. Right now, he didn't care if he was in the hull of a garbage scow, such was his mood. As he stood there, he really wasn't seeing anything outside the ship. His mind was on what the Earther had said and his response to it.

His hatch buzzer sounded but it came as no surprise. He turned away from the view port, lifted one hand to a control panel in the bulkhead, and opened the entrance to his quarters. Barst stood in the outer passageway but paused before actually entering a supervisor's living space. Darius slowly considered the glowering countenance on his friend and second-in-command. Barst simply stood in silence waiting to be asked within the space.

"Enter," Darius said as he turned back toward the view port. He heard the hatch close behind Barst but waited for the sordid conversation to follow. He declined any comment until Barst said something.

"Permission to speak freely," Barst requested.

Darius simply lifted his right hand in acceptance, but he didn't face his friend for the time being.

"We need to talk," Barst said as he moved to Darius's right and positioned himself in such a way that his presence couldn't be ignored.

Darius faced the other man squarely, clasped his hands behind his back, and lifted his chin. "Yes?" he asked, in a noncommittal fashion.

"No disrespect, sir, but … what was that all about?"

"Elucidate."

Barst took a deep breath and puffed out his massive chest. "Darius … what's wrong with you? I haven't seen you lose your temper like that in a very long time. Certainly never as an officer in a command position."

Barst only used his first name when something was both serious and personal. Given his words, the latter of the two situations now existed. This was personal.

For that reason, he let the familiarity concerning his given name pass. Instead of facing his crewman, however, he turned back to the huge view port again before speaking. "I take it our … *guest* … isn't happy with my response to her situation?"

"What was that crap about collateral damage? I know damned well you didn't mean it. At least, I *think* I do."

"That was an … *unfortunate* … choice of words," he relented. "But she needs to realize her place aboard this vessel."

"Her *place*?" Barst sighed deeply and shook his head as he did so. "She's not a member of our crew. There are no real boundaries where she's concerned."

Feeling anger rise again, Darius finally faced his friend to continue the conversation on a less formal basis. "She must accept the situation. I can't change it, and neither can you!"

"Darius, she's in the middle of a circumstance that's as alien to her as any world we've ever visited. She's also lost everything and everyone she's ever loved." He paused for a long moment then spoke in softer tone. "I think you, of all people, would understand—"

"Don't! Don't go there!" Darius angrily interrupted as he stuck one index finger beneath Barst's nose, then sighed in frustration and turned away.

"I took the liberty of explaining that your anger made you misspeak."

Darius rounded on his friend and glared at him. This time, he had no intention of tempering his words. "You overstep yourself, *mister!*"

"Don't worry, Commander," Barst placated as he reverted to more formal airs, "neither Gemma nor I referenced anything concerning Goll's past. We simply tried to explain that our intentions are to see justice done, that there are stringent, standing orders about restricted planets like Earth. She, in turn, asked a great many questions about why she couldn't go back—"

"All of which have been already answered."

"Sir, Gemma hadn't yet told her about the malfunction with the decontamination unit. But that issue is now out in the open."

Darius opened his mouth to upbraid his subordinate, but Barst put one hand up to stop him.

"Yes, I know you'd ordered her not to say anything," Barst continued. "Everyone knows about that damned order to leave the explanation to you. And once it was revealed, it caused quite a scene, but at least Laurel is now fully aware of the extent of her surgery, and that putting her back on Earth would make her a physical oddity. Her life would never be her own. And since we don't know what caused her breathing difficulties to begin with, Gemma cannot reverse the changes she made. It's just too risky. Again, Laurel has been advised of *everything* you told us not to talk about. But it was necessary so she'd understand. Then we tactfully reminded her of that which she already knows. That even if by some miracle she goes back … she'd never be able to explain what happened to any authority's satisfaction, and that she's most surely presumed dead along with her comrades. She wasn't aware that, while she's been aboard just fifteen days, more than five months have passed back on Earth given the current speed of this ship. She also wasn't aware that you'd incinerated the bodies of the victims so as not to leave any evidence of contact with advanced life forms. All her people will know is that an area of the woods was burned, but not how." Barst took a deep breath before finishing his lengthy soliloquy. "Now ... you may deal with me as you wish but it's still done. In cases like this, the truth is always best. She knew we were lying. She's not without a certain amount of astuteness."

Darius closed his eyes, wearily dragged his hands through his hair, and faced Barst squarely again. "Exactly *how* did she respond?"

"As I alluded, she was angry."

"Of course! That's why the bloody damned woman wasn't told right off, and why we were waiting to approach the subject until she'd acclimated. Did she understand *that*?"

"Would you? Would any of us?"

"So we're damned for showing compassion? Should I have just blurted the fact that I burned all her friends' bodies so that not even ash remained? Would that make her feel better?" Darius sarcastically finished.

"As I've already stated, she just wants the truth. All of it. With some people, nothing less will do."

Darius paced slowly before turning to his friend again. "Barst, she'll never believe anything anyone tells her? There'll always be doubts."

"But patronizing doesn't diminish doubt, it only causes mistrust. And it's time we quit withholding things. She's been trying very hard to act as though she can deal with this situation but it's not remotely possible when someone has been virtually abducted, told her friends are all dead, and that she's now stuck in a reality that seems more like a nightmare. Right now, the facts are her ally."

"So you're saying my initial orders not to speak to her about what happened on Earth … prompted, I might add, by her show of rage in the sick bay … was faulty. Is that it?"

"Sir … I don't know how we could have more appropriately approached the subject. I just know this woman isn't as backward as you seem to think. Gemma agrees that all questions should be answered, and that Laurel should be allowed full access to the ship's computers and any training she needs. This might help her adapt where nothing else has so far." He shrugged. "If nothing else, studying our history and our part of life in the galaxy will keep her occupied."

Darius sighed heavily and finally nodded. "I suppose so. But … and I can't put too fine a point on this … as sad as her loss is, this is a working enforcer ship. I cannot and will not spend time bending over backward to assuage her tragic life's course or explain circumstances as if she's a child. No one is sorrier for her losses than I. Indeed, all of us grieve for her and those who were murdered. But others have suffered at Goll's hands. She hasn't got the market cornered on sorrow. I won't have this ship and its crew turned into a mental nursery for one lone Earther who refuses to accept the situation. If she wants to funnel her energies into other, more positive pursuits, then she is free to do so. But we are not the enemy here! I stand by my initial orders that if she cannot or will not control her behavior, or her decorum concerning hierarchy aboard this vessel, I'll have her locked away until we land on Luster. If, at that time, she's still unable or unwilling to come to terms I'll have her transferred to a mental facility whose physicians can more suitably deal with her issues. Is that clear?"

"Understood, sir. But … "

"Yes?"

"I trust you'll let Gemma and me explain this in terms more … "

"More *what*?" Darius demanded as he put his hands on his hips.

"I was about to use the words … *more tactful*," Barst explained.

"Tell her however you will! I shouldn't have coddled the infant to begin with. In my mistaken belief that she might not be ready for the facts, I withheld them. She obviously mistook my brand of *tact* … tact only used in deference to her position as a law enforcer … for some sort of sinister subterfuge. So let her deal with the truth, harsh and blunt as it may be. Tell her whatever it is she wants to know." He drew himself up to his full height. "Whatever she thinks or feels is not my concern any longer. I want no more outbursts of temper on this ship. My sad, infantile displays inclusive!" He pointed toward the hatch to signal the end of the conversation. "Keep her out of my way and busy. Is that understood?"

"Aye," Barst uttered as he turned and left the space.

• • •

"And this control panel handles the environmental status of your quarters," Gemma said as she finished explaining how to operate life support systems within Laurel's new quarters.

"Are you sure His Highness won't go thermonuclear when he hears you've assigned me quarters?" Laurel quietly asked. "I thought he'd lock me up for sure after that little misunderstanding we had."

"You've done nothing but express your opinion. Since you're not a member of the crew the commander can hardly hold you in contempt for that. As long as you don't do it where others can hear or cast disparagement in a way that disrupts the normal operation of the ship, that is." Gemma shrugged. "You can't go on living in the med bay. Since we have space available, it just makes sense that you have a place of your own. My quarters are just down the passageway, if you need anything, or have any questions concerning access to the main computer bank."

Laurel took a deep breath, exhaled slowly, and looked around her new quarters. The bulkhead, deck, and overhead were made of shiny, silver metal, just like the rest of the ship's interior. Thankfully, crewmembers had their own bathing facilities. She meant to make use of hers soon if she could remember how to turn on the damned water.

Against the far bulkhead, a single-sized bed was neatly made. She even had a small view port to gaze out at the stars, enhanced as they were for viewing pleasure according to Gemma's description.

She walked toward the round port, stared at the coldness of space, and simply stood there, mute. What was left to say? Whatever protest she might have made would fall on deaf ears and likely get her into even more trouble. It was clear the commander of this ship was no fan of hers. For her part, she spent far too much time thinking about what *he* thought. And she didn't know why, except to explain it as his being in charge of everything that'd gone wrong in her life. Still, he had saved her. But what difference would that make if she couldn't acclimate?

"Laurel, we never asked because we thought it might be too traumatic but … "

"Go on. Ask whatever you want," Laurel prompted as she turned to face Gemma again.

"Did you leave any family behind?"

She slowly shook her head and stuffed down a smartass remark concerning the tardiness of the query. There was no sense arguing over any of that now.

"No. No husband or kids, thank God. I do have parents who won't be overly concerned after they get used to the idea that I'm gone. That shouldn't take so very long."

"I'm sure that's not true. I'm certain they'll miss you terribly!" Gemma insisted as she moved forward and put her hands on Laurel's shoulders.

"No. Not so much. They went their separate ways a long time ago. And after too many arguments about how much they paid for my very exclusive education only to find I'd underachieved by deciding to be a cop … well … we didn't have a lot to say to one another."

"What *did* make you choose an enforcer's life … if you don't mind my asking?"

The corner of Laurel's mouth lifted as she shrugged. "I'd always secretly wanted to. When I was a kid I watched every show I could that had to do with cops, detectives, and solving crimes. My parents always had different plans so I never told them what I wanted to do with my life until after I'd signed up for the police academy."

"Well … I'm sure you're a very good enforcer. Especially after what I saw in the tavern. You aren't afraid to stand up for yourself, that's for certain."

"Yeah. That's me," she muttered sarcastically, "I'm all up for a fight." Then she shook her head and snorted in disdain.

"What's wrong?"

"It's a damned shame. Ironic really."

"What is?" Gemma asked.

"Out of all of us in the park, I'm the only one who had nobody to go home to. But I'm the only one to survive. Whoever made that decision really humped the bunk."

Gemma briefly bowed her head.

"My partner was a couple of weeks away from getting married … " Laurel began, but then let her words trail away. Nothing was going to alter what happened. Talking about it wasn't going to do her any good.

"Is there anything I can do to help?"

Laurel noted the sincerity in Gemma's voice. There was only one thing she wanted. "Yeah. Put my organs back where they belong and take me home."

"I wish that were possible. You'd probably end up in a stasis cell for the rest of our journey, just so we could keep you alive until we got back to Earth."

"And the second part? There is one, isn't there?"

"Actually getting back to Earth again isn't within my power to grant. Nor the commander's. But he'd have still asked on your behalf. That much is true."

"So it's pretty much etched in stone, then?"

"Laurel … how could you explain what'd happened were such a request to ever be granted? Assuming miracles in this regard were possible, you know your life would be highly scrutinized. Authorities on Earth would never believe your story concerning our existence. They might even institutionalize you for mentioning the incident. You couldn't tell the truth, and you'd most surely be caught in any lie. What's more to the point, a lot of time has passed since you left your world. Far more than you can account for. And the faster this ship goes, the worse that situation gets. People you left behind are aging as we speak. Laws of the universe can't be changed in that regard."

"Even if that *wasn't* the case, it's like you said. They'd probably lock me up and throw the key away. Everything that's happened to me sounds like a very bad movie." She sighed heavily, lifted her hands, and let them fall to her sides again. "So here we are."

Gemma simply nodded.

Laurel kept her silence for a time, moving about the quarters opening and closing containment units meant for uniforms or other clothing and belongings she obviously didn't have. Eventually, she moved closer to Gemma and pretended to rally. Sadly, her poor acting skills to this point hadn't fooled anyone. Gemma and Barst had known she was scared and had been trying hard not to show it. Still, there was no sense screaming, crying, or venting. Not until she was alone. There was nothing anyone in this strange, futuristic existence could do for her. And if she pushed *Commander Inflexible* too far—if she showed any outward appearance of how unraveled she really felt—he might follow through on his promise to lock her up for good.

"Are you sure there won't be any trouble with me accessing the ship's library? If I've gotta be here, I need to catch up on about three hundred years of technology. Otherwise, you and Barst will end up babysitting me for the rest of my life."

"There'll be no problem. I assure you the computer system is intuitive. It will suggest searches and techniques as it analyzes your needs and skill level," Gemma promised. "But if you have any questions you want personally answered, you must come to Barst and me. Of course, we'll take meals together in the galley." She paused for a moment before offering a friendly smile. "It won't be long before you start to see how things work. I'm sure you'll catch on, Laurel. The technology may be advanced but it's just a matter of learning to access data and use it to your advantage. You'll have all the time you need."

"Speaking of which … how long will this trip take to … where was it again?"

"I'll take months to get home, give or take, depending on new worm hole mapping and requests for law enforcement assistance along the way. You can start by searching through the database concerning our home planet of Luster. It's where the commander was born and raised. Barst and I had families that immigrated there some decades ago. We're considered citizens now. I'm sure the same privileges will be offered to you."

Laurel lifted one brow in disdain. "And how is the commander going to explain my presence? I'm sure my being here isn't considered normal since my world is off limits."

"The commander, Barst, and I will offer testimony as to your injuries. We're certain special dispensation will be made. No one would have wanted you to lie there in the dirt and die."

She considered that piece of information wryly. There were moments when she wondered if that scenario wouldn't have been better. But the survivor in her wouldn't consider anything as depressive as suicide. She was alive and meant to stay that way, if for no other reason than to inflict the high-and-mighty commander of this ship with her continued existence. She'd live for those who hadn't had another night of life after Goll. That thought brought up another query.

"And I *will* get to say something at Goll's trial?" Laurel slowly asked.

"Almost certainly! You can give better testimony than anyone so far. You have firsthand experience of his cruelty."

"Yeah. I certainly won't ever forget it," she muttered as she turned away, trying to control anger Gemma didn't need to see.

"I suppose I should get back to my duties now. Later, we'll have the ship's quartermaster issue you clothing. I'm sorry that enforcer uniforms are all he has. But you can take the emblems off, as we did with the clothing you now wear."

Laurel glanced down at the tall boots, skintight leggings, and unmarked black tunic she wore. "What I wear really isn't important."

After a long moment of standing there, it was clear Gemma wanted to be away. And *she* had centuries of learning to start if she wasn't going to be consigned to some schoolroom for the rest of her life. And then there was her idea to find Goll, wherever he was on this ship, and make sure the punishment he had coming was accomplished. There was no way she'd trust justice to beings who considered her world so inferior. Some bleeding heart might just find a way to let that butchering son-of-a-bitch go. And if that happened, he'd head back to where pickings were easy and more people would suffer as she had. For her idea to work, she needed the computer and some time alone. Up to now, no one had asked what she'd been researching. She prayed no one would and that whatever she studied wouldn't be worth such *superior* intellects' time. Still, she'd be as careful as she could.

"Well … I'll leave you to get acquainted with your surroundings, Laurel. Again, if there's anything you need, just use the communication panel on the wall. You remember how to—"

"I remember how to call," Laurel quietly insisted as she tamped down irritation at being treated like a child. It wasn't Gemma's fault she was so ignorant about the technology. "Just one quick question?"

"Yes?"

"Your and Barst's surnames. If I need to contact you and you aren't on duty or near some kind of communication device, what *exactly* do I say to anyone else?"

"Simply access the bridge controls, ask the com officer for Med-Tech Gemma Tocurus. Since Barst is second-in command he'd be addressed as Bridge Officer K'rad. But everyone knows us, Laurel. You can use our given names. You aren't bound by any uniform codes or etiquette. Just be yourself. No one expects you to comfortably accept all this. It'll take time. We understand. Just come to us if you're feeling depressed or angry. Don't try to bottle things up the way you have been."

"Sure. Fine," she awkwardly responded. The fifteen days she'd already been aboard seemed like an eternity. And how much worse would it get when she eventually got to Goll?

What she had planned for the savage incarcerated aboard meant there was no reason to get to know the occupants of the ship. Not when she'd surely be punished. Still, she had to act the part of a compliant passenger but only up to a point.

"I'll see you for chow. Barst and I will pick you up—"

"No. I'll get the ship's schematics from the computer and find my own way. I need to learn how," Laurel murmured.

"Very well. Six bells then. You'll hear the signal throughout the ship."

"Thanks, Gemma."

Gemma unexpectedly offered a vigorous hug then quickly left.

As the hatch automatically closed behind her new friend, Laurel stuffed down an overwhelming desire to cry. She blinked hard and tried, but tears still came.

In her entire life, she'd never felt so alone, so utterly helpless. But she didn't have to stay that way.

She rubbed the tears away with the backs of both hands, shook her hair back over her shoulders, and went from one bulkhead panel to the next. Slowly and painstakingly, she began to familiarize herself with every single button in her quarters. It didn't matter if it was turning on a reading light, or getting a glass of water, she meant to conquer at least this part of what was now her world.

The only person who could make a fool of her was herself. After joining the PD, she'd learned to fire assorted weapons, go over a seven-foot wall, complete twenty pull-ups in a single session, and run mile after mile right alongside the men in her academy class. She'd learned to fight hand-to-hand and had got pretty good at it. All that had been scary, especially for a young debutante who hadn't ever had to do her own laundry prior to joining a police department. But she'd done it.

This was one more challenge. It was new, bizarre, and overwhelming. But it could be done. Even as her brain told her she had no choice, pride wouldn't let her just sit down, give in to tears and give up. This wasn't about what she had to do, but what she *could* do if she tried hard enough. Those dead men on her shift wouldn't have wanted to see her surrender to emotion. She owed them her best effort and she owed it to herself. More importantly, she meant to show that damned giant who was running things that she wasn't excess baggage he could treat as he pleased. She wasn't inferior.

Eventually giving in to the desire for a long warm shower, Laurel played with the buttons in her bathing cubicle and discovered there were actually laser treatments for the removal of unwanted body hair, and treatments to highlight or dramatically change the color of the hair she wanted to keep. It was little consolation, but such a small discovery boosted her confidence. If she didn't have to ask for little things like a razor or shampoo from now on, it'd go a long way toward proving her independence. She was even able to ask the computer questions concerning how to use the infrared system to dry off.

So far so good.

After figuring out how to freshen the clothing she had on using a cleanser unit very much like a personal dry cleaning system, she redressed and sat down at a console where she had access to the main computer system, as Gemma instructed. Her very first entries into her personal computer had to do with the ship's schematics. Though she had the prison section in mind, it'd look as though she was trying to memorize how to get to the onboard gym, the rec center, music room and other places no naval vessel back home would ever accommodate.

She kept her butt parked there until the bell signals throughout the ship indicated she was to join Barst and Gemma in the galley. Again, as small matters went, finding her way to the dining area aboard a ship carrying over one thousand men, women, and creatures of assorted sizes and shapes was a big deal to her if it meant nothing to anyone else. The idea was to *not* make it look like she gave a damn. She had to tamp down surprise and any expression of sudden shock as she passed beings in the passageways that were odder and differently colored than anything in any science fiction movie. She repeated one phrase over and over.

I'm the alien here. Not them.

When she entered the galley area she found it very like a large restaurant. As with everything else aboard, it was constructed of metal with a high sheen. Cloths covered the round tables as they would have in dining places back home.

Unfortunately, this wasn't home and there was no way to forget it. She kept her gaze up, and not on the varied appendages of assorted creatures too numerous to count. Until she could put races to body types, it might not do to stare at someone and cause some kind of interstellar incident. Being on the commander's bad side was dangerous enough.

It was with great relief that Gemma's and Barst's familiar, smiling faces were soon located among the sea of so many others. She was aware of being stared at, again reminding her of being the only Earth person these people had ever seen. In many cases, her peripheral vision indicated she wasn't so very unlike a lot of the crew. A few others besides the commander looked positively human but who knew what really lay beneath the exterior? What looked normal could be egg-laying, face eating parasitic worms for all she knew.

She slowly approached Gemma and Barst, smiled unsteadily and sat when Barst was kind enough to pull out a chair. The table accoutrement looked familiar enough. There were plates, spoons, forks, napkins and glasses. But the food was another story. The protein squares available in the med bay—used by Gemma to make sure she could tolerate certain food substances from alien worlds like those on Chamron—were now a thing of the past.

She simply waited until general hubbub around them was loud enough to ask questions.

"Would you like some jerva fruit?" Barst asked as he picked up a bowl of bright green, huge plum-looking items.

"It's very good," Gemma insisted. "I promise it won't upset your system. Since everything seems to have stayed down after your meal on Chamron, regular galley food will make a nice change from the med bay ingestion tests." She winked. "Just watch what I eat if you don't think any protein is for you. We get a lot of variety. The commander insists his crew has a lot of choice. But what some of the meat eaters dine on might not be up to your taste. And ... "

"And?" Laurel prompted.

"Um ... don't look at what Barst eats. He's strictly a meat kind of guy." Gemma winced when Barst broke into a loud laugh and wagged his brows in appreciation of the food.

When he grinned and picked up a plate full of very odious looking, sausage-like red meats from a passing hover tray, Laurel quickly lowered her gaze to her own plate and the greenery Gemma was serving her. She didn't want to know what their male companion consumed.

"I can't stand meat myself, but what can I say? He eats it, I ignore it," Gemma muttered as she shook her head in obvious distaste.

Laurel sipped water from her goblet and more-or-less pushed her food around her plate. There was something that smelled very citrusy. Eating some of the so-called amber fruit was satisfying so she left most of what else was offered alone.

As the meal and the polite conversation progressed, she tried her luck at covertly glancing around the room. At the far end, *Herr Commander* was dining with a lot of very officious types in beribboned uniforms. Apparently, when one dined with him, one must look appropriate.

When she caught him lifting a glass of what looked like wine and actually staring in her direction, she quickly lowered her gaze and started a conversation with her companions.

"Um ... I-I was reading what appeared to be shipboard communication via some kind of newsletter. There was some information in it I had questions about."

"Of course," Barst acknowledged with a bright smile. "And good for you! Uh, not to imply you couldn't learn to access it," he quickly offered, "but it's good to know you're interested. So ask anything you like."

He was trying to be kind. There was no need to take offense at his almost-slip concerning any implied ignorance of the technology. If she took umbrage to every single thing anyone said, she'd soon be by herself. And that would get her nowhere. On the other hand, it'd do her no good to get too close to these beings since her plans included murdering what she now referred to as the Butcher of Balboa Park. If the commander believed Gemma or Barst had helped her get to Goll, they'd likely be judged as harshly as she would. She'd simply ask her questions and hope no one caught on to her plan.

"I ... well ... information I came across in the bulletin had to do with some group calling themselves ... *Warlords*. Did that communication thing Gemma put in my head translate correctly? Are we in their area of space? Is that why the information was warning all hands to be on their toes? And did I get it straight that Goll is a member of this faction?"

"Indeed!" Gemma readily responded in apparent appreciation of her comprehensive abilities. "We've taken a course that's less traveled, but Goll's people will attack if they locate us. You see, the Warlords don't want Goll to talk. He *allegedly* killed a peace negotiator on a planet called Minion. The League is certain the Warlords, as a group, were behind the assassination."

"But their *official* position is that the negotiator's death was a conspiracy cooked up by the Constellation League ... *us*," Barst added. "They keep lies stirred up like this so planets outside League jurisdiction have doubts about the League's peaceful intent."

Gemma leaned toward her with an expression of urgency pasted on her face. "Warlords will stop at nothing to disrupt all peaceful negotiations, and certain planets tend to side with them. In those instances where planets abstain from any opinion one way or the other, there's no unified law enforcement to keep pirates from smuggling, raiding, or doing anything else they want. Using raiders and killers like Goll to do their dirty work is nothing new for the Warlords. Then, if their henchmen get caught, they disavow any knowledge of the behavior and say that the League superiors make it all up."

"We have countries on Earth that seem to operate like these Warlords," Laurel grudgingly admitted. "Seems like that's something we have in common." Then she edged into the next part of her query. "So … if there's a general alarm, does that mean we've come under attack?"

"Just stay in your quarters or head to them as quickly as possible," Barst advised. "I don't say this out of disrespect for you or your abilities as an enforcer, Laurel. But each person aboard is assigned a duty station if trouble breaks out. The general alarm mentioned in the news feeds will be obvious when all the red lights in the passageways come on. If you ever hear it or see such an event, you'll know exactly what's happening."

She nodded. "I'm sure I will. And don't worry. I certainly won't get in anyone's way. I just wanted to ask what I was supposed to do."

"You might see armed guards roaming throughout the passageways but don't be alarmed," Gemma said. "A League vessel has never been boarded. It's standard operating procedure."

Laurel slowly munched a little more fruit, drank her water, and stored all this information. She didn't dare ask more, but let the conversation segue into politics and a general description of the planet Luster. She pretended to have an interest in what Gemma and Barst told her, but everything being discussed was accessible from the general computer. They were being polite. She might even be interfering with an ongoing romance she perceived the two shared, just by being in their presence.

That, more than anything, prompted her to deny too many social engagements with the couple. She needed their friendship, but sometimes three was a crowd. She'd overstay her welcome if she insisted on eating with them every single night when, as the computer relayed, she could have her meals in her quarters.

Glancing back at the commander's table, his insistence on staring at her from across a crowded galley made her believe that dining in her own space would be a better idea. It was the stoic man's continued surly and uncalled for scrutiny that plucked her nerve, and made her consider an idea she might not have otherwise condoned—the one concerning the death of a vampire prisoner.

Her brief contact with the ship's computer in the med bay prompted what she'd initially considered a make-believe scenario. Later, the plan didn't seem so farfetched, especially if it'd wipe that nasty gaze off the big, tanned man's face. What also made the mock scenario so easy to entertain *now* was the overall opinion that she simply wasn't advanced enough to implement it. Her ignorance was basically implied in everything Gemma and Barst said. That situation was being rammed home with every passing moment though she was certain her dinner companions didn't mean for it to be so obvious. Still, the idea of pulling off something so daring just wouldn't go away. As moments passed, all intents to play it cool, calm, and collected melted away. Her stubbornness took over one more time.

She glared back at the commander with all the enraged feeling she'd stuffed deep down. Their gazes met and she saw his eyes narrow, even from the distance across the galley. Due in no small part to her open, blatant glower and deliberate accusatory stare, he threw his napkin onto the table, put his wine glass down, and stood. He turned to his companions, apparently to dismiss himself, and stalked across the room, straight toward *her*. She was aware of others watching his stormy progress. Even Gemma and Barst turned when the look on her face went dark and she put her full attention on the approaching giant. They knew something was up, but were clueless as to the silent, less-than-cordial exchange she'd just had with their superior.

Never in her life had she wanted to irk someone as much as she wanted to pester, provoke, and mentally duel with Commander Darius Starlaw. They had about as much in common as whale shit has with moon dust, and he had it in his power to bring her real grief. But rather than stay out of his way as she'd originally intended, his uncalled for hostility in staring so ungraciously brought out the very worst in her. He wasn't even pretending to be gracious now.

And as he approached—his hostile gaze still riveted with hers—she pasted on her most assertive, kiss-my-ass sarcastic smile. Some part of her, albeit a very sick and dangerous side, wanted to finally have it out with this guy and in no uncertain terms. If she could get under his skin, there was nothing that would make her feel better. This was something she could control when everything else was overwhelming.

Bring it on, big man. I've finally had a gutful of you.

Chapter 5

Gemma and Barst simultaneously stood as their commander moved closer to their table.

Laurel did so as well, but only because it would have appeared rather churlish not to. If he wanted to start an argument—and the look all over his face indicated as much—it wasn't going to be over her lack of manners. There were much more serious matters between them.

She didn't like him. He didn't like her. It was that simple. There was no reason to drag anyone else into what was an obvious lack of respect on both sides.

Darius nodded at his crewmen and exchanged a few pleasantries with them before turning to her. She stepped back only so she wouldn't have to tilt her head at such a ridiculous angle just to look him in the face.

"Are you enjoying the ship's fare?" he asked as he glared down at her.

"Everything's fine," she abruptly replied, resisting the urge to remark that it wouldn't matter if she liked the food or not. She had to eat and he knew it.

"I take it your quarters are satisfactory?"

Of course he'd know she'd been issued a space of her own. He'd probably approved its assignment. She simply nodded, but gave nothing else away.

"Since Gemma and Barst are due back at their stations in short order, I suggest you head back to your area of the ship. If you'd like me to escort—"

"No thank you! I can find my way back," Laurel curtly muttered then turned to Gemma and Barst. "Thanks for the invitation to join you. It's clear I'm done here." She tossed down the napkin still in her left hand and summarily marched away. He didn't call her back. She didn't know what she'd have said or done if he had.

If anything was said by the commander's subordinates, on her behalf, she never heard it.

Controlling her temper was no longer an option. She just couldn't do it, no matter how hard she tried. Every bit of common sense regarding the matter floated away in the face of her very real fury.

The man wasn't going to let her even eat in peace. This cemented her resolve to take her meals in private. That was clearly what he wanted. Rather than be embarrassed again, being dismissed from the galley in front of everyone and much the way a small child would be sent to bed, wasn't going to happen a second time.

"Son-of-a-bitch!" she angrily muttered as she entered the passcode into her quarters, strode through the opening, then locked it behind her.

For a long time, she paced. Part of her—the more balanced and fair side of her better nature—kept insisting that she'd started the issue with her very curt and angry confrontation after that tavern incident. But another part, which was the side that hated his control over every aspect of her life, just couldn't get over his disproportionate anger where she was concerned. Why the hell confront her in the galley? What the fuck was that all about if not to make sure she understood her *place* and in such a way that anyone within four tables heard it?

Finally, she plopped down in front of her computer workstation, and opened files she'd recently learned to save on equipment that was so far superior to anything she'd ever seen that she congratulated herself on even being able to turn the damned thing on.

That dangerous idea concerning Goll's demise by her own hands was insane. If anything could have cemented her resolve about that ongoing plan his actions in the galley just had.

"If he thinks he can order me to stay put like a *good little girl* … he can kiss my Earth butt! Let's see how big, burly, and bombastic likes this!"

• • •

Hours later, when the entire ship seemed at rest, Laurel carefully left her quarters and made her way to the aft section. It was no short trip, and took the better part of what she guessed was half an hour. Once committed, she had no intention of turning back. Goll was meeting whatever maker he believed in tonight. Whatever happened, it'd be worth seeing the commander's face when she was done. And she *did* mean to succeed.

If there were security devices in the gangway, nothing on the schematics said so, but then there were likely a lot of such devices no one would put on a blueprint. She took her chances anyhow. And the farther she got, the more it looked like no one was watching her. Then again, she'd been deemed very ignorant by all those she'd met so far. That underestimation of her abilities and sheer, unmitigated gall, might be working to her advantage.

Her destination was the armory. She had no idea what she'd have to do to get her hands on one of the laser weapons or how she'd even use one. Parameters for their operation weren't in any schematics and she decided not to search too hard in case her computerized informational requests set off some kind of internal alarm.

Still, if someone had been silently alerted to her searches, they hadn't made an appearance yet. And as long as she wasn't stopped, nothing was dissuading her. Where there was a will, there was a way. And *Commander Bastard* had given her all the motivation she'd needed.

Anger gave her courage.

She simply didn't care what happened any longer. By all reasonable standards, she should have been dead along with Cory and her other friends. Instead, she was here. Pride made her act even where prior common sense made her hesitate.

She'd tried. God knew she had. But she was done walking on eggshells. If the man in charge, the same one deemed almost godlike by the rest of the crew, wanted to kill her for what she was doing, then that was acceptable. Better to die acting out of courage than live, cowering in fear. She couldn't exist with every tiny aspect of her daily life governed in such fine detail. That wasn't living. It was an eternal, hellish prison, one she meant to escape as soon as possible. And if the rest of Earth was to be judged by her actions, let the fellow citizens of her planet be thought brave if nothing else.

Coded symbols on passageway signs led her in the right direction even though she'd memorized every turn and curve. Luckily, she hadn't had to enter any of the elevator-like lifts, and punch in access codes, as she'd seen other crewmembers do while on her way to the galley. The armory was conveniently on the same level of the ship as her quarters. That was one of the design aspects of the ship that'd given her this crazy idea to begin with.

When she got to the entrance to the armory, she ducked behind a support beam in the passageway. For what seemed like an interminable length of time, she simply stood quite still. No alarms sounded.

Eventually, several uniformed crewmembers looking more fishlike than humanoid exited the armory. They laughed and joked with each other, headed in the opposite direction and down another passageway. Before the double hatches closed behind them, she ran from her secreted position, and prayed no one in the armory itself would see her entrance.

From the schematics, the room was quite large. If luck was with her, anyone within the space would only glance her way. Her clothing was enough like the other uniforms that, without closer inspection, she might pass for a crewmember.

Once inside the space, with the hatches closing behind her, she relaxed and acted as if she utterly belonged. There were a few crewmen milling about. Some had green faces that looked trollish. Others were tall and angular, reminding her of pencils. But no one seemed to notice her slow, ambling walk around the space. Everyone had jobs to do. They seemed inordinately interested in paying attention to consoles whose lights and beeping function indicators took precedence. With so many crewmembers, it was clear they hadn't all met one another. In darker portions of the massive space, where cavernous cabinets likely contained all kinds of weaponry, she was just one more person appearing to do her duty. How long her game lasted depended on how well she could act.

She simply kept to the edges of the space and wandered until a weapon storage cabinet came into view. The schematic that got her this far was all very general. Likely, it was the same in all such vessels. What got more specific was what *kind* of weapons the ship held and where, in the large recesses of the space, they were located.

A computerized clipboard of sorts lay on a nearby console. She picked it up and pretended to check it randomly. What seemed like many minutes were probably only a few. She didn't count herself so lucky as to have been there long without notice. Sooner or later, someone would say something and the scheme would be undone. She had to pick up the pace.

Finally, her slow sojourn around the area was rewarded. An entire bulkhead display unit bore all kinds of nasty-looking side arms. Only one was all she'd need.

She carefully put her clipboard down and moved to the display. One wrong move would surely set off an alarm, but nothing happened as she reached out and actually grasped the handle of something that looked very like a nine millimeter. It was a bit bigger and had a larger barrel but she recognized what might be a safety catch on the side.

Surely it was charged? If it wasn't ready to fire, she'd soon find out.

After having the weapon firmly in her right palm, she slipped it beneath her tunic and into the waistband of her pants.

It can't be this fucking easy. What's wrong with these people?

Almost angry that she'd made it so far without being questioned, she simply shook her head in disgust, even as she slowly walked toward the hatches. When they opened and she was in an empty passageway once more, she blinked and gazed up. Someone upstairs was with her. That was the only explanation for having gotten so far.

She shrugged, turned to her left, and continued.

The next part of her journey would take even longer. She had to move faster. Crew would scramble when a weapon was discovered missing. That could be at any moment.

She recalled every turn again. Every passageway and symbol leading to the other side of the ship and the prisoner section was memorized, down to the exact distances. Still no alarm sounded.

That made her more nervous than the silence. Something had to be wrong, but she'd committed to this act. There was no turning back now.

A symbol on a large hatch indicated her destination. The hatch opened without any problem and she found herself alone in a very large space containing square, black boxes that looked like refrigerated units. These were what the commander had referred to as stasis cells. A brief study of the ship's glossary left her in no doubt about what stood before her.

All the units were darkened but one. It was very near the hatches, situated on a bulkhead or wall. Inside the lighted cell, along with a lot of mist and fog, was the very same creature that'd attacked and killed her friends. Goll stood there, frozen in time. His eyes were closed but his gaunt, emaciated body was being kept alive. It was a sort of cryogenic freezing technique that kept him going while preventing him from making any escape attempts.

For a long moment, she simply stared. Anger, loathing, and rage filtered up from deep inside her gut.

In front of her stood the reason she was there. The officers who'd locked Goll up hadn't even bothered to offer him a change of clothing. He still wore the bloody garments that, even in the dim light of Balboa Park, couldn't be disguised. The gore from her friends' murders was right in front of her, a few inches away.

An alarm sounded. She glanced backward and knew there was no time left.

She raised the weapon and aimed it. Her thumb came up to turn off what she assumed was the safety mechanism.

Fire! Do it!

She fixated on the gruesome image in front of her, but her hand began to shake.

He deserves it. And I'll be done. What happens afterward won't matter. Just fire. You can't miss from here.

As it had on other occasions when considering the matter, she entertained the idea that his ilk might have visited Earth before. Hence the similarities between the name these aliens used and the terms Earthlings would employ to describe him. If she didn't fire now and make an example of him—to show what Earthlings would do to his kind if they decided to visit her world again—then history could repeat itself. More cops or those even less able to defend themselves could be slaughtered.

The alarm got louder. There were voices in the passageway outside the stasis cell area. It was now or never.

Her hand shook worse. Tears filled her eyes.

I have to do this. I have to do it now or it's over.

The oath she'd sworn echoed in her head. To serve. To protect. To defend.

Self-loathing bubbled up. She cried out in rage as her free hand balled into a tight fist.

"Goddammit!" she whispered as she lowered the weapon, took a deep breath, and put the safety back on. "Damn me to hell!"

A long moment passed. She stared at the deck.

Voices in the passageway outside the stasis area faded. The crew was looking for someone with a stolen weapon. This might be the last place they expected to find a thief but find her they would. Once caught, she'd be locked up forever or maybe even put to death. This entire plan had come to nothing. And she'd still pay for it. All because she couldn't pull the damned trigger.

"It may be hard to believe right now, but you've done the right thing."

Laurel lifted her head, briefly closed her eyes, and slowly turned. That deep, baritone voice was all too familiar. She gazed into the shadows as a very large, looming figure stepped into the light.

He put out one hand.

She squared her shoulders and placed the weapon on his upturned palm. Her gaze met his. She refused to look away, ready to accept punishment. No excuses. She'd expected disdain or even triumph, but the expression in his eyes was surprisingly gentle. Still, she knew the consequences and accepted what he'd do.

"I knew this was too damn easy," she admitted. "Why did you let me get this far? Or was I tonight's entertainment?"

Darius moved so that he stood inches from her. "I didn't believe you'd be capable of going through with it. You're an enforcer, not a murderer. But *you* had to know it, too!"

"I-I don't understand."

"I've stood in that exact same spot, wanting Goll dead. I might have done what you just attempted except I suddenly realized that what's waiting for him will be far worse than anything I could ever do. Trust me, Laurel … he won't get away with his crimes."

He turned his attention to Goll for a moment. The brief silence that followed puzzled her. "Aren't you going to call for your guards?"

"No. I'm not."

When she would have voiced more questions, the hatch suddenly opened, and Barst walked in with a half-smile on his bear-like, amiable face. "The uh … *drill* … we arranged is over. I'll take the weapon back to the armory."

Laurel glanced between the two men. They both bore expressions of amused conspiracy. As the commander handed over the weapon she'd stolen, she nodded in understanding. "Of course! All the other weapons were locked away in containers I couldn't get to. There were just a few available, on open display. I'll bet that thing isn't even armed, is it? None of those I could have grabbed are armed."

"Correct," Barst answered. Then he turned to his superior. "The security chief is a bit confused but I'll calm him down. And I've called an end to general quarters. As far as anyone knows, this is another one of your impromptu tests, sir."

"Good," Darius responded. "I'll escort *her* back to her quarters and fill 'er in on the story," he advised as he nodded toward Laurel.

She simply stood there blinking. She was apparently not under arrest, nor was she to be charged with a very serious crime. Somehow, with Barst's help, the commander had made her escapade look like some kind of training session.

Filled with questions, she opened her mouth to speak but he held up one hand to silence her.

"Wait until we get to your quarters. We'll talk there." He nodded toward his second-in-command. "Let me know if there're any problems. I'll see you tomorrow morning for briefings."

Dumbstruck, she let him take her arm and guide her through the many passageways, back to her small space down the hall from the med bay. They met a few crewmembers along the way. All greeted their superior cordially. None of them seemed the least bit put out by the alarm or her presence with their commander.

Once inside her quarters, with the hatch closed safely behind them, he walked to her miniscule view port and considered the sights before him before turning to speak.

"Go ahead now. Ask what you will," he instructed.

"How the hell did you know I'd even do such a thing? How *could* you have known?"

"You've been aboard for less than a month but I've seen this coming. I've ordered the security chief to take the guards off the armory hatches. I've issued orders to allow you full access to that area, and instructed personnel to let you take unarmed display weaponry at your discretion. I didn't know *when* you'd do it, but there was no doubt about your eventual intent. If it wasn't tonight, it would have been the next night or the one after." He lifted one brow and nodded. "After that rather angry and uncalled for display I put on in the galley, I figured I'd pushed you into acting tonight. I was correct."

She unceremoniously plopped down on the edge of her bunk. Shock and utter amazement kept her from gracefully taking a seat. "You pissed me off on purpose. But … I still don't … I don't … "

"I told you. I understand better than anyone else what you're going through. A few nights after you came aboard, I took a fully armed weapon from the armory and meant to blow that damned, savaging bastard all over this part of the galaxy." He took a deep breath, briefly closed his eyes, and continued more calmly. "I couldn't do it any more than you could. We aren't Goll. We could never kill unless it was in self-defense."

"But you didn't know for *sure*."

"That was why I allowed only unarmed display weaponry to be made available. What I wasn't sure of before, I know quite decisively now. You couldn't do it. You'd have always wondered had I not allowed you to make the decision yourself. And now that we know, we'll both sleep better."

She shook her head in confusion. "But h-how will you explain my actions tonight? And yours?"

"Section heads have been told the entire thing was another of many drills I occasionally think up. I was the one who issued the general alarm so as to make the circumstances seem realistic. The theft of the weapon from the armory was to have simulated a real theft by someone having full access to that area of the ship. What was being supposedly tested wasn't the actual theft, but the crew's *response* in searching the passageways and living quarters."

"But—"

"The particulars won't matter. The crew will believe what I tell them. Trust me when I say I've thought up far more bizarre drills. Tomorrow, I'll issue critiques on the crew's response times, and they'll be better off for the experience."

"Normally, someone like me would have never even been allowed so near the armory. Is that it?"

He simply nodded.

She took a deep breath, let it out slowly, and watched as he sank into an oversized console chair across the space. "You wanted this to happen, didn't you?"

"There was no other way, Laurel. I went through it. I knew, from the look on your face when I confirmed your friends' deaths that you'd end up wanting blood. I just pushed enough buttons to make you ready. My actions only facilitated the inevitable. I let you make a choice to the good of your soul, and without any harm being done."

Angry that she'd been so easily manipulated, Laurel clasped her hands in her lap and stared out the view port for a long time.

If he knew her that well in such a short time, what else could he glean? And when had she become so transparent to begin with? The man had almost turned psychic where she was concerned, and his understanding of her rage was frightening.

He leaned forward. The position put him very close to her.

"Would you like to hear a story that better explains my actions?"

She lifted one shoulder and let it fall. The gesture was far more nonchalant than she felt. Of course she wanted to know where he was coming from but was afraid to ask.

He leaned back in the chair and stared into the distance.

She got the impression he was trying to find the right way to say something that wasn't coming easily.

"About thirteen years ago, a young woman boarded a transport vessel with her two-year-old child. They were bound for Tarsus Minor. It's a garden world but a few weeks from Luster. She … she'd … decided to escape an unhappy relationship." He paused as if he was trying to keep his composure. "The … vessel wasn't heavily armed. Not many luxury class ships really are. The trip should have been uneventful."

Laurel's mouth went dry. Some part of her didn't want to hear what he was about to say. The commander got up, paced around the small space, and then finally sat beside her on the small bunk. The expression on his face was terrible. His deep green eyes were almost glassy as he stared into the distance.

"A vamphiere pirate contingent happened upon the ship. A short battle ensued when the transport captain wouldn't let the pirates aboard. He made the mistake of trying to outrun his attackers. It didn't take more than a few minutes for the pirates to blow the transport into a thousand pieces. Of course, there were no survivors. But the vamphieres were successful in making an example of the captain's escape attempt."

For a very long time, they sat in silence. He kept staring at the far bulkhead. She sat there, staring at him.

"Who w-was this woman and child?"

"My wife and little girl," he softly told her. Then he shook his head slightly as if trying to rally. "The leader of the vamphiere contingent was a man named Gorm. He was Goll's sire. Goll was said to have been at the helm of the pirate ship when the order was given to kill eight hundred men, women, and children who were only emigrating.

"My god!" she whispered.

"Gorm openly bragged from one end of the galaxy to the other. He was particularly proud about that … *victory*," Darius bitterly said. "I spent the next two years of my life chasing him. From one nebula to another, from one sector of darkest space to the next … I finally caught up with him and had him cornered on a small mining colony in the Vega system. My superiors ordered me to hold off making any arrest. They wanted him cornered to stand trial, and being so personally involved with the man's deeds put me in a precarious position." He sneered. "I didn't give a damn! I issued an ultimatum for total surrender. I knew Gorm would never accept and that he'd attack a better armed war class Constellation League bird-of-prey rather than submit to arrest. Vamphieres are nothing if not arrogant bastards!"

"You killed him," she whispered.

"I ordered truncheon bombs aimed into parts of his hull where he and his minions would surely survive long enough to suffer. I wanted him to live just long enough to know who'd beaten him. I drew the situation out for as long as possible, just for the satisfaction of watching his ship and every one of his henchmen burn." He turned toward her. "Fire is one of the things they fear most. I felt nothing but satisfaction when I saw their vessel burn from bow to stern."

"But Goll—"

"Wasn't aboard. For whatever reason, Gorm's misbegotten by-blow escaped. But I later learned he was alive and where he might be. I went after him with all the zeal I'd used to chase down his sire."

Laurel swallowed hard. Clearly some part of the vampire legend didn't hold true if the species could breed. Sadly, Goll was a result of that mistaken mythology. She wasn't sure she wanted to know more about the creatures than she already did.

She licked her lips, moved closer to him, and gazed up into his eyes. Rage had darkened their color. Anger over his behavior in the past now warred with pity. In the past half hour, everything had changed between them and she wasn't sure she could deal with the difference.

"I-I told you I took a weapon from the armory and fully intended to go to the stasis center and see him fry. *Slowly*. All I could think about was Kyrie ... " His voice broke, his hands clenched into fists, and he quickly stood and faced a bulkhead. "She was so little. She shouldn't have had to suffer the fear she must have ... in the moments prior to ... there were other children on that ... "

"Stop! Please stop," Laurel begged as she got up to join him. She put one hand on his back and stood by his side.

He finally faced her.

The expression he wore now was stoic and fearsome. "Astral and I shouldn't have quarreled. My duties kept me away from home and we'd grown apart. She hinted she'd leave but I didn't believe her. She threatened to take Kyrie away. I warned her about even trying. I wasn't about to let anyone separate me from my little girl. She and I couldn't ... " His words trailed away and he simply stopped talking.

In telling the reason for why he'd wanted Goll dead, he'd revealed how he'd risk his career and probably his life toward that end. He'd begun to explain the history behind his hate.

Laurel didn't want to hear it. The gut-wrenching tale made him seem all too human when she didn't want to recognize him as anything but an autocratic, arrogant bully.

There was no denying the validity of every syllable. Before her stood a man who'd have broken any rule and ignored any order to take down creatures responsible for his family's death. He'd probably been brought up on charges stemming from his actions and it might have taken a very long time to recover from the circumstances. But he hadn't mentioned caring about any of that.

The thought that a child had been involved was too awful to contemplate. But she now understood exactly how and why he'd known *her* intentions.

On his face was the rage and deadly resolve she'd felt. To keep her from ending up another victim, through killing an unarmed vamphiere in a stasis cell, he'd set up a scenario by which he'd let her decide what was right, and mitigated the circumstances all at the same time. But why go to all the trouble? If she'd killed Goll, two of his worst problems would have been solved. Goll would've been dead. She'd have been charged with the murder and probably executed for it. That was her summation of the situation. So all that really needed answering was *why*.

She stepped in front of him, put the palms of her hands on his chest, and stared up into his eyes. The anger eventually left, leaving only pain and regret behind. "Why didn't you just turn me over to the guards? Why were you so willing to lie on my behalf? After every offensive thing I've said to you—"

"Because you'd have been one more victim." He took a deep breath and let it out slowly. "After I knew I could stand in front of that stasis cell and walk away, confident he wouldn't make me destroy my life, I finally felt free. Hatred of him and what he's done doesn't own me any longer. I know he's going to get what's coming to him. For me, it's finally over." He put his hands on her shoulders. "Think about it. Think of how you feel now as opposed to how you felt when you were trying so hard to appear brave and utterly in control. You had a weapon trained on him. Regardless of how you got it, or whether it was even armed, you thought you could fire and kill him. But you made a better decision. You did what a good enforcer would do."

She nodded in understanding. "I still want to see justice done. But I *am* in control now. He doesn't own me. I can look at him and hate him for what he's done, but he's not going to force me to do something stupid."

"He loses. We win," he murmured as he slowly nodded. "So how could I hold you responsible for something I'd been through myself?"

They stared at each other for a very long time. Neither spoke as minutes ticked by. Some understanding that was deeper, richer, and lasting was forged. She couldn't put a name to it, but he wasn't the fierce, unfeeling man she'd thought. He was a *hurt* man. That was quite different.

"There's something you should know," he eventually told her in a voice that was very low and quite unlike any tone she'd heard him use before.

"Yes?"

"When we got to Earth, your friend Cory was still alive. I held him when he spoke his last words."

Tears immediately filled her eyes. She shuddered and blinked as they fell down her cheeks.

"His last request was that I look after you. I hadn't time to respond but my personal oath to do as he asked stands. So do not think me impertinent if I seem to overstep certain boundaries. I couldn't help my family. But I can help you … if you let me," he softly finished.

She turned away, crying in earnest now. It no longer mattered who saw how she really felt.

He gently turned her to face him again, pulled her into his embrace, and held her tightly, rocking her as if she were a small child. The warm protection offered was unbelievable. She couldn't have torn free if her life depended on it.

...

As moments passed, everything changed for Darius. He lifted the thick mass of sun-streaked brown hair from her shoulders and let it sift through his fingers.

She eventually gazed up at him, bearing a shattered look in her blue eyes. He couldn't help himself. Her lovely face was so close, her eyes so intense. He slowly lowered his mouth to hers and tasted her sweetness. The gentle kiss was meant to comfort, nothing more. But as she responded with fire and passion it went on and deepened. Their tongues entwined and caressed. Her hands flattened against his back, stroking and urging him on. If he'd known nothing else concerning her race, the kiss they shared was a form of intimacy with which she was obviously familiar. He savored this one as a starving man craved food.

He lowered his free hand to her hip and pulled her against him as heated blood flowed into his groin. Every drop of it engorged his cock. And when she moaned softly, the small sound turned his blood into lava. With a temperament such as hers, this woman could make love with ardor that would stop a man's heart.

Guilt tore through Darius. She was mourning, confused, and in need of comforting, not seducing. He pulled back and gently pushed her away, though doing so would leave him in painful need.

"I'd better go back to my quarters," he softly insisted while his hand still rested on her shoulder.

"I ... I guess ... you'd better," she softly agreed.

Her hand came up and she pushed his hair back. It was such a gentle gesture that he pressed his cheek into her palm. He wanted nothing more than to pull her back against his chest but this was not the way an officer behaved. Later, she might not thank him for the liberty taken while her soul was under such duress. Still, the loss of her body heat left him feeling colder and more alone than he had felt in a very long time. He slowly turned away. But when he reached the hatch and glanced back over his shoulder, he could have sworn she was about to ask him to stay. Her lovely, full red lips parted. The remains of tears were still on her cheeks. It would have taken very little for him to remain the rest of the night. He didn't give her the chance to say another word, but quickly walked out of her space.

As he strode through the passageways back to his own quarters, his heart wouldn't stop pounding. In his life, he couldn't recall experiencing such quick, all-encompassing, and uncontrollable passion. Something was connecting them. Perhaps it had to do with similar losses suffered at the hands of vampieres. Maybe it was just fear of being alone. But where she had good reason to lose control, he did not. Though she wasn't a member of his crew there were rules concerning those taken aboard for humanitarian purposes. She definitely fell into that category. Then again, he'd broken several *other* codes this night. One had to do with actually helping her get to that stasis cell. Others circulated the lies he'd told about some idiotic drill, meant to cover her actions.

Try as he might, he felt no pangs of professional conscience. He told himself he was only helping by gaining her trust. But would he have put his career in jeopardy for anyone else in a similar situation or was it just her?

Moments after reaching his quarters, he pulled his uniform off, showered, and collapsed onto his bed. The artificial breeze supplied by the circulation system drifted across his nude body. He lay there for a while thinking he'd never get to sleep, just as he hadn't rested well since bringing the Earther aboard. But his lids soon drifted down and he utterly relaxed. Something about the evening's activities made him less anxious, more connected.

He dreamed of being back on Luster, in the sunshine. Friends and family were all there. A warm, gentle hand slid around his waist from behind and he turned to look into eyes of sapphire blue. The woman smiling up at him wasn't one of his regular female companions. She wasn't from his world at all. She was a fiery Earther, with such hot desire in her gaze that the dream soon had him bedding her in some of the most exotic positions he could have imagined.

The dream segued from one sexual fantasy to the next. They made love in the gardens surrounding his family's estate. They enjoyed wild intercourse on the back of a personal transport shuttle, stopping on the way home to address passions that couldn't wait. He took her in a warm, bubbling hot spring that dotted the forests of his world. Each and every time, she cried out loud and long, while begging for more. His orgasms were intense and enduring.

He writhed in pleasure as another fantasy filled his dream world. Sheets wrapping around his body felt more like a lover's arms. Every caress with his hands became strokes she lovingly bestowed. Over and over the scenes played out and he moaned in expectation of sweet release.

When next he woke, the sheets of his bunk were tangled around him, his body was covered in a fine sheen of sweat, and evidence of his last orgasm lay all over his abdomen. Even in his youth, he'd never had such a wild night.

He simply lay there panting, when another round of desire and fantasizing coursed through his body, making him hard again. He had time to enjoy the respite before rising to shower and take up duties.

Somehow, this shift was going to be different. His attitude had changed about a few things, among them the status of his personal life.

Laurel Blake hadn't survived by accident. He believed that with all his heart. She'd come into his life in a hailstorm of fire and death, rocking his world to the core in the process. And whatever happened from here on, he meant to enjoy the ride thoroughly. But not until they reached Luster. After he was on the surface of his world again, rules wouldn't apply. She'd be off his ship and he could pursue her the way his passion demanded.

Chapter 6

A full three months later, Darius stared at the bulkhead in guilt.

Laurel hadn't approached him again, but her gaze when joining friends during meals was quite different. It was softer, more inviting. She often stared at him across the galley, when she thought no one was looking. Questions in her expressive eyes made him want to get her alone. But he could do nothing about his feelings while aboard the *Titan*. He still had a job to do and rules prohibited any fraternization. At least, they prohibited *him* from such involvements.

As the ship's highest ranking officer, he was expected to live by much more stringent regs than others. At all times, his mind must be clear, his only concern the safety of his crew. He wryly assumed that was why he was paid an almost obscene amount of credits. But remuneration didn't make up for the lack of other, more intimate pastimes. And that kiss they'd shared broke more than a few regulations.

For that reason but more because Laurel was still suffering deeply, he'd kept his distance. She needed space and time. What'd occurred between them came on so strong and suddenly that they both needed to see things for what they were. After all, neither of them could be referred to as children. They knew the score; Laurel seemed to accept it though her lovely eyes still beckoned.

His guilt in regards to her was in direct response to having hacked into the computer in Laurel's quarters. This was how he'd really known she'd eventually go after Goll, though he'd had to guess at *when*. Still, his actions were beneath contempt, certainly not worthy of a ranking League officer or renowned citizen of Luster. His only justification was in keeping her from doing something he'd so badly wanted to do himself.

Now, to have contact with her at all, he still maintained that computer vigil. Though rules allowed him to review any research made from the *Titan*'s computers—and the crew knew it— he trusted his subordinates to the point he'd never made use of that statute. In Laurel's case, there really was no excuse. He was almost certain she didn't know about that tenet. Worse, Barst and Gemma kept reminding him she wasn't part of the crew. It was almost as if his two subordinates knew he was hacking and were warning him off the pastime. Of course, they *didn't* know what he did in his quarters. His guilt over the issue just made him feel as if he were being watched and judged. Like the non-fraternization edict, he had no right prying into the personal business of a non-crewmember. No excuses.

The situation was confusing. He adhered to the one rule concerning not having too much contact while completely ignoring the other concerning what she did with her research, in her assigned private quarters.

What kind of person was he to decide which regulation to obey and which to cast aside?

Still, he felt the need to know her better. Her research gave him an insight into what she viewed as important.

Among the subjects of her studies, everything about the ship seemed of high interest. Then she'd located and read information about Luster for hours and hours on end. Animal life, plant life, or anything else she could find about his home world's industry, traditions, or history was accessed. Even the kind of transportation used and who owned the companies building shuttles was investigated. He found her interest in that bit of boring trivia odd, but there was nothing illegal about it. Certainly, whatever she gleaned wasn't as inappropriate as what *he* did in regard to her computer studies.

I'm disgraceful. Utterly and irrevocably vile. What kind of man hacks a woman's computer when he practices the discipline required in keeping his distance?

He couldn't do it to her any longer. He had to end it. The best thing for him to do was throw himself into work. In that regard, a new day approached; duty called. He wouldn't look at what she studied, accessed, or read one more time. Sadly, that meant the next months were going to be long and arduous indeed.

He made his way to the bridge, considered incoming data for a full half hour, then issued orders for their next refueling stop. Given its importance in League dignitary circles, he had to keep his mind on every detail of what would otherwise have been a routine chore.

"Dock and run a complete system check as quickly as possible. I want to get off Arjus and back into open space," he ordered, as he restlessly paced the length of the bridge.

"Yes, sir. If you have no objections, I'll run a standard check on our armament, given we're in a dangerous sector of space," Barst said as he piloted the *Titan* toward Arjus's landing field.

Darius sighed heavily as he nodded. "Things have been too quiet. At the very least, we should have run up against some of Goll's mercenaries before reaching the second moon in this system. Either they're still plotting an attack to get him back, or they really *don't* give a giant jekari's red ass that he's incarcerated," Darius pondered as Barst maneuvered the battleship into position for landing.

"Commander, we're receiving a general greeting from Council Leader Char," Barst advised as he considered the communication screen in front of him.

"Put it on the main panel," Darius commanded.

As the large, bridge vid screen activated, Darius saw the familiar, pale but humanoid face of the Council Leader as it morphed into view. He'd dealt with the man before when patrolling this quadrant.

As leaders went, Char was fair and tolerant if too indecisive about whether to deal with the League or the Warlords. As a result of such vacillation, the planet Arjus was aligned with neither faction. Ambassadors had tried to convince the ruler that the Warlords would come armed and ready to take over one day, but Char steadfastly remained neutral, playing both sides against the other.

"Greetings, Council Char," Darius acknowledged. "What service can I offer?"

"Please, Commander Starlaw, it is I who offer services to you," the man replied quickly.

"How so?"

"While your crew refuels your vessel, perhaps you would take advantage of my hospitality this evening? As I'm sure you'll admit our ale and women are among the finest in the galaxy."

Something wasn't right. Char had never made such a gesture before. Indeed, previous refueling stops had barely purchased any interest at all.

"I'm afraid my crew is anxious to begin their shore leave on Luster, Council. We'll be taking off as soon as we possibly can," Darius prevaricated.

"*Please*, Commander Starlaw. I have … urgent business … I'd like to discuss with you. It will only take an hour. We can meet at my residence as I'm sure you know where it is. Your crew can't possibly have your vessel ready in that time."

"May I ask the nature of such a meeting?"

"I've … well … I've had a change of heart concerning neutrality. I believe, as do my advisors, that alignment with the League may now be in our best interests. But this is something I wish to discuss with you privately. Please, Commander, I promise to be succinct."

Darius considered the man's announcement. Civility required his presence even if he couldn't technically speak for his home world in any ambassadorial capacity. "Very well, Council. I'll call at your residence within the half hour." He ended the transmission and turned to face his second-in-command.

"Darius," Barst began while temporarily dropping titles, "after all the time ambassadors have spent trying to convince that man to align with our cause, I find it highly suspicious he'd want to do so now. His timing is a bit too coincidental. I don't like it!"

"I agree. But on the off chance he's sincere I'd be insane to pass up the opportunity. Besides, diplomats and my own superiors would find me lacking in manners if I didn't at least listen. I can't afford to cause an incident."

"You *will* go armed?" Barst insisted.

"I'll go armed and *traceable*." Darius smiled and sharply slapped Barst's broad back. "Come on, I'll need your help."

Ten minutes later, Darius stood on the ship's gangway giving orders to Barst and Gemma. If anything untoward happened, his last orders were firm. He ignored his crew's insistence that one of them be allowed to accompany him.

"The invitation was personal," he said, denying their requests yet again. "You both have orders. If I'm not back within an hour … leave. I want Goll back on Luster as soon as you can get him there. The tracking device I'm wearing will allow you to find me, assuming a return rescue mission is even needed."

"That's if there's anything left to find," Gemma sourly declared. "Sir, I protest. Council Char isn't overly fond of League officers and never has been. Can't you at least take—"

"No. Let Arjus's refueling staff do their work with all hands safely aboard. Don't open the outer hatch for anyone but me," he commanded as looked into their faces.

He noted their concern and tried to act as if nothing was amiss. In that effort, he pasted on the best smile he could. "Don't worry,

We could be wrong. I might find myself enjoying a fine meal, and signing up a new League planet."

He strode away with a decided chill crawling up his spine.

No one was buying this. Not his crew and not him.

If Char wanted to barter for League membership, the commander of an enforcer vessel was not the proper authority. Still, he had to yield to Char's simple request or risk open, diplomatic criticism of the entire crew.

Perhaps they were all on edge due to the length of the mission, and their need to return home to see Goll finally stand trial. Maybe this was nothing more than a simple, informational consultation and Char was being melodramatic as he so often had been in the past. If that was so, why were members of his own crew— consistent with his own instinct—on full alert?

● ● ●

"Please, come this way, Commander."

The female servant at the front door to Char's gray, stone and castle-like residence led him inside to a large chamber. Darius took no more note of it than he had the bland streets or thoroughfares, so like those on Chamron. One after another, refueling planetoids seemed to mimic each other in almost everything.

"The council leader will be with you in a moment," the woman said as she bowed and left.

For several quiet moments he stood where he was. Surely, if the meeting was so urgent, Char should have met him by now. He was about to leave when the door behind him opened. He turned to greet his host, pasting on a smile as he did so.

"Commander … thank you for coming," Char said as he moved forward to clasp Darius's hand. "I'm sorry. So very, very sorry!"

Darius briefly clasped Char's hand in greeting, noting the extensive contrition on the man's face as he did so. Another chill went up his spine but he guarded his expression, posture, and tone of voice.

"Council … why would you … "

He stopped in mid-sentence when several vamphieres and a Gloxynian wizard entered the gray stone room. Each had weapons drawn and aimed at *him*.

"I see the reason for your apology," Darius said as he rounded on Char. The man still wore a remorseful expression, though it was clear he'd helped orchestrate what was clearly a kidnapping.

"Please understand that I wanted no part of this," Char explained. "These gentlemen, as I'm sure you're aware, are members of the Warlord faction. You must understand … they have my family, my advisors, and *their* families held hostage here. Every one of them was to die if I didn't cooperate. Please, *please* forgive me?" The man hung his head in despair.

Though none of what was happening came as any surprise, Darius was still concerned to see a Gloxynian wizard among the vamphieres. These wizards were known for their ability to extract information from their hostages in creative ways.

One of the vamphieres stepped forward. A look of utter contempt was pasted all over the gaunt man's face.

"We'll take your weapon," the vamphiere leader warned as his fangs elongated.

Darius slowly raised his hands to shoulder level. One of the other vamphieres quickly removed his sidearm while another produced a length of rope and proceeded to bind his hands behind his back.

"We want Goll. If he isn't delivered to us in an hour, we will make good on our promise to kill the Council and the other hostages. And you will die as well," the leader advised.

Darius shrugged. "I don't know what you're talking about. We were on patrol in this quadrant and stopped for fuel. Who is Goll?"

The vamphiere leader struck Darius hard across the face.

He recovered quickly, spat out a bit of blood mingling with the saliva on his tongue, and slowly faced his tormentor again.

"Don't waste my time, Starlaw! You have my brother and I want him back." The leader of the captors then turned and walked toward Char. "Open communications between yourself and Starlaw's crew. I want them to see what will happen to their commander if they fail to meet my demands within the allotted time."

Char raised shaking hands in a supplicating gesture. "I-I'll do as you a-ask. But please don't harm the c-commander or any of the other hostages. I'm sure there'll be no problem with compliance."

Darius shook his head in denial. "I wouldn't, Council. They're going to kill us anyway. They won't leave witnesses behind. Without us to say otherwise, they'll claim pirates landed on your world and committed the murders."

The vamphiere leader quickly walked to Darius and struck him again. Darius simply glared back at the man, daring him to strike one more time. His attacker moved very close.

"I want my brother. I'll not stop at killing hostages. I will destroy everyone on this backward world if I have to." The leader snarled then turned to Char again. "Now … make the call to Starlaw's ship or die!"

Char nervously nodded and turned to his communications console. In a matter of moments, he established contact with the *Titan*.

Darius breathed slowly, trying to control rage at having been so duped. And when Barst's face appeared on Char's large holo-screen, he remained silent. Orders had been given. They would be followed.

"Crew of the *Titan* ... I am called Garron," the vamphiere leader announced as he took a pretentious stance before the two-way viewer and gazed into the faces of his enemies aboard the enforcer ship. "I am brother to Goll."

Darius saw Barst's chin go up and an angry expression entered his second-in-command's dark eyes. Several other bridge staff took a stance behind Barst. Their expressions were equally hostile. But his best friend and current the commander of the vessel in his stead said nothing, and waited for the vamphiere to continue with his demands.

"We have your commanding officer, Char, and other members of the populace under our direct control." The lanky vamphiere put his hands on his thin hips and threw back his shoulders. The gesture only enhanced the man's hollow chest.

Darius rolled his eyes. Why hadn't he just refused and accepted the consequences for poor diplomacy? But then, there *were* the other hostages to consider. Garron would kill them anyway, no matter what he'd done.

"If my brother isn't released to me ... unharmed ... I will slaughter the hostages beginning with your commander. You have one hour."

Garron motioned to the two vamphieres standing on either side of him. They tried to push him into line of sight with the viewer so his crew could see him.

Darius resisted until he saw one of the vamphieres raise a laser short rifle to Char's head. To keep the other man from being slaughtered then and there, he ceased struggling and grudgingly moved as his captors bid.

"So you know I am serious, I will give you a sample of what will happen if Goll isn't released," Garron asserted. Then he turned and motioned the wizard forward.

Darius couldn't imagine what Barst was thinking, but he hoped his friend would realize the captives were doomed. Vamphieres wouldn't leave them alive. It was likely their blood would be drained, then their flesh torn from their bodies. Matters didn't improve when he saw Gemma's concerned, pretty face enter the view point on the *Titan*'s bridge. Obviously, one of the bridge crew had alerted her to his physical danger. As a med-tech—but more as a friend—she'd joined other concerned members of the crew who were gathering on the bridge. Each of their faces displayed anger, outrage, and concern. He barely nodded in acknowledgement. They still had their orders.

The Gloxynian wizard moved in front of him and raised one be-robed arm. In the elderly, bearded man's hand, a clear crystal shard sparkled from the light of an overhead chandelier. The sparkling quickly morphed into a bright glow.

Darius said nothing but put his full attention back on Barst. He stared at his friend and attempted to communicate—with nothing more than his insistent expression—that his last orders should be strictly obeyed.

As the midnight blue-clad wizard began to chant and slowly walk around him in a circle, nothing happened. Darius opened his mouth to utter a sarcastic remark concerning the failed magical properties of a cheap, open-market crystal but the words never came.

The room began to spin. His blood heated.

Soon, every cell in his body felt as if it was being utterly torn and disrupted. It took all the strength and concentration he could muster not to cry out with the onslaught of sudden, immense pain.

He dropped his head back as the agony wound its way like a snake into his very bones and outward to his flesh. Darkness closed in. And though he fought it, he knew he'd eventually lose.

"Release our commander immediately!" Barst shouted.

Darius heard the rallying cry and clung to it as the last friendly voice he'd likely ever hear.

"Give me my brother and I'll see that your commander is returned," Garron shouted back. "Fail to meet my demands and you'll find pieces of Starlaw and the others all over the surface of this planet … and that's *after* my wizard has a chance to practice his special talents on them. You have one hour. No more!"

Garron passed one hand over Char's communication console, effectively cutting off the transmission and the conversation.

"Garron, the commander is in terrible pain," Char advised.

From the place on the floor where he'd fallen, Darius tried to speak but the attempt only hastened unconsciousness. He heard Char's plea on his behalf and felt sorry for the man.

"You gave your word that nothing would happen if your brother was returned to you," Char anxiously insisted.

Garron laughed cruelly as he faced the council leader. "You're a fool, Char. Starlaw was right! You and your family will die … it's just a matter of *how*."

"But you promised—"

"If you cooperate, you'll be quickly incinerated," Garron said. "But if you resist, I'll let the wizard have you. One look at the commander should tell you how horribly one *might* die."

"The commander's crew won't let you get away with this," Char warned. "The Constellation League will send every enforcer in the galaxy after you!"

"It's as Starlaw said. With all witnesses killed, there'll be no proof. And proof is what League justice demands before taking action."

Darius was vaguely aware of the wizard moving away. Though he couldn't speak, the pain diminished, but only slightly. He was meant to lie there, unable to fight back or even advise Char.

All he could think about—besides the daunting, horrific, and electrical quality of the pain in his body—was how easily this entire scenario had been coordinated. He was glad to pay the price for stupidity, but Barst and his crew should not. They had to remain aboard the *Titan*.

Within the protective confines of its superior hull, they stood a chance against any weaponry the vamphieres' vessel might unleash. They must *not* attempt a rescue. That his mind wandered to that possibility resulted from either his need to be rid of the pain, or his knowledge of his crew's loyalty. Despite other mistakes in his personal life, engendering their loyalty was one thing he'd done right.

"What will you do with the commander now?" Char softly asked in a dejected tone of voice.

"Take Starlaw away," Garron ordered as he nodded toward the Gloxynian and his comrades. "It will do me good to watch him suffer."

Darius was aware of being lifted. The foul stench of vamphieres told him who carried his limp frame. The darkness he'd so valiantly fought now claimed him.

. . .

Laurel boldly stepped onto the bridge. Since red alert lights had come on all over the ship, and she couldn't find either Gemma or Barst, she headed to the bridge. Gazing around, she saw that most if not all the crew was there. With one very large, tanned exception.

Scanning bodies and faces, she couldn't see Darius Starlaw.

Since the incident involving Goll's stasis chamber, three months ago, the dauntless commander and she hadn't seen that much of each another. Encounters were limited to passageway conversations of limited and cordial length and quality. She'd dined with Gemma and Barst or alone in her quarters, using computer research time to advantage.

But in those brief passageway encounters with Darius, she'd come to learn he wasn't the taciturn, harsh individual she'd once believed. In fact, he'd become much friendlier, much more approachable. There were several encounters, during times when her heart ached, when she'd wanted to ask how he'd survived the deaths in his life. The question would have only been posed as seeking advice concerning her personal losses. But on every occasion she'd found a way to tactfully word her queries, doing so had always seemed inappropriate. Especially since she'd have to reveal an utter lack of experience in such matters as loss. A pampered upbringing shielded her from strife. In her job as a cop, she'd yet to witness the loss of brethren. But when it *had* happened, it had been massively tragic. She'd not only lost her best friend and partner, but her shift mates and her entire world. How did one deal with it? How had he gone on after the loss of his wife and little girl?

She'd kept her feelings and thoughts to herself. She'd kept her distance from the commander of the *Titan,* which resulted in no more trouble. It had also resulted in no opportunity for physical contact. And that, she found, left her feeling somehow starved.

When he'd held her and kissed her, time stopped. All anger and pain fled, if only briefly. She'd felt needed and trusted. The contact was the most riveting of her life, and she wasn't without experience in such matters.

All other men aside, Darius Starlaw was the most enigmatic yet breathtakingly virile male she'd ever met. If she'd been angered to the point of hatred before, the other side of that coin now applied. During that almost sacred contact of their kiss, the softness of his breath on her skin, the gentle way he'd caressed her, and the heat of his lips pressed to hers were the only things in existence. And though she wanted more, she knew why he kept his distance even as she'd kept hers.

Whatever had happened between them, that night—whatever caused the significant change between them—they needed time to sort it out. He was the superior officer on a spaceship commanding many; all their lives were in his hands. She daren't attempt to move closer to the man, physically or spiritually, until the time was right. They'd both know when that was. But the feelings were still there and had increased. She'd seen it in the way he looked at her, heard it in his voice when he'd spoken softly and without the previous rancor. She knew it in the very air around them. Instinct any law enforcer possessed didn't go amiss. They were attracted to each other and were biding their time. For her part, she had to wait until they could truly be alone and without duties or her insecurities getting in the way. But once they *were* finally alone— and there was no crew, no duty, and no trial ahead—she meant to find out the deepest secrets of a spaceman who was quickly becoming the center of her life. She no longer feared him. With each passing day a growing yearning took the place of any fear at all. And now, something about his absence signaled trouble that frightened her on his behalf.

Tonight, anxiety concerning some unknown circumstance— along with the alarms signaling it—drove her from the serenity of her quarters and into the company of others. Whatever was happening, it involved every man and woman aboard. This included the only person from Earth.

"What's happened?" she asked one of the crewmembers as she searched for familiar faces.

When a gray, tentacled being with gill slits might have answered, Gemma came into view, pushing through the crowds to get to the bridge hatch where Laurel stood.

"Gemma ... what the hell is going on?" Laurel asked when her new friend was close enough to query.

"Vamphieres. They took Darius hostage during what was supposed to be a diplomatic meeting," Gemma responded, anxiety causing her to use her superior's given name. "There are others being held. Everyone will die if we don't release Goll."

"If you let them have your prisoner it won't make any difference. From what I saw the night my friends were killed, vamphieres aren't partial to mercy," Laurel insisted. "Why doesn't someone arm a rescue team and go after the commander?"

Gemma put her hands on her hips and sighed in frustration. "That's just it … Barst was given strict orders to keep every crewmember aboard. When an Arjus official asked to see him, Darius knew he might be walking into a trap and planned for it. He's made himself expendable."

Laurel considered the news then put one hand on Gemma's shoulder. "The commander gave orders for every crewman to stay aboard? Are you sure about that?"

Gemma simply nodded then absently turned to look at the large holographic view screen—now darkened—mounted on the bulkhead, opposite the commander's chair. It was as if she hoped there'd be some transmission from her superior, a transmission that likely wouldn't ever come if someone didn't do something right away.

"He's being tortured, Laurel. We saw it—"

The look on Gemma's face as well as the faces of others was telling. They believed their commander would die excruciatingly. "Get Barst!" Laurel demanded. "He's still second-in-command. I need to speak to him … *now!*"

Gemma's head snapped back in her direction. "Why?"

"*Please* … just do it. I don't think we have much time."

• • •

The black uniform that comprised Laurel's only choice of clothing was gone. In its place she now wore borrowed brown leather pants, soft high boots in a matching shade, and a green leather jerkin with a white blouse beneath it. It was clothing that looked very similar to what was being worn by the townspeople milling around in the marketplace.

To further blend in, she wore her hair loose like other women. No one seemed to notice her as she moved toward the most prominent stone structure in town.

As she'd been told, the large gray stone structure—appearing more like a castle than any home—was where Council Char lived. It was also the place from which Darius had last been traced.

When she'd conveyed her quick plan to Barst and Gemma, they'd resisted—as did all of the bridge crew. But she'd severely reminded them of her status as a civilian and as a law enforcer with experience in her own right. She'd persisted, and with such virulent passion, that they'd given in. Moreover, there simply wasn't any other choice.

As to her own feelings, she drove out thoughts of what Darius must be going through at the hands of vamphiere torturers. She had to shove down what could be one more death she'd have to endure, and one that was now so precious to her that she couldn't imagine going through life on another world—at least not without seeing his face from time-to-time or hearing the gentle timbre of his voice. Of late, that voice was so caring during even the briefest of encounters. Whatever that distant horizon brought, he was part of it. He couldn't die now.

Everything was conflicted and confusing. But she knew another good man couldn't die. Not if she could stop it. She couldn't help Cory or her other friends, but she could damned sure do something now. In the end, the crew had seen that her plan might work; it was all they had, there was no time left to plot anything better.

Now, she was alone on the alien world of Arjus and the plan was enacted. Somehow, she wasn't afraid but excited and worried for Darius's sake. Still, she drove one thought in her head above all others.

Get the job done.

As she moved, the city to her appeared positively medieval. The exception in the Merlin-era scenario was the appearance of so many creatures of various shades, heights, and builds. Many of the denizens had multiple eyes and limbs. Some of the appendages were of a number and size that was startling. But as she moved among them, she understood every word being said. Gossip about someone's husband sleeping with someone else's wife, a bad deal or the state of politics, reminded her of Earth. She tamped down a wave of utter homesickness and kept to the task at hand. It took everything she had to paste on what she hoped was her best nonchalant expression. She moved from one venue to the next as if she were examining sales goods.

A credit to her acting—or to her utter unimportance on this planet—most of the traders and market people had their own business to mind.

Without being questioned, Laurel strolled from one place to the next and finally ducked into an alley to check her bearings.

On the chance Darius was no longer in the council leader's residence the pocket-sized device Barst provided would lead her to the commander. No matter where he was, its vibrating speed was supposed to increase as she came nearer to Darius. The small black box, barely the size of a deck of cards, was supposed to be covert enough to escape electronic detection, but advanced enough to react to some transmitter Darius concealed on his body. All this was assuming Darius's device hadn't been located and disabled.

There were so many things that could go wrong. For starters, the enemy should have known some sort of tracking device would be installed on the *Titan*'s commanding officer. If that were the case, she could be walking into a trap. Darius, along with the other hostages, might already be dead.

Laurel tried not to think about that possibility. She simply kept moving and forced herself to assume all was going as planned.

As she moved northward in the alley, her device indicated she was very close. The vibrations from her receiver were faster and stronger. She was at the back entrance to Council Char's residence. Darius, or his tracking device, was still inside.

She leaned against a wall, pretending to straighten her jerkin. There were no guards at the rear, ground entrance. But no one was leaving, either. Anyone looking her way shouldn't believe she was up to anything.

She took a deep breath and walked toward the arched wooden doors. The laser weapon in her tall right boot was ready if she needed it. She prayed there'd be no devices inside that might indicate she'd entered and was armed. Barst had given her a tiny deactivation cube in that event. But as she saw it, if vamphieres were present and they were alerted to her presence, she'd be set upon before any piece of equipment could silence an alarm.

She put out one hand, then took a deep breath to stop shaking. As she pushed down on the first, old-fashioned latch she'd seen since leaving Earth, elation filled her. The servants' door—as schematics perused aboard the *Titan* indicated—was unlocked. She glided inside and found herself in a darkened foyer. No one was near.

It took time, but rushing now wasn't going to help matters. Clearly, the vamphieres and the so-called wizard Barst told her about were nowhere in sight. Neither were the employees. She guessed they were all being held with the other hostages, in some room away from any access point. Sad for them, this made any escape attempt very difficult.

With such enhanced powers as vamphieres possessed, they obviously believed themselves superior. Only three had been seen in the holo images transmitted to the *Titan*, but there could be more. But *if* three was all Garron brought with him, so few could still do a hell of a lot of damage. She'd seen the carnage wrought by one.

Taking great care, Laurel slowly walked down a hallway past a huge, unbelievably equipped kitchen. There was no time to study alien cooking apparatus; the tracking device in her left hip pocket vibrated even faster.

The sound of voices made her stop and move behind a large, white floor planter bearing a tall purple plant with orange blossoms. Armed vamphieres strode by her location. Her hopes for only three were dashed.

She sent up a silent prayer for their not having advanced senses legend attributed to mythic Earth vampires. But as the cadre moved by and took no notice of her in her hidden niche, she took heart. It might be that there were too many *other* humanoids near to discern her presence. For whatever reason, she was still alive and still undetected.

Once again, the vibrating functions on her tracer silently whirred harder as she moved from her hidden location to the left. If Darius's tracker had been located by his enemies, all this was for nothing. But she had to try.

With her heart pounding so loud she was sure someone would hear, she moved on.

Chapter 7

Darius woke slowly. The pounding in his head subsided only slightly as time passed. He heard voices around him long before his eyes focused in the torch-lit room. Typical of many old-style residences, Char evidently preferred the ambiance provided by antiquated lighting. Without the harsh glare of modern fixtures, the lower light actually helped him concentrate.

His uniform tunic had been removed, leaving his chest bare. Ropes were tied to his wrists and booted ankles, stretching him between two columns. The wizard who'd rendered him unconscious could have easily killed him, but that wasn't the plan. The vamphieres wanted him to suffer. That was apparently why the skills of a master wizard had been employed.

"So … you're the famous Commander Starlaw."

The Gloxynian wizard moved from the shadows and stood before his captive. A gloating look was plastered on his face. Darius silently noted how his captor's dark blue robe swirled. He saw the older man thoughtfully stroke his long white beard as if considering the next round of torture. There was nothing to say. He steeled himself for what was to come.

"You made no sound when my sensor crystal electrified your body. That was most unusual," his captor mused. "We shall see if you can maintain control or if, like so many of your kind, you die screaming. Don't disappoint me, Commander. I become inventive when I'm disappointed."

Darius's eyes narrowed. He strained at the ropes binding him only to find they tightened with struggling.

"Whip," the wizard ordered as he simultaneously held out his right hand and turned to one of three vamphieres present.

He was handed a whip with various pieces of glass, metal, and rock shards tied within its flailing straps.

The wizard slowly smiled. "The flesh must be readied."

Darius stared blankly ahead. Gloxynians prided themselves on the fear they induced.

The wizard circled him slowly. When the man stood behind him, the whip was applied. Darius gritted his teeth and clenched his bound hands. The whip came down on his flesh over and over, but he made no sound. He looked straight ahead and fixed his mind on getting home.

For the first time since Astral and Kyrie died, he feared his own demise. He thought of his parents and siblings. Barst, Gemma, and especially Laurel. He'd have given anything to hold her for just one long night.

Suddenly, the beating stopped. His torturer threw the whip to the floor in frustration and moved in front of him. The wizard's yellow smile was uneven and sickening. It occurred to Darius that this man liked his job far, far too well.

"Well done, Starlaw. But we'll see how you fare against *these*."

The wizard walked to a nearby table and picked up a large jar. When several nearby vamphieres moved away, Darius's heart sank.

As his torturer approached again, he literally felt blood drain from his heart. He would rather be incinerated outright than to have the creatures in the jar placed near him. With his back scored open and bleeding, the slug-like, fat animals with glowing red eyes—known to just about every enforcer as *drillers*—would have a ready entrance into his body. These were particularly large, spanning the distance of his index finger. Still, he fixed his mind against flinching or crying out. The Gloxynian would have to glean pleasure from some other source.

"You're not impressed?" the wizard asked. "When they enter you, everyone in this building will know. Even *you* cannot withstand that kind of pain, Starlaw. And what a story I'll have to tell. I'll relate how the legendary heir to the throne of Luster begged to die. I'll even have my vamphiere friends record it for posterity." The wizard sneered. "Shall I tell you what these creatures can do to a man? Or perhaps you've heard."

When the wizard moved closer, Darius smiled slowly then spat right into his face. If he could anger the man enough, the torture wouldn't go on much longer.

His enraged captor shrieked in rage, pulled the lid off the jar, and threw it to the floor. It broke into shards as the wizard purposely moved closer. Each step was meant to extract fear. Darius vowed to show none, whatever it took.

The wizard held out his hand and one of the guards placed a pair of tongs in it. With these, he extracted one of the creatures from the floor where they lay amongst shards of broken glass. Then the wizard slowly and deliberately moved to stand behind Darius.

At first, he felt nothing. When the stinging began he stared at an old tapestry across the room and firmly planted himself into the bucolic landscape portrayed there.

"You will respond sooner or later," the wizard promised.

Darius felt more of the creatures being applied to open wounds. The slimy, gray slugs writhed on his flesh as they tasted blood. He swallowed hard but made no sound.

Eventually, his intentions weakened. The pain endured from the wizard's crystal was nothing next to what he felt now. He truly wished for death.

From his peripheral vision, he noted how even the vamphieres lowered their heads and backed away. Even *they* didn't want to look as the beasts ate their way into his body. Worse, they'd grow as they gorged.

"We'll see, Commander. We'll see who wins!" The Gloxynian backed away to admire his handiwork.

●●●

Laurel heard a cackling voice coming from the chamber directly ahead. The door was cracked open. From it, flickering light illuminated shadows of moving bodies. According to her instrument, Darius's tracking device was in that room. Whether he was still attached to it was another matter.

She lowered her hand to her boot and pulled out a small laser pistol. Had security on this planet not been so lax, she'd likely not have gotten this far from the airfield with it, nor would she have been able to exit the *Titan* from a service duct far beneath the ship's belly.

She breathed deeply, reminding herself how to aim and fire the sidearm as Barst instructed. The thing was as automatic as it got. Using it was the least of her troubles. First, she'd have to get past any vamphieres that might be present.

Thanking her mother for the endless ballet lessons she'd once hated, she employed that grace now and moved closer to the door. From there, she quietly gazed through the small crack as she raised her sidearm.

What she saw made her back into the shadows again, wincing in horror. Darius was tied to a set of wooden beams; his body was scored and bloody. God only knew what he'd endured. The blood she'd glimpsed on the floor was like something out of a horror flick.

A combination of anger and protective instincts she'd never believed possible surfaced. Darius's torso was horribly pale. The intense pain he suffered was almost palpable and her heart broke for him. Even when they'd been at each other's throats, she'd have never wished this kind of anguish on the man. Now, after understanding him so much better and sharing a moment of ultimate connection during that magnificent, universe-shattering kiss, she wanted to kill anyone and everyone who'd dared hurt him. All she could think about was getting to him and removing him from the source of his pain.

Forgetting caution, fear, or strategy, she rounded the corner firing her weapon in straight volleys, toward anything *not* tied to blood-covered beams.

Three vamphieres and an elderly, human-looking man in a long blue robe were so shocked that they barely had time to react.

Two vamphieres hesitated too long. Surprise at her appearance was written on their faces as they went down. She didn't hesitate in unloading on them with all she had.

According to Barst, she had enough firepower to take down fifty men, but who knew if a blood-sucking creature of legend might not just take it on the chin and get up. For that reason, she felt no remorse as she kept aiming and firing.

• • •

Like some avenging, wraithlike entity from a dream, Darius watched her enter the room. His savior moved like a graceful feline; righteous fury etched itself into her beautiful features as she dropped each of his tormentors, one after the other. And though one vamphiere got off several volleys, she ducked and dodged with such athletic elegance that the man repeatedly missed his target and eventually joined his comrades on the wooden floor.

Darius couldn't remember seeing anything so lethally lovely. Pain mingled with some other emotion too raw to name. Then anger flooded him. His fists clenched.

She has no business being off the ship.

Surely, Laurel must have plotted this scheme. Barst and Gemma wouldn't endanger the life of an unqualified civilian and risk their careers or his crew's safety by disobeying orders.

For a moment longer, he fought off pain and actually won.

With the torturers lying on the floor, either unconscious from stun mode or dead from a more lethal setting, Laurel moved swiftly. She grabbed a knife from the belt of one of the vamphieres and began cutting his ropes.

"What are you doing here?" Darius croaked as the blood in his mouth threatened to choke off words entirely.

"I think it's called saving your ass, and you can thank me later. The weapon fire made a lot of noise. I don't think we'll be alone very long."

His bindings fell away even as he took several staggering steps forward and gasped. His slightest movement drove the creatures within his body deeper.

"Are you good to fight?" she quickly asked.

"Yes. We n-need to move," he rasped out.

"Okay. Here's another weapon," she told him as she pulled a backup laser pistol from one boot. "Having never fired one of the damned things, I really didn't want to use both at the same time. My left-hand aim isn't that great." She shrugged as her gaze wandered over his bleeding chest. "Anyway … I didn't need it." She took several steps toward him and haltingly put out one hand as if to help him. "Are you sure you can you move by yourself?"

Her words were fired as fast as her weapon. He took a deep breath, along with the laser pistol she offered, and willed himself to stay upright, all of which was done while ignoring the arm she offered for support. "I don't know how you got here … I'll address somebody's failure to follow orders later. Right now we have to make our way upstairs. While they thought I was unconscious, I overheard a vamphiere saying that's where the hostages are being held."

Laurel quickly moved to each of the downed foes. "I-I think these bastards are dead … if *not breathing* passes for it in this part of the universe," she quipped.

"We need to move," he harshly reiterated. "Their friends will have heard the laser fire, just as you—"

"Don't worry, Darius. There's a plan in place!" Laurel countered as she moved to the door and carefully checked the hallway.

Approaching voices made her pull back, into the room.

"What *plan*?" Darius demanded. "We'll be trapped here—"

"We're supposed to get as many of these vampire-things to follow us as we can … assuming you can move."

"I can hold my own!" he growled.

"Then follow me."

Angered by her pompous behavior while simultaneously being fearful for her safety, he stuffed down any comments along with the pain, and did as she commanded. If they survived, he'd deal with her later.

As a team, they bolted out the door and ran down the hallway in the opposite direction from approaching guards. Unfortunately, their forward momentum toward freedom was short lived. Another group of angry voices sounded from the opposite direction.

Laurel turned to him. A look of chagrin was pasted on her face. "Okay … I got us this far. You're up, spaceman!"

He stared at her, wanting to shake her and then pull her into his embrace. A quick glance showed him the only exit available—a large, stained-glass window to their left.

"This time you follow *me*," he said as he grabbed her free hand. "We go through that."

"*Are you crazy?*"

"Debate it later … close your eyes!"

He leaned forward and put all his remaining strength into charging through the window. Before he leapt, he made sure his grasp was firm on the pistol she'd provided, and her wrist.

The once-lovely artisan glasswork, mounted in a window several times taller than most men, shattered around them as he pulled them through. The resulting jolt his body took while landing on the well-manicured lawn of an Arjus garden was almost more than he could stand. But he managed to push himself upright as he glanced to his left where Laurel landed beside him. She was also standing. Shattered glass flew from her hair as she shook it free.

In that moment, even through pain that was almost unendurable, he noted the courageous look on her face and the absolute, resolute determination to stay alive at all costs. In her, he found strength and renewed will to live.

"If you wanted them to follow us, you've got your wish," he told her as he glanced backward in time to see vamphiere guards athletically bounding through the hole they'd made in what was probably one of Char's prized artistic possessions.

He re-gripped her free hand and ran.

Together, they bolted into the safety of nearby woods. Lasers burst in the air around them as they moved, ducked, and outdistanced their pursuers. The vamphieres apparently had second thoughts about following. Though they could move faster and with greater agility, they were nothing without their leader. They'd consult Garron before taking action. None of them wanted to die this day, and the cowards now faced foes armed with weapons that *would* destroy them.

As he moved and felt the effects of the parasites within his body, he prayed their luck held. Eventually, the adrenaline in his body ran out. The creatures were doing their job and he could fight them no more. Tall trees, plants, shrubs, and vines sheltered their escape. His beautiful, brave companion might at least have a chance to get to safety.

When a small clearing no larger than the space of a personal transport shuttle came into view, he stopped and sank to his knees. There was no further escape for him. He'd moved his last. Only the thought of outwitting his foes and seeing her to safety after having so brilliantly rescued him had kept him on his feet so long. But no longer.

"Darius, we have to keep going," she insisted.

He finally let go of her hand and shook his head. Conversation was hard. Energy ebbed. He made good use of the time and fought off the darkness threatening to overwhelm him. "Wh-what was this plan you s-spoke of?" he gasped.

"We were supposed to be a diversion. Barst was going to engage a rescue operation for the hostages if we could get the vamphieres to follow us. Or at least one of us," Laurel replied. "I-I guess it didn't work. If they came after us, I haven't heard them."

"They knew we were armed and reached the cover of the woods. The vamphieres are probably where they always were ... inside Char's residence. That probably means there are a lot of dead, innocent people back in that house! Whose insane idea was this?"

"If you thought they wouldn't follow us, then why did you pull me through that damned window? And by the way ... you're welcome!" she snapped.

"What?" Darius weakly asked, his breathing labored and heavy.

"I said ... you're welcome! For saving your ungrateful, alien ass."

"*Why you little* ... did it ever occur to you that you're the alien among *us*? You unappreciative little ... I don't know whether to shake you or hug you ... "

He stopped and slumped forward. Having contained any sign of pain before, during the torture and in front of the wizard and his conspirators, he could no longer stop the low moan emanating from deep within his lungs now.

"Fuck ... Darius ... how bad are you? When you took us through that window I thought maybe you weren't so bad off ... sweet Jesus!" she anxiously muttered as she placed her hands on his shoulders. She rummaged beneath her dark blue tunic to produce a small medical kit. "Gemma gave me a medical recorder and a few emergency supplies. Everyone on the *Titan* saw you being tortured ... oh, God! There wasn't time before ... "

He shook his head and waved off her attempts to use equipment that was as far above her ability to comprehend as the stars were above the forest leaves on which they stood.

"At least let me try," she coaxed.

Using what precious little strength he had, he grabbed the small, handheld bio unit in her palm, turned it on, then pressed it back into her hand. It would only diagnose injuries, not treat them.

"I-I don't know what … Gemma told me how to read the screen." She paused and shook her head in confusion. "I-I'm getting different sets of vital signs. How can that be?"

"Just attribute it to my alien physiology," Darius said, mocking her earlier use of the term describing him.

He wasn't about to tell her she was reading the recorder correctly. There were three parasites in his body. Four different readings were what she should see. His and *theirs*.

Laurel gazed around her quickly. "If we weren't followed, I can at least try to do something about the pain and dress those wounds."

"No … we s-should get b-back. If Barst is trying to free the hostages, he'll need help … "

Darius tried to stand but the pain was far too intense. He fell to the ground, and darkness closed around him. He heard Laurel calling his name. He felt her hands on his face and body but even the blessed softness of her touch quickly faded.

•••

"Darius, can you hear me?"

Laurel tried talking to him but he was well and truly out. Nothing she did or said made him respond.

The whip wounds on his massive back and chest were deep and ugly. But the bleeding had long since stopped. He'd made it through that huge window, out of Char's residence, and into the woods. She figured they'd run for a couple of miles.

Something about his having passed out now wasn't right. And why was Gemma's black bio-thingy not showing correct readings? If she'd heard the instructions right, there should be one set of vital signs. A blue gauge on the read-out should have shown how badly his body varied from norm. Anything to the left of center wasn't good. His readings came in at almost all the way to the left.

"Dammit! Your wounds are nasty, but not so much for someone of your size … you big-ass, tanned giant! Don't you dare die on me. Don't you dare."

She pulled some white, sterile-looking dressing from the small kit. It was covered in yellow paste that Gemma referred to as *antibiotic fixative*.

She could neither leave him nor go back. Barst was supposed to have used the tracker in Darius's body to send help if his commander couldn't get back to the ship. As it was, she didn't even know where the hell his tracker was.

"Probably in his gravity-defying left butt cheek," she angrily muttered as she continued to dab at the long gashes on torso. "Where the hell is everybody?"

She sighed heavily, shook her head, and moved closer to her downed comrade. Light was fading and it was getting harder to differentiate between where she'd cleansed and those places on his body where she hadn't.

As she put her face only inches away from a very bad gash near the base of his spine, movement just beneath the skin caused her to fall backward in shock.

"*What the fuck!*"

When a wriggling, worm-like thing—about five or six inches long and as round as her thumb—repeatedly moved several more times, her eyes opened wide in horror.

"What the hell is that?" she whispered as she slowly turned her face to consider Darius's blank, unconscious countenance. Even in the fading light his pallor stood out.

"What if that thing's *supposed* to be there and I somehow pissed it off?" she softly muttered as she considered, for the thousandth time, how very different these beings were from her. "What if there're more?"

She jumped again when Darius's moan echoed through the clearing.

"Okay … okay … big guy. I-I'm gonna roll you over, onto your back. J-just don't turn into something ugly and b-bite my face off. All right? We're on the same side here."

Slowly, carefully, she completed the task, hoping not to awaken some living appendage that might take offense to her having touched him at all. At any moment she expected five inches of wriggling, wormlike critter to break free from his skin and do something terrible—something she'd only seen in horror movies.

"Darius? Talk to me, spaceman," she begged. "Wh-what am I supposed to do?"

"Astral … I thought … I thought you were gone," he whispered.

Laurel stared down at him. If the man thought she was someone else, then he was in worse condition than she'd assumed.

He began to tremble. There was only one conclusion to draw. "Darius … if you can hear me … it's Laurel. We have to get you out of here. If your physiology is anything like mine, you're going into shock. All I've got are bandages. Where's your tracking device? I think it might have been damaged 'cause nobody's showing up. I-I don't want to leave you but I might have to."

"K-keep me warm," he uttered.

She had to move closer to hear. Part of her was scared of getting so near someone who had a critter embedded beneath his flesh. But she couldn't just let him lie there shivering, either.

The same reason she'd left the safety of the ship applied. He'd suddenly become too important in her life. Nothing in the world mattered so much as making sure he made it through this mess.

She pulled off her tunic and shirt and began to shiver, too. The sleeveless compression top she'd been given to wear under the garments did nothing to ward off the evening's chill.

"Okay … I'm putting some of my clothing over you … so don't grow some third arm or something and attack."

She took a deep breath and dropped her garments over his chest. They were far, far too small to cover his frame but it was all she had. They still held her body heat and might help.

When nothing happened she let out a long sigh, unaware she'd been holding her breath.

Some minutes later, he showed signs of consciousness. He turned his head toward her and sighed deeply. Whether it was in relief or pain, she couldn't tell. But his trembling resumed moments later.

"I-I won't let you go this time, Astral. Nothing can take you from me again," he softly murmured.

Laurel leaned toward him and was immediately shocked by his next action.

As if he knew exactly where she sat, how far away she was, and what it took to get her closer, the man pulled her onto his chest. Seconds later, he buried one hand into her long hair as it cascaded over his shoulder. His emerald-colored eyes slowly opened and he gazed straight up at her. In them she saw pain and terrible sorrow. It was enough to almost break her heart.

She struggled and tried to speak, but he lifted his head quickly. His mouth made contact with hers.

His lips were hot. Their full, luscious movement against her mouth was sensual, sweetly passionate, and not-to-be-forgotten. Even she momentarily forgot the bad timing of the loving contact.

He parted his lips and his tongue touched hers.

In that split second, she closed her eyes and moaned into his mouth. If there was an alien thing living within him, the presence of it didn't matter at all, not at that moment in time. All she cared about was how desperately tender the connection was, how a jolt of pure energy shot straight down into her abdomen. In less than a heartbeat, she was wet with desire.

His free hand slid around the small of her back, just where the compression top fell short of the top of her leggings. She wanted to kick off the tall boots she wore and writhe against him like a thousand-dollar whore. His palm was warm. His strong hand caressed her spine like a soft summer breeze. The feel of it was infinitely tender and made her pelvis thrust forward automatically.

She lifted her face a scant inch from his. She felt his breath on her lips but had to stop while she could.

"D-Darius, I'm *not* Astral. L-let me go," she murmured as he pressed oh-so-soft kisses into her left cheek, chin, and throat. The pressure of his palm on her back became more insistent.

"No. You're mine," he softly responded. "Locking doors between us won't stop me this time. Out of respect for your wishes I held back. But no more."

The words weren't stammering or disjointed as before. They'd been uttered as if he was in full control of his faculties but she knew he wasn't. Something was obviously very, *very* wrong.

Darius rolled over, pinning her body to the ground. It was as if he was being forced to behave this way. For whatever reason, the man wasn't in his right mind. Thinking quickly, Laurel decided to humor him long enough to find a way out.

"All right, Darius. I'll do whatever you want. It's time to stop fighting." She stopped struggling and caressed his shoulders instead. His size and strength, with her current position beneath him, prohibited a fight.

He rose slightly and looked at her as if the words confused him. She pushed his dark hair back, trailed her fingertips across mammoth biceps to his strong, hairless chest. Her caresses lingered on his nipples. He actually shuddered at the contact.

"You never touched me like this. Not even when we were trying to conceive," he said as he gazed down at her with an expression of great tenderness in his eyes. "I know we were both so young. But … " His words suddenly trailed away. He stared at her for a very long moment before continuing. "You're eyes are blue. So very blue. Just like a mountain lake." He pushed himself up and off of her. "You're *not* Astral!"

"No, I'm Laurel. The Earther you picked up out of the dirt … remember?"

Darius hung his head and moaned.

The man was in deep pain when he'd been about to make love to her a moment before. It didn't make sense.

"Listen to me … *Laurel*," he said, as if trying to reinforce the name of the woman with him. "I-I can't control what's happening. The n-next time will be worse unless I go unconscious. You've got to leave. Find Barst or Gemma, but don't come back. The pain is … I can't … "

He plunged his hands into his hair and dropped his head back. His eyes rolled upward as if he was going into a seizure.

"I can't just leave you like this. We don't know where those vamphieres are. But I know Barst will put together a search party and come looking, even if your tracker has been damaged. I believe it must have been or we'd have been located by now." She sat up and moved closer to him. "If you can still hear me and understand … just try to hang on."

He passed out and became so still she was afraid he'd stopped breathing. When she checked, his chest still moved up and down but barely.

Time crawled by. She lay next to him, trying to keep him warm and murmuring any nonsensical thing she could think of, hoping he could hear. All the while, she prayed he'd be all right. Nothing else that happened mattered if he didn't make it through. Even the thought of his having some other life forms within him no longer mattered.

Eternities passed before Laurel heard the familiar sound of Barst's deep voice. She cried out for help and a dozen crewmembers from the *Titan* rushed forward, Gemma among them.

She backed away, giving the medical technician room to work. Only a moment later—after Gemma pulled out a larger version of the palm-sized bio reader she'd been given, and took the time to take more readings—she saw the med-tech glance at Barst and slowly shake her head in sadness.

"Wait … he's not that bad," Laurel blurted. "He's a bit out of it, but I think anybody would be after being whipped like a medieval serf."

Gemma gazed up at her from her kneeling position by the commander. "It's not the wounds, Laurel. It's what's been put inside him."

"Drillers," Barst uttered as he knelt to view Darius's back and saw a wiggly creature still moving beneath his skin.

"Oh … my … God!" Laurel uttered in absolute shock as she stared at Darius and the things wiggling just beneath his flesh. "Who the hell would do something like that? What kind of sick bastard would … my God!"

"It's all right, Laurel. I know what to do," Gemma announced. "There are three inside him. We need to get him back to the *Titan* as soon as possible. If his damned tracking device had been embedded anywhere but in his left shoulder, we'd have located the both of you sooner."

Laurel blinked back tears and simply nodded. She was momentarily unable to speak, probably one of the few times in her life that'd ever happened.

Her assumption about the damage done to his tracking device was correct. It might have been severely damaged or destroyed by the flails that had been applied to his skin. If the situation had been less dire, she'd have suggested embedding it into deeper body tissue, like his thick brain. But this was neither the time nor the place for such levity. Darius actually had creatures forcibly rooted within his body. At that moment she knew she'd kill every vamphiere—or their cohorts—whenever or wherever she came across them. Not content with slaughtering, as if that wasn't bad enough, they had to do it in a way that was both gruesome and agonizing. Any race that'd do such a thing wasn't worth the space they occupied.

She said nothing else as Barst pulled a six-inch black rod from his belt, pressed some lighted buttons on it, and tossed it a few feet to the right. The rod instantaneously folded out, into a floating stretcher.

With one more of a million wonders to learn, she simply followed as the procession quickly made its way back to the *Titan*.

She wanted to ask about Char and the other hostages but Darius's safety was still uppermost in her mind. She just assumed the situation had been dealt with or Barst and the other crewmembers with him would be chasing homicidal maniacs with a penchant for embedding foreign creatures in other folks' bodies.

Explanations would come. For now, she just wanted this incident over. More importantly, she wanted to be home again, away from all the intrigue space people inflicted on one another. She'd have given anything for a plain old burglary or a simple smash-and-grab of a couple of pieces of jewelry.

Only when they were in the med bay and Barst stood to one side giving orders to his crew did she finally ask the one pertinent question of immediate concern.

"Okay … will someone please tell me what the hell a driller is? Besides being unbelievably sickening to watch, what do they do?"

"They're sentient parasites," Barst said. "The things eat their way into the central nervous system, move to the brain stem, mate, and lay eggs there. Their intent is to totally control their host. Through reading synapses the way we read a star map, they can use any part of the consciousness or memory to render their host malleable. This makes it much harder for their removal. The pain they cause by noncompliance is excruciating." He shook his head and shuddered. "I think they found his tracker and ate it. If they perceived it might be used to get medical help, they'd do so."

"Sweet Jesus!" She rolled her eyes and briefly stared at the deck. What other horrors were there in the universe? She was beginning to even appreciate a common cockroach. They might be nasty, but she knew how to deal with them.

Gemma called to Barst from across the med bay. "Let's do this now. I have to get all of these things. Not one cell can remain or Darius will be worse than dead," she urgently told them while automatically using into her commander's given name.

It was clearer than ever to Laurel that the three of them were very close. Barst and Gemma had probably been with Darius for a long time. That would explain the looks of severe concern and solemnity on their faces now. Their commander wasn't just a supervisor. He was a best friend.

When Gemma and Barst drew nearer to the examination table where Darius was laid out, Laurel followed. They silently watched as Gemma placed a white disc against Darius's neck and then pushed it.

"This will bring him around while blocking a portion of the pain," Gemma said.

"Is that necessary?" Barst asked. "Can't we do this while he's still out?"

Gemma shook her head. "No! He's going to have to tell me where they're located. Part of the little bastards' survival technique is to throw off intermittent, false life signs. And we don't have time to hook up a special incu-unit to the main computers." She paused, then put her full attention on Laurel and the second-in-command.

"Laurel … can you stand in front of him? Keep him focused. Barst, you and a couple of crewmen will have to hold him still if medical restraints won't work. Obviously, he'll have to remain in a seated position so I can get to his back."

Laurel slowly shook her head. "Gemma, is this wise? You didn't see him in the woods. Can't you do something more than just block a *little* pain?"

"If I give him any more than what I just shot into him, he'll die. That much painkiller would have already stopped a smaller man's heart." She began to say more, but stopped when her patient moaned. "He's coming around now."

Darius raised his head, opened his eyes, and gasped.

Laurel stepped in front of him when Gemma nodded. And doing as the med-tech instructed, she placed her hands on either side of Darius's face.

"Good, Laurel! Now get him to talk," Gemma instructed as she prepared a hover tray for her needs.

"Darius … you're back on the *Titan*," Laurel said as she gently shook his face to get him focused. "Gemma is gonna help you. Do you understand?"

From his seated position, Darius strained at his bonds but nodded.

Gemma slipped on surgical gloves and a mask then picked up a wicked looking probe-like device. It was about eight inches long, as thick as her thumb and had a hook on one end. To Laurel, it looked like a small version of an old whaling harpoon.

Gemma spoke straight to her patient, clearly and loudly. "Commander, if you can hear me, I'm going to take the drillers out. How many of them are there? My equipment says three but my readouts may be wrong."

"Yes. Three," Darius whispered.

The med-tech asked yet another question. "Where is the most painful one now?"

"R-right shoulder," he replied.

"Watch Laurel, Commander. Keep your attention on *her*," Gemma told him. She glanced at Laurel before beginning. "Barst and these other two crewman will hold him if the pain gets too bad."

Laurel nodded at the others in attendance. None of them was particularly up for this task, as evidenced by their forbidding expressions. But if Gemma said it had to be done, then it would be.

"Laurel … he might say things that don't make sense. That'll be the drillers making him remember things to get him to fight us. Okay?"

She nodded, took a deep breath, and moved closer. She kept her hands on either side of Darius's face and tried not to notice the horrible pain in his eyes.

As Gemma moved to Darius's back, lifted her probe, and inserted it into one of many whip wounds, Darius fought his restraints. Barst and the two crew alongside the examination table crowded together to hold their supervisor steady. In that moment, she'd never felt sorrier for another soul in her life, not even herself.

As Gemma dug, sweat broke out on Darius's face and he pulled against the friends holding him. Every muscle in his gargantuan body bulged. She was sure if they let him go, he'd break any of the restraints Gemma already applied. If he got free, it was possible for him to take all of them out.

"Darius, look at me! Don't fight … look at *me*," Laurel begged.

Even from her position in front of him, the fresh flow of blood on the sheets behind him was evident. His wounds were reopening due to either his struggling, Gemma's probing, or the creatures' will to survive.

"Got it!" Gemma cried as she lifted the probe and placed one gray, worm-like thing in a jar her assistant held.

Laurel felt bile rise all the way from her gall bladder.

The creature that'd been extracted looked like it'd grown. But that might have been her imagination, augmented by how horribly awful the entire procedure was. It shouldn't have ever happened. Any vamphiere, wizard or anybody else who did this to another soul wasn't worthy of any kind of life. The desire to kill them all welled within her again. At the same time, respect for Darius and his ability to withstand the pain grew immensely.

She looked away from the jar and into his face again. He was staring at her as if she were the only anchor in a very terrible storm.

She licked dry lips, composed her features into a mask of complete calm, and acted for all she was worth. From that moment on, she refused to look at what Gemma did. Instead, she gazed into a pair of forest-green eyes, trying to infuse some of her strength into him.

For another fifteen minutes, Gemma dug, probed, missed, and finally located one driller after another. But Darius kept his gaze locked to hers. He made no more attempts to fight. He answered Gemma's questions as to where he thought the creatures were located, but remained perfectly still.

As the last driller was removed and Gemma's triumphant smile indicated success, Laurel let out a long sigh of relief. She kept her hands on either side of Darius's face even as tears trembled on her lashes. If the situation had been reversed, she'd have turned a weapon on herself.

"We have to leave him tied for a few minutes," Gemma softly told everyone as she waved them away from the exam table. "I want to get to the lab with these damn things and make sure nothing was left behind. To do that, I have to put them under a photo-cosmic amplifier." She pulled off her gloves and her mask. "Barst, could you give him this? I think he can have it now. And he can lie down."

Gemma handed Barst another white injection disc. And when the med-tech hurriedly left the med bay, the second-in-command—bearing a look of utter relief on his fuzzy face—gently pushed the contents of the disk into Darius's neck. With great care, he lowered his commander backward, into a semi-lying position against soft pillows.

Laurel swallowed hard. Clearly, there were those on this ship who would give their lives for their superior—their friend. That kind of loyalty was hard-won and everlasting. She could respect that more than any rank.

"Untie me," Darius ordered as he blinked and took his steady gaze off Laurel's face.

Barst slowly shook his head. "Gemma said—"

"For the love of Perdian's Moons … untie me and do it now," Darius insisted, his voice still shaking.

When he was finally free of restraints, Darius shook his head as if he was trying to clear it. His skin color was much better. The pallor was fading, leaving in its place a deep tan, muscular hue. Laurel moved to support him on one side while Barst supported the other.

"I think we can actually take him to an incu-unit. Gemma won't mind. He can rest more comfortably and it'll be easier for further treatment," Barst suggested.

"Just one damn minute," Darius said as he glanced at each of them in turn. "What happened? I specifically gave orders for the crew to stay aboard and lift off if I didn't return."

"We did lift off," Barst admitted as he suppressed a grin. "We finished refueling, took off, and moved the *Titan* due west, closer to the Council Leader's residence. The vamphieres probably thought we'd left you. Our deep space concealment arrays hid us from their vessel's tracking console."

Darius shook his head and blinked. "My orders—"

"I followed them to the letter," Barst interrupted. "You said for the crew to stay aboard and refuel. They did. Laurel isn't part of the crew. She's free to leave and do whatever she wishes. But you never said what to do directly after taking off."

"You were to get to Luster!"

"But you never said *when*," Barst smilingly finished.

Darius glared at both of them. "You ... I don't ... if I have to reword every command to account for semantics ... then ... "

"Darius, everything worked out fine," Barst insisted.

Darius dragged air into his lungs, continuing to stare at them both. Anger was pasted all over his face. Eventually he sighed and passed a weary hand over the back of his neck. "What happened at Char's residence? Are he and the hostages all right?"

Barst raised one brow. "Not sure what happened when Laurel found you, but the diversion she gave us seems to have worked. She used your tracker to find you before one of the drillers destroyed it. Garron was found dead with the wizard and a couple of goons. The other vamphieres fled the home and headed for their ship, just to the west of Char's estate. We picked them off with photon cannons from the *Titan*."

Laurel nodded as the pieces started fitting together. "If one of the vamphieres I killed was their leader, then the others probably thought they were under attack and took off like the low-life cowards they are." She moved closer to Darius. "*Was* one of those things I shot a vamphiere leader?"

"I-I don't know. It could be," Darius admitted. "I don't remember much after that damned wizard pulled out a disrupter crystal and went to work on me. But Garron's minions would certainly run if he and their wizard were taken out. When they aren't used to being on their own, the savages follow whoever's alpha."

"At any rate ... when the vamphieres ran toward their ship, we couldn't let them take off and attack some other planetoid or colony," Barst explained. "Following League codes, we warned them, then blasted them and their small light-cruiser when they didn't surrender. One of our crew found Char and the other hostages on an upper floor of his residence. They were safe, if scared out of their wits." Barst paused for a moment then smiled and chuckled. "Char is ready to join the League and has offered any amount of coin, jewels, or women to service *you*, Darius. Of course, I told him you could take no remuneration, but he's determined to that see that superiors on Luster reward you accordingly."

"I'm flattered. *Really*!" Darius responded sarcastically. "All I did was get myself captured and tortured while you used semantics to pull off a victory by the seat of your pants. And, might I add, with an Earther who's barely able to open a hatch on this ship without help!"

Laurel gasped and would have walked away except for Barst's gentle grip on her upper left arm. The gentle shake of his big head told her not to take Darius's comments to heart.

"That's hardly fair," Barst defended. "She saved your life and provided a distraction that protected innocent people. One might say we pulled it off more with luck than skill. But it turned out all right. The best part is that another of Goll's kin is dead, and we'll have a new ally in the League. You'll get the credit, Darius."

Laurel simply glared at the man in charge. She would never be anything to him other than a primitive Earther. She thought she could be something more than that. A friend, at least. Perhaps a lover one day, when she could get over her own, numerous insecurities about people from other worlds. But she'd misread the signals or maybe she'd inferred things a man from another planet wouldn't want her thinking.

Hurt and unable to respond because of what he said, she simply remained silent. At least Barst afforded her the opportunity to do something besides sit in her quarters and vegetate. Bear man trusted her. Even Gemma was more inclined to respect her lately. Their confidence in letting her go to their beloved supervisor's aid spoke for itself. But what must she do to get Darius's simple thanks? What did she have to do to be an equal? Why, in his view, was an individual's intelligence always linked to their world's technology? And finally, where was the gentle man who'd kissed her so tenderly?

Darius blinked several times, shook his head, and put one hand to his temple.

"We'd better get him into an incubation unit. The drillers may be gone, but those whip marks aren't," Barst suggested. "I think I can manage getting him up if you can get one of the unit sides down so he can lie in it."

She would have refused the request and told Barst to leave the ungrateful bastard where he was, but the more genial of the two didn't deserve her tantrums. Barst knew what she'd done in Char's residence. She wouldn't ever have to prove herself again, at least not to *one* member of the crew. But the pain of rejection threatened to make her act ill-bred.

Without any further comment, Barst helped Darius up. They moved slowly but finally crept across the length of the med bay.

When they approached the largest of the incubation units, the second-in-command helped his superior lie down, after Laurel lowered one side of the coffin-looking, silver box.

Just looking at the device made her shiver. But if it healed without surgery in most cases then it was worth its weight in gold. More to the point, if the incubation unit kept Darius asleep and out of her hair for a while, so much the better. More than ever now, she needed to think and analyze her feelings. This would be better accomplished with her current, biggest obstacle out of the way.

As the bigger of the two men lay backward into the box, and Barst turned the unit on, Laurel took a brief moment to gaze into

Darius's eyes. He was still angry. Had his stare been a bullet, she'd have been well and truly punctured. She didn't understand him and likely never would.

The entire incident on Arjus might be over—and a grand success to everyone on the ship—but he'd have words with her later. She was sure of it. Somehow, he saw her as an incendiary element that was inappropriately influencing his crew. To him, she was a floating ember that needed to be stomped out. She'd seen that very same look on other supervisors' faces. In this instance, however, she wasn't a subordinate. Like Barst said, she had every right to leave the ship when and as she pleased.

Thankfully, Gemma walked back into the space. The med-tech smiled happily in recognition of a successful operation. "Great! You've got him in an incu-unit. The good news is … I got all of those foul things out of him. Every piece. The better news is … it'll be a short trip home!"

"What will you do with them … the drillers, I mean?" Laurel asked.

"Put them in an air lock and space 'em!" Gemma replied. "That's standard operating procedure when we come in contact with particularly tenacious parasites. Drillers are so bad that not even our decontamination unit can deal with them."

"As far as spacing nasty little creatures goes, it'll be my pleasure," Barst added as he smilingly left to find the jar in which the creatures had been placed.

For a moment longer, Laurel stayed to watch Gemma push buttons on the incubation unit. As the med-tech worked, the pain-filled look on Darius's face diminished. But he wasn't healing so fast that he'd relent. His probing stare in *her* direction was still very effective.

Laurel shook her head in frustration. "If I'm not needed here I'll go back to my quarters and plant my primitive butt in front of a computer," she muttered as she stared back at Darius. "God forbid I find a way to be useful!"

With that, she strode out of the med bay vowing to apologize to Gemma for the less-than-cordial exit.

Chapter 8

With minimal time, the healing properties of the unit did their job. The pain suffered was only a memory but Darius knew how close he'd been to death. Unsure exactly when he'd become so careless of his own life, he evaluated the future and what he wanted from it.

After being released from the med bay, he'd taken up duties again with many congratulatory comments being offered. The daring and spontaneous nature of the mission wasn't lost on his crew. Down to the last man and women, each was in awe of Laurel Blake and how an untrained, backward Earther so easily managed to thwart the threat to their superior's life. Darius, too, was heaped with accolades for his having endured such atrocious behavior. With every tribute, he was quick to remind his crew that no one achieved anything without the help of all.

Secretly, he burned at the thought of having been rescued by a woman who—even as he watched her join newly-made friends among the crew at meal times, and in the recreation area of the ship—was still unable to open intricate hatches, operate certain food dispensary machines, or figure out what to do with her day without help. He'd watched her accept aid from others, help she'd never request of *him*. But then she'd pointedly kept out of his way. The woman even went so far as to get up and leave the galley when he approached her table. Even common cordiality was lost between them. There were certainly no more questioning, warm stares sent his way.

She was as angry with him as he was with her. But where her ire was directed at his tactless comments—made out of fear for her life—his outrage originated from the terror of losing someone he now cared for deeply, just as he'd lost Astral. And even as he recognized the foolhardiness of her actions, that part of him where fairness dwelled felt shame. He shouldn't have been so harsh. What was it about her that made him want to either strangle or embrace her depending on the moment or the situation? And why had he so willingly walked into what he'd innately known was a trap? There'd been other ways to handle the situation. And though Char might not have agreed, those alternates would have been vastly safer for all concerned.

The more he thought on the subject during the long hours alone in his quarters, the more he realized the answer. Guilt still ate every waking moment of his life.

Astral and Kyrie were dead. He was alive and nothing was ever going to bring his family back. There were nights in the past when he believed death was the only solution to the pain. But then everything changed once Goll had been captured, and that Earther torpedoed into his life.

Now, every waking moment was consumed with thoughts of where she was, what she was doing, who she was with, and how was she getting along. Sadly, his poor behavior put her in no mood to seek his company. No, she'd found the *rest* of the crew, down to the lads who kept the passageways clean, much more suitable. He'd seen her speaking to them, and had caught the end of conversations having to do with their duties. On seeing his approach, she'd quickly left and strode the other way. A solid look of resolve, the likes of which he'd never seen, was constantly pasted on her lovely face when cast in his direction.

She made friends easily but he was not among them. He knew she missed her planet and her friends, just as he missed his family. He should have been more understanding. More sympathetic. But the constant worry over something happening to her and losing her made him say and do things he'd not otherwise engage. Honesty made him recognize the foul emotions and their cause: he didn't want to see her die.

If he let himself, she could so easily worm her way into his life. All he'd have to do was approach her, apologize, ask to start anew, and see her cast one hint of a smile in his direction. And if she did, he'd be lost. But amending what he'd said wouldn't be that easy. Not with her. She had a will of iron and was out to do anything she had to, to prove it. That very same ornery characteristic would likely get her destroyed.

Still, Laurel Blake was everything he'd ever wanted in a woman. He was far past those days when just a pretty face and toned body turned his head. She was fearless and intuitive. She was an enforcer and would understand the life of a mate in such an occupation. But she took things too far, especially for one so primitive.

Astral had at least known the dangers in traveling through a section of space deemed unsafe during tourist season, when attacks of travel vessels were at their peak. His dead beloved had made a choice based on knowledge.

Laurel, on the other hand, knew absolutely nothing. Sadly, the Earther's steely tenacity when it came to involving herself in dangerous situations was every bit as powerful as Astral's had ever been, even stronger. That was the only similarity the women shared.

It was Laurel's persistence to be included in all the crew's duties, no matter how hazardous, that he most dreaded. He dared not let anyone so determined and reckless come close to his heart. Not ever.

But what did he want from here on? Was his love life now relegated to passionate moments within some Lusterian brothel? At least there, he need not fear any emotional ties.

But nothing could convince him that was living. It was slaking lust. Nothing more.

All his life he'd wanted a large family. How much longer was the past going to own him? Alone in his quarters, he stared out his view port and considered options—just as he had almost every night since that insane Earther arrived.

His family pitied him, along with his crew and the commanders and crews of other enforcer ships. He was nothing if not the personification of tragedy. Bits of gossip about "poor Commander Starlaw" floated back to him. The pity got on his nerves, and it wore thin.

He could end that well-meaning but demeaning empathy, open his heart, approach Laurel, and offer to be her tutor on a new world where every small thing would be so difficult for her to understand. He could make himself so necessary in her life that she'd need him as she seemed to need all the rest of the crew. But then what?

She was not the kind of woman to constantly lean on others. She was not some vine to cling to him for every decision. Poor Astral had been like that when they'd first been married. The young man he'd been was flattered. That neediness had bolstered his protectiveness and masculinity. But that kind of relationship was one-sided. It was cloying and claustrophobic. It was also in the past.

What he craved now was a woman who wouldn't leave. One who'd stand her ground and fight to the nth degree, especially if it meant keeping a family together and safe. The Earther was such a woman. But how did he get past the fear of losing her when she'd accept nothing less than the kind of life she'd had back on her home world? One filled with excitement and intrigue.

He ran one weary hand over his face and walked toward his bathing area. At least he could do what he'd been doing almost every night since Laurel had come aboard. He'd slake his body's needs while fantasizing about her beneath a long, warm shower.

•••

"How close are we to Luster?" Laurel asked as she stood on the bridge beside Gemma and gazed out the main view port.

"Less than half a shift and we'll be home again. Finally!" Gemma smiled. "The crew needs shore leave badly. We'd been chasing Goll for such a long time before his ship's tekion engine left a trace leading us to Earth. He'll be turned over to League investigators in short order. His case and all the horrors associated with him will be put to rest. And I, for one, couldn't be happier."

"What will happen when he *is* turned over?"

"Superiors will question him. He'll be given a fair hearing and the right to representation though I don't think he's going to deny his crimes. He'll know that, since you survived, your testimony will be utterly devastating. At this point, he'll want to look like a martyr for his kind."

"And will all this take very long?" Laurel asked.

"Some weeks. But that's short compared to how long he's been out there murdering people."

Laurel simply nodded and took a better position to see out the bridge view port. She was only allowed into that secured area due to Barst's and Gemma's vouching. But she'd wanted to join them, eager to use the better vantage point to see what would likely be her new home. Luster was supposed to be many times larger than Earth but populated with much less density. Wild animals, plants, and cultures she could never have imagined were waiting to be explored. Putting the computer in her quarters to use paid off as she'd researched whatever she could get her hands on. Knowing everything she could was vitally important now.

From this point forward, nobody had mentioned what she was supposed to do with her life. How was she supposed to make a living? How would she even eat?

But as time passed, one thing became very clear. As much as she hated to admit it, there was one simple truth concerning her future.

She couldn't go home again, either by law or choice.

Others she'd spoken to were right. There was no way to explain her lengthy absence after surely being declared dead along with her comrades. A group of think tanks back home were probably still considering circumstances surrounding the heat that'd destroyed her friends' remains. But the charred grass and shrubbery were the *only* bizarre signs associated with the events of that night. If she showed up back on Earth—never mind the physical changes Gemma had made—she'd be right in the middle of a controversy that would last the rest of her life. How would she ever explain the fact that she was still young while at least a decade had gone by on Earth? And when she was obliged to tell her fellow Earth citizens about advanced life forms from other worlds, they'd want technological information she didn't know how to provide. She'd never be free from serious scrutiny again.

So what of the future?

She didn't want to end up begging for whatever might be given to her. The very clothing she wore was borrowed or loaned from the ship's stores. Every morsel that went into her mouth was being paid for by someone. Even advanced societies had monetary exchanges, and she couldn't live on the ship, off someone's grace forever. Worse, she felt the commander was probably the one footing her bill or explaining the added responsibility on her behalf. Since that was likely the case, she hated owing the man. He saw her as an encumbrance even though *he* owed *her*.

As to his close call on Arjus, she was pretty damn sure the man was fed up with living. That was why he'd actually ordered the crew to leave him behind at the first sign of trouble.

How hard it must have been for him after losing his wife and little girl. Long hours in her quarters put everything into perspective.

She'd lost friends who were cops. They'd all accepted the fact that they might not go home one night. Their families would grieve, but would have each other for solace. It'd taken time for her to get that through her thick skull, hating the idea of kids growing up without parents whose deaths could never be explained. But that scenario back on Earth just wasn't the same as what the commander had experienced. His wife and child weren't professionally putting themselves in harm's way. They'd been innocents who'd been in the wrong place at the wrong time. She couldn't imagine how she'd have felt if that little girl had been hers. Perhaps she'd throw herself into her work, to the exclusion of all else, the way Darius Starlaw seemed to have done.

After considering all the facts, she was on the verge of giving the man a break. His rigidity and taciturn expression were outward signs of his loss. He wasn't getting close to any damned body if he could help it. While she was no psychologist, she knew the signs of severe grief when she saw them. She'd at least had that much exposure to how others dealt with loss back home.

The crew respected the hell out of the man. They'd regaled her with his heroic exploits. But all those stories of his bravery pointed to a person who was pushing himself into situations where, sooner or later, he wouldn't come back.

He'd lost his future. However strange and hard it might be for her to adapt, she at least had one. She hadn't lived through her family dying.

When everything was considered, her anger with Darius's treatment was constantly at war with pity on his behalf. She'd stayed away from him just so there'd be no more angry outbursts on either side. There was no point in stirring a pot when he'd made his choices and she had several thousands of them to still consider. Besides finding a way to fit in on a new world—with about three centuries of learning to make up—one more thing was perfectly clear.

She had to go her own way.

He and his crew would continue their duties and leave her to her own devices. The sooner she broke any kind of dependence on Gemma, Barst, or anyone else she'd befriended, the better she'd be.

No … there certainly was no going back now. And the safe harbor that'd been her quarters would be gone. She'd simply have to go somewhere else.

"Look … not much longer now!" Gemma cried out as she pointed to the view screen.

Laurel couldn't see anything other than a brighter star enhanced so that astronomical events were more easily viewable. But as the *Titan* flew through space, the star became the super-sized sun that warmed a very massive planet just to the left of it. Other planets came into view behind this larger one. Like Earth, Luster was green and blue—though it had landmasses that dwarfed anything considered a continent on her former home world.

Laurel swallowed hard. She noted the smiles on the crew's faces. They greeted their commanding officer as he walked onto the bridge, wearing a black dress uniform that probably signaled a meeting with dignitaries on landing. The big commanding officer barked out commands in his typical, reserved style.

"Barst … signal headquarters we're approaching. Have a detail of eight ground enforcers meet us at the landing field. I want Goll off this ship and into their custody as soon as possible."

Darius paused and gazed at the crew around him. Their silent return regard was nothing less than epic. Laurel didn't regard him with so much heroic grandeur. She simply looked away when he might have caught her staring.

Darius took the commander's chair from Barst. He sat but everyone still gawked expectantly in his direction. Every crewmember within sight was frozen in place, waiting to hear whatever he'd say.

"Log a long shore leave for the entire crew," Darius announced. "We've earned it!"

That announcement was met with cries of joy, backslapping happiness, and a sense of impending celebration.

Laurel took that opportunity to back away and off the bridge before Darius even noted her presence. In a matter of seconds, she was in the passageway, on her way to her quarters without as much as a question.

Her throat closed, and tears stung her eyes.

Now's not the time to cry like a baby. I got that outta my system when I was alone in my quarters, struggling to learn how to use an alien version of a commode without embarrassing myself. So I can either give up or stand strong. I'm representing an entire planet. And by God, I mean to show anyone having doubts that an Earth citizen can shine.

With that, she lifted her chin, blinked harder, and quickly made her way to a space where she could think alone.

• • •

Darius noted her presence. He knew the exact moment she left the bridge and felt pity on her behalf. The Earther among them was so clearly out of her league. But he'd tried to approach, offer support in his own way, only to be silently rebuffed when he came physically near.

One didn't have to have a sign posted to know the woman simply didn't want to have anything to do with him. She hated her circumstances and still blamed him for them even though she'd tried to make the best of her lot. At least her attempts were lauded by Gemma and Barst and many of the crew.

It was through his ship's med-tech and his second-in-command that he meant to offer support, if she'd accept. His family had numerous empty cottages on their large, country estate. These were set aside for special occasions, when large familial gatherings overflowed the castle compound.

Gossip might make of the situation something different than a simple friendly gesture. As a younger man he might have taken more care with the reputation he'd worked hard to cultivate. But Laurel was a special case, and he was long over the blathering others chose to engage. If his deeds didn't command respect at this time in life, then no amount of respectable behavior concerning what would likely be deemed a kept woman would make any difference. He'd always found it strange that what others could do so easily and without comment was considered off limits for *him*. As his father so often repeated "more is expected of us." That unfortunate code was what prompted him to marry Astral when it'd become clear, shortly after the ceremony, that the two of them were ill-suited.

As he stared at the view screen—wishing himself back on solid ground so vehemently that he almost smelled the clean Lusterian air and felt the cool breeze against his skin—he wondered what Laurel would make of her new home. For all intents and purposes, Luster would be her planet of origin. And to help her establish a new life, he'd made special requests to have proper ID and citizenship documentation recorded. He'd relayed her need of a home to his family and there were no objections to his plans.

He tried, for the thousandth time, to put himself in her place. How would he fare on her world, living an existence so antiquated as to almost become an exercise in survival? Still, he firmly believed it would be easier to go backward in time and live life according to antiquated norms, than to have so many centuries of advancement to absorb. Becoming comfortable might well take the woman the rest of her life. But she was no fool. She knew she'd never be allowed to see Earth again. No amount of begging on her behalf would lift the ban concerning official contact with her planet.

He leaned forward and put his attention on their landing. When it was the proper time, later in the evening, Gemma would approach Laurel with the news that her residence, and therefore her safety, was secured.

She'd resent his help, even when cajoled by her friends to take it. But that's where things stood. She really had no other choice. He kept telling himself these well laid plans were for her good. In reality, the thought of losing complete contact was intolerable.

• • •

Laurel felt the crew's excitement as they prepared to land. They ran everywhere and energetic happiness was etched in their features. Even those whose faces were alien and whose mouth location was questionable seemed ecstatic. Their eyes revealed the emotion if nothing else did. Though some of the crew was not originally from Luster, as she'd been informed, smatterings of conversation mentioned celebrating at local taverns all over the capital city of Crystol. She remembered late night drinks with her comrades and mourned the loss of even the simplest things. But no one must know. Her regrets and fears had to remain her own. Even Gemma and Barst surely had limits as to how much self-pity they'd endure. She vowed to show none. The life she'd lived was over. This was a new one. On the bright side, she could make herself over, into anything she pleased. Be anyone or anything if Lusterian edicts she'd studied on the ship's computers were to be believed.

As the ship landed later that evening, the crew gathered near the *Titan*'s large landing bay hatch. Outside it, families and friends were said to be waiting.

Over what served as the ship's intercom, she heard Darius's deep voice resonate throughout the ship. He officially ordered the bay exit open and gave permission for his crew to disembark. She assumed this was her chance to leave. Gemma and Barst were nowhere to be seen, and she tried not to panic. No one was going to hurt her. Nothing lurked on the other side of that hatch that was so terrible. She'd seen and experienced far worse than traveling to a new place. But her heart still wouldn't stop pounding as she moved forward among the throngs of departing crew.

The outer gangway gracefully fell into place and the crew pushed their way outside. She was among them.

For Laurel, it was like watching shoppers at a Christmas sale. Every conceivable body shape, appendage size, and skin color milled around in happy, embracing clusters. At a loss of which way to go, but certain she'd be found if needed, she stood near the bottom of the gangway.

Minutes later, Gemma, Barst, and Darius exited. The commander of the vessel was regaled with rounds of applause and well wishes. He simply lifted one large hand in acknowledgement. Only the corner of his lip shifted upward by way of a smile.

She licked dry lips and tried to quell childish fears threatening to overwhelm. This was no nightmare. She was on another planet witnessing a scene that could only have been produced at great expense had it been depicted by some Hollywood mogul.

A stray strand of hair blew across her face. The air smelled fresh. It wasn't the recirculated, if clean, artificial breeze experienced on the ship. Somewhere nearby, flowers were growing. Their scent was impossible to disguise. But she couldn't see the landscape beyond the many crew and family members present on the landing field. The gray, solid surface beneath her booted feet was reminiscent of cement, absent any stains of oil, fuel of other signs of ship repairs.

Gemma suddenly bounced toward her, looking so much like a young teenager—blue color notwithstanding—that is was impossible not to smile.

"Come on, Laurel. This is going to be terrific fun. Let me show you the sights," Gemma offered as she gaily laughed and beckoned her Earth friend to follow.

Suddenly, Gemma went quite still. Her attention was captured by approaching beings that looked like her.

Almost in tandem, Gemma and Barst ran forward and cried out heartfelt greetings to what Laurel assumed were either siblings, parents, or other very close friends. These arriving individuals opened their arms wide to accept the med-tech and the *Titan*'s second-in-command.

The breeze blew cooler. Laurel held back. She wasn't used to happy homecomings on Earth, never mind some strange world where her presence might be perceived as an intrusion.

Among the crew she'd befriended, many were locating and loudly welcoming their families and friends. She didn't back up but was actually pressed backward by the advancing crowds. With not so much as a piece of luggage, she stood there feeling like a piece of the *Titan*'s hull. No one would ever welcome her again. Not that her family *had*, but the emotional outbursts around her reminded her of the isolation of the situation.

To get out of the way, she put her back to the hull and concentrated on seeing anything of the landscape she could. With so many present, her only clear view of anything was straight up. When she lifted her gaze, she saw a huge, moon-like body overhead. Behind it, several other planets in hues of purple, blue and gold hovered in the Lusterian evening sky. Surrounding these bodies were clusters of celestial events that made her think of some telescopic view of space dreamed up by science fiction writers. Her mouth dropped open at the beauty of an alien evening so lovely that fears suddenly diminished. No planet she'd seen so far rivaled this spectacular presentation of nature.

My God! I'm the first from Earth to ever know. I'm the first to ever see this.

Time was lost. She simply stared up and wasn't sure how long she stood there in awe. Sounds of revelry seemed to fade. There was nothing but her and that unbelievable alien sky.

If the rest of the planet was as lovely as her research indicated, she might drown her insecurity in the wonders of the environment. Surely no one would care if she wandered and explored. What harm could she possibly do?

Despite the absolute riveting nature of the celestial presentation, a deep familiar voice dragged her gaze downward, back to the throngs and reality.

Before her, the crowd parted. The crew and their families slightly bowed their heads as a powerfully built man moved closer to the ship. This dark-haired giant was dressed in a deep green, belted tunic, black pants, and polished, high black boots. He wore a cloak bearing an insignia over his left breast. It looked as though it had some majestic significance.

Next to this older, warrior-like figure, a diminutive woman of wondrous beauty strode. She had long pale hair that had been braided. It hung down her left shoulder and glistened in the evening light. The color offset her lovely blue eyes. Her bright, open smile lit the coming darkness. And though her long gown exactly matched the clothing of her male companion, she stood out like one of the seven-pointed stars in the twilight sky. There were those in the crowd who actually gasped in wonder of her awesome appearance. Where gleeful greetings had been heard, silence now engulfed the landing field. The style of the significant arrivals' garb appeared almost medieval except for the sparkling quality of the expensive-looking fabric. The pair seemed like some mythic king and queen from a fairytale. Compared to others who were dressed in floating, gossamer fabrics that moved in the slightest breeze, or to the League enforcers whose dark uniforms were meant to make them look more official, these new arrivals clearly meant to stand out. She heard someone mention the arrival of the royal couple. Her summation of their importance was correct.

What was more interesting than the clothing was the regal man's eye color. Even as far away as Laurel stood, the glowing, deep green hue matched that of the *Titan*'s commander.

She looked closer. Yes. The resemblance was inescapable.

The stately, older man greatly resembled Darius—or perhaps it was the other way around. The man's long black hair, streaked with gray, couldn't diminish his handsome face. His joy in being present was obvious. Unlike the man who commanded the *Titan*, this newcomer's countenance was kind and open. There was nothing stoic or somber in his bearing. He greeted those around him with a slight, congenial nod and murmured what she assumed were quiet welcoming messages to those nearest his location.

These people had to be Darius's kin. They made a breathtaking family who were happily acknowledged by those on the landing field. It was clear they commanded and received the greatest respect.

No one dared touch the ethereal duo. In fact, the crew and their friends and family made a path that equaled one given for the impromptu visit of dignitaries. Behind the couple, others of equally royal bearing approached. Smiles were plastered over their faces. Some of these new arrivals were very young, some were older, but all had those piercing green eyes.

"The royal family is welcoming home their son," someone commented. "It is fitting after the controversy allowing the commander of the *Titan* latitude in arresting one whose kin killed his wife and child."

Laurel turned her head to see who'd spoken but those nearest were already moving aside and forward to get a better view. Small, crystal orbs appeared from folds of clothing. She assumed those raising the devices were trying to keep the event intact for posterity. Her research indicated the shimmering round objects now being lifted by the onlookers were recorders and used much the same as Earth video devices or smart phones. She neither knew nor cared how they worked. What was most important was that no one, Gemma and Barst included, had ever said Darius was part of some royal family. It was likely the pair she so admired were his parents. They appeared old enough to have sired him.

"Hail to King Dar and Queen Maelle," a League officer suddenly shouted.

Laurel retreated toward the stern of the large, silver bird-of-prey shaped vessel that'd been her home since having been taken from Earth. Why had no one bothered to impart that little bit of trivia? Why did she now feel so insecure? Would that knowledge have made any difference in the way she'd treated Darius? And finally, if his family was so powerful, and she *still* wouldn't be allowed to go back to Earth, then her summation of her status was correct.

She truly was a denizen of Luster, for the rest of her life.

She stood a bit apart from the massing crowd and watched as Darius slowly approached his family with all the pomp of a returning prince. His head was slightly bowed. He knelt before his liege and lady, just as if he were in some children's story she'd read so many years ago when cynicism hadn't dimmed her belief in such pageantry.

For some strange reason, she wished herself anyplace else. She tried to remember the rude things she'd said to Darius and knew that piper would be paid. As a supervisor back on Earth had told her over and over, it's better to keep your mouth shut and be thought a fool than to open it and remove all doubt. Well, she'd truly opened hers and proved herself a total malcontent at best, a troublemaker in need of incarcerating at worst.

What would he say to his parents about her? Had her temper finally sealed her fate, and would Darius use his influence and his belief in her inferiority to quell any plans she might make for this new life?

She took a deep breath and waited.

Chapter 9

Laurel felt her heart pounding but couldn't say why. After having confronted a man many times larger and more powerful than she, why the sudden desire to run? Perhaps she'd be locked away as Darius once promised.

Darius's mother held her arms wide and tearfully pulled her very large son into her petite embrace, holding nothing back as far as emotion was concerned. Maelle—if that really was the queen's name—was a lady who was obviously happy to have her child home. Several women dressed similarly to the royal couple pushed themselves forward and held the *Titan*'s commanding officer as though they'd never let him go. Who were these new additions to the spectacle? Friends, relatives, or lovers?

The crowds suddenly seemed overbearing, too besotted and too fan-like with their recording globes held high and reverent smiles pasted on their faces. Everyone's attention was riveted on Darius, his father, and mother. Laurel couldn't locate Gemma or Barst. Without their camaraderie, some of her swagger disappeared.

Laurel slowly backed away. In the throngs, no one noticed one person wearing an unmarked League-looking tunic, pants, and boots. She should leave now, before the royal family learned of the disrespect she'd shown their titled son.

She slowly turned. The bright lights of the city were impossible to miss. Research told her that Crystol was populated by about eight million beings that'd either immigrated to Luster or were born there. Surely no one would notice one more walking peaceably about the streets.

Likely, she'd pass as Lusterian. They were a human-looking lot despite their taller frames. But she could fit in. She had to. Where else could she go?

As she sauntered slowly away, making sure not to move so fast as to garner notice, she congratulated herself. Even the less-than-human sentient beings scattered about the massive gray landing field paid her no attention at all. Eventually, she walked through a very large containment apparatus that looked like the pearly gates of heaven itself.

Lights from city power sources beckoned her forward. Not knowing where she was going or even caring, she took fate in hand and acted as if she belonged.

...

Darius stifled his amusement. Ever the perfect hostess, his mother was in the process of graciously welcoming friends and dignitaries to their home. It'd taken the better part of two hours to shuttle everyone from the airfield to the estate, but celebrations for the *Titan*'s homecoming were in full swing. He sipped Anphrasian brandy, smiled at his sisters' antics in flirting with various members of his crew—crew who were too wise to take up the invitation lest they find their hearts broken or become the subject of gossip among citizens.

"Barst and Gemma … you are always welcome here," Maelle announced as she greeted Darius's best friends and their extended families. "Please join us in the great chamber. We've missed you all so much."

While others not afforded the privilege of entering the inner, more secure sanctum of Starlaw castle's great chamber mingled, dined, danced and drank themselves into stupors, Darius and his crew followed his mother, sire, and siblings into the large hallway off the dining area.

The great chamber was a massive room decorated with gilt treasures of another era. Tapestries, ancient armor no longer used, and heraldic symbols hung everywhere. Heavy, dark colored furniture made it possible for even the largest, off-world species to sit in comfort. A thick burgundy carpet muted the sounds of booted feet as well as the lighter taps of ladies' sandals.

"You should sit down, Darius. I know you reported that nasty encounter with those driller things as history, but you look stressed to me."

He waved off his eldest sister's concern. Lovely, blonde Nyssa—a perfect copy of their mother in every respect—was forevermore trying to nurse someone or some*thing*. If it wasn't some wounded creature, it was anyone claiming a scratch or a cut. In his case, the incident with the drillers had been over for months. Nyssa wouldn't be satisfied until he gave her some *other* project to attack.

"Nyss," he addressed using the nickname he always had, "there's someone I'd like you to befriend. She's the Earth woman I spoke of."

"Ah yes! Laurel Blake. I've yet to see anyone matching her description though I have searched for her," Nyssa claimed as she glanced around the chamber. "With so many revelers present, perhaps she's still in the dining area or dancing with the others."

"Perhaps," he said with a decided nod. Since Laurel had kept her distance on the ship, he readily assumed this was the case. "Is the cottage ready?"

"Certainly! And I'll be happy to help her acclimate, in any way possible."

He smiled down at his sibling, loving her for her open, sweet heart. "Gemma and Barst will know where she's got to. Likely the woman is somewhere with the ship's crew, trying to figure out some dance step or bit of trivia having to do with local custom. She may be from a primitive world, but her tenacity when it comes to learning is nothing short of mind boggling. At least that's the word I have from my staff."

"Don't you know her well enough to judge such things for yourself?" Nyssa asked as she tilted her head and gazed up at him.

"I've had a ship to run and a prisoner to deliver. Since both chores are now completed and I'm on leave, I'll put more attention on our sad little victim." His smile faded. "Truly, she's in need of guidance, Nyss. And I thank you for your offer in that regard." He finished his drink and put it on the tray of a passing waiter. "If you'll excuse me, I'll fight my way through these bodies and attempt to locate our little charity case. She has no idea I've secured a residence on her behalf and I fear the news will be met with more hostility than happiness. With her, it's all about pride."

"Just use that Starlaw charm, brother. I'm sure she'll come 'round," Nyssa teased.

"You don't know this woman."

He stepped away from Nyssa and searched a half hour but still couldn't find the tall brunette that was the center of his existence these days. But he *did* locate Barst's large frame near the chamber doors. As ever, Gemma was by his side.

He quickly greeted his comrades, motioned them onto a balcony away from the crowds, and put voice to his queries.

"Have either of you seen Laurel?"

"Indeed we have not," Barst answered. "Gemma and I wanted to introduce her to our parents and a few other friends who'd be eager to offer support in her new life."

Gemma nodded in agreement. "I rather thought she might be with some of the crew outside. She's made a number of friends among them."

"I thought of that, but still can't find her," Darius relayed as he anxiously gazed out at the gardens and the guests who strolled there.

"Stars! All I could think of was finding my parents … poor Laurel … " Gemma uttered as her smile faded. "You don't think she got lost, do you?"

Feeling embarrassment and shame, Darius dragged one hand through his hair in an agitated gesture. To his consternation, the thick mass he'd carefully tied back as uniform codes required came loose. Strands of it sifted forward even as he tried to shove it all back. "That woman! Where by Orion's balls could she have possibly drifted? I should have put an ID chip on her before she left the ship. She's the only one on the entire damned planet without any identification whatsoever. It never occurred to me she'd have the gumption to actually go off on her own. What was I thinking?"

"I'm sure she's all right," Barst placated. "Perhaps we've just overlooked her in the throngs. There are a great many in attendance, after all."

Darius sighed heavily. "Barst ... check the dining area and the ballroom. Gemma, check the great chamber and the ladies' dressing rooms. The crew knows her. Ask around," he ordered.

As Barst and Gemma hurried away to begin their search, he strode purposely into the garden area, trying not to interrupt trysts between members of his crew and the lovers with whom they'd so recently been reunited.

With each passing moment he was more certain that Laurel had never made it on one of the shuttles headed to the castle. He'd given her the space she'd seemed to crave and was now sorry for it. Without a communication device of any kind, how would she know where she was or where the airfield was if she got lost?

He dodged well-wishers and those who'd comment on political decisions having to do with Goll's capture, and made his way to a communication console in his father's study. Several vid calls to the airfield proved fruitless. A cleaning supervisor, whose crew was sprucing up the *Titan*, hadn't seen a lone woman matching Laurel's description. The man confirmed there were no enforcers remaining on the ship. Gate guards couldn't remember who, among all the enforcers, had left the airfield alone. Without any reason to ask for ID from those *leaving* the field, they hadn't noticed anything amiss—even though she was in an unmarked League uniform.

"Fools! The guards should have at least noticed that much about her," he angrily muttered as he shut down communication to the airfield.

Furious over having to leave the celebrations, he knew there was simply no other choice. If Gemma or Barst didn't find her, and none of the crew had seen her, then she was not on the premises. He found his parents and dejectedly made explanations for having to leave the celebrations.

"Mother, Father … please, excuse me. I have to find the Earth woman we took aboard the *Titan*. Creator only knows what she thinks of us for departing as we did. As a primitive, we can't leave her on her own. There's much she doesn't understand about our society."

"Of *course*," Maelle agreed. "This is unbelievably awkward. That poor young woman was simply left behind? Part of tonight's festivities was meant to be in her honor; she's the first Earthling on our world."

"Don't worry, Your Majesty," Barst addressed Maelle as he joined Gemma and Darius, "if there's anyone in the star system who can look after herself it's Laurel. Our mutual ignorance of her whereabouts is still incredibly tactless."

After bidding their families a brief goodbye, Darius, Gemma, and Barst left the palace and made their way back to the ship. Where the gate guards hadn't remembered her, perimeter guards had. Several had seen Laurel leave toward the main thoroughfare. Because the *Titan*'s arrival was being celebrated, the shopkeepers and street merchants would be doing business day and night. Thousands of people crowded the area.

Darius took communicators from the ship's inventory and the three of them split up. As he left to search the central section of the city, he couldn't help but wonder why she hadn't simply followed the crew to the celebration. It wasn't as if they'd *meant* to leave her. Knowing the woman's damned pride, she probably stayed behind on purpose.

•••

Laurel lost track of time. She wandered the streets seeing things a science fiction writer would give their right arm to witness. There were creatures of every imaginable shape, size, and color meandering about. And, to her amusement, they appeared in every stage of dress and *un*dress. Women of some species bared their breasts for men who eagerly suckled nipples and fondled shapely curves. This was Lusterian nightlife, in no way similar to the austerity—and chastity—of a deep space enforcer's existence. What she had seen aboard the *Titan* hadn't prepared her for this strange but exciting multitude. It was surreal, dramatic, and even comical. The new quickly wore off, however. She was reminded a million times over, and in every small way, how alone she was on this world. As they had on so many occasions, feelings of inadequacy threatened to overwhelm. Her jaw clenched, bolstering courage that suddenly threatened to desert.

But no one acted threatening. The passing crowds didn't even seem to notice her. Once more, as she had so many times, she tamped down paranoid thoughts, took a deep breath, and continued. It wasn't as if there was no diversion.

Merchants offered wonderful cloth, exotic scents, fragrant and tantalizing dishes. She only wished Gemma were with her to explain things. The blue woman had become quite important in her life and Laurel missed their shared, first real outing on Luster. But she understood. Gemma had a family and wanted to be with them. *Hers* would obviously believe she was dead by now. As things in her family stratosphere went, she was pretty sure they'd eventually got on with life. She'd be a fond memory, replaced by the new children her father would get by a girl near her own age. Her mother would take extra trips to Italy, buy gold jewelry to assuage her pain, then return home to California with a new lover.

She stopped in the middle of a gray stone thoroughfare and wished Cory were still alive. *He* got her. That was why she'd spent so much time with him and his fiancée.

Her throat tightened.

How in God's name would she ever adapt? It was a necessity. She knew it. But how did a person keep pretending to be all right? What resources were there for coping?

"Are you in need of help?" a strange voice asked from behind.

She whirled to see a very dark blue, tall man wearing a silver jerkin, pants, and tall boots. His square jaw, straight nose, and electric blue eyes were startling. But he was a handsome male. With his bald head, standing there smiling down at her, she was reminded of Mr. Clean. He gazed down at her with concern in his eyes. As a defense against pity, she immediately pulled her shoulders back and smiled brilliantly. "Oh no … I'm fine, thank you! I … I'm new to Luster. Just enjoying the sights."

"Strange. You wear an enforcer's uniform with no visible markings," he said. "Is this some new style?"

"No. I'm not an enforcer. I'm sort of a refugee. The clothing was loaned to me until I can acquire garments of my own."

"Ah! You must have just arrived on the *Titan*? Am I correct?"

Laurel nodded.

The big man stepped closer. "You looked a bit lost. If I can be of assistance … "

"No. I'm fine. *Really.*"

A woman with scarlet skin, flame-red hair and a diaphanous dress that sparkled in the light from nearby shops suddenly latched onto Mr. Clean. This new being looked up at dark blue guy with lust in her eyes.

"There you are, Crecian. I'm in need of you," scarlet woman announced while staring aggressively at Laurel, and staking her claim by running her hands all over Crecian's body.

Laurel realized she was being warned off, but dark blue man still stared at her intently and spoke again.

"Would you like to join us?" he asked. "We're celebrating the monthly glow of Luster's two moons. He reached for the gown scarlet woman wore, and pulled one shoulder of it down to more fully reveal the lady's very large right breast. "We can share coitus tea. It induces lactation. The drinking of breast milk is a custom during such celebrations here."

With that announcement, he grasped the scarlet woman's breast, and massaged it enough that droplets of milk actually fell from the orange-red female's nipple.

Laurel stood in shocked silence. What could she possibly say and not sound incredibly inane?

"I hoped to have you to myself, Crecian," the bare-breasted siren complained as she lifted her breast for Crecian's inspection.

"This lady is new to our world, Fior. We should make her welcome," Crecian gently insisted as he spoke to his companion.

Laurel finally found her voice. Her next words came out sounding a bit high-pitched but firm. "Um … thanks for the offer. I-I'm … trying to cut down!" She turned and strode away quickly.

Before dark blue floor cleaner man and flame-woman could follow, she jogged around the nearest street corner.

With the same glee a lost child might experience on seeing familiar faces, she caught sight of some of the men and women from the *Titan*. The glass-front tavern they stood before—with its neon-looking signs and cosmic, planetary statues outside— must be the Nebulae Bar. Some of them remarked about the place while aboard the ship. There'd been enthusiastic discussions about visiting the hangout after other, official landing obligations were attended to.

She smiled heartily. Thankfully, all of the crew she saw were dressed in their uniforms. None seemed interested in participating in bizarre lactation events, much to her relief. And like a lot of friends she'd partied with back on Earth, the shift seemed to be enjoying each other's company, making toasts with various beverages in multi-colored, oddly shaped glasses. A few were enjoying the night air by sitting at scattered café tables that appeared to have been carved of heavy white marble. The scene vaguely reminded her of sailors on leave at the 32nd Street Naval Base back home.

One of Gemma's assistants saw her, ran forward, and pulled her into the amiable rowdiness. So happy to be among beings she at least knew, Laurel laughed outright.

A white, snake-looking man pressed an impressive fuchsia-colored drink into her hands. She gazed at the bluish fog drifting off the top of the beverage, but the crew around her dared her to drink it. After what she'd just witnessed around the corner, a good stiff drink seemed appropriate.

She shrugged off any misgivings concerning the fogging nature of the beverage, took a sip, and found it wonderfully refreshing. It tasted like champagne but with a decided kick.

Someone told her it was called Falconian Ale. It was a good name for the effect it had. She felt as though she was flying. Everything between her throat and her crotch suddenly warmed quite nicely. More importantly, she didn't feel alone anymore.

• • •

Darius only searched a short time when he recalled the favored, late night hangout for a few of his crew—the Nebulae Bar. Some found their way to the establishment after the more formal welcoming events at the palace. This was the last logical place to ask about the Earther's whereabouts.

He walked down the street and smiled when sounds of singing filled the air. There was a time when he would have joined them, but that was many years and responsibilities ago.

From his position near the rear of the crowd, he heard someone in the center of it garnering attention. Amused laughs and encouraging remarks were egging someone on to greater drink.

One of the engineers noticed him and, as if an alert sounded, the crowd instantly stilled. He was confused for a moment. Even a ranking officer did not warrant *this* kind of attention, especially not during shore leave. Salutes, yes … total silence, no.

"Three cheers for Commander Starlaw," the engineer shouted. "No driller could daunt him!"

Cries of hurrah rang out and Darius felt something in his chest tighten. He still hoped someone there might know Laurel's whereabouts. But after the initial recognition of his presence, the crew instantaneously regained their former celebratory revelry, and put their attention back to the center of the large group. He was quickly relegated to one more in their number.

Sensing something unusual was taking place, he moved toward the center of the boisterousness. Once there he understood the crew's brief acknowledgement of him, and why their attention went back to the entertainment.

An Illusion dancer with bare breasts was diverting the crew. A few of the more rowdy individuals urged the entertainer on— including the one person he'd been seeking.

I should have known.

Once again, Laurel had found her way into the hearts of his subordinates. It appeared as if she hadn't been alone or lost at all. She fit in with them, the way a fuel gauge custom fit into the side of a carbrundium engine.

He pressed forward and dodged several of his bawdier crewmembers' attempts to get him to drink. Finally, he made a space by her side.

"Laurel, are you all right?" he loudly asked as the din nearly buried his voice. "Barst, Gemma, and I have been searching for you. In our haste to see our families, we were incredibly ill-mannered. I apologize. It wasn't intentional, I assure you."

Laurel simply shrugged. "No problem," she responded. "A homecoming wasn't exactly where I belonged. Besides, I wasn't alone."

Her response came a little too easily, and he doubted the truth of her words. Her voice made light of the entire night's events. Her eyes, however, were a bit cool even considering the same brisk responses she'd given of late. Where he was concerned, she either gave very frigid answers or avoided him entirely. He would have asked her more about what'd happened since landing but the drink in her hand caught his attention.

"Is that Falconian Ale?"

"That's what they tell me. It goes down smooth, what*ever* it is!"

He frowned. "How many of those have you had?"

"Five … I think."

"Mother of Kronos … I'd better get you to the palace."

"Why?"

"Because you're safer where I can keep an eye on you."

"Holy crap … I thought I'd proven I can take care of *myself*. And who died and left you babysitter?" she daringly asked as she sipped more of the drink.

"*Excuse me?*" Darius was certain he'd misunderstood her amid all the merrymaking.

"Why can't I just go back to the ship? Is there some reason I have to go with *you* … back to the palace that everyone tells me *you* live in?"

"But for my diverted attention earlier this evening, that's where you'd be. The accommodations I can offer you are far better than those on the ship. No one expected you to stay aboard forever."

"No one *expects* me at all, spaceman. I'm excess baggage. *I* know it and *you* know it. And I don't belong someplace where your family wants you to themselves. You need time with them alone, Darius. I wouldn't feel right imposing."

"That's the ale talking," he said as he vehemently shook his head. "Now stop this craziness and come with me."

"No! I'm not some stray puppy that you, Gemma, and Barst have to feel sorry for." She shook her head and spoke more genially. "I know I sound ungrateful. I don't mean to. But it's time for me to pull my own weight. At least until this business with Goll is over."

He softened his tone in order to gain compliance. "Laurel, *please*. There's no other motive for wanting you home except friendship. Gemma and Barst will be staying with me for a few days. Along with my family, I'd like to have my friends near. *All* of them. Besides, everyone wants to meet the woman who saved my life. If you don't come, my family will find you and drag you back to the palace. The women in my household would castrate me for being so inhospitable."

"Friendship? Since when did our relationship … if you can call it that … evolve?" She snorted and shook her head in a belligerent fashion. "As for the castration, I'm sure that'd prove most unpleasant."

"Castration usually is. Or so I'm told." He had to grin at her audacity. In a world many light years from her own, Laurel was still unmanageable. She remained undaunted as ever.

She finally raised one brow and put her drink down. "All right. Since you've gone to all the trouble of finding me, I'll come quietly. But would it be acceptable if I met your family tomorrow? You really should be alone with them tonight, and I'm not in any condition to be presented to polite, *royal* society.

"Ah … you're upset that no one told you about my ancestry."

"I thought it might have at least come up in some conversation or other. But it didn't," she said as she stared up at him.

"My crew wouldn't have mentioned it. I've made it quite clear that while we're on duty only my rank matters. Not my ancestry. All the regal trappings in the universe wouldn't help if I weren't able to command my ship. Besides … my family's place in Lusterian society is more honorary. They're more figureheads than anything else."

"And that's really why I wasn't told?"

The look in her eyes grew even colder. She was angry over the matter, there was no denying it. But once she understood the situation, perhaps her anger would diminish. First, he had to get her home.

"Will you come now?" he asked.

"I'm not only a bit sloshed … but I'm hardly dressed for such an occasion."

He gazed down at her immaculate, if plain, enforcer clothing. "The garments you wear don't matter. My family won't judge you by such trivialities. As to the rest—"

"Won't your family have been in bed for some time?" she asked.

For some of his family members that was true. But he knew he'd still be expected to introduce her as soon as circumstances allowed. He took a deep breath and finally nodded.

"Alright. You can meet them tomorrow. I'll put you in the room across from mine. Since my parents will have likely celebrated with great zeal, they'll probably rise later than usual and need time to recover. Indeed, I don't expect to see much of them until tomorrow evening." He sighed and held out one hand in supplication. "You can sleep in and meet my family then."

She put her drink down and stared up at him for a long moment before nodding. "I just want you to know something."

"Yes?"

"I don't want or need special attention, Darius. I just want to be treated like anyone else."

He took her arm and led her from the merriment. They were hardly noticed now by members of his inebriated crew. By the looks of things, there'd be a great many of his underlings rising late the next day.

Once they were some distance from the bar, he glanced down at her and might have spoken except for her rather hard expression. Such a look was easily distinguishable under the city streetlights .

He'd have liked to ask about the sights she'd seen and help her understand them, but silence was the better part of tact for now. As to treating her like anyone else, that would never happen. He couldn't imagine anyone *less* like others of his acquaintance.

•••

After briefly using his communicator to let Barst and Gemma know Laurel had been found and was with him, Darius took her back to the palace.

The walk out of the city and to his residence was some distance, but he felt she needed the time and exercise to regain composure. Falconian Ale was a strong beverage and he meant to make sure she suffered no ill effects from its consumption.

When they approached the arched entryway into the palace, he acknowledged the ceremonial High Guards who were currently dressed in their best black space armor and battle helmets. But when he would have led his guest inside, he suddenly walked alone. Instantly turning, he found her frozen in place. Her eyes were as wide as any orbiting planetoid.

Laurel was pointedly glancing between the guards, and the massive heights of the structure he called home.

"I thought everyone was using the word *palace* metaphorically. But they meant you really live in an honest-to-God palace! With guards who look like something from a Hollywood space epic."

"That reference to something called Hollywood escapes me." He moved closer. "What is your point?"

"How royal *are* you, Darius Starlaw? And don't feed me a line about your family being figureheads, either."

"That part is quite true. My father is king of Luster, from a long line of ancestors who ruled by popular consent."

"King?" she croaked. "After the greeting you got at the airfield, I thought that might be the case. I j-just wasn't sure until now."

He had to smile. The look of incredulity on her face was priceless. In that moment, he'd witnessed her as speechless as he was likely to ever see her again. But she finally swallowed hard and gazed up at him with something akin to respect reflecting in her eyes. The softness of the two moons' glow couldn't diminish what he witnessed. She was either afraid, or inclined in that moment to show less disrespect. Somehow, he felt a little sorry for her but tried to hide it. A shrewd woman, she wouldn't endure such compassion. Nor would she understand it. Indeed, she'd view pity on her behalf with the same disdain as weakness.

"Are you the prince and heir?"

He simply nodded.

"Christ! No wonder you're uppity."

He actually snickered in response. No one had ever used that adjective when describing his personality.

• • •

Hell…he's probably never known anything but golden goblets and magnificent garments. And I was opening my mouth, dissing the guy as if he was just one more supervisor in a huge fleet of civil servants.

Laurel looked back at the huge structure, trying to guess what it'd been like to grow up in a real castle. Moreover, it was just like all the castles she'd ever seen in movies. Truly, there had to be *some* distant star travelers who'd visited her world and his. Hence the strong resemblance to this place and European holdings of the same size. But the alcohol in her system wouldn't let her consider much more than what she'd already processed. She shook her head and lifted one hand to push strands of hair out of her face. A sudden cool breeze wafted around her, temporarily subduing her resolve to remain so aloof.

"Darius … I'll try to remember my proper place and act appropriate. I'll be the definition of demure." She curtsied to make her point. The idea of being thrown in a dungeon wasn't attractive. A prudent person would guard their mouth more than she had. Especially now she realized who he really was.

"Laurel … I don't think demure is a word anyone could remotely associate with you. You're neither shy, nor retiring. And frankly … I prefer you just as you are. Assuming my opinion matters," he countered, clearly trying not to smile too broadly at the sudden show of subservience.

She remained silent. That was the very first time he'd ever said something like that to her. Internally accepting the compliment, if it could be called that, his words actually made him seem more human. What rejoinder could she have given that would have sufficed? In those few words, he was back to the man she'd kissed on the *Titan*.

He gently took her by the arm. "Come on. Let's get you inside before that ale makes you do something for which *I'll* be sorry. You need rest and I need to attend my family."

"I-I'm sorry you felt it necessary to leave them to look for me. I'd have been perfectly all right," she assured him.

"Perhaps I was more concerned about the city's population while you were free to walk among them," he joked. "But don't worry about the absence from my family. I've … I've come to a conclusion." He hesitated before continuing. "I believe that I've accepted more than my fair share of deep space missions. Perhaps it's time to ask for reassignment. Goll has been captured and my duty in that regard is done. I think my decision will be well met. My family has long hinted they'd rather see me home, after this last task was complete."

"But *tonight* I've taken you from your responsibilities and your welcome home. If you'll show me to my room, you can rejoin them. I can sleep off the effects of the ale, and meet whomever you please tomorrow. I'll … I'll be ready then," she confirmed with a nod.

"As you wish."

Ten minutes later—after walking through white marble hallways draped with tapestries like those in any similar structure on Earth—Laurel was comfortably situated in the most beautiful and luxurious room she had ever seen. Like the *Titan*, all she had to do was make a request of the holographic computer within the bedroom, and the computerized voice from within a wall accessed data, walking her through where toiletries could be found, and how to make use of a shower system that could exfoliate, provide tint for hair highlights, and even offer small manicure and pedicure cubicles within the walk-in, closet-sized shower. Within those small spaces, she could ask the computer for the mechanical application of whatever nail shades she could possibly dream up.

There was even a recessed wardrobe of makeup. When opened, the computer offered to produce images of how she'd look after donning certain shades of eye shadow, blush, foundation, and contour powders. She could actually see how different shades of hair or styles would look before committing to anything.

Then she stopped exploring, sat on the bed, and took a deep breath.

She thought back to her childhood.

Her parents were obscenely wealthy, so she'd had advantages others couldn't imagine. She'd stayed in some of the best hotels in the world, while traveling in foreign countries. But those facilities couldn't compare to the high-ceilinged, crystalline blue bedroom in which she found herself. All the furnishings were draped in silken-looking fabrics of the same deep shade of cobalt blue. Even with her benefits, she'd never been asked to sleep in a castle.

Darius had left with a cursory goodnight. But he'd instructed her to address the computer, and specifically ask for him, if she needed anything. What could she possibly need? Everything was provided.

Exotic, unknown fruit graced a white marble table along with an assortment of wine. While the walls were white, they seemed to glow from within. The carpet was thick and deep blue; matching blue drapes framed an open balcony. Outside, shooting stars fell every few seconds. The shadows of trees and gardens were punctuated by moonlight.

While she could walk into the night air, none of its coolness entered the room. It was as if there was an invisible barrier between the entrance to the balcony and the room itself.

With distant planets retreating now, two gorgeous moons hung from the sky like lanterns. Each was a different shade of green, probably due to some atmospheric property she didn't yet understand.

The air was clean, cool, and fragrant with the scent of unseen flora.

To keep from thinking about how far away from home she was—and dwelling on constant, if stuffed-down, fears—she took off her borrowed uniform, strode into the oversized shower and made good use of the hot water. After taking a very long time figuring out what was actually available for use, a gentle flow of air from various ports left her body dry. It took only a few moments afterward to locate a deep blue robe hanging in an alcove. This, she wrapped tightly around her body.

The massive oval bed located at the end of the huge room was eminently more comfortable than her small bunk aboard the

Titan. Shimmering sheets enveloped her in softness that defied description.

But after lying there and staring up at the gilt ceiling with its jewel-like ornaments hanging down as if they were stars falling from a midnight sky, she sat up. The bed and her surroundings felt wrong.

She finally grabbed a lush pillow and a thick, mink-soft blanket and stood in the middle of the room gazing around at the sumptuous decor. After so many nights spent within the confines of a crewmember's space aboard the *Titan*, being outside appealed. The night called and she felt less like a prisoner when she gazed outside, beyond the glimmering folds of draperies and toward the balcony. Eventually, she pushed what looked like a large daybed out there, and decided to sleep whilst staring at the stars and moons. More quickly than she believed possible, weariness finally took its toll. Darkness of sleep called.

• • •

Past the midnight hour, Darius finally made his way to his room, leaving his family and friends to finish celebrating the *Titan*'s return. Those still awake begged him to stay and greet the dawn with them, but weariness made him seek rest. He also had an overpowering need to be out of the ornate dress uniform donned for the occasion. And then there were memories to be expunged. Every homecoming brought them. With Goll's capture, perhaps this was the last time he'd experience the joy of family mingled with the pain of regret.

The only sad things about being back were memories of Astral and Kyrie, and why he'd set out to find any vamphiere remotely responsible for their slaughter.

Once the door to his chamber was closed, he stared at his image in the full-length mirror across the room. The man looking back at him was older, wiser. If he could go back in time, things would have been different. Since that was impossible, he must look to the future. Indeed, he'd spent far too much time from family and friends.

Life was short. Once the coming trial was over, he must find a new purpose.

Sighing and turning away from the image of a man whose primary drive concerned revenge, he removed his uniform, showered, and slipped into a warm robe. Without regard to what he'd already drunk after so many welcoming toasts and speeches from friends and superiors, he threw caution to the wind and poured a good measure of Lusterian brandy. The crystal tumbler he held sparkled in the light. Something about the amber color of the liquid and the cut of the glass mesmerized him for a moment. His mind seized on the information he'd just been provided and its impact on both him and the Earther in his charge.

Anxious to have his mind at ease concerning the loss of his wife and child, and the family of vamphieres who'd plotted the murders, his father had pulled strings concerning the trial. To affect a quick end to a situation that had lasted far too long, Goll would be brought out of stasis tomorrow. League investigators would begin questioning him. Charges would be brought and he'd go to trial immediately.

If Goll could be made to talk, Warlord sympathizers on Luster would be named. It could be the end of that warring faction's existence.

He closed his eyes and sighed heavily. There was but one down side. Laurel would be asked to testify, to relive the night her friends died.

It was one thing to state facts before magistrates when one wasn't personally involved. As an enforcer on her world, she'd surely have testified. But there was a difference between that and being forced to endure gruesome accounts of friends' bodies having been torn asunder. Those facts would be repeated by Gemma, Barst, and himself. As he sipped his drink, he considered the outcome.

He had a feeling the composed, strong persona she'd so carefully constructed would crumble. Laurel would be reminded again that she could never go home, that whatever her life had been bore little resemblance to what she'd have to learn and withstand now. She'd be forced to face how inadequate she was, on a world many times more advanced than hers. He feared for her future and how she'd face it, even as he embraced his.

"Computer on," he softly announced.

"Computer on."

When the deep female voice programmed as a communication option spoke, he quickly relayed his command.

"Computer … switch on coms for the room across the hallway from this location."

"Opening communication to the designated area."

A moment of silence made him reconsider the late hour and any attempt to check on Laurel. But the woman wasn't as sturdy as she pretended. And when the façade she so carefully built fell and cracked, he wanted to be there. Right now, his concern was for how she was resting and if she had everything she needed. The Earther would go hungry or thirsty before asking him for help. The room computer in her quarters wasn't exactly like the one on the *Titan*. To allay suspicions concerning his desire to check on her status, he'd lie and say *he* was the one in need of *her*. And if she took on that obstinate air that marked her response to anything he said or did, he vowed to hold his temper and remember the deep-seated fears she tamped down.

"No response to hail."

"Open voice-to-voice com."

"Accessing."

"Laurel … will you speak to me, please?"

He waited a full minute, but no one responded. "She might be sleeping," he muttered.

"*There is no response. But there are sounds of distress. Enhancing vocalization now,*" the computer responded.

Darius put his glass down and his body went rigid with concern. "Computer … open the door to that room immediately!" he ordered.

"*Doors have been sealed for the evening—*"

"This is a code red emergency … break the seal," he demanded as he bolted from his quarters.

As he reached the massive arched wooden doorway of her room, the latch slid open and the door swung inward. He surged into the room, found the lights still on, and glanced at the bed. There was no one there, though the bedclothes were disheveled.

"Laurel, are you all right?" he shouted.

Soft cries filtered into the room from the balcony. He followed the sound.

She lay there, stretched out on a daybed, writhing as if she were in agony.

He knelt beside her and realized she was having a nightmare. Her eyes were closed and it appeared she fought some unseen demon from the darker regions of her brain. Her words were unintelligible, but her body language spoke of great conflict. Her hands gripped the bedclothes and her body suddenly tensed.

Without thinking of any consequences, whether she'd accept his presence in her room or his embrace, he reached out and wrapped his arms around her body. Then he stroked her long hair and lowered his voice.

"Laurel, wake up. You're safe," he crooned.

In the next few seconds her cries stopped. Her eyelids fluttered as she came back to the real world, from whatever tortuous place she'd been plunged. In short order she awakened more fully and stared up at him in shock.

"What … what are you doing here?" she whispered.

"You were having a nightmare."

"How did you—"

"That's not important. Just know you're safe. Nothing will hurt you, I promise."

"It was dark. I saw Goll. He said … he said he'd kill me," she softly relayed as she stared up into the vastness of space over them.

"He can't hurt you here. He can't hurt anyone anymore, Laurel."

"Promise me … *promise*!" she demanded as she grabbed his robe with fierce determination.

"I'll kill him if he tries. I swear it!"

She blinked, nodded, and released her grip. "I … I … believe you."

"Lie back. If you want to sleep on the balcony, inside, or anywhere else, that's fine. But just try to calm down and get some rest."

"I d-don't think I can."

She stared over his shoulder and the light from the moons' glow revealed how frightened she was. The woman wasn't hiding the real fear that likely lived with her every moment. Not now.

He pulled her closer and nuzzled his cheek against hers. "How many nightmares have you had? And don't lie to me.

"I don't know. A few."

He pulled slightly away so he could see her face. "It's all right to admit it, you know. We all have bad dreams."

"Not you. Not the great commander of an interstellar starship. Not the prince and heir to an entire planet."

Now the look in her eyes was calmer. And it might have been a trick of the light, but he thought he saw the shimmer of tears.

With one hand, he smoothed back the tangled mass of her long hair and slowly shook his head. "I have nightmares, too."

"A-about vamphieres?"

He slowly nodded. "Sometimes, they're about … " His words trailed away, and he shook his head in sad remembrance.

"Tell me. Please?" she begged.

"Sometimes … I'm … I'm in a very dark place, too. I think I hear my little girl. She calls for me and I can't find her … then she's gone. I wake up feeling like I've lost her all over again."

"God! Darius … I'm so sorry." She leaned into him and wrapped her arms around his shoulders.

"It's just one of a few bad dreams. They fade. Yours will too." He tried to make light of his sudden, unexpected input concerning a very sad and personal occurrence. But he wasn't able to withhold telltale sorrow from his voice. The shake in it was clearly audible.

She suddenly released him from her warm embrace, straightened her body, and the robe she wore. Then she tossed back her hair and took a deep breath. Her next words were as unexpected as her very presence in his life.

"Would you stay with me? Just to lie next to me, I mean. I-I don't want to be alone. And I don't think you do, either," she quietly said as she placed one palm on his cheek.

He didn't have to think twice.

The daybed was large, but became much smaller as he lay beside her and pulled her firmly against his body. Even through their robes, he felt her heat. And he felt how very, very soft she was.

"Darius?"

"Yes?"

"Y-you've had a lot of nightmares about your deceased wife and baby, haven't you?"

He didn't answer.

"Goodnight," she murmured as she tucked her head against his left shoulder, just over his left breast.

"Goodnight, Laurel."

Common sense bid him leave.

He asked himself why he stayed. She relaxed and her body simultaneously molded to his.

She would likely resent his interference tomorrow. But it'd be easier to move the moons from their orbit than leave. He just couldn't. And for once, in a very long time, he indulged himself and closed his eyes.

Her scent, her soft warmth, and the way she snuggled next to him were the only things he craved. Such small gifts were all he thought lost in life.

I can't want her. She's not from this world and will never fully adapt. I need someone with whom I can share life. Not constantly worry about. That was Astral. I can't do that again.

Even as these thoughts filtered through his tired brain, he pulled her closer and gave into sweeter dreams.

Chapter 10

Bird song awakened Darius sometime near dawn. For a moment, he forgot where he was. Then a warm, cuddling presence brought him back to reality. He looked down at her, halfway beneath his body, and sighed in contentment. It had been so long since he'd slept the whole night with a woman.

Memories of Astral came to mind but no shame emerged.

He rose on one elbow and looked down at Laurel's lovely face. Her gracefully long fingers were spread against his chest. She must have sensed his movement, or felt the change in his posture.

Her eyes opened and she presented him with the sweetest, most beautiful smile he'd ever seen. The woman, on waking, was exquisite. And she was in his arms.

"Good morning," he murmured softly then felt her shiver. His response was to pull her even closer. "What made you sleep on the balcony?"

"I-I don't know. I think I might have felt a little trapped."

Such a revelation was unlike anything he'd ever heard. "Why? Why do you say that?"

She shrugged. "Maybe I'm not used to space travel, and all those months in crew quarters got to me."

"Extended space travel isn't for everyone," he said as he pulled the blanket around her and tried not to think about what he had to say. But news from last evening had to be relayed. Better that it came from him. "Laurel … I have to talk to you."

"That sounds ominous," she replied as she pushed away from him, sat up, and shook her hair back. She tightened her robe about her slender frame and stared at him expectantly.

"My father used his influence to move up Goll's trial. I … I think, for my sake and for the wellbeing of the entire family, he wants one of the last vamphieres associated with Astral's and Kyrie's deaths … dealt with."

She took on a thoughtful expression. "Well … that's understandable. If you've been searching for him for years, your family would see the trial as closure. They probably want you home as much as you want this over."

"Yes. But you must know what will be asked of you."

She tucked one long strand behind her ear.

In that moment, he wanted nothing more than to lock the door and stay there until the entire business was over. She wouldn't understand until she experienced the trial firsthand. How could she? But he still had to *try*. Her lack of aptitude when it came to such matters as justice on his world mustn't sway attempts at an explanation.

"You'll be asked to recount what happened the night you were attacked and your friends were killed. Can you imagine what that will entail?"

"I've testified before—"

"But not like this. Goll and anyone who supports or defends him will have the opportunity to do a cross-examination, if they wish to. Are you ready to relive that night on Earth again?"

She shook her head and the soft gaze she'd bestowed on awakening drifted away. He now witnessed that familiar hardness filter into her gaze. It was the very same severe expression she held in reserve for him and no one else.

"Do you think I'm incapable of this? Is that what you're saying?" she slowly asked.

"I think that … I might be able to petition the judges. It *might* be possible to set aside your testimony. We have many other witnesses to Goll's crimes, eyewitnesses from other planets. These are individuals who're fully aware of our justice system and how it—"

"If I have the right … and you've said I do … then I want to have my day in court. I'm owed that, Darius, and I won't be denied. If I have to, I'll go straight to your father to demand it!"

"All right, Laurel. I *have* tried to warn you. After last night and your confession of nightmares brought on by your past, I'd think you'd welcome the chance, however slim it might be, to walk away from this. I'm the only one who can ask for your abstention. Be sure this is what you really want."

"You had no right to even consider such a thing. My testimony represents what happened on Earth. Without me, there's no one to speak for my planet."

She stood and glared at him as if he'd committed the last, final sacrilege. He opened his mouth to speak, but she wouldn't allow it.

"No matter what I do or say … no matter what I admit to or how I share my innermost feelings, you'll never see me as anything other than some primitive victim from a backward world. A world you hold in complete disdain."

He also stood. "What *feelings* have you ever shared that would change that opinion?" he tersely asked.

"Last night. I shared my nightmare. You shared yours, too. But I see now that you were just humoring the little Earthling again." She tossed her head and crossed her arms over her chest.

He took a deep breath and sighed heavily. Nothing he'd say would make any difference. Facts were facts. He'd done his best to mitigate further suffering. She'd have none of it. So let her deal with the repercussions. Martyrdom was what she wanted. Let her have it.

"I have matters to tend," he told her. "If you need anything you can access the holo—"

"I know what to do, Darius! Stop treating me like a child."

"Then quit acting like one."

She pointed toward the door. "Get out … now!"

He took one step toward her, then another. Anger over being treated like some lingering inferior rankled. "You dare order me in my own home?"

"It's time somebody refused to kiss your ass. I'm not a citizen of this world and you don't have any control over me. Not now. Not ever." She poked one index finger into her own chest. "I'm still free. I didn't ask to be brought here but as long as I *am* here, you won't deny me the right to testify. Quit interfering."

"I was trying to save you from—"

"How many times do I have to tell you that I can take care of myself?"

She drew herself up and moved closer.

When she stood only a breath away and tilted her head back to gaze up at him, he actually felt her anger. It was like a wall of heat between them; she shook with it.

At that moment, he'd never wanted a woman more in his life. His cock was hard with need. He briefly clenched his hands to keep from putting them around her slender body and ravaging her décolletage with kisses. The V of her robe had widened, showing the full swell of her breasts.

"You saved my life, Darius Starlaw. And then I saved yours. We're even. And we're *done*. I'm not on the *Titan* any longer. And as soon as I can, I'll find another place to stay."

"That's not necess—"

"I don't think you and I need to be around each other. I'm too ignorant. And you're too arrogant. Now get out!" she repeated.

Never having been ordered to leave quarters he considered *his* had a nasty, belittling effect. He wasn't leaving with her having the final word. "All right, you little nova! So much for your so-called intent to show respect." He put his hands on her shoulders and pulled her up against his body. "I don't think you know what that word means, and I still have grave doubts about whoever put you into an enforcer's position. But I won't leave until I extract payment for rent, and anything else offered to a very thoughtless, spoiled little harridan."

He ran one hand up the back of her neck, gently grasped a handful of long, luxurious hair, and pulled her head back. When her neck was exposed, he lowered his head and kissed the deep valley between her breasts. Then he worked his way slowly upward.

To his surprise, she didn't fight but wrapped her arms around his waist and held on as tightly as he held her. Soft moans of desire slipped from her lips as he kissed her left cheek then pressed his mouth against hers in what became a savage, deeply passionate kiss.

When she actually took one of his hands and pulled it to cover her left breast, he moaned back. The sound of it echoed around the room.

With experienced tenderness, he massaged the full orb for a few seconds before breaking their kiss and covering her nipple with his lips.

She inhaled, then gasped and arched upward toward his mouth as he suckled. Nothing in life had ever tasted as sweet as that pink, soft nub. Sensations filled him and threatened to take away all reason. He craved her the way some men desired riches.

In the entire universe, what lay in the embrace of a beautiful woman was the best treasure any man could find. And he wanted this particular plunder for his own.

Then, as he almost made the decision to pick her up and carry her to the large bed to finish what would be the hottest encounter of his existence, some spark of reason and sanity set in.

Years of discipline and the certainty of disdain she'd show over his lack of control halted him. He let her go, backed away, and turned toward the door. Taking only a few seconds to catch his breath and force some semblance of normalcy into the sound of his voice, he finally addressed her in his best command speech.

"Someday I'll demand the rest of payment due, for all services rendered. Until then, your demand will be met. We should see as little of each other as possible. I won't be accused of rape!"

Her loud gasp made him wince, but she couldn't see his expression with his back to her. "One more thing, Earther. Don't leave this room without a communication device on you. That you did so last night will be forgiven this time. But our laws are clear concerning this issue. All those on this world are to carry such communicators in case of general emergencies. Weather, security alerts, and any environmental problems notify the population of problems. I'll have a servant fetch one and show you how to use it. But be sure it's on you at all times. Is that clear?" he finished, enunciating the last three words with forceful resolve.

When she made no sound, he nodded as if her silence was acceptable. Then he strode from her room. The echoing noise caused by her slamming the door behind him made him pause only a second before reentering his own quarters.

• • •

It hadn't been necessary to leave the warmth of home so early and head into the city. But anger drove him to do anything but sit and dwell on what'd occurred. Only moments afterward, he was both sorry and ashamed. They'd both behaved like recalcitrant children.

One her side, she was not the kind of woman to be bullied, nor would she silently stand for disparagement of her world or her intellect. To even imply inferior status was to brook dissent. And in truth, Laurel's intelligence appeared as sharp as a dragon's barb. She worded her objections with clear, precise language and didn't play semantics with definition. She had the ability to see through deceit. That was why he'd always striven to relay the truth.

On his side, however, the tactlessness in *how* that truth was relayed seemed obvious. He'd been around those expected to blindly follow commands. Clearly, the Earther had no such experience. He suspected that when she complied during the regular commission of duties on her own planet, she did so only as long as her conscience was clear.

Perhaps that was the best definition of a good enforcer—someone who *wouldn't* follow questionable orders without resolving their origin or their necessity.

He hadn't meant it when he suggested they not see much of each other. Considering her out of his life seemed so very wrong as to make him pause and turn back toward the castle. He almost went back to her to retract statements made in anger. But she needed time. And he needed to choose his words and how he'd approach her more carefully. For now, he must focus on what'd dragged him from his room and toward the city—Goll's interrogation.

If the vamphiere didn't give up his contacts on Luster—the very same ones who'd likely supplied him with blood from some gruesome source so the bastard could escape this part of the galaxy—then some *other* vamphiere just like him would take his place. Warlords and their minions were making a great deal of money by attacking and looting colonies whose constabularies weren't as strong or as honest as Constellation League enforcers.

He put thoughts of Laurel and how he'd apologize out of his mind for the moment. He couldn't protect her any longer. She was, as she'd stated, free. There was no way to properly explain what she'd endure when Goll testified. At least *he'd* not found a good way.

Some hours later he returned to the castle in an even worse mood than when he'd left. Sounds of merriment coming from Laurel's quarters via her now fully open doorway, made him pause. He recognized his sisters' giggling, Gemma's gay interruption into some story or another, and even his mother's lower, more mature but amused voice. Apparently, they'd tired of waiting for his introduction to the Earth woman and had forged their way, en masse, to her temporary quarters.

As Barst was also staying at the castle for a few days, he'd contacted his second-in-command with the news he must now relay to his family. Sure his face would project anger and frustration, he took a deep breath and hoped his father or one of his sire's many advisers could put a different complexion on the issue. As of right this moment, bringing Goll back to Luster had accomplished only one thing—closure for his family's deaths. While Goll hadn't ordered Astral and Kyrie's shuttle attacked, he'd certainly watched Gorm, his sick, detested father, do it. Indeed, Goll admitted to standing by, watching and even picking off survivors who'd exited the vessel in escape pods. The idea that pirates of any kind would murder with such depravity left him feeling hollow.

He slowly strode forward, and paused outside the door but not within eyesight of anyone in the room. Inhaling deeply, he briefly made his presence known by knocking. Then he stood in the entrance awaiting Laurel's permission to enter. He was half certain she'd tell him to leave, and use short, rude verbiage to do so.

Silence followed his knock. Surprised to see his entire family in Laurel's quarters, including his sire, he simply drew himself up to his full height and waited.

"Darius … where have you got to?" Dar asked. "And why are you in dress uniform?"

Once again, tact seemed less important than just spitting out the truth. He was in no mood to play politics. He bowed his head slightly, in deference to his parents' presence, and spoke bluntly.

"I went to League headquarters. Goll has been brought out of stasis. He's defiantly refusing to give up his Lusterian contacts though he readily admits there are Warlord traitors in our midst. And he was quite adamant, even jubilant, when mentioning his father's destruction of civilian shuttles that refused to be boarded on demand of common criminals. Especially the one containing my family."

Whatever merriment ensued within the room previously, saddened and shocked expressions now prevailed. He glanced at Laurel as she stood there in a lovely new dressing gown likely provided by his mother or sisters, staring at the marble floor. Her face held an expression of utter sorrow.

"Sorry to break up your revelry, but it's been decided that Goll will be tried tomorrow. Since he's of no use, League bureaucrats have chosen to end his effrontery as quickly as possible. I, for one, agree with their decision. And I thank you, Father, for pushing the matter forward. At least Goll will face justice at last. Even if we *don't* know who, among our elite, have been helping him."

Dar stood and nodded.

Darius squarely faced him, and waited whatever chastisement might come for having approached the interrogators at all. He hadn't long to think on the matter.

"Son ... we should talk elsewhere about these matters. Come to my quarters and we'll discuss—"

"I see no reason to keep Mother and everyone else in the dark, sir. As of this morning, it's common knowledge that League directors ordered the *Titan* to find Goll at all costs, and that I used my influence to pursue him even though a conflict of interest existed. It's also known that we approached and landed on a banned world to affect an arrest, and that we brought back an Earth citizen ... an *enforcer* ... to testify. The members of Goll's defense team are voicing their protestations. It's likely they'll say the arrest wasn't legal since we were never supposed to land on Earth to begin with. In effect, I committed a crime to make the arrest!"

"Son ... we were fully aware this very defense might be used, and are prepared to counter it. But we should discuss this matter *elsewhere!*" his father curtly responded.

Darius glanced at Laurel once more, but stubbornly ignored the warning in his sire's voice. He put his full attention back on Dar before continuing. "I was aware such accusations might be made. But not for how quickly the news spread to the populace. If there's any further proof that Goll and his minions have friends in high places, then please tell me." He lifted one hand and curled it into a fist. "He should be questioned more forcibly. When the people know just how many of our officials are accepting bribes from the Warlords, or just how many are in collusion with them, then any defense will be impossible. Too many of our citizens have lost loved ones to our enemies. The people won't stand for—"

"What the people will or won't stand for is my business, my son. It is the business of my advisers and those duly elected officials of the League. You've done your job. Goll's interrogation and the resulting fallout is not your concern. You're on official leave, are you not?"

"Father … have you not seen the news coming from every source on the planet? Are you not aware of what's being said?"

Dar slowly walked forward. He said nothing more until he stood directly in front of his son. The king took his time responding.

"You want us to resort to torture? Is that what you're asking, Darius?"

"There are those within enforcer ranks who could extract information that would—"

"Is that what my son … my firstborn and heir to the throne … is suggesting? Is this what I've taught you? Is your need for vengeance so all-consuming that you'd forgo your oath in order to see Goll suffer? Do you want justice or do you want him to endure the same agony you have? And are you remotely suggesting, after allowing you to bring Goll safely here, that I would now let you throw your career and your life and freedom away so you could somehow witness or even participate in such an interrogation?"

"I want the truth!" Darius loudly confirmed.

"The truth will come out." Dar put one hand on Darius's right shoulder. "Until further notice, you are officially relieved of duty. You will remove your uniform, turn in your weapon and identification to League headquarters, then remain on palace premises."

"*Father!*"

"You'll be allowed to attend the trial and the administration of any punishment, assuming officials deem it necessary. But you will remain within the compound or you will be arrested by the household High Guard. Is … that … clear?"

"Assuming officials deem it … Father … you can't be serious!"

"I won't repeat myself. You have one hour to present yourself to League headquarters and obey, or I *will* put you under lock and key."

Speechless, humiliated, and profoundly embarrassed. Darius slowly turned and walked away.

Chapter 11

Laurel wasn't aware she'd been holding her breath until soft apologies were made by the family. Regrets were voiced for having subjected her to what they referred to as "this ugly business."

Once the Starlaw clan was gone and her door closed, she sat on the bed and tried not to cry. The entire trip to Earth had been painfully put into perspective, and one thing was terribly clear.

Dar had been fully aware this might happen.

The look on the king's face, as the news of Goll's defense was delivered, had suddenly become passive. The king's choice to send a son after a murderer—a son with a very definite conflict of interest—was ordered to give Darius closure. The father was seriously worried over Darius's future as he'd seen his son become obsessed with catching *all* the vamphieres present when Astral and Kyrie were killed. This fact was revealed in words of relief uttered by the king, just moments before Darius arrived back from League headquarters. The king had just expressed his thanks to the Creator of all things for sending his son home safely and with the last vamphiere incarcerated.

But the result of Dar's well-meant intentions might now set Goll free. Dar probably believed that Goll's imprisonment would be enough, that once the pursuit was over, Darius would heal and finally get on with his life. Obviously, Dar hadn't known the vamphiere would flee to a banned planet. But the order to find and arrest the brute, wherever he was, added to the problem inherent in sending Darius to begin with.

With several legal boundaries having been breached, Goll *might* really go free. And Darius was at the point of losing his edge, possibly even his reason. She'd seen the look of stupefied shock on the big man's face. He'd stood there listening to his father at least temporarily take away the only thing he had left—his career.

What Dar had meant to accomplish backfired.

She sat there feeling horrible sorrow for a man who'd only tried to protect and serve, a man who was being punished with agonizing pain every day of his life. Years after the fact, he still loved his wife and child. He still missed them and couldn't get on with his future and likely never would now.

And she knew one thing more.

If Goll went free, Darius would become a criminal himself in the pursuit of his nemesis. No order from any constabulary would keep him from going after the vamphiere and one or both would end up dead.

"There's a solution to this. I know there is," she whispered as she stared at the marble floor and clasped her hands together.

The words of a training officer, from her academy days, suddenly came back.

"If a situation is as bad as it can get, what's the harm in trying something crazy?"

For several hours she thought. She hadn't even been on the planet a full week. Goll would stand trial that afternoon and, if he was found guilty, would be executed summarily. Darius's sister, Nyssa, had said so. There'd been so little time to get used to being on solid ground again, before she had to go right back into cop mode.

Suddenly, a very strange plan began to form. She lifted her left hand to her mouth and chewed on her thumbnail, trying to work out the details. But to enact it, she needed to work fast. And she needed to talk to Darius.

She stood and lunged for the computer console and addressed the artificial intelligence device therein.

"Computer ... is Commander Starlaw in his quarters now? Has he returned to the premises?"

Scanning for known biological readout ... presence is confirmed. Commander Starlaw is within his quarters. Initiate contact?"

"Yes. Now ... please."

"Com open."

"Darius, can I speak with you?"

For a long moment nothing happened. She opened her mouth to repeat the request, hoping he wasn't ignoring her but perhaps taking a shower and unable to hear the console com request. But then a low, familiar voice responded.

"What is it, Laurel?"

"Can I talk to you?"

"I'm not in the mood," he softly responded. "Perhaps later."

"I ... I think I might have a plan that could out Goll's collaborators."

Another silence ensued.

"Darius?"

"Come on over. I need to speak to you anyhow. Now's as good a time as any."

She pulled at the edges of the robe she still wore and tightened the garment as she bolted for her door and the one directly opposite.

His doorway swung open just as she got to the other side of the hallway.

When she entered his room, there was barely time to note the beautiful spruce-colored furnishings, and how they were so perfectly balanced by the white marble of the walls, ceiling and floor.

He stood there with his arms folded across his chest. He'd removed his uniform and now wore a dark green robe that made him look even larger, his shoulders more broad. His hair was damp. He'd recently showered and appeared to be going nowhere soon, just as his sire ordered.

She quickly closed the door behind her, took a deep breath, and squarely faced him.

"First ... I want to apologize for how I acted this morning, Darius. I-I know everything you've ever done was to protect me. I'm not used to it and I reacted badly."

His enigmatic expression faded and a gentler one took its place. "I'm sorry, too. I've never meant to imply, by words or actions, that you're inept. That wasn't my intention but I said and did things that would certainly lead a prudent and reasonable person to that very conclusion. And you're not, by any means, unskilled. But ... "

"But?" she prompted when he paused.

"I can no more set aside the instinct to protect you than I can will myself to stop breathing. I have tried," he contritely said as he shook his head. "It's just not working for me."

Deep protective instincts welled within her. She'd never seen this huge man look so confused. A telltale look of boyish pain was etched across his face. He really didn't know what to say or do now. His embarrassment over having been so terribly chastised by his sire, in front of every one of his family members *and* her, clearly humbled him. She'd never wanted to reach out and hold a man so badly in her life. But time was short now. She opted for helping him in other, more potent ways.

"I mentioned a plan."

"I'm listening," he softly told her.

She held out her hands, palms up, in a gesture of supplication. "Darius ... what if there was a way to trick some of Goll's cohorts into revealing themselves? If they believed Goll spilled his guts while being interrogated, *they* might find a way to shut him up for good."

His expression suddenly changed. Interest lit his face. "Go on."

"I know what I'm going to suggest isn't exactly procedure. We'd be endangering the life of a prisoner and that's not appropriate.

But I've seen investigators do this on Earth and it worked. It's not a good plan but it's *something*."

He motioned for her to sit on the bed.

When she plopped down, drew her feet under her body, and shook her hair back, he sat near and gazed down at her while nodding his consent to continue.

She exhaled and blurted out the rest.

"What if we put out a rumor that Goll broke down and gave up names? What would his cohorts here on Luster do if they believed the lie that they were about to be caught?"

He dragged his hands through his hair and gazed at the floor for a moment before responding. "If I were one of them, I'd try to get off the planet. I'd book a one-way ticket on the nearest galactic shuttle. I wouldn't want to be arrested for conspiracy to commit murder."

"So these traitors … these Warlord anarchists … have been involved in activities that could get them put to death? Just like Goll? And they're highly placed in your society?"

"Most certainly! They're in positions high enough to give pirates, vamphieres, and other butchers news of arms shipments, enforcer troop movements, and gem, ore, and fuel consignments. These traitors have hidden among us, on Luster, for years. They know how to do so while quietly encouraging the looting. The parasites live a life of luxury here while paying bounty to thugs who'll do their dirty work for them. A share of what's pillaged goes to them, a share goes back to Warlord based planets and their dignitaries, and a share of blood and other loot goes to vamphieres and whoever is sociopathic enough to kill for money. But I don't understand—"

"What if somebody leaked Goll's duplicity from headquarters, where I understand he's being held? That leak could be done in such a way that it appears real."

He thought for a long moment. "I … I don't think it could work. Goll was actually offered a deal to have his death sentence commuted to life in prison … *if* he'd talk. That news has certainly been spread to anyone who'd have a need to know it, including those Warlord traitors in our midst. Why would they believe he'd suddenly start talking now?"

"Maybe the leak could include Goll's sudden, last-minute desire to live. When cowards face death, they might do anything for a chance at life. Especially if the death penalty was one as heinous as the decimation chamber."

"How do you know about … aha! You've been researching the likely choices for sentencing."

"I read up about it when I was on the *Titan*. I wanted to know just what would happen to Goll when he was put to death for having killed my friends."

"Except that now, the bastard might actually go free," Darius murmured. "And on technicalities."

"Darius, it's those technicalities that make the law work for everyone."

When he drew himself up and pasted on an angry expression, she put one hand on his shoulder and spoke quickly.

"I'm not saying he doesn't deserve justice. I'm saying that justice might be served if one of his own, hidden cohorts here on Luster takes exception to his having revealed them. He won't be safe anywhere if what I've heard about the Warlords is true. They'll hunt him into infinity and even a secure cell here might not offer safety. Especially if these secret backers of his are highly placed enough. You follow?"

"It might work … maybe … "

"It's just an idea. Better than sitting here and doing nothing," she finished.

He stood and paced for a few minutes before speaking. "If we do this, we haven't much time. The trial is only hours away, sentencing shortly thereafter assuming Goll doesn't go free. But some of Goll's backers *might* be misled into believing they're in danger of arrest."

He stared into the distance, lifted one hand, and mechanically began to tick off mental notations on his fingers.

"This might work, Laurel. I think I can use my computer to compile a planetary list of every dignitary, official, and bureaucrat who might be privy to information—information that would be worth its weight in precious jewels or other plunder to the Warlords. We've compiled such lists before, but they never came to anything. We couldn't act on them without proof."

"Can you also set up an alert to flag any dignitary who coincidentally books a one-way ticket off the planet, for no apparent reason?"

"Yes, but … " He sighed and shook his head in exasperation. "That's still not enough to arrest them. Their leaving under suspicious circumstances isn't proof of any crime against the populace."

"At worst, they'd get away but still be gone forever. At best, they might be tactfully detained, questioned, and convinced to give away *other* names."

"It's worth a try, isn't it?" he softly mused. "As you've said, it's better than doing nothing! I've certainly nothing left to lose. And no one can touch you for giving me an idea."

"We can keep your father's name out of it. He can use plausible deniability if the whole thing implodes."

"The thing is … I can't get into HQ. Father has had me restricted to the compound, remember?"

"Yeah, but … "

"But what, Laurel? What are you thinking?" he asked as he rejoined her on the bed.

She saw the look of excitement on his face and plowed ahead.

"Barst could get into HQ. As your second-in-command, he'd have access to any computer there, wouldn't he?"

"Yes. And a message traced back to where Goll is being held would lend credence to the rumor. Barst would know exactly how to word it so the message would look real." He stopped and turned away. "There's just one problem."

"What?"

"I can't ask that of him. He's due to stand down from space duty, take a supervisor's job here on the planet's surface, and wed Gemma. I can't ask him to risk his career over sending a fake message from HQ—one that might get a prisoner killed."

"That's his decision to make, Darius. And no one will get killed if the guards do their jobs. It might even be a good idea to send them an anonymous warning to be careful of who comes and goes from Goll's cell and to wear protective armor. Besides, Barst wants to see Goll get what's coming to him as badly as we do."

"That much is true," Darius said as he nodded.

"And can't he send the message from some general source at HQ? A computer everyone has access to or something? I mean … does he have to be named as the sender? The message is supposed to be *leaked*, for crying out loud. Nobody leaks anything and puts their actual name on it!"

He smiled at her. "You've got a devious little mind."

"I told you, investigators on Earth use this pit-one-crook-against-another technique all the time. It's not anyone's fault if some idiot criminal buys the ruse."

"I'll contact Barst. I think he and Gemma are still on the premises," Darius said.

In the few minutes it'd taken to relay the plan, she'd watched his mood change from deathlike despair to rampant hope. His green eyes lit with conspiratorial camaraderie. Somber reflection was replaced with the excitement of action.

As he addressed the computer and she heard him request Barst's presence, his entire body seemed energized. He became the warrior she'd first met.

Finally, he turned to her with a broad smile on his face. "When I apologized to you, I meant it. And I won't ever be so presumptuous as to underestimate you again. Not on anything."

"Good," she happily told him. "And I won't lose my temper so easily. I'll ask for help when I need it, and put my pride aside."

He nodded and slowly approached her. The gleam in his eyes suddenly changed from amity to something else. His gaze now was decidedly hot.

"There is one thing about this morning that I won't apologize for. Not now or in the next life."

She swallowed hard as he moved toward her and sat on the bed, very close. "What's th-that?"

"I won't ever say I'm sorry for having done *this*."

He pulled her into his embrace and pressed his lips against hers in such a soft, tender kiss that she melted against him. Then she moaned softly, in utter capitulation. In that moment in time, she forgot everything except the feel of a godlike man's arms around her body and the passionate way he kissed. A wave of heat swept over her and settled between her thighs. She breathed in his clean, woodsy smell and would have pushed him backward onto the bed but an alert buzzer sounded. It took everything she had to break the embrace.

"Uh … is that someone at your door?" she breathlessly asked.

"Probably Barst." He cupped her cheeks in his palms and stared into her eyes. "We have work to do but don't think this is over. It's to be continued," he promised as he slowly stood.

She took that opportunity to pull her robe closer and walk toward the window where it wouldn't look as if she'd been about to ravage the man.

Things had changed dramatically.

She prayed her suggestions worked. To see Darius go back to the defeated status of only a few hours ago was unthinkable.

He turned and nodded as he let Barst into the room. The big bear man was dressed in a tunic, leggings, and boots but Gemma followed, wearing a lovely dressing gown similar to her own. The women embraced as Darius outlined the new plan.

Finally, Laurel knew she was considered one of them. And in that moment she knew that if anyone ever offered to take her home, she'd flatly refuse.

It seemed so long ago that she'd left. And maybe she'd changed, maybe she hadn't. But she couldn't walk away from the man she now knew she loved. As he animatedly told Barst of their mutual plot and Gemma insisted on joining their little conspiracy, she watched Darius closely.

Every move, every gesture, every ripple of body muscle was forever etched into memory.

Darius Starlaw was the kind of man to take action. He was bold, brave and deeply committed to doing his best at all times. He cared about his family and friends to the point of laying his own life down for any of them.

The man solved problems. He never asked anyone to do for him what he couldn't or wouldn't do himself. He'd gone into danger on a faraway planet, without asking for any help, ordering his crew to leave him behind if it meant their safety. If there was a better definition of bravery, she'd never heard of it.

He wasn't perfect, but who was? But he'd saved a stranger's life, without thinking of the trouble it might cause him, and brought her to a new world filled with possibilities. He'd expressed his heartache at her losses and every word of sorrow he'd uttered was the truth. She'd seen that in his eyes.

He lived life to the fullest and wasn't afraid of anything. She found herself wanting to share her life with him. He had a conscience whose edicts spilled into everything he did. Even now, when his friends would help him do whatever he asked, he feared for their reputations and their careers. Above all things, Darius Starlaw was a good and honest man. Though the plan they enacted might seem underhanded, no one was forcing their foes to say or do anything.

But they'd laid out this plan together. And in doing so she'd seen respect for her in his gaze; she knew he was the one she'd love forever. No man had ever come close to making her feel the way he did. Her heart surged whenever he entered a room; even when she believed she'd never have had anything to do with him his presence was always so galvanizing. They'd seen each other at their very best and at their very worst. She knew all she needed to know. He was the one.

All they had to do was get through the day. And maybe, just maybe, she could help him put his past behind him and live again. She took a deep breath and embraced the future for the first time.

Chapter 12

After dismissing everyone from his quarters with the admonition to hurry, dress, and guard their expressions and actions, Darius fastened the last, gilt buttons on his best-dress uniform. His father's edict aside, he'd not appear in civilian gear.

He left his quarters and found his comrades at the end of the hallway, waiting for his last words.

The plan was all Laurel's. But the execution of it fell to him. And if they were wrong and arrests were made inappropriately, embarrassing dignitaries and defiling his father's fine reputation, no one would take the blame but him. But since the arrests, if any were made, were so sensitive in nature, he'd had Barst call for volunteers from the *Titan*'s crew.

Without so much as asking a single question, every man and woman had stepped up to the call—sent out without explanation—to follow their commander's orders for a special, on-ground mission. Hundreds of them gave up leave time and were now gathering at the north end of the League Justice Hall, where any arrests would take place. His crew would cover all exits and access points to affect plans, escorting any dignitaries who might flee, to that north end.

Like him, Gemma and Barst were in the finest dress togs. Laurel wore the borrowed uniform, sans any patches or designators, as a show of solidarity for the crewmembers who were now her friends. He didn't dare to hope she'd worn the outfit for his benefit. But as her bright, intuitive gaze fell on him, his heartbeat quickened. He shot her what he hoped was his best encouraging look, nodded briefly, and faced them as a group.

"Everyone's communicator is in sync?"

They all checked their wide wristbands; he was gratified to see Laurel wore hers and pushed the proper buttons, indicating she'd learned how to operate the device. "Gemma, if anyone asks why you're accompanying Barst to HQ—"

"I'll tell them he's giving me a tour since the new construction took place. I haven't set foot there for over two years. And anyone who knows us knows we're on leave, and that we wouldn't be out and about without each other." She shook her head. "I don't think anyone will question us if we just happen to stop by a computer console."

"Agreed," Barst confirmed. "Everyone knows the trial is today and that if we're to attend, we'd be dressed as we are. The crew's appearance would be to back you, in negation of any attempts Goll's defense team might make, Commander. Which is the truth!"

Darius briefly bowed his head in humble acceptance of a great crew's loyalty, but quickly continued with last minute instructions. The first of these he still directed at Gemma and his second-in-command. "After you've sent the message, join Mother and Father in their seats. As guests of the estate, you'll be expected there. No one will stop you." He finally turned to Laurel. His last instructions were for her and were most crucial. Her face bore a determined expression; she awaited instructions as any eager crewmember might. It was on the tip of his tongue to tell her to be careful, but the words hung in his throat as he gazed into her lovely blue eyes.

"Any last words for me?" she prompted as he stood there staring down at her.

"You'll be given the chance to confront him. I'd rather not have you lie but ... "

"Darius, this is my choice. You don't need to warn any of us what might happen. We all know. We accept what needs to be done."

Barst and Gemma supported her with vigorous, mutual nods.

"If anything goes wrong, direct all queries to me and me alone. Understood?" The request was sent to all present, but he still stared at Laurel. She nodded in consent and he knew they'd finally reached a relationship that went beyond sexual attraction. They were a team.

Barst held out his hand. "If there's trouble, the crew knows how to respond, Darius. We all know innocent civilians are present and that anything could go wrong. We're prepared."

Darius took his best friend's hand, gripped it hard, and followed with a similar handshake for the two women. He'd have rather hugged Laurel, but the professional gesture might go a long way toward her knowing she was his equal. He'd accepted her as nothing less.

When they turned to walk away, a sudden wave of uneasiness struck. He'd have to sit and watch everything when he was used to giving commands. His father's orders concerning his suspended status kept him from leaving the viewing box and even acknowledging his crew. He was to go to the trial, accept whatever happened, then come home again. Then—if his father was satisfied his temper was under control and that he'd accept the decision concerning Goll's sentence—he'd be allowed to reclaim his ID at HQ and his command position. Currently, he couldn't officially order anyone to do anything. His crew, Barst, Gemma, and especially Laurel were all putting their lives, careers, and futures on the line, all on a plan that was scrambled together at the last moment, for no other reason than they rallied to his cause.

He swallowed hard and tried to calm his breathing as he eventually heard his sire, mother, and sisters approach.

If only Marcos were there. But his younger brother's ship was still stuck on duty, in some classified sector of space. At least that one member of the family wouldn't be blamed if something went wrong.

Determined no one else would either, he'd composed a letter of admission on his personal room computer and would automatically send it from his wristband communicator if anything went wrong. Everything in it pointed toward *his* being the mastermind behind any attempt to oust dignitaries allied with the Warlords.

"Son … you look like you've been waiting for a while," Dar quietly acknowledged as he looked his son over. Then Dar tilted his head and gazed at him with such intensity that Darius had to look away. "Are you all right, Darius?"

"Yes, sir. I … I just want this over. I assume you won't mind the uniform I chose."

"It is right and proper for you to wear it now. Despite my most recent edict, I will not deny you that."

"Stand to my left," Maelle told him as she regally looped her right arm through her husband's. "Girls … stand to the other side of your eldest brother, Nyssa first."

Many times they'd appeared in public, similarly arranged. Darius knew his mother need not have spoken about protocol, but she acted as if she *did* know something was afoot. His lovely mother—the very first love of his life—squeezed his arm hard and gazed up at him with a look of such trust in her gaze that he hated himself for lying. But the plausible deniability his family might claim would only work if he could swear, and *they* could, that he'd never uttered a word to them about upcoming plans.

All fault for failure must be relegated to him.

"Ready?" Dar asked.

Darius simply nodded, squared his shoulders, and escorted his mother and siblings toward their waiting royal shuttle. As he did so, media announcers crowded around the palace, anxious to view and report on the family's departure.

•••

Barst and Gemma gave Laurel a ride in their shuttle, letting her out within sight of the Constellation League Hall of Justice.

She was a good hour early but felt more at ease not having to rush in with any crowds already gathering to witness what had to be a very important trial.

Just like on Earth, news crews who'd obviously be broadcasting the latest events were setting up equipment that looked as odd as it was advanced. Small earpieces replaced any bulky, portable microphones. Cameras were operated by floating, pod-like android devices in front of the newscasters. Crews applied makeup and tested sound bites.

As soon as she approached, broadcast crews pointed at her and shouted her name. She had no idea how they knew who she was but suspected either the defense team or the prosecution had cited her as a key witness. No one instructed her not to speak to them, but Earth experience in these matters led her to understand she shouldn't. To avoid any queries, she simply turned away as several green-looking, dragonish reporters, with glowing yellow eyes, approached. She did what she would have on Earth and kept her mouth shut. She looked neither to the left nor to the right but kept walking.

After about a hundred yards of avoiding queries from reporters, several members of the *Titan* crew spotted her, escorted her into the hall, and told her where to stand. She was to be ensconced in a white marble witness box, about ten feet square and directly in front of a viewing dais, many yards below her. That dais was also made of marble. From her research aboard the *Titan*, she knew this was where Goll would stand. He'd be contained or restricted in his movements, for her safety as well as the magistrates' and court employees'.

A long box, directly opposite her, indicated where the judges would sit. Goll would stand between them all and before crowds who'd sit in the galleries. The entire setup reminded her of the Coliseum in Rome. The accused, in this case, wouldn't be fed to any lions, but would still stand in the center where everyone could see him and hear his statements, assuming he made any. And *that* was her active part of the plan: to make him talk. She knew now that she could. Darius had no idea just what she *did* know and hadn't said. She'd kept information from him that was vital to the trial, things she'd learned during her computer research aboard the *Titan*. And just as he was going to take the blame if this entire plan went awry, she'd do so if the facts she'd gleaned had somehow been misinterpreted. Darius had enough on his shoulders. What she'd testify to was all her doing and she'd own it.

She sat there, stoically silent. Crowds began to fill the building. She saw Darius and his family being seated in a box, some distance to her right. The accommodation for the king and his family was decorated in dark green cloth. Again, the similarity between the scene and an old Roman gladiator flick was uncanny. There was one exception.

Instead of open air overhead, there was some kind of clear, dome-like glass that let all the light in but protected against the elements.

Sunlight sparkled off some mica or quartz-like mineral within all the marble of the viewing stands and columns holding them upright. She tried to concentrate on the décor and not on the stare of one very large, tanned commander sitting so far away.

She covertly glanced down at her wrist communicator and shock almost made her lose her barely-maintained composure.

The plan was working.

Names of officials were coming across her small, wrist view screen. They were men and women who'd suddenly decided to leave the planet, and who were privy to classified information that might have been imparted to Warlord contingents—contingents just like the vamphieres. They'd likely bought whatever message Barst sent, implying Goll had talked or was about to.

As she surreptitiously glanced upward and toward Darius, she saw him nod, cover his wrist as a sign he'd received the same information, and turn to address his father with some mundane comment or other.

Some minutes later, Gemma and Barst joined the royals in their private box. Neither gave anything away, but she didn't miss a smile Gemma shot her way.

Guards in gray uniforms, wearing sidearms, approached her witness box. Two on either side stopped and stood at attention. Ostensibly these were court officers, assigned to protect her and to keep anyone away who didn't have a need to speak to her.

She sat on her sumptuous, green velvety cushion and waited.

If the rest of Luster believed in Earth's inferiority, as Darius had, then the citizens were about to get a shock. She had no intention of embarrassing her world but would represent it with strength of conviction and the truth. She wouldn't lie about what had happened on Earth. But she *would* make Goll talk.

The vamphiere who'd killed her friends would be sworn in just as she would. He had a right to keep his mouth shut but something told her he wouldn't, not when he was informed of what was going on. Goll knew nothing of the rumor circulating about his duplicity. But as that rumor grew and likely became public, through one news source or another, Goll's defense team would inform him. She'd be there to simply confront the butcher with questions and accusations of her own.

"Would you stand, please?"

Laurel jerked her head when a voice sounded to her left. She did as the uniformed court officer demanded. He was a grayish being with a round head and a fuzzy face. She resisted the urge to smile as memories of her mother's Manx tabby cat named Pooty came to mind.

"Place your right hand over your heart, please, and repeat after me. Do you swear to tell the full truth?"

"I do, sir."

"And are you here of your own free will, without accepting bribes or without any force or coercion?"

"I am."

"Please be seated and await the head magistrate's instruction," Pooty-man said. "You will be the only witness today since others have withdrawn their statements."

Laurel watched the officer walk away and guessed why there'd be no one else to testify. Goll, or someone working with him, had probably got to the others. No wonder the bastard had refused commutation of sentence if he talked. He never expected to be convicted.

As she'd read during her research, no one on this world could be compelled to testify against their will. This made convicting others terribly difficult. But as she had nothing much to lose, no one was scaring her off. She suspected Darius kept her at the palace compound for that very reason. But he hadn't needed to. She knew what to expect.

And as much research as she'd done during the months aboard the *Titan*, she was sure it hadn't been reciprocal. What Goll's defense team *didn't* know about Earth police officers was about to hit them deep, quick, hard, and often.

She glanced down at her wrist communicator again, and began committing names to memory. Once more, she waited.

Knowing crowds were filling the stadium and that many were anxious to see their first real Earther, Laurel kept her gaze straight ahead. Over an hour later, she refused to so much as glance at Darius, his parents, Gemma, or Barst. No one must record her having done so and therefore implicate them in her testimony.

Her part of the plan was confrontation. But she meant to do it so that only she could be held responsible for any rumors of Goll's defection from Warlord control.

Finally, after it seemed the great building could hold no more, a plethora of gray-suited court officers made their way to the central dais where the magistrates and their minions would sit.

"All stand!" one court officer proclaimed as he stood before a floating, android-like microphone device.

She complied when everyone else did. Her next words would likely be part of the testimony since she'd already been sworn in.

One official after another, of various colors, sizes, shapes, and species, flowed onto the magistrates' dais and sat as each of them was formally announced. She counted at least thirty, all robed in various colors of gold, silver, greens, reds, ambers, and every other hue known to the universe. Each of them represented various factions on the planet.

Goll had killed hundreds, possibly thousands. And at special issue was the fact that he'd been apprehended on a forbidden world. It remained to be seen whether the judges would maintain his capture was legitimate. The defense team, if they were worth their salt, would claim otherwise. But his being there to kill her friends still had nothing to do with being on Earth to begin with. Who caught him didn't matter to her, as long as he *was* caught.

There were various other introductions, and the moving of officials from one partitioned section of the building to another, officials whose opinions might weigh when the final pronouncement was made. She waited and tried to paste on a very stalwart expression, giving nothing away.

Finally, Goll was brought in.

A few specifics concerning the legend of vampires on Earth were repetitive in his case. He couldn't tolerate sunlight. He was actually wheeled in from a recessed portion of the great stadium, encased in a cage that was covered on top by some ornate, metallic roof. The entire apparatus reminded her of a small pagoda. The sides were shielded by some glassy substance that was electrified and barred. Bolts of green energy filtered over and through the bars and might have inflicted a great amount of pain if any attempt was made to even touch them. However, Goll didn't move. Not until he saw *her*.

When he did, he stared malevolently. She felt hatred emanating from him, the way one feels a blast of cold rain in the face. But she had no intention of backing down. She'd seen that merciless intimidation tactic before, in many courts on Earth. Her friends' butcher wasn't threatening her. She lifted her chin, glared back, and was vaguely aware of dark-robed figures behind the pagoda. She believed, from their repeated instructions to Goll, that these must be the defense team. They were bustling about the smaller dais where Goll's containment unit was situated. Even while staring at her attacker, her peripheral vision revealed their furtive gestures and muted agitated discussion. There was no doubt in her mind. They knew about the circulated rumors, and were probably even aware that their client's cohorts on Luster were fleeing and being arrested at various airfields around the planet.

The corner of her mouth lifted as she continued staring straight at Goll. Finally, he'd get what was coming to him. In return, his lips lifted in an ominous sneer that displayed his fangs, and his face grew even gaunter. The crowd responded with a low murmur of utter disapproval. The idiot wasn't doing himself any good. He was likely angry over the rumors concerning his disloyalty. That meant she could get to him.

Hiding from sunlight notwithstanding, one *difference* between Goll and Earth vampire legend was in the way he could sustain his metabolism. She'd read that, once he'd been taken from stasis, he'd been offered any food of his choice. But he'd refused it, demanding fresh blood instead. When his guards wouldn't provide it, they'd had to use blood substitute to indulge him. But the substitution had angered him and set off claims of unfair treatment by his defense team.

Even now, the bastard wanted real blood. She remembered the look on his face that night in Balboa Park. He'd *wanted* to kill. He liked it. It all came rushing back: Cory stretched out on the ground, her friends so still and silent.

"Will you rise, and face the defendant?" Pooty-man asked.

Her guard's cat-like face was kind and his voice was soft. There was a look of encouragement in his gaze. It occurred to her that many in the building wanted Goll to face justice. She took a deep breath and stood.

A purple-robed creature, looking very much like some tall version of a swamp alligator also stood and addressed her.

"To introduce myself, madam, I am Magistrate Orat 'Cur. If you do not understand anything in this proceeding, anything you're asked, you may query the court for any explanation."

His gaze, too, was very kind. She was either being humored or gently encouraged to say anything to convict Goll.

Orat 'Cur turned to Goll's defense team. "Sirs … we have read your client's statements concerning his refusal to speak. He is pleading guilty and has refused commutation of a death sentence … which is the only recourse of this court given his plea and the deaths attributed to him by his own testimony. Is there anything further you have to say before the Earth witness is allowed to speak?"

"I wish to be recognized," one of the black-robed attorneys loudly claimed.

"Step forward and speak, Jakus Mol. As head defense advisor to the defendant, you may now add anything else not previously mentioned, for the record."

Jakus lifted one dark-cloaked arm and pointed at Laurel.

She stepped forward as a gesture of strength and an unwillingness to cower.

"Magistrate 'Cur," Jakus began, "this woman is likely among others from the royal family that has, just this morning, circulated untrue rumors about my client's willingness to speak. The defendant has made no statements implicating anyone on Luster as collaborator in any criminal activity."

"First … I, as well as probably everyone on Luster by now, know about that gossip, Jakus. There is no law against circulating a rumor. Second, if you are accusing anyone of the royal family of any *criminal* activity, speak now or hold your accusations," 'Cur seriously advised.

"Sir … surely we are all aware that, while there is no criminal charge for having circulated such nonsense, there are ethical codes to which enforcers bind themselves. If Commander Darius Starlaw had any part in such chicanery, his future with the Constellation League, in any capacity, should be reviewed."

An angry roar from the crowd caused a court officer to step up to the floating microphone again and demand silence.

'Cur addressed the crowd briefly. "There will be no further outbursts from this assemblage or I will clear this building. *Is that understood?*"

Silence ensued with the exception of a few catcalls demanding Goll's death. These came from obvious death penalty supporters from an upper gallery. But even they quickly shut their mouths when court enforcers were sent to rout them.

The magistrate got back to the subject at hand.

"Jakus Mol … we are not here today to vet anyone in the crowd, royalty or not, for *their* behavior. That is another issue, completely separate from our purpose. The matter before us now is whether your client has anything to add to the statements already recorded when he was released from stasis. He has, as stated, pled guilty. He has admitted to being a Warlord conspirator, working on their behalf. Is there anything else he wishes to say before the only witness available makes her statement?"

Jakus and his team quickly spoke with Goll, shook their heads in apparent disagreement, and threw up their hands in confusion. Their leader turned to the court once more. "Sir … our client wishes to say nothing more. But I must elucidate, for the record, that his arrest was illegal. If the act of landing on a banned planet requires the death penalty, notwithstanding any other charges of murder, theft, or looting attributed to my client … then those who landed on that same banned world to effect an arrest are also in violation of the law. They should stand for their crimes as well, with the same penalty being applied."

A huge outburst poured from the crowds as they stood as one and blasted the attorney for his legal trickery. Despite persistent attempts of court officers to get the crowd to quiet down, they shouted their anger at this maneuvering.

On Earth, Laurel had seen this same kind of semantic game-playing. She kept her silence and didn't respond to those begging her to go ahead, step up to her own microphone, and speak on behalf of the *Titan*'s crew and her commanding officer. It wasn't time. Not just yet. But when she did speak, everyone would listen. And they'd remember every syllable.

The melee continued for some minutes. Eventually, Orat 'Cur stepped forward and raised his hands, and the crowd began to wind down. It took more minutes for some semblance of order to return. But 'Cur was a very tall man and his presence not lightly ignored.

"The court has already debated the legalities of this issue, Jakus Mol. Before we yield our conclusion on this rather inclusive definition of enforcing the laws, wherever our League ships might travel, we are as yet undecided. A legal clarification will come before the day is out. However, whatever the crew of one of our enforcer vessels correctly did or did not do in the pursuit of their duties has no bearing on the lives Goll is alleged to have taken on that world." He turned toward Laurel.

She took a deep breath, stood, and faced him squarely.

"We will hear from the Earther on this matter. Let her words stand as testimony. She has sworn to tell the truth." He then glanced at Jakus again. "Will your client remain silent and forego his right to openly question her?"

Jakus lifted one hand and let it fall impotently. "My client refuses to speak openly on any issue except to have his defense team reiterate that he did not make any accusation toward any Lusterian citizen concerning collusion. He has not asked for his sentence to be commuted for the sake of naming those who might be Warlord sympathizers on this planet. The rumors so rampantly circulating in the media at this time … are false."

When Jakus Mol turned away to join his team, 'Cur approached Laurel.

"Have you any questions … any at all … about any of the procedure, madam?"

She was being given the chance to leave and have no further part in this trial. But that wasn't happening. "No, sir."

"And do you still wish to address the accused?"

"I do," Laurel insisted loudly. 'Cur was making damn sure she wanted to make a statement and that everyone knew it. Repeated instructions or requests, like those she'd just been given, were always offered as a way out for anyone who'd suddenly gone squeamish. She'd seen that technique employed in courts back on Earth. But she wasn't budging.

'Cur returned to his place on the dais and spoke clearly so all could hear. "The Earth witness may now speak to Goll. She speaks on behalf of the prosecution and may publicly make any accusation of crimes or attempts to criminal action. She may appeal to the court for such maximum or minimum sentencing as the law allows. But bear in mind that any final judgment or sentence rendered this day comes from the court alone, based on facts heretofore gathered. Her testimony will be added to the records against the accused. As he pleads guilty, and refuses to refute accusations, this woman's statements are allowed as a matter of clarification." Orat 'Cur nodded at her. "You may speak when and as long as you please on any matter concerning the attack that prosecution has recorded from the *Titan*'s records. Those records will be weighed against your own statement for accuracy. As you've sworn to tell the truth, it should match what Commander Starlaw's records maintain. Before beginning, the law requires that you state your name and occupation before witnesses in this hallway."

She was being told to not to lie or exaggerate. Someone from the prosecution either didn't know or didn't care that she'd researched Darius's records and found them exactly as she recalled. There were no fabrications, no lies to substantiate claims. It was likely the powers-that-be trusted a League officer to the point that what she did or didn't say made no difference. Whether she'd been coached didn't matter. The magistrate's warning was clear.

She had never lied in court or on duty, not about anything. She wasn't about to start now.

She turned to Goll. His face was still a mask of hate and venomous regard. It didn't matter.

"I am Officer Laurel Hannah Blake ... badge number 4115, San Diego Police Department. I hold the same rank as one of your ground enforcers of the first cadre, with ten years of experience, thirty-one commendations and—"

"Objection, Magistrate 'Cur! This woman is not an enforcer *here*," Jakus Mol cried. "Her attempt to imbue authority, to augment her statements, is inappropriate!"

Murmurs from the crowd made 'Cur stand and hold up his hands for silence yet again. "This Earther has every right to bring forth expertise if it pertains to this trial. It matters not to this court where such expertise was obtained. Your objection is overruled, Jakus. And I warn you about interrupting the witness again, or making any attempt at intimidating her. Your client was given an opportunity to question this woman and he refused. It is her turn to speak." He faced Laurel. "You may continue, madam."

Laurel was incensed. How dare that man try to mitigate who and what she was? She walked around the partition of her witness box, down a set of steps, and approached Goll's cell. A floating microphone followed her every move.

Murmurs of shock and surprise followed her actions but neither Magistrate Orat 'Cur nor any of the other magistrates said a word. No court officer tried to stop her.

"I have no problem addressing the defense team's concern in that regard," she proudly announced. "Neither Mr. Mol nor anyone on this planet has the power to take from me what the laws of my world bestowed. As far as legal authorities on Earth are concerned, I *am* an enforcer until such time as the citizens of my jurisdiction ... who gave me authority ... rescind it!"

Applause broke out from the galleries, but she continued. The floating microphone followed her straight up to the side of Goll's containment unit. She stood only two feet from him. The bars were the only thing keeping them apart. She stared straight at him as she spoke.

"I and other officers were on duty the night Goll attacked us. Attacks of the kind he committed before my own eyes were also perpetrated against a number of citizens. I cannot and will not speak as to his guilt in those other killings, but I will testify as to what I saw right before my own eyes." She moved even closer and Goll actually snarled. "I saw this vamphiere rip open the throats of police officers with whom I worked. Then he tried to kill me. But for Commander Starlaw and his medical technician, I'd have died. The facts of these events are recorded in the commander's report. I do not object to ... nor will I alter ... one syllable of anything the commander wrote."

The crowd muttered again and she almost felt them lean toward her, lending her strength. But she didn't need it.

"This vamphiere before me is a coward. He landed on my world and committed murder. And how else was any enforcer on my planet to stop him if the commander had not landed and taken action? Goll knew my people had no weaponry that could match his. He believed it was highly unlikely anyone would chase him to Earth. On the night he attacked my friends, he'd actually landed his craft in a park where anyone exercising the next morning could have found it. According to the commander's records, it'd been parked right next to a jogging trail. That was the extent of his disdain for my people, and for any League justice."

Loud rounds of shouts and applause again broke from the galleries.

"No, Goll … I can't crawl inside your head and know exactly why you chose to land on Earth, but I can speculate as this court allows. You landed many times over a period of weeks, and I believe you killed on each and every occasion. Being there at all, so far from Luster, indicates you were escaping League justice. That seems to have been your goal. But you didn't get there by yourself, did you?"

Goll actually growled and leaned toward her. For that moment, she no longer cared what the crowd's response might be. She was talking to *him*.

"Commander Starlaw reported that his crew destroyed a Vardorian-class, light starship in the park."

"What of it?" Goll blurted.

"The defendant will refrain from—"

She briefly held up one hand. "It's all right, Magistrate 'Cur. He's only opening his mouth now because he knows exactly what point I'm about to make. And he feels I'm getting close to a truth he believed would be overlooked. Isn't that right, Goll?"

"The court is highly interested in this point of fact, madam. What is there about the craft that is condemning?"

Laurel kept her gaze on Goll, never wavering. "My research indicated that kind of ship is top-of-the-line for its class. It's highly expensive, the latest model. And there have only been several hundred produced."

"Go on," 'Cur instructed.

"I believe Commander Starlaw assumed the ship to have been stolen. Oddly, no stolen or missing reports of a craft of that type have ever been made. At least not according to the general archives from Luster's Department of Vital Records. As the name of that division implies, those records are made available to average citizens so they may, at any time, scan serial numbers and report stolen property that nefarious individuals may attempt to sell. That agency is meant to keep everyone honest."

"Yes, madam … we are all aware of why that department exists. Please get to the point," 'Cur insisted as he listened intently, leaning forward as if he knew what she might be about to say.

"Sir … Commander Starlaw was anxious to leave Earth's surface before he and his crew were discovered by members of my own constabulary or Earth's military. He didn't enter the serial or licensure number of Goll's vessel as exigent circumstances existed. Such actions were within his purview. But I find it strange that, back on this world, not one of the vessels of that type was *ever* reported stolen. Every single one ever produced is listed as having been consigned to Caprorian Industries, for the use of corporate officials here on Luster. I think it highly unlikely a vessel of that expense and design would have been overlooked from Caprorian's inventory. And for so many months."

"Indeed!" 'Cur muttered as he nodded. "Continue … *please.*"

"Sir, I believe Goll was never supposed to have been caught. A powerful vessel of that type was meant to provide him an escape to distant places. With his murdering habits I believe he'd made a nuisance of himself in this sector of space. Commander Starlaw was on his heels everywhere he was sighted. Goll and his protector simply didn't count on the tenacity of the *Titan*'s commander and crew."

"Objection!" Jakus Mol shouted. "The witness is inferring things she cannot know about."

"We'll see just what I know and what I don't," she snapped back before anyone could rule on his protest. Then she paused before saying more.

The court officials were having a difficult time containing the crowd's growing excitement. Her next words had to be carefully chosen. Darius, Barst, and Gemma knew nothing about any of this. She must make sure the court understood the accusations were her own.

"I maintain that Goll was *provided* a vehicle that, because of its speed and maneuverability, might more easily evade detection. And more ... "

"Madam ... you have this court's full attention!"

"One of the Chief Operating Officers of Caprorian Industries was arrested just an hour ago, trying to leave Luster at Crystol City's main airfield. When he was detained for simple questioning before takeoff, it was discovered that he had no less than six separate pieces of identification ... all bearing different names ... on his person. Since that, in and of itself is a major crime on Luster, he was taken into custody and is signing testimonial documentation concerning his involvement with Goll's escape. This man is also admitting his collaboration with the Warlord faction, involving attacks made on civilian transport vessels."

"You lie!" Goll shouted.

The entire building shook with shouts of anger and outrage.

Laurel spoke as loudly as she could, to get over the din. She finally put her attention on the magistrates. Information coming over her wrist communicator wasn't exactly what Barst, Gemma, or Darius received, because she'd programmed her communication device to correlate with the name of *anyone* of rank in Caprorian Industries—anyone who was or even might be connected to Lusterian authority. A few names on all those lists were connecting. All she had to do was draw lines to dots.

"This gentleman under arrest is only one of many being questioned and brought back to League Headquarters. He, like many others, assumed the rumor *I* instigated … the one inferring Goll was naming names in connection to Warlord conspiracies … was true. That corporate mogul wanted no part of a death sentence and was fleeing Luster. But he isn't just some official holding stock in a company. His name is Prafin Lon. You may also know him as Prefect of Crystol City. In that position as well as having business contacts in many industries, Prefect Lon would have been privy to shipping schedules of everything from precious ores to fuel."

As the crowd roared in fury, Laurel raised her voice to be heard over the terrible clamor.

"With Constellation League ships, crews, and assets continually weakened and spread thin in their attempts to hold Warlord cutthroats at bay, the enemies of this world know they might one day be able to attack and invade Luster itself. And anyone subscribing to the Warlord cause and aiding it might then find himself in a very powerful position indeed. Perhaps Prefect Lon saw himself as more than just a city's governor. Perhaps he actually saw himself as the new ruler of Luster—a reward from the Warlord leaders for his services … inclusive of having employed Goll … to attack cargo, fuel and even medical supply ships in order to eventually bring down the Constellation League once and for all." In the face of the crowds' growing ire, she drew herself up and continued with confidence. "I strongly maintain that Goll's services to the prefect were integral when speaking of cutting deep into League resources. Lon gave Goll whatever information the vamphiere factions needed. It's no secret to anyone what Goll has done. He has, as the records of this proceeding indicate, admitted his crimes. He simply didn't think he'd be found guilty and expects to be released on a technicality. That's why he won't testify on his own behalf! He realizes his life expectancy is severely shortened once he gives away his employers. One of whom is Prefect Lon," she boldly claimed.

As she'd spoken the obvious, the crowd's cries for justice were so loud they might have opened the heavens.

Magistrate 'Cur stood when all the other magistrates did.

Goll shouted in rage. "She lies. I have never met Prefect Lon. I never obtained shipping information from him or attacked at his command."

With every word he uttered, he sealed his fate. His denial of her speculations fired the crowd rather than supported his guiltlessness. He wouldn't have opened his mouth at all if the accusations weren't true.

She stared at Goll once more, but lowered her voice and pushed the microphone away. "Lon or one of his cronies gave you that ship, you son-of-a-bitch! And he's as much as said so already. So you might as well spill your guts about the rest. They'll have no problem hanging your rangy ass out to dry. And anyone you care about, extended family, friends, lovers, or even kids, won't be safe now. The Warlords won't ever believe you didn't talk. So even *if* your attorneys get you off on a technicality, you're gonna wish you were dead a thousand times over."

Within his cell, Goll went berserk. He grabbed his head, thrashed about madly, and didn't care whether the electronic bars came into contact with his body.

Guards rushed forward to move his cell back, within the confines of the building. The crowd was on its feet, screaming for action.

Only *then* did she turn to look across the stadium, into the eyes of the man with whom she'd fallen in love.

Chapter 13

Primitive!

What had he been thinking? Though she'd forgiven him for a few transgressions, he still had a lot of apologizing to do.

Darius stood when the crowd did. Laurel gazed at him across the distance and he could almost read her mind.

But now, he must do his part.

"Father," he blurted as he put on hand on his sire's shoulder and spoke above the roar, "I need to be reinstated. My crew is detaining, questioning, and even arresting Warlord collaborators as we speak. I need to get to them. I need to coordinate their efforts. So many suspects are admitting to conspiracy that someone needs to be in charge."

"Darius … what by Kronos's balls is going on?" the king asked.

"I'll explain later. Right now, I need to resume my command."

For a long moment, Dar stared at him.

Darius saw utter confusion in his family's expressions. The crowds got even louder and he feared for their safety. "Father, there's no time. If there're any Warlord sympathizers here, the family shouldn't be sitting together, making themselves one big target. You'll undoubtedly be asked to speak to the magistrates. Mother, as ambassador to the planets of Ikaena and Chokar, will likely be asked to speak to representatives from those worlds, especially since it appears Prefect Lon might have assisted the very vamphieres who attacked them and destroyed agricultural concerns last year. They'll want reparation and will likely demand some say in Lon's sentencing, assuming it comes to that. And I insist that I need to coordinate my crew's efforts," he repeated.

"All right, Darius. You may resume duties," Dar advised. "But someone must see your sisters safely back to the palace."

Gemma spoke up. "Majesty … I'll do that, and take Laurel back as well. If anyone requests further testimony from her, I'll let the court officers know where she is."

Darius immediately took control of the situation.

"Barst, we need to get to the north end of the building. The crew will be bringing any detained or arrested suspects to that location," he brusquely ordered. "We need to have all defendants taken to HQ for questioning, especially those wishing to admit conspiracy. Keep them separate from one another."

Barst glanced at his wrist communicator. "The information is coming in fast, but it looks as though many of the bastards were, indeed, fooled by the rumor. They want to spill their guts while they still have information that can be used to bargain down a possible death sentence."

Darius nodded then grinned. "Yes. Cowards always turn on one another. I've counted over thirty dignitaries who suddenly found Luster a bit too crowded. "Come on, we've got work to do."

As Barst left the viewing box reserved for royalty, Darius made one loud request. Gemma's attention was fixated on gathering his youngest sisters, who were confused and almost terrified by the shouting and angry commentary of the people around them. He shouted one last instruction to the eldest of them, the one who was closest to where he stood and who could hear his words clearest.

"Nyssa … when you get back to the palace with the girls, tell Laurel I'll want to speak to her later. I don't know when I'll return, but make sure the guards are informed of the situation. No one is to leave the palace for any reason, and reinforce the perimeter with all the Household Elite Guard you can muster. As soon as Gemma safely can, have her join Father, Mother and me at HQ. Understand?"

"Yes, Darius!" Nyssa shouted. "Don't worry about us. We'll be all right. Just check on Mother and Father as soon as you're done with your crew. I'll send palace guards to escort Mother and

Father wherever they need to go later. That way your crew won't need to assume the extra duty. Seems like your people will all be needed elsewhere …like near the airfields … arresting escaping traitors," she finished with a firm nod.

He beamed, then set off to join Barst and his crew.

• • •

Almost seven hours later, Darius, his entire crew, his parents, and the magistrates were cloistered in a secure room at League Headquarters. Gemma confirmed that his sisters and Laurel were safely within palace walls, with extra guards and hover cameras patrolling the grounds.

More than seventy arrests had been made. Most of those were clandestine Warlord extremists, wishing to come clean about their activities before they were discovered and formally charged.

As he'd suspected, those who conspired with—or in any way provided a means of escape for—Warlord spies, almost fought each other to see who could hand over the most damning information. Anyone without a bargaining platform knew they'd receive the most serious sentencing the law allowed, which was death. They were all trying to save their skins, possibly their family's lives from Warlord retribution. The traitors knew their former extremist benefactors wouldn't care who started a rumor, or why. Warlord leaders would want immediate, serious reprisals for anyone having spoken up, and for breaking their secretive foothold on Luster. They didn't tolerate traitors to their cause any more than they endured peaceful coexistence with planets siding with the Constellation League.

All the uproar originated from one lie concerning Goll's non-existent plea bargain—a lie broadly circulated where crew most powerful entities within Lusterian society might know of it. The entire plan was utterly simplistic. It'd taken Goll's capture for the plot to work. Within only just a few days of landing on Luster, the heavens had opened and sent that part of the galaxy a blessing. Laurel's idea depended on the lack of trust one traitor had for another. It'd worked shockingly well.

Tired as he was, elation filled him. If there were any more defectors on the planet's surface, they'd hide from Lusterian enforcers *and* their Warlord benefactors. None trusted any of the rest. Their powers had been severely crippled, possibly for good.

He dragged one hand over his face and the back of his neck before addressing Barst with his latest command. "Have the crew stand down and continue their leave. I'll thank them personally for their loyalty. I don't know how … but I'll find some way to do it."

Barst grinned broadly and waved away Darius's concern with one hand. "They loved it. Of course, there are a few commanding officers who'd have liked to be included in the arrests … and who may have had their noses tweaked because they weren't … but they'll eventually understand the need for secrecy and quick action. The crew of the *Titan* chased Goll the longest. They were separated from home and family most frequently. They deserved the chance to arrest the people who helped him escape."

Darius glanced at his wrist communicator and noted the lateness of the hour. All he could think about now was getting back to the palace and to a woman who'd caused more trouble in the time he'd known her than all the spoiled debutantes to whom he'd ever been introduced.

After Astral's and Kyrie's deaths, he'd shunned sexual encounters entirely, until over two years had passed and physical need eventually drove him to frequent a few of the better brothels in the city. But that was carnal release. He craved more in life than hopping in and out of strangers' beds.

Now, everything was different. He hadn't imagined the look in her eyes the last time he and Laurel had spoken. Even after angry exchanges, he felt closer to her than to any woman he'd ever known, poor Astral included. He was a much older man now, not a boy. Thoughts of career and grandeur were replaced with need of family and for one soul to share his dreams. Where he hadn't been ready to assume responsibilities of family life then, he was now. Astral hadn't been wrong. They'd just been wrong for each *other*.

But he could live now and remember the past with less pain. Yes. Everything had changed indeed.

"Darius … are you listening?" Maelle loudly asked as she snapped her fingers in front of his face.

Darius turned to her with a start, not having realized his mother was speaking to him. Gemma, Barst, and his father were staring at him, smirking as if they knew where his mind wandered.

"I-I'm sorry, Mother. Please go on."

"You're drifting, dear," Maelle gently criticized. "I was asking what you're going to say to the magistrates." She gazed across the room, where an intense conversation took place between Chief Magistrate Orat 'Cur and the other lesser court justices. "Now that certain vermin have been swept from the shadows, the justices will likely question you about Laurel's testimony."

"Indeed," Dar affirmed. "I haven't commented because it seems to be a personal matter between you. All this business about spreading a false rumor is a bit alarming. Gemma and Barst's part in it is obvious. The Earther's part … not so much. But you seem to trust her implicitly, son. This being the case … curiosity regarding her place in your life now bids me speak."

"I don't understand, Father."

"Let me put it this way … what's up between you and the Earth woman?" he succinctly asked, with a saucy wag of his right brow.

Everyone else in the group chuckled.

Darius glanced at the faces of those he cared about and was, for once in his life, speechless. How could he answer when he hadn't had time to consult the other party first—alone, where they could work out what indeed *was up*?

Darius opened his mouth, intending to say something tactful and off-putting, but a loud summons from the chief magistrate saved him.

"Commander Starlaw," Magistrate Orat 'Cur announced as he and his official group approached. "There are a few questions I'd like to ask. But doing so in any legal capacity will require you being sworn in before the citizens of Luster, as law requires."

"As a Constellation League officer, sir … I'm always bound by honor and my oath to provide truth in any legal proceeding. You may ask what you will. Now or in public will make no difference. My answers will be the same," Darius humbly offered.

"Very well." 'Cur cleared his throat, glanced as his compatriots and began. "How is it that this Earth woman found what you and your crew obviously overlooked?"

"If you're referring to Goll's ship, sir, I have no excuse. As she testified, Laurel Blake was an enforcer in her own right. Her training allowed her to detect that which went unnoticed by me."

"If I may speak," Barst broke in.

"You may," 'Cur confirmed with a slight nod.

"In all fairness, Magistrate, Luster's best prosecution team did not detect that fact, either. Commander Starlaw never actually saw Goll's vessel on the surface of Earth. As his report states, I was the one ordered to destroy it. *I* did so and later reported the specifications concerning the type and model of craft Goll used. The Commander entered that data into his own report, as procedure allows. We *all* overlooked the significance of the craft. And as the Earther truthfully testified, circumstances were exigent. We needed to get off the surface of her world, get her to medical help since Goll left her close to death, and get our own light transport back to the *Titan* before any Earthers arrived at our location. Since we had Goll in custody and since everyone presumed his guilt would be easily proven, what kind of craft he operated was a minor detail. Besides, we no longer had it, or any part of it, as evidence."

Orat stroked his chin thoughtfully. "Indeed, our own prosecution team *did* fail to even notice Goll's ship. It fell into the category of minutiae where all else was concerned. But this Earth woman seems to have grasped its importance. As investigators have confirmed, she used computers aboard the *Titan* to trace its probable origin, and suspected Prefect Lon's duplicity for some months ... but did not tell any of *you*. Is that not so?" he questioned as he raised one brow. "Why?"

"No, sir. She didn't tell us," Darius readily defended. "Her reasons now are quite understandable."

"Elucidate."

"She was a woman torn from her world, injured and with the recent deaths of her friends to contemplate. She was inflicted with a new life and new technology not of her understanding. She was in the middle of a culture that was as alien to her as hers would be to us. I wrongly assumed her to be inferior in every way, intelligence included. She was cordial to my ship's crew, even to the point of becoming quite popular among them, but who could she really trust? After all ... if a major dignitary from Luster might be a conspirator involved in her fellow Earthers' deaths, to whom could she go?" Darius searched the faces of those around him as he spoke. "She bided her time and learned. She figured out who she could trust, but withheld that evidence until she could reveal it in such a way that only she'd take blame for any misunderstanding. She knew one of two things might happen. Either revealing Prefect Lon's involvement would get her in serious trouble, *or* she'd draw out others of his ilk, and make them believe their names were next. She made them consider running—and face eventual capture—or throwing themselves on the mercy of the court."

"For all intents and purposes, she became like a member of your crew?"

"Not *like*, sir. She *was* a member of my crew, in every way that mattered. She even risked her life to save mine on Chamron. That incident is recorded in the ship's log."

"Hmmm. It appears that the Earther has shown ingenuity and loyalty beyond expectations," the magistrate noted.

"I have no reason to believe she's an exception to her culture," Darius said, knowing Laurel would heartily approve of that comment.

"It still bothers me most grievously that all of us overlooked the very thing that damned Prefect Lon," 'Cur said. "To have disregarded the craft Goll used for escape was … profoundly unprofessional and decidedly embarrassing. For everyone."

"May I speak, sir?" Gemma chimed in.

'Cur nodded as he lifted one hand and let it fall.

"Sir," she began, "I understand Laurel as well as anyone aboard the *Titan*. I believe she was curious as to how Goll's ship evaded detection and landed on her world. She might not have understood terminology concerning advanced shielding capabilities, but she'd conclude that an escaping criminal would not purchase such noticeable transportation. And minus any kind of theft report—"

"Yes … that was the key to the prefect's duplicity. Hence the rest of her testimony," 'Cur concluded as he crossed his arms over his chest in contemplation. "But to have kept that information to herself was most unusual. It leaves a bad taste in my mouth that an Earther, centuries behind our own culture, discovered it."

"She's an unusual person," Darius advised. "Laurel looks beyond the obvious and finds what's important. She is, in every way imaginable, most extraordinary. Where I attributed her behavior to stubbornness, she was guarding herself. Watching and learning. She may assume her entire race … everyone on her world … is being judged by what she does in front of us. And if any of us were faced with that kind of burden, how much information would we share? How much would we keep to ourselves?" He shook his head. "I judged her too harshly. I was stern and prejudiced. She withheld information because of me, and I take full responsibility."

He'd stared into the distance as he'd spoken, and thought of nothing but what he'd say when he saw her again. What could he do to apologize for those days aboard the *Titan*? Especially their first few encounters, when he'd said and done everything wrong.

He suddenly realized everyone was staring at him, drew himself up, and assumed a more practiced, commander's stance. He pasted on what he hoped was a very stoic expression. There'd be a time to express himself. First to *her*, then to everyone *else*.

The magistrate had a contemplative look on his face.

Barst and Gemma were trying to suppress laughter, as was his mother.

His father cleared his throat and spoke next. "Son … I think you just answered that question I put to you earlier. Now … if we're done here for the night, I suggest we head to the safety of our various abodes."

"There is but one more matter to discuss," 'Cur added, then sighed heavily before continuing. "We have made a decision concerning Goll's sentence."

Darius stiffened. His family and friends drew closer, as if they were protecting each other.

"Goll will get his wish, whether he thought it would actually occur or not," 'Cur declared. "The death sentence will be carried out tomorrow … midnight. I will not risk having some vamphiere clansman covertly landing on our world, attempting to free him, and taking more lives in the process." He slowly bowed his head before turning away.

The chamber slowly emptied.

As they walked to their transports, Darius silently contemplated the news.

An impending execution didn't deliver the triumphant feeling he'd expected. But after all that'd happened, pity was too much to ask.

• • •

Events of the last days filled Darius's mind. His transport driver's alert was the only thing that brought him out of his reverie.

As they approached the castle, hundreds of small craft, ground shuttles, and vehicles of various sizes were scattered across the great lawn, leading up to the front of the structure.

"Kronos's blood! Now what?" he sullenly muttered as he halted the other transports behind him, especially the one carrying his mother and father.

Once he was sure they were secured by guards, he took action.

Leaping from the deck of his small, oval-shaped, silver vehicle as it hovered several feet above the ground, he unlatched the trigger guard on his sidearm. Along with the restoration of his position, he'd been given back a duty weapon but prayed he'd not have to use it.

In his life, he'd never seen so many people and craft milling around the palace. He approached at a fast lope, praying something heinous hadn't taken place during the day. His beloved sisters, Laurel, and all of the household staff were inside. Members of the Elite Household High Guard were nowhere to be seen.

His heart was in his throat as he took three steps at a time, up the main outer marble stairway, through the foyer, and into the entrance gallery.

Dignitaries in every state of dress and undress turned as he barreled into the massive, ancestral hall bearing tapestries and banners of every Starlaw to have ever occupied the dwelling.

Nyssa spoke with the Regent of Askarid, the next largest city on the planet. Members of the High Guard seemed to be escorting other recognizable dignitaries. Servants were busy carrying luggage and offering trays of food and drink.

"What in the name of all creation is going on?" he loudly asked.

"Maybe I can explain."

He turned when he heard Laurel's voice. Her hair was down and floated in long soft waves around her shoulders. She was dressed in a midnight blue gown he recognized as one of Nyssa's.

"Laurel? What is all this? Why are these people here?"

"Darius … come with me," she softly requested as she turned and walked toward the great library.

As she strode away, obviously expecting him to follow, he briefly dropped his head and stared at the floor. Weariness mixed with the realization that yet *another* drama was playing out almost did him in.

One thing struck him above all else.

Since having met the Earther, life had been one series of tempestuous encounters. He shrugged, felt the corner of his mouth lift, and gave in.

If loving her meant being thrust into one fracas after another, life would certainly never be dull. And with someone so challenging in his existence, it was a good thing he'd decided to take a ground position. As of tonight, he'd be replacing a man the traitorous Prefect Lon had appointed as Crystol's Chief of Enforcers. Anyone associated with ousted Warlord sympathizers would likely forfeit their positions. Perhaps the dignitaries, staff, and assorted flunkies' presence in his home was part of an all-out power grab—sure to rock the entire planet's government to its core.

First, he had to question the one person who seemed particularly good at attracting controversy. With a deep sigh, he picked up his booted feet and headed to the library, anxious to get this new scenario straight as well as the future.

As tired as he was, he'd stay awake for the next month if the result was making Laurel a permanent fixture in his life.

Chapter 14

Laurel shook her hair back, tied her gown's sash more securely about her waist, and turned to see the eldest son and heir to the throne walk through the library.

He looked like hell. If ever there was a man who needed sleep, food, and down time, it was Darius Starlaw. He'd uncharacteristically pulled his long, black hair loose. The left epaulet of his dress uniform tunic was undone. The sidearm he wore trailed down his right hip, reminding her of the town sheriff in an old Hollywood epic.

Weariness made the few wrinkles around his dark green eyes more pronounced, but his jaw wasn't nearly as set and intimidating as it'd been when he'd first burst into the gallery.

Because she'd been helping prepare rooms, food, and beverages for arriving dignitaries all night, she had a better understanding of where everything was, including the library. It was the one spot no one currently occupied, hence the only choice for having a conversation of the type that needed to transpire.

"Are you okay?" she softly asked as she approached him.

He put his hands on his hips, briefly tilted his head back, and took a deep breath before responding. "I suppose that depends on what's happening *now*," he joked.

"We weren't back to the palace very long before a lot of bureaucrats started arriving with their families and entourage. Seems there are a lot of highly placed friends of your parents who're worried they might be targeted by as yet undiscovered vamphiere and Warlord sympathizers. Some are asking for a few days of protection behind palace walls. Most want to journey to the execution with your mother and father, as a show of solidarity for the royal family. We heard about the magistrates' decision concerning Goll," she supplied. Then she took a deep breath and quickly continued. "Nyssa and the rest of your sisters have things well in hand. She'd have contacted your parents or you, but I suggested it might not be a good idea to broadly telegraph the fact that the honest legislators and dignitaries on the planet have temporarily taken up residence on palace grounds ... all in one place." She lifted one hand and tucked a strand of hair behind her left ear.

She was babbling and knew it. Nyssa should be explaining all this but, as Darius's oldest sister, the girl had been officially in charge for the last six hours. In fact, Nyssa and the household staff didn't have time to mollify and pamper the elite *and* explain everything to the absent members of the Starlaw family. That left her.

"Uh ... the outbuildings and cottages are full. The overflow will be assigned guest rooms upstairs," she quickly supplied. "Nyssa ... she couldn't just turn people away, Darius. Some were really frightened by what happened at the trial. And with all the terrorists turning themselves in ... some of whom were once very trusted members of Lusterian society ... they're afraid for their children and need your parents' stalwart presence to soothe them," she finished. "They want to assert their loyalty. But, all that notwithstanding, I suggested the guards search everyone for weapons. Tactfully ... *of course.*"

He dragged both hands through his hair, nodded, and slowly walked across the room. Then he poured a very large amount of alcohol into a crystal glass and drank it down in one smooth gulp. He took still another drink before finally putting the glass down and standing in silence.

Laurel understood weariness and frustration with the day's happenings. She put her gaze on ceiling-high shelves filled with ancient tomes. Nyssa had told her that that no one ever used paper anymore; the resource was considered too valuable and was reserved now for the most important documents of state, where actual signatures were required. The relics she gazed on were part of a carefully archived and preserved library—a library she'd been given permission to use. So far, however, anything she'd needed to learn had been gleaned from computers. But nothing in one of *those* was going to help her tell Darius how she felt. Still, he had to know. If he didn't reciprocate, it wouldn't be the first time she'd loved someone who didn't wholly and unreservedly love her back. Her parents were included in that list. But she'd learned one thing from all her adventures—just one simple truth that made all the difference to her attitude.

Life was damned short. When one loved someone else to the point that everything else fell by the wayside, that love should be unequivocally expressed. She hadn't told Cory he'd been the closest thing she'd ever had to a brother. She'd assumed he knew. That was a regret she wouldn't repeat.

Darius slowly faced her, leaned on the corner of a massive marble desk, crossed his booted ankles, and stared for a long moment. His face was a mask of determined strength. She couldn't guess what he was thinking but was sure to hear it now.

"Before one more damned thing gets in the way … before some other catastrophe or incident takes place and we're thrust in the middle of intrigue … you need to hear me, Laurel."

"You need to hear me, too. I want to go first."

"No. This can't wait another moment."

"Darius—"

"I love you!" they both blurted in unison.

She stared at him and shook her head, sure she'd misheard. "Y-you *what?*"

He smiled, pushed himself away from the desk, and slowly advanced with all the stealth of a lion. "I said … I love you. And you said it, too."

She simply nodded, swallowed hard, and stood her ground.

He didn't stop until he was a few inches away. She had to tilt her head far back to gaze into his face. The weariness he'd displayed was gone. Now, there was an open vulnerability in his dark green eyes that almost broke her heart. She was pretty sure her face bore a similar expression.

"I do love you," she whispered. "I do."

He pulled her into his embrace so fast that she had no time to feel her next heartbeat. One millisecond she was standing there declaring her love. The next, he was kissing her breathlessly. And kissing, she now knew, was one form of intimacy that seemed universally accepted. Unlike turning on a computer or finding her way around an alien starship, no one could claim she didn't know how to do it.

Without wasting one more precious second, she kissed him back with all the passion she'd kept bottled for months.

She looped her arms around his neck and moaned as their tongues met. He pulled her so close and held her in such a way that her feet were no longer in contact with the cool white marble floor. Their bodies blended as they embraced.

And when he hungrily let his kisses wander from her mouth to her left cheek, and then her neck, she whispered encouraging words. His reply wasn't what she expected.

"I think I loved you the minute I saw you lying in the *Titan*'s med bay, so badly wounded," he softly murmured. "You opened your eyes and I felt like I'd lost control of everything. I knew you were afraid. But you had the guts to tell me where to get off and in no uncertain terms. I don't think I've ever had someone throw a specimen bottle at me. I knew even then that I didn't ever want anyone touching you but me."

"I thought you hated me back then," she quietly responded as she ran her hands through his hair and nuzzled his neck.

"I hated how every minute was consumed with thoughts of you," he admitted. "I'd never met a woman so determined to get herself into trouble. I've never been driven so nearly crazy by anyone."

"And do you prefer things safe and sane? Because if you do, Darius Starlaw, we might have issues. I'm not and never have been predictable. I don't do things the way other people expect," she told him as she stared into his eyes. "You've figured out that I don't always follow rules. I had a hell of a time trying back on Earth."

He laughed as he held her closer. "Yeah … I get that about you. That's why I'll be as near normal as possible. I'll follow the rules for both of us. And you … you just be you, beautiful. I wouldn't want it any other way."

"So … is this gonna work?" she tearfully asked.

"Why else would you have come into my life if somebody hadn't wanted us to be together? I feel … "

"What? What do you feel?" she prompted.

"Alive. I feel like everything is new. I don't feel like I'm in some kind of cage anymore. Does that make sense?"

"Yeah. It makes sense to me," she said as she hugged him hard.

"All we have to do is take one day at a time, Laurel. Just let me help you. You don't have to do everything alone. Everybody needs help, no matter who they are. Understand?"

She smiled. "I-I'll try to put my pride aside."

"And I'll try not to become the officious, overzealous prick in a uniform. I'm not like that, you know. Not really."

"And you don't think people from Earth are primitive and backward now? I mean … I know we don't have your technological advantages but—"

"Creator's balls! That was the biggest mistake I ever made."

"Yeah?" she softly asked.

"The terrible error I made was in judging your world by the tools available to it. Instead … I should have considered the content of character, the courage, and the honesty you've displayed. While I was disparaging your people, some of mine were betraying us all, and with all the power of those same technological advances you just mentioned. I had no right to judge. None at all. And … there's something else as well."

"What?" she asked as she gazed deeply into his eyes.

"Having just been put on report by my own father, I had no right second guessing how you got to be an enforcer." He slowly nodded. "Only someone who really cares about what they're doing questions authority. It's those who *don't* that we have to worry about."

She nodded back. "So … "

"So?"

She put the fingertips of her right hand on his full lips and would have kissed him again but the library door suddenly flew open with such force that the sound of it reverberated off the marble walls. Maelle stood there with her hands on her hips, framed by the white marble opening, staring at them. A look of outrage was pasted on her lovely face.

Laurel didn't try to pull herself from Darius's embrace, nor did he make any attempt to release her.

"Mother? What's wrong? Is there something you needed?" Darius carefully asked.

"I pray to the Creator I'm interrupting something important? Something that will, when some kind of announcement is made, makes us all very happy … something of such monumental importance as to warrant official announcements in proper social circles! Am I right?" she implored as she pointedly glanced at them both.

"Yes, you're interrupting something," Darius glibly responded. "If you'll be so kind as to close the door, we'll get back to it."

"You've been in here for almost half an hour, and you haven't asked her to marry you yet?" Maelle squeaked. "Darius … are you waiting for the sun to go nova? Your father and I saw the way you looked at Laurel while she was testifying. We've known you were in love with her since you first brought her home. And while she hadn't been on the surface of Luster for three days, an idiot could figure it out even if your family took a little longer. What will it take to motivate you?" She demanded. "Do you think women like her grow on trees?"

Laurel tried to stifle a laugh, but wasn't successful. As far as Maelle was concerned, Laurel wasn't present. The audacity of the situation was too funny. At that moment in time, they could be any family on Earth.

Darius gently lowered her until her feet touched the floor again. With an exasperated sigh, he slowly faced Maelle and put his hands on his hips. "Mother … see to our guests. Let me see to my love life. All right?"

"Son … I want this settled. *Tonight*!"

"Mother, I know what you're doing and you can stop—"

Maelle interrupted by pointing one long, red-tipped, and well-manicured finger toward the floor. "I want things arranged … now … and I mean it." She put her attention on Laurel. "If he comes out of this room without having proposed, I'll declare he did it anyway. I want him home, out of space, away from murdering, savage vamphieres. I managed to wheedle information out of Gemma though it took hours to do so. She tells me her medical records indicate the two of you are perfectly compatible, reproductively speaking."

Darius rolled his eyes skyward.

Laurel simply shook her head and tried not to laugh. The fact that the *Titan*'s medical officer revealed personal information of that nature—and to Darius's mother—was more than inappropriate. But it was equally wrong for Maelle to have asked. Still, it made no difference now since that cat was well and fully out of the bag.

"Laurel … have you any aversion to children? Will you agree to bear my son's babies?" Maelle determinedly asked.

"Uh … y-yeah … y-yes? I mean … I love kids."

"Mother ... that's none of your—"

"Quiet, Darius! I was speaking to your future bride," Maelle asserted. "Then she put her full attention back on Laurel. My dear, you may be assured of finding employment in any occupation you seek. I'll see to it myself," she promised as she turned to Darius. "You see? How hard was that?"

When Maelle turned and strode away, Laurel pressed her lips together and stared at the floor. When she finally spoke, her voice was reverently low, in direct opposition to the tirade the queen of Luster just displayed.

"I-I haven't known your mother that long. Is she always so ... "

"She drives my father crazy. But he loves her to distraction. That's why there's so many of *us*."

It suddenly dawned on Laurel that her own mother wouldn't have cared where she was, who she was with, or why. Having failed to live up to expectations, having settled for what'd been referred to as "employment fit for mentally inept fascists," she suddenly felt cared for.

Something in the vicinity of her heart cracked. She blinked as tears filled her eyes.

Darius immediately tried to comfort her. "Laurel ... don't take anything Mother just said to heart. You know what she was doing, don't you?"

Not trusting herself to speak, Laurel shook her head.

"As an ambassador for the past thirty years, she's learned more than one or two tricks about how to get information out of people. You see ... she really didn't have any idea how you and I felt about one another, just a suspicion. A best guess, if you will."

"Wh-what?"

"It was a fishing expedition. Now, she knows we're in love without any doubt. She knows I'm serious and so are you. You even promised to marry me and have my babies. And all in the few seconds she threw her tantrum. You see ... if the woman was only surmising before, she just got you to remove all doubts." He displayed a broad grin.

"S-she uses this attack-and-watch technique to draw out information from dignitaries?"

He nodded. "She's very good. She's been doing this to Father, me, and everyone else in the household for years. You'd be surprised how much she learns by just pretending to be outraged or even obnoxious at times. I've even seen her make believe she's utterly clueless. That one seems to get the best results of all. You'd be surprised how much someone will reveal if they *think* they're spilling their guts to some poor fool."

Laurel blinked in shock. "Wow!"

"Indeed. And she did one more thing," he added.

"Yeah?"

He lifted one hand in a supplicating gesture then slowly let it fall to his side again. "She made sure *I* know how you feel. Not having heard any part of our conversation prior to entering… *that* was probably her real intent. All that's left to do is to officially put the question of marriage to you, arrange a wedding big enough to satisfy protocol, and have us both moved into the estate my grandparents left me."

"I-I feel … used," she jokingly told him.

He laughed. "So … is it? Settled, I mean?"

She lifted her chin and poked her index finger in his chest. "Not so fast, mister. I haven't gotten what I want out of this deal."

"Laurel, you can have anything you desire. Though you're not shallow enough to ask for jewels, fine clothing, or introductions into the finest social circles or the brightest minds of our era, Mother will likely insist on all the above if only to make up for my lack of motivation. She doesn't understand how desperately I wanted you and how afraid I was of rejection. That last part, her little well-acted tantrum didn't reveal."

"Darius—"

"She wants you for a daughter-in-law and no one else will do. I want you for a wife. And no one else will do. So … I'll ask in a more romantic way later. When all this craziness concerning the trial and everything to do with it is over and we can finally be alone. But put me out of my misery now. *Please?*"

"Keep your jewels and introductions to the proper social circles," she softly murmured. "I'll marry you and follow through with all the rest, spaceman. But I want something right now."

"Name it," he said as he pulled her into his embrace again.

"Take me upstairs, to your room. Take my clothes off and make love to me until neither of us can walk. 'Kay?"

"Creator's blood, woman! That's the easy part." He kissed her hard, then released her and took her hand in his.

In a breathless display of determination, Darius led her out of the library using a patio door. They avoided everyone else in the household and all the questions, requests, and concerns others still had about Goll, the trial, Laurel being from Earth, and minutiae that could wait or couldn't be changed.

Once the door to his room was locked behind them, he pulled her robe off with such ease that Laurel didn't remember it being removed. She vaguely remembered pulling his clothes off him, running her hands over his broad, bronzed shoulders, and feeling his lips on hers.

Any final misgivings as to physiology were settled.

From his circumcised, hard penis to every muscle of his body, he was as human as any male she'd ever known. But that was where all similarities ended.

The man made love with all the stamina and strength of a mythical god. But every single touch was gently and carefully crafted so that screams of delight and moans of utter fulfillment poured from the bottom of her lungs and into the night.

His words were equally tender. Over and over again, he encouraged her to surrender and give of herself. And only when he was deeply inside her body and sure she'd been satisfied did he suddenly stop, shudder, and grip the bedclothes on either side of her head.

His moans of absolute, perfect delight caused multiple, rolling sensations to cascade forward in strong bursts. His hips circled and then thrust hard as testament to his completion.

Never in her life had she experienced multiple orgasms. And these were of such intensity that her body shook with sweet convulsions. Even her hands shook to the point that he gripped them in his, to steady her and move her into the next wave. Even as she thought she could endure no more and a new wave pulsed forward, he held her as if she was the most precious thing in his world.

Sheets of perspiration poured from their bodies. As she lay there panting, he kissed his way down her throat, between her breasts, and then let his lips hover over her left nipple.

When he lowered his head and suckled deeply, a heavenly, unreal sensation filled her entire body. She pressed his head into her chest to continue the lovemaking. Eventually, he switched sides and moisture pooled between her thighs again.

He kissed his way down her body, exceedingly slowly. She spread her thighs as his tongue tempted the soft flesh between them. One more orgasm tore from her body and her entire back arched off the bed. He moved over her, wrapped his hands around her body, and kissed her as she gasped. This was what it was like to be filled by a man from the stars—*her spaceman*.

Sometime early the next morning, wonderful weariness crept over them both. He fell asleep in her arms. She held him and closed her eyes as the first rays of a large sun crept in through crystalline windows. A soft breeze filtered through one of the windows that'd been left open, and it traveled softly over their bodies.

Then, in that stillness, he whispered her name in his sleep. She pushed back long, long strands of his midnight black hair, and caressed his back and shoulders as tears filled her eyes. They fell down the sides of her face and onto a very large pillow that was clad in some kind of soothing silk-like fabric.

In this new place, she could be anyone she wanted. She could reinvent herself and make up for mistakes she'd made on Earth.

He'd driven fear away. In its place was acceptance. The thrill of new chances took over.

She finally closed her eyes and felt peace in his arms. She was finally at home, with a mountainous man from the stars. And in this new life, all things were possible.

Chapter 15

Five months after Goll's execution

Darius stood on the balcony of his estate and looked out onto the lush gardens. He glanced at his wrist communicator and sighed in frustration. She was late from duty *again*.

His mother's promise had been kept. Once Laurel wed him—in a ceremony that was sure to go down as one of the most extravagant ever to grace a royal household—Maelle had sponsored Laurel's entrance into enforcer academy.

For months his lovely once-Earther bride had studied, worked physically harder than he was sure she'd ever done in her life, and, in all mental ways, pushed herself until she'd finally graduated. She hadn't been at the top of her class but, in a turn of tradition, she'd been voted as its captain. Such was her popularity among her classmates.

That left him in somewhat of a quandary.

Because Laurel had been assigned ground patrol within Luster's capitol city of Crystol, he'd been hard-pressed to explain *his* position as the New Chief of Enforcers of that same city. It put Laurel in the rather awkward position of being employed as one of his subordinates. Rules formerly disallowed such nepotistic relationships, but *some* unknown soul had made it their personal goal to have the rule changed. As it now stood, his wife could work as an enforcer, but she would not answer for her actions to anyone but her precinct commanding officer. And *that* man made every excuse imaginable to keep his lovely, newest academy graduate after hours, for one special assignment or another.

Laurel loved her work. Moreover, she was good at it. She made no excuses for having a lot to learn, but her instincts were impeccable. She was already making arrests.

Two months ago, a smuggling ring selling everything from stolen artwork to dangerous, illicit drugs, had been broken, and with her in the middle of the entire operation. She and her coworkers were now after a particularly insidious ring of criminals. The vermin were actually kidnapping children from outlying colonies to use as slave labor in fuel mines. The mines were located somewhere in the Beta 1254 sector of space, but the leaders of the setup were located on Luster. He knew the specifics of the operation, not the actual duties of his wife in locating the criminals responsible.

He feared for her safety. But this was her life; it was what she wanted. And after work each day, she came home, held him in the night, and chased away any vestige of pain or loneliness. He'd learned to get on with life, and to remember what he'd lost with love and patience.

Such was a very nearly perfect life together. It was marred only by her absence.

His thoughts had circled back to the one thing bothering him at the moment. She was late *again*. Mother and Father had made a family gathering of an important evening. They were to all meet with ambassadors of Gerent and Pabrara—two outlying colonies with which Luster hoped to develop agricultural trade.

In the room behind him, a maid was humming happily as she laid out Laurel's latest gown, a midnight blue confection that sparkled in the sunlight. The gauzy fabric was cut low enough to make his mouth water. The fabric, he was told, had been a gift from Gemma. His former med-tech—who was now expecting her first child with Barst—had purchased it for Laurel, in some marketplace or other while on their way back to Luster from Earth. He hadn't paid a lot of attention back then to his crew's relationship with the woman who was to become his life mate. He wished he had.

Back then, he'd existed in utter turmoil. He hadn't wanted to admit he was so desperately in love with an Earth woman. Now, he couldn't imagine life without her. And soon, as she promised, they'd work on that baby his parents were so eager to announce.

But before any of that could happen, she had to get home. The hour was growing later. And every time this happened, fear for her safety almost froze him. Of course, someone would notify him if she was injured. But the angst in even considering such a missive was terrible.

He suddenly vowed to get her pregnant so she could take leave. Then *he* could take leave, and they'd have more time together. At last.

"Sorry I'm late, baby. We got caught up in a meeting," she called as she breezed into the room, removing her tunic as the maid smiled, nodded, and left them alone.

He walked back in through the open patio door, pulled her into his arms, and kissed her hard. "Can't you contact me when that happens? You're going to drive me crazy, Laurel. You won't let me call you, so I have to sit and wait … "

She stopped undressing and stood there in a tight, sleeveless compression shirt, tighter black uniform leggings, and tall boots. She unpinned her long hair from its neat bun and shook it loose. "I promise. I won't do it again, Darius. I'm sorry."

"That's what you said the last time," he murmured as he nuzzled her neck.

"I didn't know about this meeting. Commander Kkurian asked me to stay … "

"He and I are going to have a serious talk about when and how he breaks rules. He has no grounds for keeping enforcers after hours. Not when it doesn't have to do with duty. Meetings don't apply. Especially when they only involve *you*."

She slowly smiled up at him. "Don't be jealous. I don't care about him other than as a co-worker."

"I know that. It's *him* I'm worried about."

She looped her arms around his neck. "The problem's been solved. He's been put on space duty. Deep sector, area 43MK. Commander Letor is taking his place. Kkurian just kept us *all* late … the entire shift … to thank us for our service. It was a sort of cake and coffee send-off. At least what passes for cake and coffee on this world." She shrugged happily. "Okay?"

His mood brightened considerably. "Commander Letor is a very good supervisor. You'll enjoy working with *her*."

"You know what?"

"What?" he asked as his body responded to her sudden closeness.

"Since you haven't changed into your dress uniform yet … and since I'm home now … we've got just enough time to take a warm shower together." She ran one index finger down the center of his chest and began to unfasten his uniform tunic.

His cock went granite hard, and every problem in the world fled. "Sounds like a very good idea. And if we're a little late, Barst and Gemma will make some excuse or another since they've been invited by the family. Besides … I'm sure my parents will get over it."

She cupped his erection and gently squeezed. "Don't plan on getting much sleep tonight or the rest of the weekend. I'm really, really hot for you," she said as she nibbled on his left earlobe.

He closed his eyes, breathed in her unique, floral scent, and hurriedly pulled his clothing off. He got down to the pouch he wore to cover his genitals and would have removed that, too, but Laurel ran her hands over his hips and untied the bindings for him. In turn, he took his time removing her uniform and a lacy pair of shocking red panties.

Soft afternoon light glittered through the crystal panes of their windows. And as a breeze blew in from the gardens, lifting her hair off her shoulders and back, he wasted no time. He'd learned to seize the moment, before some incident or other, relayed by a servant or over a computer, got in their way. There were days when he thought he'd go insane from wanting her. They'd get close only to be called back to duty. Enough was enough.

He pulled her into the large shower stall. She commanded the bath area personal computer to turn on the water, but barely had time to face him again before he backed her into a white, marble wall and kissed her soundly.

She broke the contact with one breathless confirmation. "I love you, spaceman. God ... what you do to me." She seductively ran her hands over her body, but paused to lift and gently squeeze her breasts in a way the drove him crazy with desire. As she did it, she closed her eyes and dropped her head backward. The motion exposed her soft, white neck. He ran his lips over the soft flesh there.

"I love you, too, little Earther. And ... "

"And?" she prompted.

He dropped his hand to her flat abdomen and gently pressed inward. "I know we haven't been together all that long but—"

"You want that baby bad, don't you?"

"Have I been that obvious?"

"You've been talking about nothing but Gemma's baby ... when it's due and if you'll be one of the first to hold it."

"All right," he admitted. "Yes. I want a child very much. And more after that. I want a very big family so that there'll always be rooms filled with laughter. It's my dream to have a smiling face gazing out each window, waiting for me to come home."

"Darius, that's a lovely thought." She slowly smiled.

There was a moment of silence between them as he gazed down at her, longing filling his heart. He waited for her answer.

She lifted her left leg high and wrapped it around his waist. "What are you waiting for, spaceman?"

Her blue eyes glowed with need. And when she thrust her hips forward, his entire body flamed.

With one thrust upward he entered her deeply. She cried out and he felt the tight heat of her body surrounding him. It was exquisitely addicting, and he knew he could stay like that forever, needing nothing more than her softness to encompass him.

"Darius?" she gasped.

"Yes," he breathlessly responded.

"Have you ever heard of coitus tea?"

He grinned as he kept thrusting slowly into her. "Yes, baby. Where did you hear about it?"

"When I was wandering about the city that first night we landed, someone on a street mentioned it and what it did. I-I found a place that sells the stuff. Could we try it?" she whispered.

He grinned broadly. "That's a rather kinky beverage, little Earther."

"Gemma says it's harmless. We're adults and it's legal," she said in response while ignoring his query. "Could we?" she asked as she moved her body in time to his thrusts.

He thrust harder and she moaned so loud he was sure the servants would hear. But never mind. Their employees already knew what the lord and lady of the household were doing. They did it most nights and most mornings. What difference did it make if the sounds of their lovemaking filtered through the entire countryside now?

In asking for such an erotic addition into their lives as coitus tea, she'd just displayed complete trust. And what better way was there than to spend the weekend, ensconced in their room enjoying their sexuality?

And to think he'd once thought her repressed, along with everything else considered backward and uneducated. He'd been wrong then and was glad to make up for his mistakes now.

"We'll leave the party early," he softly promised. "We'll get your tea, and do things the galaxy has no name for. I have a few positions in mind that you'll enjoy. I really get off when you cry out my name in the middle of a climax."

"That's because I love you, Darius Starlaw. So much."

"And I love you," he told her and kissed her harder before issuing one last sexual demand for the evening. "Now hold on. And don't let go."

"Never. Never spaceman. Never *ever*."

About the Author

Candace Sams (aka C.S. Chatterly) graduated from Texas A&M University with a BS in Agriculture, worked as a police officer with the State of Texas, did a brief stint with the Texas Department of Public Safety Undercover Narcotics Task force, and was also with the San Diego Police Department. She taught for the San Diego County Sheriff's Department and worked in law enforcement in Alabama.

She currently trains as the senior woman on the US Kung Fu Team (working on her fourth black belt), and has been awarded the Medal of Putien from China and the Statue of Tao for her work in martial arts. She holds several international martial arts titles. In 2000, she was one of a fifteen-member team—authorized by act of Senate—to represent this country as a martial arts ambassador to mainland China. Experiences in law enforcement, martial arts (Shaolin Kung Fu) are frequently used in her career as an author—she is known for writing fight scenes into her fictional works. As an added note, Ms. Sams is also a Master Gardener and loves working outdoors.

After publishing over fifty titles in the fantasy, science fiction, paranormal, and action-adventure genres, she's received more than thirty awards from various organizations, including five National Readers' Choice Awards and a *USA Today* Best Book nomination. Her *Tales of The Order*™ series, as well as several other works, are now being vetted for movie options.

Hailing from Texas, Candace loves the country life. She and her husband of more than twenty-five years live in a rural area of the US. A plethora of dogs and cats have adopted them. She loves to hear from readers and can be contacted through her website at *www.candacesams.com*. Candace also writes erotica as C.S. Chatterly and can be contacted from *www.cschatterly.com*.

More from This Author
(From *Fusion* by Candace Sams)

Reisen Four
Behind enemy lines
Earth year 5037

To save what ammo she had, Lyra Markham jammed the butt of her photon rifle into the face of the charging Condorian. The resulting thud was exceedingly gratifying.

Her foe fell into an awkward heap. His head lolled to one side and his eyes immediately assumed a deathly, hollowed glaze.

It'd been a very good hit.

She tossed her empty rifle aside. It was added weight she couldn't afford.

A quick search of her dead foe's arsenal proved pointless. Though the fool was out of ammunition he'd still had the balls to charge, brandishing a horrific looking, ten-inch boot blade. Aside from that weapon, which she summarily shoved into the barrel of her tall desert boot, there was nothing else to be scavenged from his body. No ammo. No grenades. Nothing.

Scrambling sounds made her glance backward.

Unfortunately her dead enemy's nasty-looking friends witnessed her attack from about a hundred yards away. They grouped for the chase.

As they ran toward her, firing, she ducked and took off northward, as fast as her body armor allowed. She now counted seven Condorians breathing down her neck.

Sweat poured down her face as she gazed ahead, hoping to get to the far, rocky hills where she'd have the advantage of being on higher ground.

As Lyra ran, she was forced to jump over the bodies of Delloids, Capricans, Startsur warriors, and Freermen. All of them were Earth allies in the war against the Condorians. All were spilling blood just as freely.

No matter how many allies came to the front, intending to beat back the enemy ravaging the entire galaxy, the Condorians kept bringing more. The only thing that kept her world and other allied planets from being overrun were these desperate stands in space—diversions meant to slow the enemy while allied commanders fell back and reassessed battle strategy.

Annihilation was only a matter of time. She knew it; so had all the dead lying around her. But no one was giving up. The Condorians wouldn't take hostages. Innocent inhabitants from hundreds of allied planets would die horrible deaths. It now came down to a matter of how one died. Her course was in battle.

She rounded an outcrop of rock and stopped to lean against it, dragging air into her lungs while she could. Every detail of this stinking, blood-soaked battleground blended together.

There were almost no colors on Reisen Four. Sepia-tones obscured some of the rocky escarpments in shadow. There was no grass, sparse plant life of a higher order, and precious little water. Whatever the cost, Lyra vowed not to be taken alive.

Approaching boot steps signaled her brief respite was over. She gripped her sidearm and ran again. She'd have taken her helmet off for better maneuverability, but the only long-range transmitter she had was built inside. Even though she was sure her superiors had given her up for dead, she couldn't relinquish the last communication device available. And some part of the helmet might deflect incoming fire.

As one of thousands of Class M planets, Reisen Four's air was breathable. Lyra and other allied fighters had been given orders to leave air packs behind. In this environment, the oxygen canisters would have weighed fighters down. That brilliant foresight helped her make good time now. But without filtered oxygen, the dirt in the air penetrated every part of her uniform, including the damned helmet. Still, she clung to the last hope that a signal might come from an allied vessel. With her own fighters scattered to the four winds, Earth Forces deployed in this battle were quite gone or dead.

There'd originally been three other women in her platoon. She was the last and had seen the remains of her friends and what had been done to them. That image was burned into her brain and was the only thing keeping her from turning around and shooting into the pack chasing her. Her pursuers had picked up the pace. She was pretty damned sure they knew she was female.

Hours went by. She dodged, hid, and ran but it made no difference. After only a few precious moments to rest in every few hundred yards of running, her foes kept up the pursuit. Their persistence had less to do with losing their friend to her rifle butt, and more to do with catching a woman and slaking their lusts before slowly slaughtering her.

It was now late into what passed for a Reisen Four night. The sepia-tones were only a little darker to delineate the passage of time. She had no idea where she was and didn't care. The Condorians were still running her to ground like hounds on a blood trail.

With her body and wits taxed, she turned into a small, narrowing canyon. Without energy reserves, she suddenly realized she couldn't climb up its side fast enough to keep from being hauled back down the rocky slope. It was there she turned to make what she assumed would be her last stand.

I'll take a few of you bastards with me.

She squared her shoulders, determined to save one last round for her head. She'd be dead before they actually began tearing her apart.

As she raised her sidearm fear gripped her soul. It was then she realized she really wasn't ready to die. A noise from behind signaled she wasn't alone.

In an instant someone from behind clamped a large, strong hand on her shoulder. She was hauled off her feet and bodily thrown into a dark, cavernous space. Her weapon fell from her grasp and she scrambled to retrieve it.

Her attacker pulled her backward. That was the last thing she remembered.

• • •

It might have been hours or minutes later when she opened her eyes. She felt her neck being massaged by huge, gentle hands. When her foggy wits cleared, she eventually pushed herself away from the enormous, crouching figure next to her. Since she'd be dead if he was a Condorian; the reasonable assumption was that this darkly uniformed fighter was an ally. He'd most likely saved her life.

"Wh-what the hell happened?" she murmured through her helmet mouthpiece.

Her helmeted savior stared at her.

The huge megalithic creature before her tilted his black, armored head, as if he hadn't heard her correctly. She repeated her question and added more.

"I'm Lyra Markham . . . Master Sergeant, Tenth Earth Regiment. Who are you and what happened?" she demanded again.

When he kept staring down at her—his face as invisible as hers behind the anti-glare plexi-shielding—she kept trying. "Is your communicator working?" She tapped her head to indicate a communication device that should be located within his helmet.

Since learning that other races occupied the outer reaches of space many centuries ago, universal communication technology had been developed for the benefit of all who wished to speak freely. Unfortunately, better communication hadn't worked with the Condorians. They had but one desire—to take everything and kill anyone who wasn't one of them.

Lyra's comrade continued to stare at her without making a single sound. "Can … you … understand … me?" she asked one last time, enunciating every word quite clearly.

He finally stood and backed away.

From where she sat, she felt at a decided disadvantage. The figure towering over her had to be nearly seven feet tall, as wide as a hatch on a cargo frigate. His shoulders, even without the black, unmarked armor, spanned the distance of a full yard and then some. Unlike her headgear, *his* had a pronounced front-piece that appeared very avian in nature. It was as if the designer was trying to emulate the head of a very large predatory flying creature. She'd never seen its like before. Still, there was no doubt in her mind that he was an ally.

Finally, she hauled her tired frame to a standing position then removed her helmet so he could see her more clearly.

Sometimes these alien beings didn't take to speaking without eye-to-eye contact. She couldn't afford to piss this mountainous person off. He represented the only help available.

Her companion simply tilted his head the other direction and kept staring down at her. She knew she wasn't the most attractive human at the moment. Grime and sweat ran in rivulets over her face, neck, and body. She could feel it even if she couldn't see it. Without oxygen canisters, the body armor was left unsealed so the user could breathe. That resulted in every bit of dirt getting in.

He seemed to study her uniform markings carefully. Even from a great distance, anyone as familiar with allied patches could tell she was an Earther and was ranked Master Sergeant. She'd only announced that fact along with her name and unit designation as a matter of habit. Still, the painted emblem of Earth, surrounded by its telltale starry circle, was clearly emblazoned on her right shoulder and over the left breastplate of her armor. Her helmet had the same emblem plastered all over both sides. He couldn't mistake her origin, but he just wasn't communicating.

She stood for a long moment considering what to do. Her last thought before blacking out had been of death. Not rescue. And this silent giant wasn't helping her overtired brain make sense of the situation.

...

Soldar Nar had heard of Earth women being sent to fight on behalf of their world. But her sudden appearance in this desolate, lonely place was utterly astonishing.

Women from his home world of Craetoria simply didn't battle.

Indeed, women in most of the Allied Forces were rare. *This* one was not only in the middle of a very deadly confrontation, but happened to be quite arresting despite the dust and sweat all over her face. Once her helmet was off, he took full stock of a suddenly beguiling sight, something surreal and incomprehensible in this horrible combat zone. Her eyes stared up at him questioningly. Because of the hazy, dirty atmosphere he guessed they might be bright blue. For a moment, he found his mind consumed with the hue. Then he mentally shook himself and considered the rest of her appearance. She didn't seem harmed by his having jerked her into the cave.

Her short brown hair curled just beneath her chin and fell over her forehead in long, wavy wisps. She had a straight, perfect nose that spoke of fine breeding. Her cheekbones were high and elegant. Moreover, her full lips were slightly parted, as if she was about to speak again. Clearly she was as at a loss as he.

Right before he'd grabbed her, the woman had turned to fight her last. Her steadfast inclination to accept fate was apparent in the way she'd leveled her weapon against the oncoming enemy. She'd spread her legs and assumed a stance of absolute resolve. The exhibition of courage cemented his determination to save this noble ally. At that time, however, he hadn't known this valiant fighter was a woman. He'd believed *her* to be a *he* of very small stature. Now he knew her gender, everything changed.

He felt parts of his body respond magnificently. Except for the absence of a left cheek mark, she could be any woman on his world.

More to the point, he had hadn't seen a woman of *any* race in more than a year. If the Condorians had gotten their hands on this one, he couldn't imagine what she'd have suffered.

Thoughts of his sisters, his mother, and other kinswomen came to mind. If anyone had touched them the way the Condorians would have ravaged this stunning creature, he'd have butchered every last one of them no matter how long it took.

How could Earthers allow their most prized citizens into the middle of battle? Were they really as foolish as others claimed?

He'd seen their men as gallant fighters. Why would they so risk their women? Why would this questioning beauty be in this Creator-forsaken wilderness, fighting all alone and with no hope for survival?

"It's clear there's something wrong with your communicator," she told him. "There are no markings on your uniform but I know damned well you're no Condorian." She suddenly coughed to get a thick layer of dust out of her throat and mouth. When she recovered, she tried to communicate her intentions. "Look … I'm checkin' outta here. You can try to get back to your unit or you can follow me. That second option is best since two of us are more likely to survive." She raised one gloved hand and pointed toward the cave entrance. "We … can't … stay … here. It isn't safe. Those Condorians might be back and the sniveling cowards will come with company. Do you understand?"

He remained silent. His mind just wasn't absorbing her presence. Something deep in his head told him she wasn't supposed to be there. He kept searching for an answer to her presence but his intuition revealed nothing.

"Leave or stay … what's it gonna be?"

He mentally shook himself back into reality and finally responded.

"The Condorians are all dead," he electronically blurted in perfect English. "They didn't call for backup or reinforcements would have been here by now." His helmet speaker blocked more of his voice than hers had. His mouthpiece made his response sound quite automated.

It was her turn to be taken aback. He saw her brows rise. Her pretty, bow-shaped lips fell open, probably shocked to hear him speak her language so proficiently. He was still struck by the twisted situation. Her presence was wrong. He couldn't dispel the shock of it.

Finally, he haltingly raised his hands and considered removing his helmet. This Earther might have never seen a Craetorian's face. His people were ordered to keep their helmets on and speak as little as possible to allied brethren. It was thought that fraternization might prove demoralizing. His superiors believed it was hard enough watching those from one's home world die. How much more difficult would it be to have troops inflicted with the site of newly befriended, slaughtered allies. All this considered, the circumstances surrounding his presence—and hers—called for creativity. His mission came first. He must do what he must. She wouldn't find his face shocking. His features would be the same as her human countenance with but a singular difference.

. . .

Lyra couldn't place his armor or helmet at all but that really wasn't unusual. With so many different worlds fighting the

Condorians—whose silver and metallic armor was arrogantly meant to be visible—it didn't matter where any allied warrior originated. All that mattered was that they kept fighting.

There were a few planets, including Earth, whose dignitaries and generals regularly conferred as to battle plans. At Lyra's low rank she wasn't privy to their strategies. She just took orders. So if there was a new, friendly race in the battle she welcomed their presence. It wasn't as if the enemy was running out of fighters.

When her comrade took off his helmet, Lyra barely saw his face in the half light. He seemed to realize his body was shadowed and quickly stepped into a brighter area. This was how she got her first good look at a race that was at the front of every battle. She'd heard of them but had always been sent to fight in areas they weren't present.

"I'm Colonel Soldar Nar, Fifth Planetary Pulsar Unit for Craetoria. At least, my rank translates to Colonel in your language," he announced.

She shook her head in vague recollection. Earth English was rumored to be one of several dialects spoken on his world. Since it was the most universally broadcast, a lot of other races used it. His unexpected familiar greeting made her feel easier. It was a relief to know that neither of them would need any translation devices.

"I've heard of your race," she congenially acknowledged, "but I'm afraid I've never seen one of your people, sir." With that being said, she'd still have recognized the piercing eyes and long blond hair that spilled onto his shoulders when his helmet was removed. The black slash mark originating from the corner of his left eye down his strong cheekbone bore further proof of his heritage. That feature was one of the Craetorian attributes about which her Earth colleagues regularly gossiped. As they'd described, it *did* look exactly like a black electric bolt.

"Where is the rest of your platoon?" Soldar asked.

She briefly lowered her gaze.

"I see." He gestured to the empty cave around him. "My insertion team met the same fate when we landed. I heard the howling of those brutes chasing you and knew some allied fighter was their target. I took position in this cave and waited, but you'd turned to fight off the whole pack by yourself." He waited for her response, but she made none. "I apologize for having incapacitated you, but it was necessary. As I said, I don't believe they had time to call for backup or we'd have been attacked." He sighed, pushed his hair away from his face, and turned his head away to spit dust out of his mouth. When he gazed on her again, his words conveyed his admiration. "You're quite the bold one, Sergeant. The cowards had you at seven-to-one."

Lyra snorted. "Sir, couldn't you have just called out that you were here? Then we could have taken that pack together."

"I hadn't time. And I'm not supposed to be seen by anyone, not even one of the allies. I've told you, I was part of an insertion team. I'm under top secret orders. That means *you're* under those orders now."

"Excuse me?"

"I'm pulling rank, Sergeant. General Elias Shafter sent us here. I'm in his command. That makes me, as ranking officer, your superior. And no, you may not ask why an Earth general is issuing orders to a Craetorian colonel."

"Christ! I don't even want to guess," she readily confirmed as she straightened her body armor and shook her head in amazement. "Whatever the hell is goin' on … I don't mind you being responsible. I'm just here to fight." She shrugged and stared up at him. "So what're our orders?"

"I suggest you get some rest. We sit tight for another hour. Then we move due east."

She watched him lean against a far wall and toss back the thick blond hair that, even in the dim light, draped down his body like a shimmering cloak. She surmised his helmet would be back in place before they left the cave, otherwise that glowing pelt would be plainly visible in the half light of the Reisen Four evening. The presence of such long hair was another unusual characteristic of his race. Locker-room gossip had bestowed some very godlike characteristics on his people.

Was it true they were stronger than almost any other ally and could fight like madmen? Could they go without water for days, and did they have no problem eating rodents and insects they found under logs and rocks?

She tried not to smile as she recalled other, more intimate gossip concerning his race.

Was it true they made love with all the stamina of a photon infusion engine? Were they able to please their partners so thoroughly that their mates stayed by their sides for life?

She looked away before he caught her staring, but lifted one hand to her own short locks. They were matted and dirty. She was sure they didn't shine the way his thick mane did.

When she'd first left Earth as a cadet, she'd had her entire head completely shorn. Over the years, she'd let it grow and now kept it below ear length. It fit uniform codes, was easy to maintain, and didn't obstruct her view. Nobody out here cared what she looked like. Even the Condorians didn't give a damn. That she was a woman was enough for them.

For some odd reason, she wondered about the women of *his* world. Was it true they were as tall as the men? Did they crave Earth chocolate so much that they'd really smuggled it through blockades?

She shook her head. The inappropriate nature of these queries was obvious. What did any of that matter? None of them would live long since the Condorians couldn't be stopped. There were so damned many of them. They'd taken over almost half the galaxy and were on their way to finish the job.

As she leaned against a wall and slid to the ground, she looped her hand on her now empty holster. The hole where her weapon *should* be made her go rigid. She gazed down at it and felt her heart begin to pound.

"Son-of-a-bitch! I lost my sidearm. It's still out there somewhere." She stood and quickly began to search the immediate area around her before making her way outside the small cave.

"You didn't lose it," he advised as he pulled her weapon from under his armor. "I picked it up after rendering you unconscious. I only had three volleys and hoped you had more. Luckily you did."

"Sir?"

"I took out seven Condorians so we now have two volleys left. Both of them are in my weapon. The men chasing you had no remaining laser power. It appears they intended to do you in with one of these."

He showed her a long knife within his right boot top, then carefully handed back her empty sidearm.

She angrily slid her empty pistol back into its holster. The top of the Condorian blade she'd liberated still stuck out of her own boot. "I know you must have been firing fast, sir, but couldn't you have left me one round … in case I get caught?"

"Master Sergeants who lose their weapons don't deserve spare rounds."

She scowled. "Sir, you clearly saw my uniform. You could have stood beside me and helped. Instead of acting like any other ally, you rendered me unconscious, emptied the only weapon I had, and are now insinuating I was careless in losing my sidearm. I hardly think that's a fair summation—"

"Cool off, Earther. It was a joke."

"By the way … what *did* you do to me?" she asked as she rubbed the back of her neck.

"I used a lateral vascular neck restraint. I think that's the politically correct term nowadays for a choke hold." He smiled. "Its effects are only wearing off, or you'd have been questioning me about my actions sooner."

She put her hands on her hips and glared at him.

"I am sorry about taking you to the ground," he apologized. "But when I grabbed you, you turned to fight. I had a few seconds before that pack came barreling down the canyon. I didn't have time to answer questions."

"I suppose this is the part where I'm supposed to thank you?"

"Your sarcasm isn't welcome, Sergeant. I should have left you safely in this cave, coming back to consciousness on your own, without seeing me." He shrugged. "I had a surge of conscience and couldn't leave a comrade alone in this wasteland. You've seen me now and I've conscripted you for a mission. My actions make me responsible for your safety."

"Really? I thought that was *my* job."

"Get over it," he shot back. "We're a team now, whether either of us likes it or not. But to set the record straight as to your ability to look after yourself, I require an answer to just one question."

"Sir?"

"Why did you run into a canyon with no outlet? Were you not properly briefed about how many were present in this area? You're a supervisor. Did you not check maps before landing to fight?"

She rolled her eyes and let out a long, frustrated sigh. "Okay … I made a wrong turn. I screwed up!"

"I can live with the explanation, though you may *not* have. Let's just say we've both had better days. You and I have survived to learn lessons."

"What lessons?"

"You won't run into dead-ends … and I won't lose my weapons, inclusive of all the ammunition, or my entire team!"

He stood, angrily thrust his helmet back on his head, and stalked toward the cave entrance. Once there, she saw him gaze outside.

She finally understood.

He was feeling guilt over surviving. When she'd run toward him—being chased by Condorians bent on peeling her skin off—he saw his chance at vengeance. She'd just been in his way.

This cave, wherever it was, was probably the place where he and his team were supposed to have waited until later in the night. Then, they'd probably have gone about finishing whatever mission they'd planned. But, like so many plans the allies composed, nobody could maneuver against twenty-to-one odds. As she saw it, they were both lucky to be alive.

She almost let the incident go. However, her rescuer now had two shots in his weapon. He'd used hers on the enemy and that situation had to be addressed. She pulled on her helmet and approached him once more.

"Sir?"

"What now, Sergeant?"

"If we get caught you've got all our firepower. Will you make sure they don't take me alive?"

He turned his helmeted head toward her. "Count on it, Sergeant Lyra Markham!"

The corners of her mouth lifted.

His powerfully worded promise to see her die painlessly was acceptable. They now had the makings of a team. For however long they lasted.

Also check out *The Peacekeeper's Soul* by Candace Sams.
In the mood for more Crimson Romance?
Check out *A Demon in Love* by Holley Trent
at *CrimsonRomance.com*.

www.ingramcontent.com/pod-product-compliance
Lightning Source LLC
Chambersburg PA
CBHW010857100726
47905CB00011BA/3234